DUANE DE MELLO

THE WAVE OF THE FUTURE

[illegible]N:
Be alert
Be cautious
Keep watching
Stay alive
[illegible]
5.15.10

ISBN: 1-4392-6009-5
ISBN-13: 9781439260098
LCCN: 2009910381

The Wave of the Future

For
Joan
and
Mark, Susan, Sasha,
Dewey, Cary, Alexa and Nick

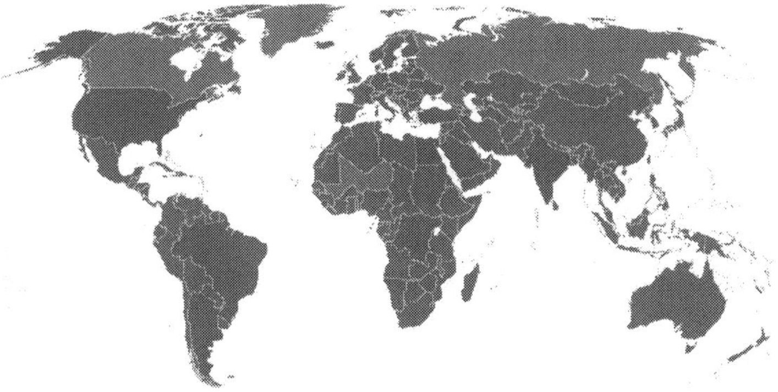

CHAPTER 1

At one time or another during our lives many of us have wondered what it would be like to be a covert operative of the Central Intelligence Agency working under deep cover throughout the world in places ranging from the most exotic, beautiful, and sublime, to the most dangerous and life-threatening bottom-feeding locales imaginable.

Mitch knew exactly what it was like, and as the hall clock struck midnight, he sipped the last of his Amaretto and reluctantly headed for his bedroom. The next day's trip to Oslo held the promise of another operational assignment, and Mitch was anxious to learn if it was, once again, the sort of case he relished and eagerly sought to be assigned. A good night's sleep seemed unlikely.

As he packed his bag, Mitch glanced beyond the balcony of his twelfth-floor apartment at the scene that seemed more beautiful each time he returned from an assignment. Below, San Francisco's Marina District lay clouded in a light mist, and he could barely make out the lights of Berkeley and Oakland beyond the choppy waters of the bay. For someone in his line of work, this place near the Hyde Street Pier and Ghirardelli Square had been his private refuge time and again.

Mitch Vasari, a thirty-seven year-old operations officer of the CIA, operated under deep commercial cover, known as non-official cover (NOC) in Agency parlance. Standing six feet two inches tall and weighing 190 pounds, he had an olive complexion and a fine head of jet-black hair. Lean and muscular, the result of twenty years of cross-country running, he maintained himself through regular weight training and marathon events whenever he could fit them into his life.

Mitch was born in Florence to an Italian father and an Egyptian mother. His father, Nicolai, was a metals commodity dealer who had perfected a method for analyzing the best times to buy and sell metal stocks. Nicolai Vasari's success, particularly in gold and platinum trading, enabled him, when Mitch was three years old, to realize a lifelong dream and move the family to Southern California. Tragically, Nicolai succumbed to a massive heart attack when his son was just starting high school.

Amira, Mitch's mother who was by then an American citizen with no interest in returning to Europe, set about seeing to her son's education and preparation for success in the business world. From the time she first started to teach Mitch to speak her native Egyptian Arabic, she placed emphasis on raising him to respect and understand the meaning of the Quran. He responded by growing up having faith, hope, and trust in God, seeking out the love of truth, practicing patience, being humble, and always listening to God's message.

After his arrival the next evening at Oslo's nineteenth-century Grand Hotel, Mitch studied his city map and carefully planned his movements in the Oslo area. The next morning he had breakfast in the Grand Café on the ground floor of the hotel, a warm and welcoming spot, particularly in the chill of November. Following breakfast, and in preparation for his scheduled late-morning meeting in the nearby town of Lillestrom, Mitch set out upon a measured half-mile walk that took him past Johan's Gate, Slottsparken, St. Olav's Gate, Henrik Ibsen's Gate and Biskop Gunnuru's Gate at the foot of the Central Train Station. In Agency procedure, this walking routine is known as a surveillance detection run (SDR).

During the walk, Mitch stopped at a church, a bookstore and an antique shop. No one appeared to be following him or paying attention to his presence. Satisfied that he was "in the black," or surveillance-free, Mitch boarded the train for a twelve-minute ride to Lillestrom, where he walked three hundred meters from the station to Nesgata, the street where the Thon Hotel

Arena is located. From the hotel lobby, next to the Lillestrom Trade Fair Center, he climbed the long, straight staircase to the second-floor restaurant

Mitch looked for the Stockholm Station case officer, who had been described in cable traffic as sandy-haired, thirty years old, dressed in a dark suit and solid yellow colored tie, and sitting at a table with a folded copy of the *Financial Times* off to the side of his right hand. Mitch spotted him, glanced down at his watch, and walked to within fifteen feet of the man's table before turning away. The time was precisely 11:15, as specified, and the *Financial Times* was correctly positioned. Feigning a slight frown, Mitch continued past, as if seeking a friend who had not yet arrived. After viewing people at all of the occupied tables, Mitch turned and descended the staircase walking to the rear of the lobby, where couches and coffee tables were arranged.

Mitch sat down, and the sandy-haired man in the dark suit and yellow tie approached and took a seat facing him with a coffee table between them.

"Lee Denning?" Mitch asked.

"Yes," he replied.

"Mitch Vasari. Good to meet you, Lee."

"Glad you made it," Lee said. "I'm pleased to be able to meet with you like this. I know meeting with a NOC is very unusual for an inside case officer working overseas. At the onset, Mitch, please be assured I've had the same kind of training you've had in surveillance detection, running SDRs, and even working on counter-surveillance teams."

"I appreciate you saying that," Mitch replied. "That hasn't always been true when I've had to meet with a case officer out in the open like this."

"I know that you're assigned to the Counterterrorism Center. I'm also aware you only get involved in working the most sensitive of terrorist cases against the radical Islamist fundamentalist targets."

"So far so good," Mitch replied. "You were read in correctly."

"I likewise am from CTC, and serve as the singleton terrorist referent case officer in Stockholm Station," Lee said "I expect to be assisted this year by another CTC case officer who will move here from headquarters. But for now, I basically oversee and represent the station in all the local terrorist cases in our territory."

"Are you involved in liaison work with the local Swedish intelligence services in any of these cases?" Mitch asked.

"No. Actually, I'm not. That is why I was able to come out to meet with you. I'm sure you are also aware that since the station here in Oslo does not have a CTC referent, they aren't involved at all in our meeting here," Lee said.

Yes, I am aware of it and have a lot of appreciation and respect for the territory you are required to cover. I am also quite satisfied with this arrangement and look forward to what you have to tell me about this new case," Mitch replied.

"OK. Here's the issue," Lee said. "Over in Ireland, Dublin Station, a small station as you know, is turning up a few good leads lately that offer potential against radical Islamist targets. Their case officers, however, not having backgrounds in counterterrorism, are quite limited in trying to work against this kind of target. At best, they are way out on the fringes and can't develop even indirect access to Islamist terrorists."

"Believe me," Mitch replied, "even with my fluent Arabic – my mother is Egyptian, and I was raised speaking it – I can't maintain direct contact with any Arab or radical Islamic terrorists. It's difficult to get very close because they have a heightened sense of security. They compartment themselves off from one another, and they rely on family members, tribal connections, and highly vetted affiliates.

"I know that so well," replied Lee.

"Tell me then," Mitch said, "what is it you have for me?"

"One of Dublin Station's recruited agents, actually a retired Irish police inspector," Lee said, "has owned a pub there for the last five years. Frequently, as you can imagine, he gets to know all sorts of old sods who, for one reason or another, come to confide in him."

"So you're offering me up an old Irish guy?" Mitch asked.

"Hardly," Lee replied. "He spotted a fellow known to him for several years, from a family with an Irish Republican Army background with, as expected, hatred for the British."

"I don't mind the hatred of the Brits, but the IRA connection is something else," Mitch said.

"We want your input and suggestions on this, but we believe we may have a scenario that may enable you to make direct contact with this guy and see what kind of information you can develop from him."

"What else have you got on the guy?" Mitch asked.

"We think you may be compatible at the onset with him," Lee said. "He's an electrical engineer and I understand you're one as well."

"Yes, I graduated from Stanford as a double E and worked for a firm in Silicon Valley before coming on board with the Agency."

"That should allow you to at least engage in initial conversation once you're able to make your own introduction to him," Lee added.

"Do you have anything else?" Mitch asked.

"When you get back stateside, you'll have a detailed cable scenario waiting for you that spells out what we have in mind."

"You mean I've been brought out here to hear this limited amount of information on a currently nonexistent case, and then you tell me to return home and see what it's all about?" Mitch said. "This information could have been sent to me by cable without me coming all this way."

"That's not the case at all," Lee replied. "Return home, think about it, and read the cable traffic. Should you believe we may have the makings of something, your meeting with me today will set the stage for this potential case, as well as our own relationship."

"What does that mean?" Mitch asked.

"If we can get something off the ground, headquarters and my station believe you'll need an inside point of contact in this area, specifically outside of Ireland. Because you're a NOC, despite your secure laptop commo system, you'll still need to meet with someone to provide the detailed assistance this kind of case will require. That's why you were asked to come out and meet with me," Lee continued. "I'm the primary CTC station officer in the region best able to work with you."

"I can understand that," Mitch said. "I do like the way you talk and how you handle yourself."

"Thank you, Mitch."

"This is going to require some thought on my part. I want to make this a case that we can pursue. I leave optimistically."

***

Lee departed the hotel, made his way to the train station and returned to Oslo International Airport for his short flight back to Stockholm. He thought about the way Mitch handled himself during their relatively brief meeting at the hotel. Although his initial impression of Mitch was positive, they shared a quickness of tongue such as the way Mitch questioned having to fly to Norway for their meeting. He knew Mitch had a favorable reputation in CTC for running successful operations against Arab and radical Islamic targets. He also understood that their supervisor at headquarters in CTC, Jack Benson, viewed Mitch as his obvious most accomplished amongst the NOC cadre assigned to him. Nevertheless, Lee expected he would be able to develop a good working relationship with him and, with Mitch having several more years' experience in working CTC ops, he would show initial deference toward him should this case involving the Irishman get off the ground.

* * *

On his way back to Oslo, Mitch also thought about the meeting. He had worked on several similar radical Islamic cases in the past involving the use of Europeans to gain access to terrorist groups. Unfortunately, these turned out to be nebulous, complicated cases to make headway with, especially when trying to determine whether a provocation was involved. He liked the Irish angle of this one, but he was concerned about the degree of IRA connection and the problems that could portend.

With this case starting out in Dublin, he knew that the headquarters position would be don't bring British or Irish intelligence services in on the case. Obviously, that was why they would allow him, a NOC, to be called in to try to get the case off the ground.

He also knew that radical Islamist terrorist groups were making more and more use of Europeans in their planning for attacks and, in some cases, were allowing them to participate directly in the attacks. Mitch was well versed in what went into the planning for these terrorist operations and was itching to get recruited agents as closely involved as possible. Only in the most select and compartmented ongoing Agency cases were recruited non-Muslim and non-Arab agents actually involved as penetrations of terrorist groups and subsequently able to keep the Agency abreast of a group's plans and intentions.

For now, Mitch mused as the train was pulling into Oslo's Central Station, he only wanted to get back to his hotel, change into his running gear, and explore more of Oslo on foot before having dinner. He also knew he would have a lot to think about during the long flight home the following day.

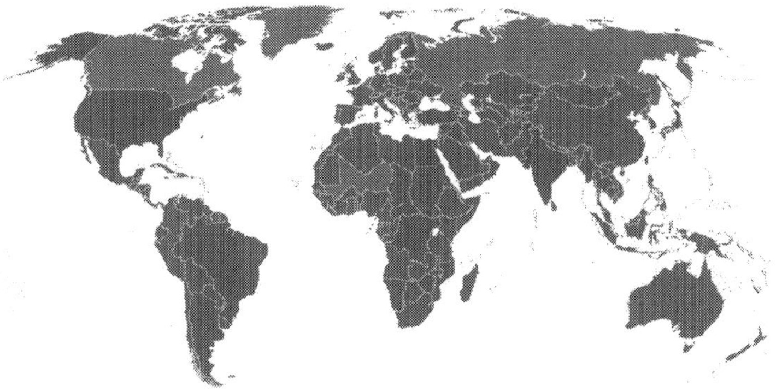

CHAPTER 2

McKinsey and Trotter, a relatively new executive search firm, was located at the foot of California Street, in San Francisco's financial district. Robert McKinsey founded the firm, M&T, as it was called, as a retirement afterthought following a successful career as an investment banker a decade earlier. He had no idea the firm's success would mean millions of dollars added to the already sizeable fortune in his investment portfolio.

McKinsey, or Mac, as he preferred, convinced his old business confidant and silent partner, Gene Trotter, to come in on the project with him. Mac was an alumnus and mentor at Stanford University, so their initial understanding was that Mac would come up with two Stanford graduates who were currently working successfully in the local area to manage the company. Mac did not let Gene down.

Dane Ashton, an MBA graduate, had developed highly polished management skills within five years after leaving the university and joining a Silicon Valley software firm. For Mac, Dane was a natural to follow his own example to business success. Mac, as chairman of the board of M&T, chose Dane as his president and chief executive officer.

For chief operations officer, Mac selected Mitch, an electrical engineering graduate who possessed scientific and technical skills as well as perhaps unexpected "people person" attributes.

A close friend and business confidant had cautioned Mac that choosing two young newcomers to the field of executive search could be courting disaster. Nevertheless, Mac, having served as a mentor during their undergraduate years, believed they were two exceptional people able to run the firm. Besides, starting the firm was really an experiment, if nothing else. Given his stage in life and financial security, he was intrigued by the idea of seeing if two quality individuals could drive a firm upwards based upon a formula for success he'd give them to carry out.

Dane's family was from old Boston money interests, banking and investments, and they were disappointed when he chose to go to Stanford instead of Harvard. Years earlier, Mac had numerous investments with one of the Boston banks owned by Dane's family. He also became a good friend to Dane's father. As a result, it was Mac's pleasure to serve as Dane's mentor throughout his university schooling.

Similarly, Mac was on intimate business terms with Mitch's father, Nicolai. Mac had become a firm believer in Nicolai's commodities analysis techniques as a result of one particular gold stock purchase that, over the course of eighteen months, involved several buy and sell periods that resulted in a net profit of $1.5 million on an investment of $2 million. Such profit was unheard of at the time. Mac continued to invest with Nicolai whenever the opportunity arose.

After Nicolai's death, Mac stepped in and became Mitch's godfather. When Mitch entered the university, Mac became his mentor as well. Mac never had a son of his own and found Mitch a delight to counsel toward a successful career.

Dane and Mitch roomed together for two years in a university dorm and then shared an apartment in Los Altos for the next three years. In that time, they both received bachelors and master's degrees, Dane in business administration and Mitch in electrical engineering.

Dane was more outgoing and extroverted while Mitch was more of a loner. However, their opposite personalities came to bond them together as the closest of friends. Mitch initially viewed with envy Dane's people skills. When together with a group of friends, Mitch would watch how Dane dealt with them. As a result, by their senior year Mitch found much to gain by emulating Dane's outgoing ways.

In terms of their major fields of study, their differences came to the forefront. After classes, Dane would attend business club forums and excursions to local Silicon Valley firms, making new personal contacts all along the way. Mitch, on the other hand, preferred conducting experiments in the engineering lab, mostly in the area of laser optics. He also thoroughly enjoyed track, namely running sixteen-hundred-meter races, as well as cross-country and marathon running.

Being a singleton runner in a long race, the excitement and pulse of the chase grew exponentially with each step. He could feel the vibrations down to the soles of his feet. With his senses improving as the race progressed, he drove himself forward, becoming possessed with achieving success. This was the same kind of driving energy he would later bring to bear when working as a NOC for the CIA. With single-minded purposefulness, he relentlessly pushed himself to seek out potential target individuals who would have information of intelligence value to the Agency.

Although Mac had mentored other students at the university prior to forming M&T, Dane and Mitch clearly were his favorites. Both turned out to be very levelheaded, forthright, and strategic thinkers in outlook. What sold him for the subsequent M&T endeavor, after both Dane and Mitch had graduated and had been working for several years, was the strong friendship they had for each other and their ability to commit to the subsequent forging of a business relationship. As a result, M&T became the new upstart in San Francisco's business community engaged in executive search recruiting and personnel placement.

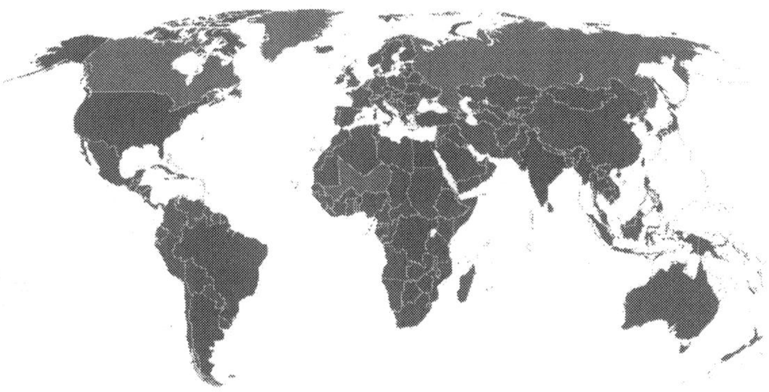

CHAPTER 3

"Good day to you, Paddy," the bar hostess said, with a twinkle in her eye, as Padraig Cahill made his way to the bar to order his usual pint of stout.

Slattery's Bar, on Capel Street, remained his favorite hangout in Dublin. It was half past four in the afternoon and he had just gotten off the day shift at work.

Patrick, as he preferred to be called, was in a foul mood, as if it was not unexpected lately.

"Caitlin, regardless what you call me, I still love you dearly," Patrick replied. "But why don't you just leave me alone to drown in the glass of heaven you're going to pour for me?"

"What is it now," she asked. "Is it the job or are the poilini still giving you a bad time?" she asked.

"Poilini, peas, the Guards, police, bastard Brits, whatever you want to call them, they are still showing their ugly heads around me too often," he said.

"They just won't stop, will they?" she said.

"I am the best supervisor and troubleshooter on the biggest assembly line in the fucking plant, but when management finds out who I'm related to, they start giving me a bad time," he replied. "The Americans have a major stake in the plant and I'm neither concerned nor bothered by them. Except for a couple of senior types, I hardly see them at all anyway. But it's the influence of the fucking Brits that's caught up with me once again," he said.

"I thought you were interested in moving across the pond to see if California was the place to be for awhile."

"I've got the money saved up now," Patrick said, "and I'd definitely like the change, but I'm convinced my commitment is to remain here for the time being."

"Well," Caitlin said, "I don't want to see you go anyway."

"I believe my family was right all along in how to best deal with the fucking Brits," he said.

"I know where this is going, Patrick, and I don't want to hear anymore about it," she replied.

"That's fine with me," he said. "If you don't want to see me around here anymore, just say so."

"That's not what I said," she replied.

"You know how I feel about the way you pour heaven's dew," he said. "So I'll still be around to see you whenever I can."

"Thanks, sporting man," she said. "I really needed to hear that from you and the hundred other gents who stumble in and out of here. Don't do me any favors," she added.

With that, Patrick downed his stout, forgot about wanting to have another, and said goodbye to Caitlin and Slattery's Bar.

As a 31-year-old electrical engineer in charge of running an assembly line producing electronic sensor components at one of the largest assembly plants in Ireland, just outside Dublin, Patrick was proud of his chosen work. He had hoped his penchant for quality design work, along with troubleshooting existing components would be his entry into the next level of accomplishment – namely, systems design, rather than just components.

However, as the nephew of Joe Cahill, born to one of Cahill's firebrand sisters, much less being the godson of Seamus Twomey, Patrick had his work cut out for him. Cahill and Twomey, two of the legendary leaders of the Provisional Irish Republican Army, had preached full-scale guerilla war against the British. They were the key figures behind "the Troubles," from the late 1960s through the late 1990s.

Patrick knew he was marked, according to the British, as someone who had to be watched to see just what he was really up to besides holding down a good-paying job. The fucking Brits were a thorn in his side.

Fortunately, starting when Patrick was eight years old, he was taught by his uncle and his godfather in how to watch and check for people following him. As a result, he became deftly alert to people around him and any strangers that might be surveilling him during his travels in the cities and the countryside. When he was older, he thought the move from Belfast to Dublin would enable him to get a good job and settle down on his own. He also thought the move would get him away from the frequent surveillance tactics and accosting by his sworn enemies, the peas and the hated Brits.

On occasion, while at work in the plant, he would notice a stranger talking to his supervisor, accompanied by a glance his way. Much the same after work while on his way home, as well as into the evening. The notice of a stranger standing in the shadows of a building, or the car driving slowly with two occupants inside, told him he was not yet free and truly on his own.

As a result of always being watched, and his staunch unionist family upbringing in Belfast, he was left with nothing in his heart but hatred for the Brits. Fortunately, though, while growing up there he had pretty much stayed out of trouble. He experienced only a few encounters with the peas, similar to that of a young teenager growing up most anywhere.

Now however, over thirty and still bothered by the watching and surveillance from those suspicious of him in Dublin, he felt it was time for a change.

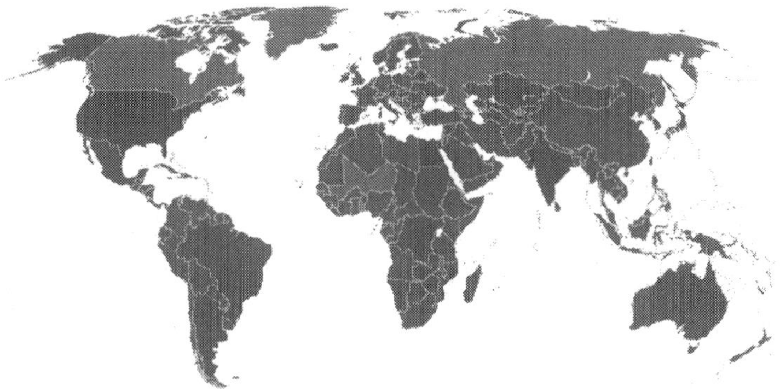

CHAPTER 4

The first morning back from Oslo, Mitch brewed a pot of coffee, had a glass of orange juice and started reading the *San Francisco Chronicle*. From the balcony view eastward across the bay, he could only see part of Alcatraz Island due to the early morning fog that had not yet fully lifted.

He knew that before going into the office he would boot up his laptop and check for encrypted cable traffic from headquarters. After finishing the paper and starting on his third cup of coffee, he checked the incoming cables and found what was foremost in his mind – the proposal for him to approach the Irish engineer in Dublin.

DIRECTOR 19648 191420Z NOV 11
TO: PRIORITY KINTARO, DUBLIN, STOCKHOLM, OSLO INFO SAN FRANCISCO
SECRET RESTRICTED HANDLING
WNINTEL
SUBJECT: PROPOSAL TO APPROACH DUBLIN STATION LEAD IDENTITY A

REFS: A. STOCKHOLM 22376 (NOT SENT/NEEDED SAN FRANCISCO)
B. DUBLIN 16424 (NOT SENT/NEEDED KINTARO, SAN FRANCISCO)
C. OSLO 14986 (NOT SENT/NEEDED KINTARO, SAN FRANCISCO)
ACTION REQUESTED: NOC KINTARO COMMENTS AND SUGGESTIONS AND, IF AGREEABLE, TIMEFRAME FOR INITIATING APPROACH TO IDEN A.

1. HQS APPRECIATES STOCKHOLM STATION OFFICER BRUBACHER (P) MEETING WITH HQS CTC NOC KINTARO (P) IN NORWAY. THANKS ALSO TO OSLO STATION FOR MEETING VENUE.
2. DUBLIN STATION LEAD, IDEN A, BASED UPON COMMENTS MADE TO STATION ASSET, TRTWITTY/1 (T/1), WOULD APPEAR TO OFFER POSSIBLE POTENTIAL FOR USE AS PENETRATION AGAINST RADICAL ISLAMIC TERRORIST TARGETS IN THE UK.
3. RECENT COMMENTS MADE BY IDEN A ARE STRONGLY ANTI-BRITISH AS BASED UPON IDEN A'S PROVISIONAL IRA LEANINGS AND FAMILY BACKGROUND. IDEN A ALSO EXPRESSES INTEREST IN "GETTING EVEN" AS RESULT SURVEILLANCE EFFORTS AGAINST IDEN A THAT INCLUDES REVEALING TO IDEN A'S EMPLOYER, IDEN B, MI5 AND GARDA SIOCHANA (POLICE FORCE OF THE REPUBLIC OF IRELAND) KEEPING TRACK OF IDEN A'S ACTIVITIES.
4. HQS PROPOSES THAT NOC KINTARO, USING THE PIPESTEM COMMERCIAL COVER, ADVISE ADDEES OSTENSIBLE APPROACH SCENARIO FOR MAKING DIRECT CONTACT WITH IDEN A. THIS COULD BE UNDER GUISE OF OFFERING FUTURE ASSISTANCE IN LANDING A POSITION WITH A PHOENIX OR BOSTON AREA ELECTRONICS FIRM.
5. OBJECT IS TO INITIATE CONTACT AND LAY GROUNDWORK FOR SUSTAINED CONTACT IN ORDER TO DETERMINE DEGREE OF HOSTILITY TOWARDS BRITISH AND IRISH AUTHORITIES, AND HOW SERIOUS IDEN A IS IN WILLINGNESS TO SEEK RETRIBUTION.

6. IF KINTARO ABLE TO MEET AND ULTIMATELY DEVELOP FAVORABLE ASSESSMENT OF IDEN A, HQS, DUBLIN STATION AND KINTARO CAN DEVELOP SUBSEQUENT RECRUITMENT SCENARIO. HQS LEAVES OPEN POSSIBILITY FOR USE OF STOCKHOLM STATION OFFICER BRUBACHER IN A RECRUITMENT ROLE.
7. HQS TRACES ON IDEN A WERE NEGATIVE.
8. FILE DEFER. E2IMPDET.

A second identity cable followed, giving IDENTITY A as Padraig Cahill, IDEN B as 5Com Ireland Electronics Limited, located in Blanchardstown, a suburb in the northwest of Dublin, and PIPESTEM as the encrypted cover name for Mitch's commercial alias cover company in Phoenix, Arizona.

Even after serving as a NOC for seven years, Mitch still liked to see his pseudonym name of KINTARO being used in all Agency cable traffic. BRUBACHER was the pseudo for Stockholm Station officer, Lee Denning. Mitch did not much care for headquarters mentioning use of Lee for the possible recruitment pitch, instead of himself. But in many of the cases involving pitches against members of terrorist groups, an inside station officer, or a CTC case officer sent out from headquarters, was invariably used to make the pitch.

Mitch was reminded of his first recruitment pitch several years earlier. A member of an Arab terrorist group was originally spotted by an inside station case officer who proceeded to assess and develop him over a period of time. Another inside case officer was brought into the picture and the target individual was further developed and brought to the point of making a recruitment pitch based on his access to excellent information of high interest. Headquarters and station management decided however, that Mitch, due to his NOC status, his ethnic background, and his Arabic language capability, would be the most suitable officer to make the pitch and be the subsequently handler.

The turnover was actually affected however, when Mitch was successful in introducing himself to the target individual without any involvement of the other inside station officers, typically referred to as an indirect turnover. After a short period of time, Mitch recruited the target and proceeded to regularly obtain from him excellent intelligence information. After about four or five meetings over the course of just over a year, the Arab, to Mitch's surprise, named the two inside case officers by the alias names they had used with him, and asked if Mitch happened to know them. Obviously, Mitch denied any knowledge of the other two officers and the subject was never brought up again. Mitch concluded that the Arab made a connection between the other two officers and him in what is termed a daisy-chain technique. Fortunately, due to the Arab's recruitment vulnerability of wanting to substantially improve his financial situation, he was willing to go along with the recruitment pitch and subsequent work as an agent penetration of a terrorist group regardless the individual officers involved.

The mid-morning sun had burned the fog off the bay by the time Mitch finished reading all of his cable traffic. Except for the two cables from headquarters CTC on the Irish engineer, the remaining cables dealt with routine administrative support issues and assorted worldwide terrorist actions and individual cases of interest.

As a backup to his laptop system, Mitch occasionally had direct contact with San Francisco Station. However, because he was a headquarters NOC, working under CTC direction, contact with the station was sporadic at best. As a courtesy more than anything else, the station was sent an info copy on all traffic between headquarters and Mitch and any other stations involved.

In an emergency or anything that required direct contact, either Mitch or the station could initiate a personal meeting. The meeting sites were all pre-arranged and held at locations outside of San Francisco proper. Because of M&T being located in the city, not far from the station's location, Mitch's preferences on where to meet prevailed, much to the chagrin of the Deputy Chief of Station, who served as Mitch's designated inside point of contact. The Deputy did not like to travel far from the station. Mitch, however, did not want to be seen anywhere near the station, let alone seen in the presence of someone who worked there. Maintaining his own personal operational security was paramount and, as a result, his favorite venues were in the town of Sausalito, in Marin County just north of the Golden Gate Bridge, or across the Bay in the cities of Berkeley and Oakland.

Dane, working a short distance away at M&T, was fully witting of Mitch's covert status with the Agency. He was originally bothered when Mitch disclosed some years earlier that he'd been approached by the Agency to work for them. But, then it was agreed that Mitch would accept the Agency's proposal, followed by a full-time training period of one year, and then return to M&T and continue to work there on as close to a full-time basis as possible. As a result, Dane accepted Mitch's absences and their close personal and business relationship never wavered. Mitch promised Dane never to fail in sharing his half of the management load and he was determined not to let him down.

The sweetheart of a deal offered by the Agency to M&T to compensate for Mitch's absences while working for the Agency also helped to ease any potential additional burden Dane would have to shoulder in running the firm. In fact, the deal offered provided enough compensation to allow Dane and Mitch to interview and hire a Deputy Chief Operations Officer, Sumiko Kuroda, a fourth-generation American-born woman of Japanese descent. With a Harvard MBA and several years experience in the personal recruiting field, she displayed exceptionally strong management and people-person skills. As a result, she was rapidly able to take on all the kinds of tasks Mitch usually handled. This included the primary work of contracting with client firms to find suitable candidates for employment, and the searching and lengthy interviews required to fill primarily high-paying positions in technology firms.

Entering into a contract on a contingency basis, a client firm would pay a substantial fee for M&T to search for, interview and offer up candidates to work under contract. The payment of the fee would be contingent on the actual hiring of the candidate and paid within an agreed upon timeframe after work commenced.

Mac, in his role as Chairman of the board of M&T, was in total agreement with the Agency's deal for Mitch's services. Likewise, Mac fully supported Dane and Mitch's decision in the hiring of Sumiko. Only Mac and Dane were witting of Mitch's Agency work. Sumiko was unwitting and was only told that Mitch's frequent absences were for his own personal and separate business interests.

Having occasional contact with several Directors of the CIA (DCIA) over the years, usually to meet and brief them on international business prospects and developments, Mac was no stranger to how the Agency functioned and operated. In fact, over rounds of golf with DCI's over the years, he became privy to the need for people such as Mitch for deep undercover work abroad.

What made the case for Mitch unique, according to what Mac understood from the signed arrangement, is that Mitch was not hired first by the Agency, trained and then offered up to M&T. Instead, Mitch's existing position, when hired by the Agency, provided him with his already built-in cover for action. Moreover, although operating in his true name identity as an officer of M&T, he could nevertheless openly perform vitally useful intelligence work abroad in the spotting, assessing and developing of target individuals of interest. On the clandestine side, with multiple alias identities and disguises to use, he would be able to go further than the spotting, assessing and developing phases. He would also be able to recruit and subsequently handle, for intelligence production purposes, penetrations of terrorist groups of interest.

Coming up upon noontime, Mitch was ready to head over to M&T and resume work. Dane and Sumiko would brief him on developments that took place in his absence. He would plan to write his response to the headquarters cable after returning home in the evening. Not being married or seriously dating anyone, Mitch was the classic around the clock workaholic, both in his M&T work and in his covert job for the Agency. It did not matter.

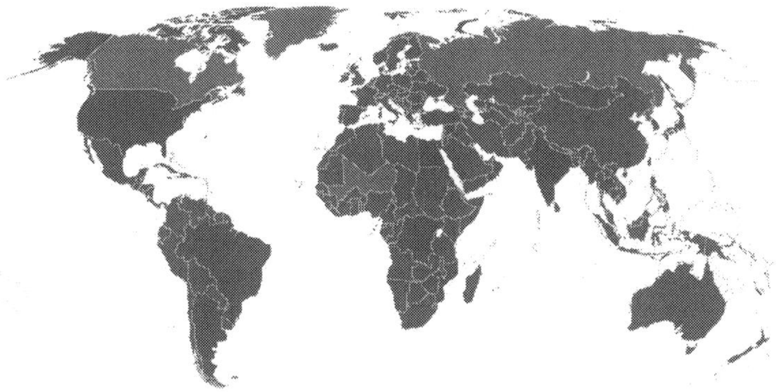

CHAPTER 5

Jack Benson, the headquarters group chief responsible for the management of all the NOCs assigned to CTC's Radical Islamic Terrorist Group (RITG), was the originator of the cables sent to Mitch. Always buoyant and upbeat, "Cowboy," as known by his call sign, was a senior career operations officer previously assigned to the former Soviet and East European Division (SE) of the old Directorate of Operations (DO). His specialty was the very difficult recruitment of Soviet KGB and military intelligence officers. However, as is usual when one is successful working the same target for a number of years, it did not matter how many alias and disguises were used, overall physical appearance alone would make a person well known to the Soviet services. As result, Jack decided he needed a career change.

With CTC in need of experienced and successful case officers, Jack landed the coveted senior position as the RITG Group Chief. With five NOCs, including Mitch, and more than twenty-five headquarters case officers working for him, Jack was up to the task. He had earned his "spurs" over the years. Best of all, it was a position he had come to relish. He was back in the hunt.

Jack brought to CTC his distinguished work against the Soviets for more than two decades. In fact, within the old KGB target spectrum alone, he was most successful against officers working in the KGB's "Fifth Department of the Directorate K." This referred to KGB officers who specialized in counterintelligence and the penetration of other foreign intelligence and security services through the recruitment of their officers.

Jack attributed his success to carefully building a personal friendship with any Soviet officer he was targeted against. He exerted no pressure or outward appearances of trying to assess and collect information over a period of time. Instead, Jack, in his fluent command of the Russian language, would let the KGB officer know he was a friend who could be called upon in a time of need. It did not matter if the officer suspected or outright knew that Jack was a CIA case officer.

What Jack hoped for was that the officer was not reporting to his management inside the "Rezidentura" (the KGB equivalent of a CIA station), and subsequently to Moscow KGB headquarters, on the personal meetings held between the two of them. Over time, Jack would use the growing personal relationship to determine if any potentially exploitable vulnerability existed. If the KGB officer eventually revealed things like not being on good terms with superiors, or failing to receive a perceived earned promotion and stay on a good career track, these represented the "hooks" that Jack could use to base a recruitment pitch. Additional vulnerabilities Jack looked for were financial difficulties, problems with a spouse or children, and illnesses in the family.

With one or more exploitable vulnerabilities being present, Jack would submit a recruitment scenario to headquarters and, upon receiving the required approvals, make a proposal for the officer to work in place for the Agency for an agreed upon period of time. Taking a KGB officer, or even a Soviet military intelligence officer, this far down the path to recruitment was a monumental accomplishment.

The capability in the language, their camaraderie, and the establishment of a growing personal relationship, did not necessarily mean the KGB officer fully trusted Jack. However, it provided the basis for Jack to proceed with his recruitment pitch and subsequent fulfillment of promises made.

Mitch rapidly rose to become Jack's favorite NOC. Jack was highly impressed with Mitch's work ethic, sound operational thinking, tradecraft skills, and growing success working the target pool. In the five years that they had now been working together, they'd had only about ten direct face-to-face meetings. Instead, their almost daily contact was via the encrypted commo capability that Mitch carried in his laptop.

A number of hostile, as well as friendly intelligence services, knew Jack as an Agency officer. Therefore, for those rare face-to-face meetings to provide for Mitch's NOC cover status and operational security, they met only in the U.S., in smaller cities away from the headquarters area, and away from the entire East Coast. Mitch, in an alias identity, would rent a room in a large hotel in the busy downtown center of the city. Jack would stay in another hotel in a different part of the city.

It was during one of those meetings, six months after Mitch's training regiment was over and he was just beginning to show what he could do operationally in the field overseas, that they got together in the early autumn in Helena, Montana. They had exchanged a number of cables and Jack thought it was time to impart to Mitch a few of the axioms from his Soviet days.

The two of them were enjoying glasses of single malt Scotch while sitting on the veranda of Mitch's hotel room. The stars that night were vivid. Occasional meteors were also quickly shooting across the sky as well.

"As you have been finding out for the last six months," Jack told Mitch, "working against the radical Islamist terrorist target is a difficult challenge. Regardless your fluency in Arabic, I can see from your reporting you have barely gotten close enough to use much of the language."

"That's right," Mitch replied. "You are always viewed as an outsider. I would not even think about trying to make an approach directly to any Arab or Muslim, either in the mosques or coffee shops where they hang out."

"You went to a mosque a couple of months ago in Hamburg."

"Yes, it was the last prayer of the day, on a Thursday, and because I was a new face I drew nothing but stares. I had even dressed down to appear like a local resident. Afterwards I stopped at a café that I'd seen some of the faithful from the mosque enter. Again, I attempted to talk to no one. I received several more stares and no approaches were made to me. Not a single one."

"Your future cover trips, in either true name or alias, will eventually result in you being approached. But, it will take time," Jack said. "You have to be seen a couple of times, be recognized from before, and you will then be queried about who you are, where are you from, any tribal affiliations and so on."

"I have an idea," Mitch said, "of setting up temporary offices in several European cities. With that, I can plausibly support visiting some local job fairs, go to pray in the mosques and visit some coffee shops. I will be able to refer to working out of my local office, and see what happens."

"I like that. Keep me advised. Between your many true names trips for M&T, combined with the alias trips under a different commercial cover, it is just a matter of time. Meanwhile, I thought you might find it useful to hear some tried and true old words from me that result from working for too many years against the Soviet target."

"Great," replied Mitch, "I like that. What have you got?"

"These were referred to as the rules of engagement when working, against terrible odds, in what was then the Soviet target. They still apply today in dealing with the Russians and any of the other hard targets for that matter. They are called 'The Moscow Rules.' I'm quite sure some of these are listed in the writings of John Le Carre, like in *Tinker, Tailor, Soldier, Spy* and *Smiley's People*, two great reads if you don't know them already. Put these rules in the context of the targets you are dealing with now, and they may prove useful to you. They represent common sense that is actually useful to an intelligence officer operating anywhere in the world. I will number them for you. Some of us in the old Soviet Division who spent years working in Moscow can recall fifteen to twenty, or more. For me, the most important ten are:"

"One, assume nothing."

"Two, never go against your gut feeling."

"Three, everyone you see and meet is probably under some form of opposition control."

"Four, don't look back behind you; it's a given that you are never completely alone."

"Five, do not under any circumstances, harass the opposition – never."

"Six, go with the flow and always try to blend in."

"Seven, stay within your cover."

"Eight, lull them into a sense of complacency."

"Nine, you can and must pick the time for action when choosing to go operational."

"And ten, keep your options open."

"I can certainly relate to all of them," Mitch replied.

"Oh, I can remember another particular one that is especially useful in developing your streets smarts – Once is an accident, twice is coincidence, and three times is enemy action against you."

Jack enjoyed his meeting with Mitch and departed late that evening to return to his own hotel. In his gut, he felt confident that Mitch was on solid ground towards becoming a superior intelligence officer. Overall, reflecting back on that autumn meeting, Jack believed it also served to cement what was going to turn out to be an excellent, even if by long distance, relationship. He saw in Mitch what he felt years earlier was his own zeal to succeed in the hunt. He wished he had Mitch's youth and future prospects so that he could spend many more years enjoying the practice of his craft.

Mitch fell asleep that night further appreciating Jack's professionalism, dedication and coming to serve as a father figure that he hadn't had since he was 12 years old. In Jack, he found respect and admiration that would further propel him forward in seeking out his own success. Jack's track record as a recruiter and producer of quality intelligence reporting was well established in the Agency. Mitch's record, while small in comparison, was starting to show results. However, with youth and time on his side, Mitch was confident of one day proving his worth, particularly insofar his growing working relationship with Jack.

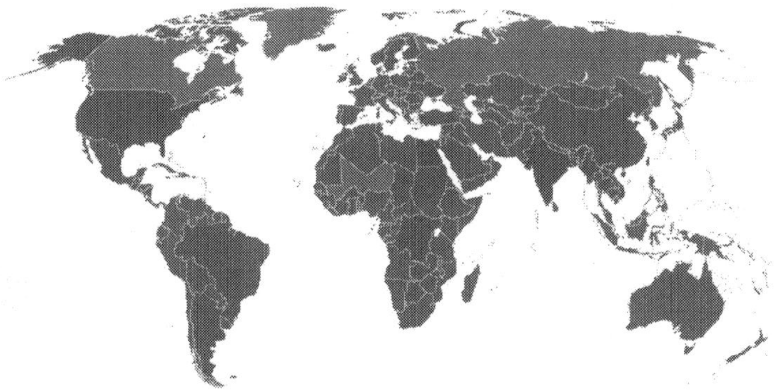

CHAPTER 6

Mitch met nonstop with Dane and Sumiko that afternoon. They brought him up-to-date on the happenings in the office, details on the signing of several new clients and an upcoming schedule of appointments for the following week. Upon leaving the office around seven in the evening, Mitch could feel the need for his favorite food before returning home.

"Ebisu Japanese Cuisine," located out in the Avenues of the City, at Irving and Ninth Avenue, was his favorite sushi-ya. Hiro-san, the master sushi chef, immediately recognized Mitch upon entering, gave him the usual "Irasshaimase," the traditional Japanese greeting, and motioned for him to take an empty seat in front of him at the counter. Mitch inquired about Hiro-san's health and the well-being of his family, who still resided in Osaka. Hiro-san expressed his appreciation and summoned a server to take Mitch's drink order.

Mitch ordered a "masu" (small wooden box) of his preferred cold sake, "Kamotsuru," from Hiroshima. The server brought it to him with the empty box sitting in a small saucer. She then filled it from a bottle she carried, until it just began to overflow onto the saucer. This was the traditional way to indicate a full measure of sake had been poured. She departed but quickly returned with a much smaller saucer containing sea salt. Mitch picked up a pinch of the salt between a thumb and forefinger and positioned it on the top edge of the box in the corner closest to him. He then proceeded to sip from the same corner and savor the dry quality of this premium sake, tinged with a slight salt taste.

Mitch made numerous trips to Japan for M&T. He would negotiate contracts with Japanese high technology firms seeking American senior management candidates for ultimate placement to operate their production facilities and offices in various locations in the US. Mitch would search for prospective candidates and subsequently hold several interviews with each of those he found suitable. He would then narrow the choices down to two or three and offer them for consideration by the Japanese client firms' management team.

The client firm would usually select one for Mitch to bring to Japan for interviewing and consideration for an offer of employment. If the firm was impressed, the candidate would be asked to inspect production facilities and offices, followed by a formal contractual offer of employment, benefits and options package included. The contract would include an agreement for the candidate to plan another trip to Japan, after the contract was signed, to undergo in-house training in the Japanese firm's products and services, as well as their style and way of doing business. At some point agreed upon between Mitch and the client firm, usually nearing the end of the candidate's training period, M&T would receive their fee for services rendered.

Savoring the box of sake until it was empty, Mitch then made eye contact with Hiro-san and proceeded to first order a sampling of sashimi. Hiro-san knew well the slices of fish that Mitch preferred: Chu Toro, or fatty tuna; Hamachi, yellowtail; Tai, red snapper; Hirame, halibut; Saba, Spanish mackerel; and Tako, octopus.

"Today I received some very fresh Aji, horse mackerel. Would you like that added to your order?"

"Thank you. By all means, I would like that as well." Mitch ordered a refill for his box of sake and serenely anticipated his enjoyment of what he would soon be served.

Since he and Dane organized M&T, both of them made numerous trips all over the world to sign contracts with clients followed by the searching out and placement of successful candidates. Along the way, for Mitch, another serious appreciation that he developed was perfecting his skills in dancing the tango. This evening however, while in the process of enjoying the first one, an appreciation for raw fish, he knew he would have no time for the second one. Once finished with his dinner, he had to return home and compose the cable reply to headquarters.

After the sashimi, Mitch ordered several kinds of nigiri sushi. This would serve to round out, as he expected, another memorable dinner in a sushi-ya where he felt completely relaxed. Along with a final box of sake, the nigiri sushi he ordered included: Uni, sea urchin; Amaebi no tama, raw fresh shrimp; and ikura, salmon roe.

During the short fifteen-minute drive back to the Marina district, Mitch finalized in his mind the subsequent cable he would write.

CITE KINTARO 2143 210514Z NOV 11
TO: PRIORITY DIRECTOR, DUBLIN, STOCKHOLM INFO SAN FRANCISCO
S E C R E T RESTRICTED HANDLING
WNINTEL
SUBJECT: PROPOSAL TO APPROACH DUBLIN STATION LEAD PER REF
REF: DIRECTOR 19648

ACTION REQUESTED: 1. HQS AND DUBLIN STATION CONCURRENCE TO APPROACH REF LEAD DURING TIMEFRAME CONDITIONS CITED BELOW. 2. HQS PLEASE SEND PIPESTEM ALIAS COVER DOCS TO DUBLIN STATION FOR PASSAGE TO KINTARO AFTER ARRIVAL. 3. DUBLIN STATION ADVISE DEAD DROP LOCATION AND DETAILS FOR PASSING DOCS, INCLUDING KINTARO RELOADING DROP WITH TRUE NAME DOCS. WILL REQUIRE SECOND DEAD DROP FOR REVERSE SWITCH OF DOCS PRIOR TO DEPARTING COUNTRY.

1. NOC KINTARO PROPOSES TO TRAVEL TO DUBLIN CIRCA FIRST WEEK OF DECEMBER TO ATTEMPT CONTACT WITH STATION LEAD CITED REF.
2. IN VIEW STATION'S LIAISON EQUITIES, KINTARO PREFERENCE IS TO CONDUCT OWN LIMITED RECCE OF AREA AND SURVEILLANCE OF LEAD PRIOR TO CONTACT. THIS WILL BE TWOFOLD: ONE, ALLOW FOR ASCERTAINING REF LEAD IS FREE OF ANY PHYSICAL SURVEILLANCE AGAINST HIM; AND TWO, IF FREE, SEARCH

OUT LOCATIONS WHERE KINTARO CAN PLAUSIBLY DIRECTLY APPROACH. NOTE, KINTARO WILL AVOID ANY KIND OF APPROACH IN TRTWITTY/1'S ESTABLISHMENT.

3. THE PIPESTEM COMMERCIAL COVER SHOULD PROVIDE PLAUSIBLE REASON FOR SUSTAINING CONTACT SHOULD INITIAL APPROACH BE ACCEPTED. IF SO, KINTARO, OVER COURSE SEVERAL DAYS, WOULD ATTEMPT HOLD TWO OR MORE MEETINGS PRIOR TO DEPARTING COUNTRY. AGREEMENT WOULD THEN BE SOUGHT TO MEET UP AGAIN, AFTER KINTARO'S PLANNED RETURN WITHIN ONE MONTH, DURING EARLY JANUARY.
4. PLEASE ADVISE.
5. FILE: DEFER. E2IMPDET.

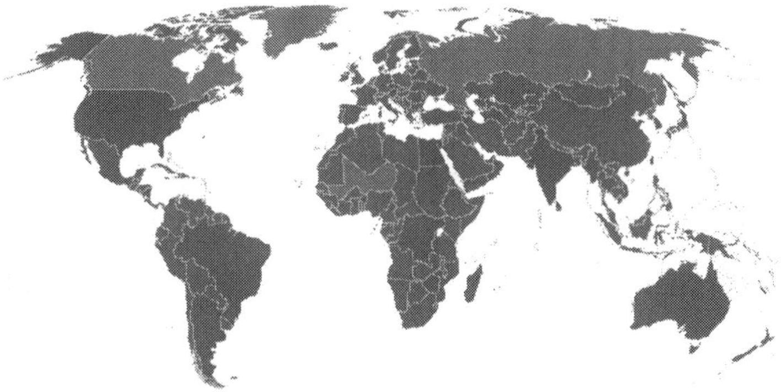

CHAPTER 7

The following week was busy, to say the least. One of the new clients Dane signed up during Mitch's absence was perfect for him to take over: a Silicon Valley laser optics firm seeking a senior physics researcher for their research and development department. Mitch thought that within two months he could have two or three candidates for the firm to consider hiring. Actually, he already had one specific candidate in mind, provided the fellow was still receptive to a job change. With the position paying a minimum $225,000 a year, plus a lucrative benefits package, he believed the fellow would be interested.

Mitch also received concurrences from headquarters and Dublin Station for the approach to the Irish engineer, along with details on the two dead drop locations, both in Dublin. What he did not expect was the phone call from Jack, setting up a meeting prior to the trip to Ireland. Usually, all meetings were set up via cable traffic. However, it was always good to hear Jack's voice and Mitch immediately agreed to meet in two days time. He made plans with Dane and Sumiko to cover what little minor items of work he would be unable to complete before the meeting.

The subsequent flight to meet with Jack, as agreed upon this time in New Orleans, was just less than three hours away and just enough for Mitch to settle into a light sleep. Before dozing off his thoughts turned to how he first came to be involved with the Agency. As he recalled, it started out following an enjoyable vacation trip to the land of his birth, Italy. Because of a purely chance encounter seven years earlier, he was spotted by a senior Agency official, subsequently vetted, screened, approached and recruited as a deep cover NOC officer.

*D*uring the early summer of 2005, while spending two weeks along the Cinque Terre and Almalfi coasts, Mitch was thoroughly enjoying working on his Italian language skills. Although he left at the age of three, Italy remained the country that held the most fascination for him. He returned there whenever possible to visit various regions and soak up the way of life he never experienced growing up in southern California.

Spending several days in the beautifully situated resort town of Ravello, on a hillside overlooking a gorgeous expanse of the Almalfi coast, Mitch was sipping a glass of chilled Pinot Grigio at an outdoor café on the edge of the main piazza. Kathleen Capps had exited a curio shop around the corner from the café, turned the corner near where Mitch was sitting and tripped on the cobblestone walkway. She went down hard, twisted her ankle, and, fortunately softly, bumped her head as she landed.

Mitch, sitting less than ten feet away, jumped up and bounded to her side. He gently lifted her to a sitting position. "Are you alright?" he asked.

She looked dazed, and replied, "Yes, I'm OK, more embarrassed than anything else. Will you help me up, please?"

He placed an arm around her waist, lifting her up so that she leaned against his side and chest. However, Mitch could see she was in no condition to put any weight on what was going to become a bruised and swollen left ankle.

"Let me carry you over to that chair at my table."

"Please do," she replied.

As Mitch gently lowered Kathleen onto the chair, her husband, Steve, came around the corner.

"Hey, what's going on here?" he asked sharply.

Before Mitch could offer a reply, Kathleen said, "Steve, slow down Marine, this gentleman just saved me."

"I'm sorry sir," Mitch said, "but she fell on the cobblestones and needed help real quick."

"It's my ankle, Steve," Kathleen said, "It's already starting to hurt."

Steve bent down and began examining her injured ankle. He stood and said to Mitch, "I owe you an apology. Thank you for coming to the aid of my wife."

"Your welcome. I was looking towards the corner as she came around it and went down," Mitch replied.

Kathleen looked up at Mitch and said, "You wouldn't happen to be a Marine would you?"

Mitch, with a sheepish grin on his face, replied, "No, but I do run a lot and try to stay in shape, if that helps."

"All the great men in my life have been Marines," Kathleen said. "Steve and my father are them and I thought I might be adding you to my list."

"That's a real compliment, ma'am. Thank you. Ever since high school and college," Mitch said, "I've been a runner. That's about the extent of my physical prowess."

"Well I thank you again. I'm Steve Capps and this is Kathleen. May we buy you a drink?"

"I'm Mitch Vasari. Sit down, let me get the drinks."

Kathleen looked at Steve, nodded, and said to Mitch: "I would like to rest up here for a few minutes and a glass of wine sounds wonderful."

For the next 20 minutes, with Kathleen showing signs of increasing pain, they made small talk about the Amalfi Coast and the beautiful setting of Ravello perched on a promontory high above the sea. Steve noted Mitch's fluent Italian when he ordered drinks.

"You sound like you're an American," Steve said to him, "but you look Italian and sound like a native when you speak it."

"Pretty close," Mitch replied. "I was born in Florence, but a few years later we moved to Palos Verdes, in southern California. My father was Italian and my mother is Egyptian."

"Where did you go to school?" Steve inquired.

"Stanford University. I majored in electrical engineering."

"You said your mother is Egyptian. Do you speak Arabic as well?"

"Yes, I do," Mitch replied. "Probably as good as, or a little better than Italian."

"Steve, I think I need to get back to our hotel, take a couple of pills and rest this ankle in some cold water," said Kathleen.

"I'll call our driver down the street in the parking lot and have him bring the car to the bottom of the hill below," replied Steve.

"Where are you staying?" Mitch asked.

"In Sorrento, at the Grand Hotel La Pace."

"That's at least an hour's drive," said Mitch. "I have a small suite right here in the Palazzo Sasso. Kathleen can rest there until she feels up to the drive back to Sorrento."

"Thank you," Steve said, "but I think it best we get her back to our hotel. You have been most kind. And again, I can't thank you enough for helping my wife."

While waiting for the driver, Steve and Mitch exchanged business cards. Steve's card only had his name on it, "Steven R. Capps,"

"This is quite a way not to advertise yourself. I like it," said Mitch.

Steve, with a wry grin on his face, replied, "I used to be in the government. The State Department to be specific, but I left after twenty years and went into consulting. With a card like this, I can pen in any additional information that I alone want to give out. Let me have it back and I will show you what I mean."

Steve wrote out a telephone number on the back of the card.

"This is the number for my Washington, D.C. office. If you are ever in town please give me a call and we can have lunch together."

"I'd like that a lot," replied Mitch. "I get to New York City several times a year, but haven't been to Washington yet."

"Better yet," Steve said, "How about joining Kathleen and me for dinner in Sorrento tomorrow night?"

"I would like that," Mitch said," but I already have a commitment here and I return to California early the following day."

The driver arrived; Mitch paid the waiter and asked to accompany Steve and Kathleen back to their car just a short distance away in the town parking lot below.

Kathleen stood up and leaned against Steve's shoulder as they made their way slowly down the hill to the car.

Along the way, Steve asked Mitch about his business card.

"You appear to me to be on the young side to be a Chief Operating Officer in a search firm," he said.

"Yes, I suppose so," Mitch replied. "I've been at it for several years now and am thirty years old. But because we specialize in the placement of primarily scientific and technical people, it is not so unusual to find someone my age in a senior position because of my technical background."

"Well," Steve said, "regardless your age, you have made an impression on me and, obviously, Kathleen. You are a gentleman and I sincerely hope our paths will cross again. Remember the invite for lunch in Washington."

"I'll take you up on it," Mitch replied. "My very best wishes to both of you. I hope Kathleen's ankle is not seriously injured and you can enjoy the rest of your vacation."

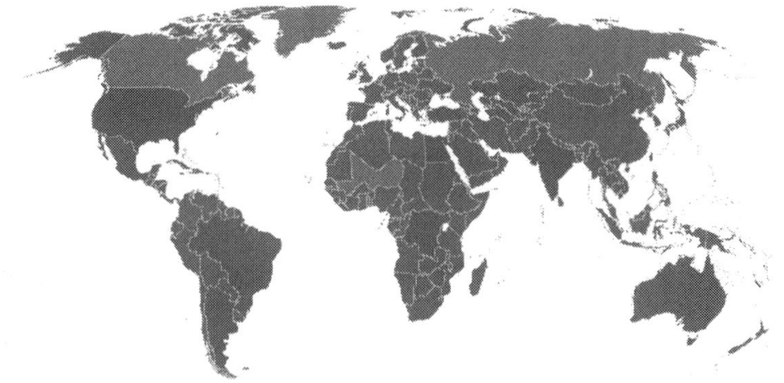

CHAPTER 8

Jack and Steve had previously worked together in the old Soviet Division at headquarters. While Jack gained prominence as an aggressive street-smart case officer and recruiter, Steve, similarly successful, rose further up through the ranks as an astute manager. After serving as Chief of Station Moscow, and Deputy Director of the National Clandestine Service (NCS), his current position was that of number two in the Agency – Deputy Director of the CIA (DDCIA).

Jack finished his preparations for the upcoming meeting with Mitch and was about to leave the headquarters building and head for home to pack and catch his flight to Baton Rouge. From there he would rent a car and take the short one-hour drive to his hotel in New Orleans.

He was interrupted by a call from the seventh floor of the old headquarters building, where Steve's office was located. Steve's executive assistant asked Jack if he could stop by for a brief meeting prior to leaving the building. Jack said he would be there in a few minutes. Steve and Jack had remained on the best of terms, even though Steve was fifteen years younger and had risen much further in the Agency. Both were professionals and respected each other's judgment and operational sense – two of the major guiding attributes for success in the world of intelligence.

When Steve and Kathleen returned seven years earlier from their too short vacation on the Amalfi Coast, Steve wasted no time in passing on a memo to the NOC office of recruitment, with an info copy to CTC. Although it would be viewed as exerting his influence, he had CTC included in the memo since he thought that with Mitch's ethnic and language background, they should have first consideration in expressing interest in him. Steve also asked to be kept appraised of any progress made by Mitch should he be contacted and agree to go through the rigorous screening and hiring process prior to being offered a position and brought on board the Agency.

Steve did not become the DDCIA because he was the brightest operations officer within the ranks. He got there because he produced results. Having been a Marine officer with many years of service behind him, he was a no-nonsense guy who could be brusque if need be. Whether it was managing the many case officers who served under him through the years, managing major stations overseas, or managing major components at headquarters, he earned the respect and admiration of not only his peers but members of the entire intelligence community as well.

Over the years, he was not only aware of the value of NOC officers and what they brought to the Agency, but also the attendant problems that existed in NOC ranks. For fifty years of the Agency's existence, the NOC program was always described to newly minted NOCs as the Agency's "wave of the future." They were to be the new breed that would rise to greatness based on their ability to go deep under cover in the world of commercial business. They would function totally outside and away from headquarters, the Washington, D.C. area, and any stations and bases throughout the world.

Yet, what happened during those years was anything but a wave of the future. They were viewed by station managers, as well as by too many inside operations officers, as less than capable to perform at a case officer level. Much of that belief was based on the perception that since NOCs never came inside a station, and instead held actual jobs with real commercial firms, they were outside of station control and direct management. Regardless that inside case officers and NOCs were provided with basically the same training, this view permeated professional ranks and led to a serious loss of morale and the feeling amongst the NOCs that they were always to be on the fringe and never really a part of the career intelligence officer service.

The screening process for NOCs, at times, also left much to be desired. As result, a number of people with personality defects and unsuitability for working as a singleton on their own in a foreign environment outside a station, found their way into the NOC cadre program. It also did not help that many of them turned in poor performances in their operational work. In those cases where they were highly successful in their cover work for their commercial sponsors, some were convinced by those sponsors to leave the Agency and work full time for these firms. The primary appeal made to these NOCs was most always increased financial inducements.

An additional complicating factor for low morale and concern amongst the NOCs were the security implications of a couple of defections by inside Agency operations officers who decided to go over to the Russians and reveal not only the names of Agency recruited Russian agents working in place, but the true name identities of a large number of NOC officers and inside case officers identities as well. When inside Agency officers turning traitor was combined with NOC disillusionment with headquarters and station management, the number of serving NOCs declined precipitously.

Nevertheless, a few bright NOC stars had indeed risen over the years. If nothing else, this was through their self-practice of excellent security and operational tradecraft, knowledge of the terrain when operating overseas, the highest of capabilities in their commercial business cover work, and consistently exceeding the expectations of headquarters and inside station management. These stars were able to securely and successfully spot, assess, develop, recruit and handle agents who produced high quality intelligence reporting. In those cases where recruited agents lost their access to produce intelligence, these NOCs were also able to terminate their relationships with the agents as well. This agent acquisition and handling cycle, for NOCs and inside operations officers alike, remains to this day the mantra that spells the success or failure of an intelligence officer.

This was the situation that confronted Steve seven years earlier as he prepared the memo about his initial encounter with Mitch in Italy. He believed the problem with NOC cadre had gotten out of hand and needed a remedy like none that had been tried before. As result, should Mitch be able to qualify for entrance on duty with the Agency, Steve was determined that he would be the real version of the wave of the future, and he would be trained in a different fashion than in the past.

"Jack, come on in, sit down," Steve said. "I don't get to see you much anymore. I wish it were otherwise."

"Good to see you," Jack replied. "Yeah, I know, we're both busy but I don't have the number of headaches you have to deal with, much less the pressure from Congress."

"You got that right," Steve said. "I don't want to take much of your time. As you may know from a read of the ops traffic today, our go-getter NOC, Mitch, is about to try to start up another case against a radical Islamic terrorist group. That's why I wanted a few minutes with you before you leave the building."

"It's always a pleasure to meet with you," Jack replied."Jack, who would have known that after I spotted this guy in Italy, he would be brought aboard and do so well?"

"I know." Jack said. "I'm proud of him too."

"After you indicated CTC interest in Mitch, I told you I wanted this NOC to be trained differently. I know I'm overdue in saying this, but I'm highly impressed by how you followed through with the training and how he turned out."

"Thank you, Steve. In looking back, our decision to train him on an individual basis, without any melding him in with other NOCs or inside officers, proved to be the way to go, as far as I'm concerned."

"All I know," Jack said, "We ended up with one hellava well-trained and capable NOC."

"Jack, I am now in process of reviewing with NOC management their latest efforts to move more NOCs into this singleton-type training mode. Don't be surprised if you get a call from their staff about making available some of the ops officers you were able to assemble for Mitch's training."

"I understand," Jack replied, "You know how I feel about the quality of CTC officers I have around me, regardless for operational tasking abroad or for training purposes. It is an exceptional group and we will do whatever we can."

"I know what you have gone through and I'm exceptionally pleased with your work. If you can help the NOC staff out, please do so. By the way," Steve continued, "I know you have a plane to catch, but I want to comment on the traffic we're reading on the current status with the radical Islamic groups assembling and operating over in the UK"

"You mean the sensitive source intelligence we are getting that is not coming from the Brits?" Jack asked.

"You got it. At least two of the groups, and we can't yet pin down their leadership or any further specifics, are indicating they realize the benefits of bringing, into their outer fringes only, non-Arabs and non-Muslims to do some of their operational tasking."

"We know the opportunity that presents, and it is great news," Jack replied.

"Be sure and bring Mitch up to speed on what we know about the few times these groups have tried this in the past. I want him fully aware of the ramifications should he get a case off the ground with the Irish engineer."

"I'll take care of it."

"Also Jack, we both are aware of the path we're going down by excluding the Brits. Nevertheless, at this very early stage, I will take care of handling our liaison responsibilities and interests."

"Will do, Steve. Give my best to Kathleen."

"My pleasure. Give my best to Mitch."

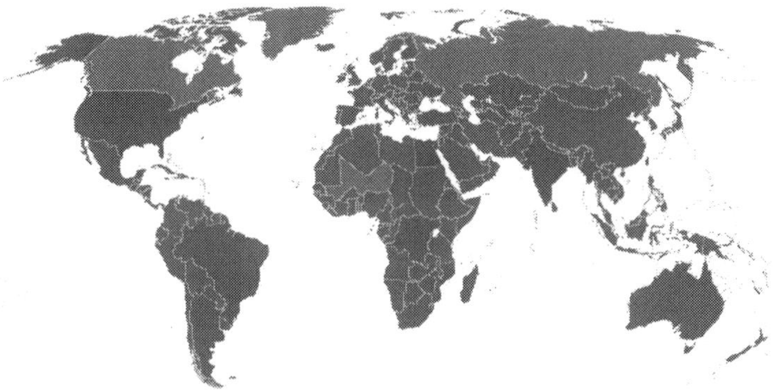

CHAPTER 9

Dr. Abdul-Karim bin Ahmad was eager to leave his homeland and return to his emergency room duties at the Royal Alexandra Hospital in Paisley, a small town along the River Cart, 8 miles west-southwest of Glasgow, Scotland. He had tired of the heat and the long wait in the dusty, decrepit border town of Miran Shah, located in North Waziristan along northwest Pakistan's border with Afghanistan. Nevertheless, the wait was worth it for the encouragement and pledge of support he received for his operational plan of action.

He had reached this point after five years of living and working in the United Kingdom in virtually a dormant, or sleeper, status. During those years, he came to be accepted as a competent and capable physician in the local community.

Because he was able to meet with Jamil Amin, while in Miran Shah, he left emboldened to begin the next phase of his operation designed to wreck havoc and destruction on the British Government. Jamil was the primary assistant and senior operative to Dr. Ayman al-Zawahiri, the number two leader of al-Qaeda, after Osama bin Laden. In returning to Paisley now, Abdul had Jamil's pledge of support in providing Muslim brothers to assist him, a commo plan for communicating with Jamil and the funds necessary to move the operation forward. With this kind of support from al-Qaeda, Abdul believed he was sure to succeed.

Abdul was born and raised in another rundown border town in North Waziristan, Mir Ali, a short walking distance from Miran Shah. A bright youngster, he enjoyed a privileged life due to his father's mercantile success in the grain business. This enabled Abdul to gain admittance into the King Edward Medical University located in Lahore. He was awarded a Bachelor of Medicine and Bachelor of Surgery Degree. He further pursued and was awarded a postgraduate degree, Master of Surgery.

Following the deaths of his father and mother while an undergraduate, Abdul, an only son, decided his immediate future would be to practice medicine in the UK. As a devout Muslim, being from North Waziristan he also possessed a singular obsession shared by many of the people in the tribal groups there – jihad against the British Government for the historical dominance of their colonial rule. As such, Abdul sought the day when he would be in a position to exact revenge. Believing himself to be a consummate tactician, he felt he had succeeded, like many Muslims in Scotland, in appearing to be a Muslim Scot.

He avoided joining any radical Islamic groups during his school years, nor publicly expressing anything close to anti-British inflammatory remarks. In Glasgow, he went to the local Central Mosque only on an irregular basis due to his emergency room duties at the hospital. At the mosque, he avoided involvement with fellow Muslim brothers there, particularly the group that advocated violence against the British authorities. Much earlier, he decided he would conduct his jihad in his own way.

Abdul learned, from a European history book many years earlier, an old proverb, "Revenge is a dish best served cold." He took this saying to heart. Coming from North Waziristan, he sought to follow in the footsteps of the Faqir of Ipi, Mirza Ali Khan. Khan, a Pashtun from North West Pakistan, was also known as "Haji Sahib" (respected pilgrim). He led and waged a successful jihad, in the form of guerrilla warfare, against the British during the 1930s and 1940s, culminating in the British departure from then British India in 1947.

To Abdul, emulating Faqir of Ipi was a noble goal. Hence, he dedicated himself to the task of staging an attack of catastrophic proportions against the British Government. Upon achieving success, he would then turn to a similar goal against "The Great Satan" – the United States of America.

First, however, he had to convince Jamil of the merit in his operational plan, and his ability to carry it through to fruition against the British.

Having first met Jamil at his father's funeral in Mir Ali some years earlier, they quickly bonded and forged a strong friendship until Abdul departed for Scotland. After that, with Jamil's involvement and rise in al-Qaeda ranks, they lost contact with each other. Fortunately, though, Abdul was able to arrange for the meeting with Jamil in Miran Shah, and present him with his plan of action.

The obvious commonality they shared was working toward the establishment of a worldwide caliphate in a single Islamic state. To do this, they both accepted that a bomb and a gun would be the only way to accomplish it.

"Tell me brother, how do you plan to proceed now that you have established yourself in Scotland?" Jamil asked.

"First of all," Abdul replied, "I have successfully assimilated into the local community, as well as the hospital where I work, by not getting overly involved in the activities of our local mosque. In particular, I have avoided involvement with our vocal brothers there who are viewed by the authorities as radical Islamists. By maintaining a low profile and working instead to establish my medical credentials, I do not believe I have come to the attention of the authorities at all. Subsequently, I have been able to move around and engage in a lengthy target selection process that has identified what I believe to be the single most vulnerable target available against which I feel I can succeed."

"Abdul, I like what I am hearing. Tell me how you came up with your choice of a target."

"By selectively using a combination of several different computers at the hospital, plus computers in internet cafes located in nearby communities, I was able to initially check on a number of potential targets. These included major sports event sites, airports, electric power grid intersections, military bases, sites for large public gatherings, major subway line junction sites and nuclear facilities. The last one, nuclear facilities, included nuclear power plants for generating electricity, uranium enrichment facilities, nuclear weapons storage sites, as well as nuclear waste processing and storage facilities."

"Are you satisfied your use of the computers appeared normal and you were able to do so without anyone being able to track your movements on them?" Jamil asked.

"Computers at the hospital as well as in the local cafes are used by so many people, I am not concerned on that score. I also deleted all my file queries as well as the results I found. Unless the hard drives are examined for all of the bits and bytes associated with my queries, and they can be reconstructed afterwards by computer experts, I am satisfied I came away clean in the process."

"After you identified these possible targets, what did you do next?"

"Whenever I had time off from my job at the hospital, I drove all over Scotland and northern England looking at prospective sites. All told, I spent about six to seven months engaged in this task."

"How about a cover story in the event you were stopped by anyone?"

"I was not stopped once. But, in the event I had been stopped or queried by anyone, I was prepared to just say I have finally found the time, away from my job, to be a tourist of sorts and get to know what the UK is all about."

"That's plausible," Jamil replied. "Before you tell me more about what you did next, what about your personal security situation where you live, work and in moving about in your own local community."

"Ever since starting work at the hospital in Paisley, I have never noticed anyone paying any kind of special attention to me, nor asking probing questions. The same goes for where I live. I lease my flat from a property management firm, 'LeasewithEase.' I completed their detailed application form and provided them with a three-month deposit when I first moved in three years ago. Thereafter, every three months someone from the firm comes inside the flat, while I am there, to conduct a routine inspection. They always leave satisfied that I am keeping it in good order. I also promptly pay the rent on time every month. Several Pakistani families live nearby and I only exchange basic pleasantries with them. Since I am single, and I work many odd hours at the hospital, it is easy to avoid much contact with them. The local Pakistani shopkeepers, and halal shops where I frequently buy foodstuffs, all have come to accept me."

"That's good. Now tell me more about your plan of attack."

"I found the sites where large public gatherings take place to be too complicated to try and succeed against. Enhanced security screening, on the day or evening when an event is scheduled to take place, would likely prevent carrying into the site any kind of explosive, chemical or biological device. Likewise, with trying to enter a site the night before and plant a device. The security measures in place do not justify trying to go up against them.

"Security is even more in effect around the military bases and nuclear weapons storage sites I evaluated. I was not able to find vulnerability points that could be exploited. However, when I saw the nuclear power generation plants and nuclear waste processing facilities, and subsequently researched details about them, I knew I was on to something.

"I researched, drove by, plus walked, in the vicinity of the Dungeness A Power Station, the Chapelcross Power Station, and the Bradwell Power Station. While these stations offered potential as targets, I researched further and found they all shared one thing – all of their spent fuel is sent to the Sellafield Nuclear Reprocessing Plant in Cumbria, in Northwest England. With that, I focused my attention on learning as much as possible about the entire Sellafield complex of nuclear facilities and determining if it represented the most worthy target of all."

"My brother, you may well be on to something," Jamil said. "Please tell me more."

"Well, it is indeed a worthy target, especially as a result of all I was able to learn about it," Abdul replied. The Sellafield nuclear waste processing and storage facilities contain over ten thousand tons of medium and high-level uranium and plutonium radioactive waste. I concluded that, for the time being, I would put aside going after nuclear power generating plants. The waste and storage facilities are my first choice as the target.

"I also learned of the poor record of the industrial processes at Sellafield that has been responsible for leaking radioactive fallout throughout the north of England, Scotland and even across the channel into the rest of Europe. That kind of fallout, carried above in the winds for those distances, is just the kind of opportunity to go after.

"The success of my plan will result in helping that leakage along by a massive explosion that will loft these toxic radioactive waste materials high into the atmosphere. The human and animal populations, plus the soil, of England and Scotland will receive the majority of the radioactive fallout, followed by somewhat less, but serious effects on the human and animal populations of mainland Europe."

"So this means," Jamil said, "you have concluded that the most vulnerable target for us is not a nuclear power plant, but rather the waste they produce?"

"Precisely."

"What do you need from us to further your plan along?"

"I want to bring together four dedicated Muslim brothers, living in either Scotland or the Northwest of England, to work with me. I will run them as a team, first in a highly compartmented fashion, until I come to accept them. Once accepted, I will be tasking them and they will come to know of each other's existence and role in the operation. I will need your help in providing me with these brothers. I cannot give my own position away in the community by trying to identify and select them myself locally. It would change my visible routine and image that I currently have there. It is also best that they not be active in any anti-British activities. Regular members of a mosque is fine. Outward activists in a mosque, no, that will not work."

"What else can I do, Abdul?"

"I will completely trust your judgment in selecting these brothers."

"God willing, it will be done," Jamil replied.

"I also hope, on my own, to be able to recruit a disaffected Scot or an Irishman, who has long held grudges against the English. I will use this person in a support capacity such as for surveillance of particular locations and people, renting vehicles, purchasing supplies, etc. I will strictly compartment him from the rest of the group and he will never come to know of the actual target or target location. I will need this kind of person due to his obvious skin color, nationality and ability to move around easier than we can.

"I will need the first Muslim brother as soon as possible. He and I will work closely together in the initial purchase and accumulation of supplies and equipment needed for the attack. The second brother I will also need soon and he will need to have well developed computer skills. Lastly, and most important as the date I select for the attack nears, you will need to send me the remaining two, who will need to be fully dedicated martyrs that can drive and handle the truck to be used in the attack. I will take care of coaching them during the final preparatory stages. They should be able to live with the first brother you send to me."

Jamil nodded his head approvingly and said, "I can see you will also need adequate funding for this operation. I will make the necessary arrangements for you to receive money immediately after your return to Scotland. A trusted brother, the first one of the four I will send to you, will approach you in your local community and identify himself as a cousin to your brother from Mir Ali. This will be the recognition signal that you can trust him. He will never mention me by name, but rather only as a cousin to your brother in Mir Ali."

"I understand perfectly."

"This trusted brother will be your link to me and he will provide funds whenever you require them. You will also need to use him as our communications link as well. No land telephone or cellular phone calls at all. This, as you already know, is the only real secure way for communicating between us."

"Yes, Jamil, this is the best way to do it."

"Actually, all four of these brothers will be sent from here. I will not have any Muslim brothers already in the UK assist you. Instead, all will be carefully selected by me only, and subsequently dispatched to you."

"That is wonderful news, Jamil. Thank you very much."

"I can see that you have given much of yourself in planning for this jihad operation. In order to be successful, we must closely coordinate in the best way to achieve it. From my perspective here, the least I can do is to see to it that your security in moving forward with the plan is adequately provided for by me from here. Unless you advise me otherwise, that is what will be done."

"I cannot tell you how much your words mean to me. I now leave you very pleased with all of your gracious support," Abdul said. "I shall now be able to proceed to work out the many remaining details for the attack. I will keep you advised."

"Go in peace, my brother," Jamil said.

"God willing," replied Abdul.

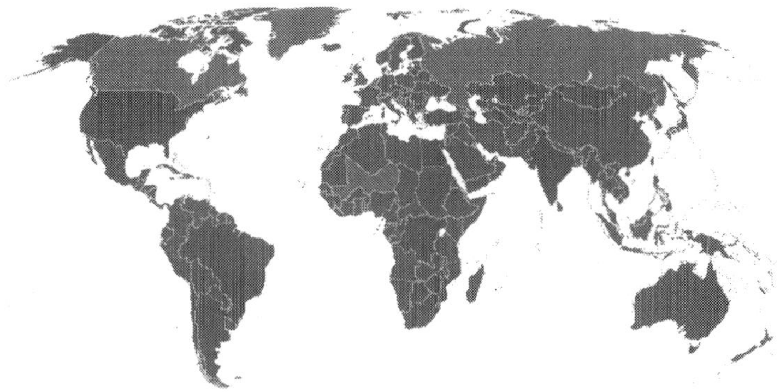

CHAPTER 10

Hotel Provincial, on Rue Chartres in the French Quarter, offered Mitch the kind of ambiance and elegance he had come to enjoy when visiting New Orleans. The hotel is located in a quieter section of the Quarter, and Mitch's room overlooked a lush courtyard and fountain. After checking in and settling in his room, he remained there waiting for Jack's call that would trigger a meeting on board a streetcar of the St. Charles Avenue Line. Via earlier cable traffic between them, it was agreed that the venue for the meeting would be on one of the line's streetcars.

When Jack called, they agreed to meet at 5:15 p.m., no location specified. This would initiate a meeting at 3:15 p.m. Whenever times to meet are mentioned over a cellular phone or land line phone, it meant to subtract two hours from whatever time was agreed upon. This gave Mitch ample time to walk from the hotel past the French Market on Decatur Street, and head straight over to Canal Street five blocks away where the line starts at the corner of Canal Street and Carondelet Avenue.

Mitch boarded the streetcar, took a seat in the back and looked for Jack to come aboard at the next stop or two upon entering the Garden District. Sure enough, when the streetcar stopped across the street from Emeril's Delmonico, another one of Chef Emeril Lagasse's restaurants, Jack bounded aboard, made eye contact with Mitch and headed straight for him. The time was 3:17 p.m.

"Hey, old sod," Jack exclaimed.

"Old sod to you too!" Mitch replied.

"We have to stop meeting like this. People will recognize us and start talking," Jack said, laughing.

"If they do we are in real trouble," replied Mitch.

"For me," Jack said, "this is the best part of visiting New Orleans. I enjoy seeing the gracious homes here on St. Charles Avenue, along with all the parks and the trees-lined streets. Even the Tulane and Loyola University campuses look good as well. It all makes for one enjoyable ride."

"I know," Mitch replied, "I feel the same way."

"As expected during this time of the afternoon, not many people are riding the streetcars. This should give us time to go over the details for your trip to Ireland."

"If we need more, I know of a coffee shop at Claiborne Avenue, where the streetcar turns around for the return trip back into the Central District," Mitch said.

"Sounds good," Jack replied.

"I'm looking forward to seeing if this Irishman has the potential to be recruited to worm his way inside one of these terrorist groups, much like the guy we succeeded with last year," Mitch said.

"Don't start bragging this soon, you haven't even met the guy yet. Yeah, I know your track record," said Jack laughing. "This will just be another scalp on the wall."

"What do you expect? You and your merry band of case officers taught me all I know," Mitch replied, also laughing.

Jack reached into his pocket and pulled out a picture. "This is the Irishman, Padraig Cahill, aka 'Patrick,' along with a barmaid at Slattery's Bar in Dublin. Burn this guy's image in your mind."

"I'll look at it a number of times as we ride along here and give it back to you before we separate," Mitch replied.

"He is shorter than you are, around 5 feet 11 inches in height. He weighs in at around 175 pounds.

"I've also got for you his home address, his work address and the neighborhood area where he hangs out in when not working."

"I'll initially try," Mitch replied, "to spot him when he returns home from work. Realizing he is sensitized and alert against the Brits and their surveillance efforts, I will be sure and keep my distance. I'll also set-up a counter-surveillance effort in order to see if I can spot any surveillance placed on him. I plan to stay away from his work area. Should he appear clean and free of surveillance, I'll contrive a plausible excuse for bumping into him when he is grocery shopping, dining, in a bar, etc. I will also stay away from Slattery's Bar in order to protect Dublin Station's equity with their source there. However, if he visits some other pub, he'll be fair game for me."

"You know the drill many times over," Jack said. "I know to expect nothing but your usual skillful approach and determination of any potential with this guy. Also," Jack added, "by tomorrow you should have Dublin Station's cable on dead drop sites for your alias cover documents, as you requested."

"That's fine," Mitch replied.

"You will also be getting a cable from Stockholm Station with any ideas they may have on a possible role for our CTC case officer there, Lee Denning, the guy you met with in Norway."

"I'll look forward to reading it."

"How are things going with M&T in San Francisco? Any concerns at all about your frequent absences when working for us?

"Work there is going quite well. They are holding their own in my absence and, in fact, increased business is soon going to require us to hire at least one more recruiter."

"That's good news. Glad to hear it. Oh, I have another question. How about the cover story you will be using upon meeting up with Cahill?" Jack asked.

"It will be the PIPESTEM commercial cover firm in Arizona, in Phoenix. I will still be in my role as an electrical engineer, but this time I will be using it in Ireland to conduct a survey of electronic parts manufacturers there.

"That is a pretty well established industry there, isn't it?"

"It sure is and it would be logical for the company in Phoenix to be interested in locating Irish facilities to assist in sub-assembly work. It should easily allow me to start up a conversation with Cahill."

"That sounds good."

"The cover company people know I will be in Europe somewhere using their firm as cover and, in actuality, they do no assembly work there at all. All of their parts work is contracted out across our border here, in Mexico."

"If the Irishman appears to buy into your story, how will you proceed?"

"As I wrote in my proposal cable, I will try and sustain two or maybe three meetings with him, including drinks and hopefully a dinner, over a five or six day period of my doing ostensible survey work there. I'll assess the degree of any anti-British views he is willing to share with me and, if I can go so far as to bring up my mother's Muslim background, I'll try to sound him out on how he feels about Muslims in the UK, and their acts of terrorism against the Brits."

"After that?"

"If it appears we have in any way bonded and established commonality due to our backgrounds, I will let him know I'll be returning for more survey work in about a month. I'll look to him to see if he suggests we get together upon my return. If not, I'll suggest it instead."

"Where do you envision Lee Denning coming into the picture?"

"If this guy looks good we may wish to bring Lee into the picture when I make my return trip back to Dublin. I realize it means moving fast, but in the real life commercial world, time means money and decisions are made much more quickly when compared to the squeaky machinery of our bureaucratic government."

"You got that one right."

"Look, we are about at the end of the line here coming up on the streetcar turnaround at Claiborne Avenue. Here's Cahill's picture back. How about we both get off here and go our separate ways?"

"Good," replied Jack. I'll stroll around here a bit and then head back towards my hotel."

"Where are you staying?"

"The Sheraton, along Riverfront Park. I'll be returning to Washington first thing in the morning though. How about you?"

"I have a late morning flight back to San Francisco."

"I wish you success in Ireland."

"Thank you, Jack. I will do my best. Say hello to the crew in CTC for me."

"Will do. Take care."

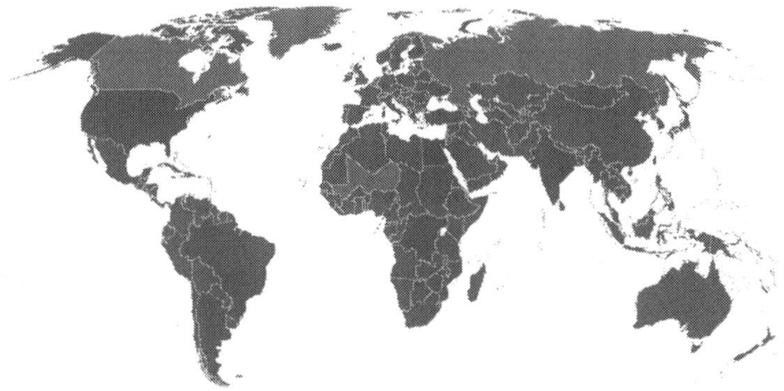

CHAPTER 11

"I am going to take you down a path that describes the art of dancing," said Mitch's first tango instructor at a "milonga" in Buenos Aires called, "Nino Bien." As a place to go to dance the tango, what a milonga path he took during that trip to Argentina several years earlier. He became a "milongueros," an aficionado who frequented the milongas in order to dance the tango. Mitch needed time to relax and get away from the double life he led as a covert operations officer for the Agency and a successful executive search recruiter, and transition into the world of the milonga that reached into his very soul.

Starting with several afternoon private classes to learn some of the basic moves, the instructor introduced Mitch to several women veterans of the dance. With the introductions and time spent with them on the dance floor, he was viewed as a friend and not a stranger in their midst. Subsequently, the women took Mitch to a whirlwind six nights of dancing, each one at a different milonga, throughout the districts of Buenos Aires. Ever since, the opportunity to spend a night in a milonga became a top priority for Mitch, whenever possible.

Now, knowing he only had one weekend left before leaving for Dublin, his plan for Saturday night was to go to his favorite local milonga, across the bay in Oakland, thousands of miles from Argentina. He started out by treating himself to an elegant dinner at Alice Waters restaurant in Berkeley, Chez Panisse, followed by an after dinner drink at Heinold's Saloon in Jack London Square at the foot of Broadway, in Oakland. Coming up on midnight, he knew it was just the right time for the short drive to Oakland's "Jingle Town" area and an all-night milonga hangout.

That first instructor who promised to take him down the path that described the art of dancing might as well have been describing the path he employed as a NOC to lead a prospective agent toward recruitment as an intelligence source of information. It was a good parallel, he thought, but dancing the tango represented a more sublime and higher plane of fulfillment.

Jingle Town, in Oakland, is located to the east of Lake Merritt, in an area that is a small part of East Oakland. It is largely a Latino populated area on the rise. Jingle town got its name in the early 1900's from the Portuguese cannery and cotton mill workers who, after being paid for their daily wages, would "jingle" the coins in their pockets to signify their pride in their earnings as they walked to their nearby homes.

The heart of Jingle Town straddles both sides of the Interstate 880 freeway between Twenty-third Avenue and Fruitvale Avenue. This area developed into one of the most thriving and fast growing art districts in the entire San Francisco-Oakland Bay Area. Located at the intersection of Fruitvale Avenue and East Tenth Street is the Las Canitas Tango Club, Mitch's destination for the rest of the evening.

Formerly a garment industry union hall, Las Canitas was perfectly suited for dancing. The open area in the center of the rectangular building measured approximately one-hundred feet by fifty feet, with a bar along one of the longer walls, and kitchen facilities in the rear. Known to a number of the regular patrons there, Mitch had no trouble recognizing several friends and engaging them in conversation prior to making any moves towards dancing. After ordering a drink at the bar, he began to cast glances around the floor and surrounding area, to see with whom he would like to dance.

Realizing he would have to engage in the ritual "cabaceo" of exchanging glances before approaching a woman to invite her to dance, he focused his eyes across the dance floor towards several woman sitting in chairs, looking for any of his partners from past visits to the club.

Sure enough, he recognized the tall, striking and raven-haired woman he had danced with a number of times in the past. She glanced his way from across the sparsely populated dance floor. Their eyes met and Mitch gave her a slight nod of his head. Upon receiving her return nod, Mitch proceeded to walk across the edge of the floor towards her table. Their cabaceo had taken place.

"Maria Luiza," he said. "It is wonderful to see you again."

She stood up and looked him directly in the eyes. "Senor Vasari," she said, with a captivating smile on her lips.

"Have you forgotten my first name already?

"Of course not, Mitch. It is so good to see you again."

"I was hoping you would be here tonight," he replied.

"You have been a naughty boy, Mitch. Where have you been keeping yourself?"

"Obviously away from you for too long."

"I am ready if you are," she replied.

"You look beautiful this evening," he said.

"Thank you."

For the next 20 minutes, they smoothly whirled around the floor for a series of five set pieces of tango music, or "tandas," as they are known. Without a spoken word between them, Maria Luiza and Mitch started to dance in close embrace. He showed a precise way of leading her as they moved in complete harmony with each other. He kept his basic turns, or "giros," tight, one after the other, as they glided effortlessly to the music. She quickly relaxed into a melodic contentment in his embrace.

When the first tanda of five pieces was finished, they exchanged small talk until the next one started up again after a few minutes of quietness on the floor. This second tanda lasted for fifteen minutes, after which they sat down and had drinks. Maria Luiza asked for a kir and Mitch ordered a glass of red wine.

What they shared in common was not the muted conversation off the floor but rather the dialogue of silence that takes place when dancing. She respected, as well as accepted, the calm sense of control Mitch maintained while leading her around the floor. This unspoken dialogue bound them together in the rhythm and melody of the music.

It was Mitch's continual placement of his feet on the floor, in essence a marking of each step, or "la marcar," in leading her, that was exactly what she expected from him.

Mitch's adroit use of la marcar, when dancing, indicated to Maria Luiza when, where and how he would lead her into the spaces he was able to create through their embrace. The unspoken control exerted by his right hand and arm determined the boundary limitations and extent of that embrace.

They found that sought-after eroticism of gliding together with four legs in unison, like the smooth elegance of a determined feline stalking its prey. The sensual motion of his leg movements, followed by her subsequent leg movements, resulted in the natural flow of their bodies together as one. While the tops of their bodies, from the waist up, appeared calm and their emotions fully under control, their legs and feet were active and moving throughout the dance. Their continuous revolutions of legs around each other, particularly when Mitch led Maria Luiza through figure eight loops, or "ochos," provided a magic dimension to their dance. It allowed them to achieve the beauty of moving in total harmony with each other.

By the time they danced their way through a fourth tanda set, they decided to sit and rest for a while. Still caught up in the intimacy of the dance, they began to speak of what tango meant to them.

"I believe it is like a mystery that I want to explore," she said to Mitch.

"Yes."

"I told you in the past that I was born and raised in Buenos Aires where my father was a struggling artist, a painter and a sculptor."

"Yes, I recall that."

"He previously studied art here in Oakland, at an arts college. After returning home, marrying and starting a family, he was not happy with the progress of his career in Argentina. He convinced my mother to move all of us here to Oakland where he would open his own studio. That was fifteen years ago and we have not been back to Argentina since.

"My father is no longer struggling. He is successfully painting and sculpting, plus teaching art to young people. However, for the rest of us, my mother, brothers and sisters, we all have a longing in our heart for home."

"And tango provides the soothing of the soul as you think of what you left back in Argentina," he said.

"I believe that is it," she replied.

"It is a dance that is steeped in a person's longing for home."

"I accept that we both have separate roles to play when we dance," she replied. "You must lead and I must follow. The better you can direct me with your feet and right hand in the small of my back, the more I can respond to your direction. This creates a balance between us. That is the appeal."

"It allows us both to explore the mysteries and searching of our souls. I feel that way too," he replied.

"Yes, yes, that is what I feel when we dance together."

"I feel much the same thing. The Portuguese actually have a word for it. It's called 'saudade.'"

"I have never heard that word before," she said.

"When I went to high school in southern California," Mitch replied, "my best friend was Portuguese. He only moved from Portugal the year before, when he was 15. He told me a lot about longing for his homeland."

"Yes, it sounds much the same."

"He called it saudade, but had a hard time defining it."

"As a mystery of sorts, I can see it would be hard to put your finger on it."

"My friend told me that with all of our freedoms here in the US, he also found he had a freedom to be sad. That is what he thought was the meaning of saudade. I would add to it though, saying that for me it is also a kind of nostalgia, even melancholy. It results in a longing for things past and what even could be a way of looking to the future."

"Yes, these are the kinds of things I feel we are exploring when we dance together. It may be sad at times, but it is also a very good feeling for me," she said.

"Talk about getting into the depths of emotion, now we know we are both souls longing for home."

"Me too," she replied.

"How about longing for a good night's sleep? It is getting close to four o'clock. Before long, the sun will be rising. Can I drive you home?"

"My younger brother, Paulie, is tending bar here tonight. He will take me home."

"That's fine. I cannot tell you how much I once again enjoyed our dancing together, and our conservation. Maria Luiza, thank you so much."

"I feel the very same way, Mitch. Thank you. I hope to see you again, soon."

"You will. Please give my very best to your family," he replied.

"I will," she replied. "And Mitch, don't forget about saudade," she added.

As Mitch was driving back home across the Bay Bridge to San Francisco, he thought back on his conversation with Maria Luiza. Alone in his car he felt like he was in a place that was far away. He was totally on his own and moving into a preparatory stage for determining how he would conduct himself in getting another operation underway. He felt good going into this frame of mind once again. It provided him with warmness and secure feeling.

This was the ambush hunter preparing to give chase and go after his prey – in this case, and much like the terrorists he sought, he would take the initiative in knowing how he would attack, where he would attack and when he would attack. Concealed by his cover, he would move into his setup position of disrupting and defeating a terrorist group bent on their waging of jihad.

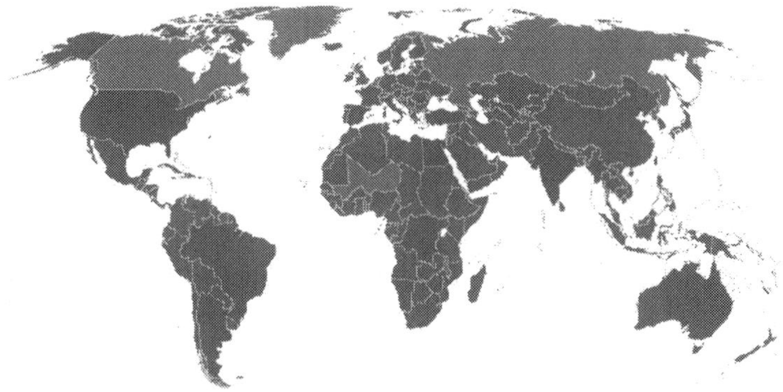

CHAPTER 12

Mitch awoke early Monday morning and did a rethink of the game plan for doing a doc swap in Dublin. Since it would involve exchanging his true name US passport, driver's license and assorted pocket litter for that of his alias commercial cover docs, he decided against it. As a result, he sent an immediate cable to Dublin Station requesting instead that they FedEx the alias docs to the Agency office in Phoenix, Arizona. He also made sure Phoenix received a copy of the cable as well. Since he would be spending a week in Dublin, plus prospects for more visits to come should he succeed in meeting Patrick Cahill there, Mitch did not want to take any risks with the doc exchange process, especially with prospects of having to go through it several more times in the future. Phoenix was the better choice. He was irritated with himself for not planning on the use of a case officer from the Phoenix office for the doc swap when making initial plans for the trip to Ireland.

Phoenix responded quickly to the cable, and provided meeting arrangements for the doc exchange. Subsequently, on Friday morning, and using a true name round-trip air e-ticket, with an open return, Mitch flew from San Francisco to Phoenix. He took a taxi from Sky Harbor Airport to the pre-arranged meeting site in the Starbucks located in Fashion Square on East Camelback Road, in Scottsdale, Phoenix's next-door city. During the drive from the airport to Scottsdale, Mitch transferred his true name California driver's license, passport, pocket litter and open return e-ticket to San Francisco, into a small manila envelope. Prior to leaving San Francisco, he booked a round-trip air ticket, with an open return, in his commercial cover alias. This would allow him to do the doc swap in Scottsdale, return to Sky Harbor Airport in alias, and fly from there to Boston for a connecting Air Lingus flight direct to Dublin Airport.

He spent 15-20 minutes walking around the Fashion Square shops area where he briefly entered two shops; looking at men's clothing in one, and sporting goods in the other. Satisfied that no one looked familiar from the flight to Phoenix or in the airport area after arriving, Mitch headed for the nearby Starbucks.

Matti Lewis, the resident Phoenix case officer sent to meet with Mitch for the doc swap, had done similar exchanges with Mitch in the past. He immediately recognized her sitting in a corner of the coffee shop, walked over and sat down in a chair across from her. He carried a current copy of "Architectural Digest" magazine, with the manila envelope inside, and placed it on the rectangular table between them.

"Matti, good to see you again," Mitch said.

"Me too," she replied. Two cups of coffee were on the table. "Do you still like a Latte in the morning?"

"Sure do. Thank you for remembering. I bet you're having an Americano, right?"

"Yes, it is still my regular morning sustenance."

"Obviously, Arizona continues to agree with you. You look great."

"Why thank you," she replied. "Do you believe it though, when I say that air conditioning has a lot to do with it?"

In front of her on the table, besides their coffee, were two magazines, fanned slightly apart from one another. The one on the top was *Wired* magazine, and the one underneath was *Laser Focus World.*

"How is Richard doing in his job?" Mitch inquired.

"My hubby physicist is overly occupied with his work, as usual," she replied.

They spent the next ten minutes engaged in small talk about the lifestyle in the Scottsdale area, the great golfing clubs that are available, and nearby sports and recreational facilities extending throughout the greater Phoenix area.

Mitch looked at his watch and said, "I am sorry to have to leave so quickly, but I have an appointment nearby in about a half hour."

"I understand. I have to get back to the office as well. Look, I have the latest *Wired* magazine for you. I know that you, like Richard, are into all the high tech gadgets and things."

"Why thank you very much. I'll enjoy reading it. Have you seen this copy of *Architectural Digest*?"

"No, I haven't"

"Be my guest."

"Both Richard and I will enjoy reading it. Thank you. Next time you are in the area, let us plan on a lunch together."

"I'd like that a lot. Give my best to Richard."

"I certainly will. Good to see you again."

With that, Mitch exited the coffee shop and Fashion Square shops area carrying the *Wired* magazine in one hand. He crossed the intersection of North Goldwater Road and East Camelback Road, and entered an office building on the northwest corner. Locating a men's restroom behind the single-row bank of elevators on the ground floor, he entered. Not seeing anyone inside, he went into one of the toilet stalls, turned around and locked the door. He opened the magazine and removed a manila envelope taped inside. Opening the envelope, he found his commercial cover alias US Passport, alias Arizona driver's license, medical and auto insurance cards and assorted pocket litter. Also inside was a small slip of paper with a local telephone number written on it. In the event the alias materials inside were incorrect or not to his satisfaction, he could call the number and make arrangements for a quick non-scheduled emergency meeting nearby in order to subsequently get the correct documents, if necessary. Loading his pockets with the alias materials, he tore the envelope from the magazine and stuffed it into one of his pockets as well.

Exiting the stall, he threw the magazine into the restroom wastebasket. Departing the restroom, he walked around the corner of the elevator and went out the building's main door. Walking westward for two short blocks, along East Camelback Road, he came upon a long arched driveway leading slightly upwards to a J.W. Marriott Hotel. He went inside and, strolling around the lobby area for a few minutes, he found a trash receptacle and threw the used manila envelope inside it, along with the torn scraps of paper that had the local telephone number written on them. He then walked outside the main entrance and caught a taxi for Sky Harbor Airport. He was satisfied that he was not under surveillance, or anyone paying undue attention to him.

Arriving at Sky Harbor, he went inside near the United Airlines check-in counter and took an escalator downstairs to the nearby baggage carousels where arriving passengers were collecting their checked luggage. He found the storage locker where he had placed his own luggage when he arrived earlier in the morning. All the clothes and items inside his garment bag and second carry-on bag had been "sanitized," meaning nothing with true name or initials sewn into clothing, or any other materials having a true name on them. Inserting two quarters next to the locker door, he opened it, retrieved his luggage and proceeded to check-in for his United Airlines flight for Boston. He was on his way to Dublin and, hopefully, making contact with Patrick Cahill there.

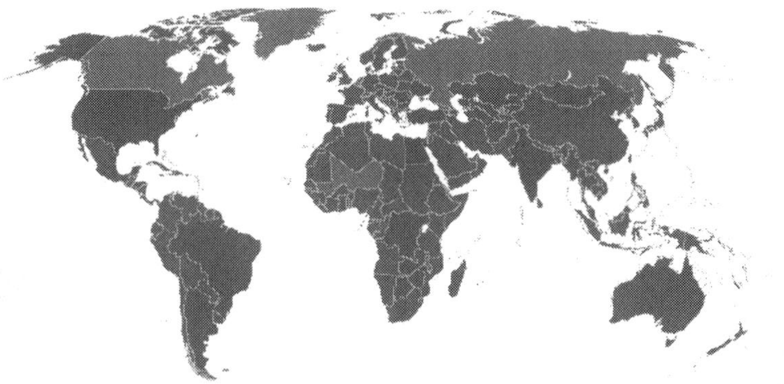

CHAPTER 13

Upon touching down at Dublin International Airport, Mitch, now in his commercial cover alias identity as Douglas Sturgeon, disembarked and proceeded to the Garda Immigration Hall. Having successfully used this alias identity for travel in a multitude of countries for over three years, he was quite comfortable with it and at ease with himself. In fact, he felt just as comfortable in this alias as the two others he regularly made use of – one as an Egyptian national and the other as an Italian national.

It was just after six in the morning and already the airport was active due to several arriving flights from the US. After going through passport control with no questions asked, he proceeded straight to the customs blue channel lane since he had nothing to declare. He was carrying a garment bag and the one other small hand carry, and therefore did not have to wait at the carousels for any checked luggage.

Mitch knew that a US citizen traveling to Europe on a direct flight from the US always quickly passes through immigration and customs. The exceptions are when that citizen would appear to look suspicious, out of place or uneasy for any variety of reasons. This could include a lack of wanting to make direct eye contact with an immigration or customs official, not being familiar with passport details, unable to speak the language of the passport country, or, possibly being of an ethnic or racial group of interest to officials in the country being entered. If an immigration officer is in the least bit suspicious of the person standing before him or her, having the person step aside and enter into what is commonly referred to as "secondary examination" is a distinct possibility. Once in secondary, there is no time limit to questioning the person under suspicion, or being subjected to an extensive luggage and body search.

With Mitch, as Sturgeon now, having an olive skin complexion, reflecting his Italian and Egyptian heritage, he had been asked a few questions in the past. However, he never had been taken into secondary for further questioning. A couple of occasions, immigration officers noticed his birthplace as Italy and questioned him about it since he was carrying a US passport. Speaking unmistakable American English, he would explain that he immigrated to the US with his parents as a young child. Combined with being able to explain in details his US background, he was always allowed through immigration. Once he was asked about having Sturgeon as a surname. He explained it away, saying his father was an American of English heritage, and his mother a native Italian.

As he was exiting the arrivals area, he decided to stop at a currency exchange booth and exchange some US dollars for Euro currency. At this point, he began his usual personal security routine of looking to see if he recognized anyone nearby who was looking at him, particularly if they had been on the aircraft with him, or in the immigration and customs area. He continued this casual looking about as he left the exchange booth and walked outside the terminal to catch a taxi for the short ride to his hotel in Dublin.

His practice was to observe the physical characteristics of a person, such as height, weight, complexion and any distinguishing characteristics, and commit them to memory. Later on, should the same person be noticed at the hotel, on the streets outside or during any of his subsequent activities in Dublin, he would be able to recall whether he had seen them in the recent past. Combined with practicing extensive surveillance detection routines, the use of good observation skills are considered to be on the level of an art form as practiced by Agency operations officers in the field.

Upon arrival at the Grand Canal Hotel, a business hotel located on Grand Canal Street, Sturgeon's reserved room was available. After shaving, a shower and changing into street clothes, he set off to explore the central area of Dublin and get familiar with it since he expected to possibly be there for up to a week. As he made his way across the lobby to exit through the main door of the hotel, he noted no one inside that looked familiar to him since arriving in country. Once outside and on the street in the front of the hotel, he glanced to both sides of the building, the taxi stand next door and the immediate dock area across the street. Again, he was satisfied that at least for the time being, he was not under any kind of physical surveillance that could be detected.

Having spent a few minutes in his hotel room looking over a local city map, he was able to get his bearings on the areas he would subsequently explore. He found Capel Street, where Slattery's Bar was located, plus Lombard Street, where Cahill lived in an apartment. He also noted on the map the area where Cahill worked, at the 5Com Ireland Electronics Limited plant, out in the Dublin suburb of Blanchardstown. For this first exploratory jaunt around the city however, he decided to limit himself to the area where Cahill lived and the Capel Street area where Cahill was known to frequent Slattery's Bar.

For a Saturday morning, the people living in the Lombard Street area, at Trinity Square, arose on the late side. Sturgeon circled Trinity College at Trinity Square, followed by most all the streets around Lombard Street. Next, he walked by the Lombard Street address where Cahill's apartment was located. In this area, there was no opportunity to stop and spend any amount of time looking at the apartment building itself. He would have stood out and attracted attention to himself as a loiterer in the area. He did notice, however, a coffee shop on a corner nearby that provided a good view of the apartment entrance two hundred feet away. He did not go into the coffee shop at this stage, preferring to make use of it later on, once he thought he was closer to making at least visual contact with Cahill. Instead, he proceeded northwest for seven or eight blocks, towards the Capel Street area. Since it was now time for lunch, he found a restaurant to his liking along Temple Bar Street, the "Elephant and Castle."

Following lunch, Sturgeon roamed the area surrounding Capel Street, including Liffey, Abbey, Henry, Talbot, Mary, O'Connell and Marlborough Streets. All told, by the time he walked back to his hotel later in the afternoon, he had spent six hours familiarizing himself with a good portion of central Dublin. After a light dinner in a seafood restaurant nearby his hotel, he turned in for the evening.

The following day, on Sunday, Sturgeon set out by bus for Blanchardstown, in the suburbs, where Cahill's electronics plant was located. The distance is approximately ten kilometers northwest of the center of Dublin, involving thirty minutes of travel time each way. He walked past the main entrance area of the plant and several of the surrounding streets, looking for suitable points of interdiction where he might make visual contact with Cahill, depending on his mode of transportation to and from the plant. He also walked around the nearby Blanchardstown Centre, a major shopping center with every conceivable kind of shop inside. Depending upon Cahill's preferences after finishing work at the plant during the workweek, the shopping center offered potential as a location where Cahill could be met.

By mid-afternoon, after returning to Dublin proper, Sturgeon ensconced himself in the coffee shop near Cahill's apartment. Recalling the picture of Cahill that Jack had shown him in New Orleans, he was hoping to spot him exiting the building and attempt to follow him to see if an opportunity presented itself to "bump" into him. No such opportunity occurred. After three cups of coffee and seeing a number of people exit and enter the building, he saw no one fitting Cahill's looks nor description of being five foot eleven inches in height and 175 pounds in weight.

The following Monday morning, early on, Sturgeon walked over to Cahill's Lombard Street apartment area, and figured out a walking route to the possible bus stop Cahill could use for going to work in Blanchardstown. He then backtracked one stop back and boarded the bus hoping that Cahill might shortly be getting on board himself. The time was seven a.m. when Sturgeon boarded the bus. One minute later, when the bus reached the stop where Cahill might board himself, two male-female couples and one singleton male boarded. All walked past Sturgeon, who was seated in the mid-section, and sat down in the rear of the bus. None of the males matched Cahill's description.

Now Sturgeon realized he had two choices. One, stay on the bus and ride out to Blanchardstown, spend the day there and hope to make visual contact with Cahill exiting the plant at the end of the workday. Or two, he could get off the bus while still in the center of Dublin, wait out the day and then go to the coffee shop to see if he could spot Cahill on his way home from work. He chose the latter.

At six-fifteen p.m., while sipping his second cup of coffee and reading a paperback novel back at the coffee shop, Sturgeon spotted Cahill walking down Lombard Street and entering his apartment building two hundred feet away. He looked exactly as he did in the picture. Sturgeon did not see any kind of surveillance on Cahill as he was walking to the apartment. However, if there was surveillance observing Cahill from inside a building or vehicle that would be more difficult to detect.

Surveilling a person's movements from a fixed observation post, like from an apartment window for example, Sturgeon knew, is an expensive proposition. Unless Cahill was known by the local authorities to be involved in activities against the state, it would be unusual to mount such a surveillance effort on him just because of his family's past background of violence against the British.

Taking the chance that Cahill would soon leave his apartment and head out for dinner or other activities, Sturgeon stayed on in the coffee shop. He was not disappointed. Within thirty minutes, Cahill exited the apartment and headed west towards the Temple Bar area. It was twilight and a distinct chill was in the air. With Cahill having about a seventy meter lead heading west, Sturgeon fell in behind him. With a number of Trinity College students out on the streets helping to mask his presence behind Cahill, he had no trouble keeping him in sight. He also was mindful of anyone who appeared to be in between himself and Cahill, or in a vehicle, should any kind of surveillance effort be mounted since Cahill left his apartment.

Turning onto the wide expanse of O'Connell Street, Cahill proceeded north for two short blocks until turning left onto Liffey Street. Since pedestrian traffic on the streets was increasing, Sturgeon stepped up his pace to move in slightly closer. After walking one block west on Liffey Street, he saw Cahill enter a bookstore and café called "The Winding Stair." This was just the kind of opportunity he sought and, if Cahill were to spend any amount of time there, he was hopeful he would be able to meet and introduce himself to him. With only three days in Dublin so far, Sturgeon thought to himself that was not bad at all to be offered up this kind of opportunity for direct contact.

With Mitch now set to enter the bookstore behind Cahill, he was once again ready to start a process that was one of the parts of intelligence work that appealed to him most – establishing contact with an individual who possibly might be of use in a terrorist operation. This was pure enjoyment for him and he relished what was about to take place.

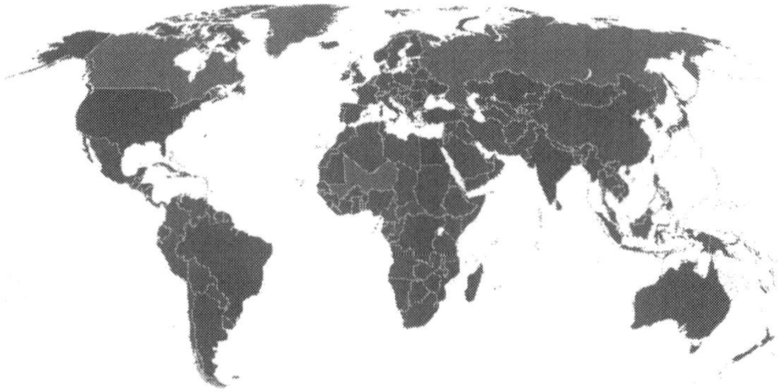

CHAPTER 14

Unexpectedly, another kind of fortuitous opportunity presented itself – this time to Abdul. Representatives from British Nuclear Fuels Limited (BNFL) extended an invitation to numerous hospitals in Scotland and Northwest England for select hospital staff members to attend a series of briefings on responding to crises involving nuclear accidents and subsequent radioactivity. In particular, the invite was for emergency room physicians, senior technicians and select hospital administrators. As a result, Abdul, along with three of his emergency room physician associates, one technician and one hospital administrator, accepted for Royal Alexandria Hospital.

Following his return from the meeting with Jamil in Miran Shah, most all of his off-duty hours from the hospital were spent working out the details of his plan of attack against the Sellafield nuclear reprocessing facility. He included in his planning the following: a) how critical the choice of target would be to the British Government; b) the tactics to be employed in the attack; c) how and when to overcome armed security guards to gain direct access to the target area; d) determining the exploitable vulnerabilities of the target; e) charting out the logistical and financial help that would be required; f) developing a communications plan; g) drawing up a training regimen for team members; and h) working out the details of the timing of the attack.

In looking at the hoped-for results of the attack, he considered the overall destructive effects on the local population, distant populations and even out-of-country populations. These after-effects would be particularly applicable due to expected winds and rain during and immediately after the attack – factors that would significantly increase human casualties, affect water supplies, take a toll on local and distant animals and livestock and cause a decrease in crop yields due to soil contamination. Lastly, he planned for the exfiltration of himself and team members from the affected areas after the attack.

Abdul took two extended driving trips to the area around the Sellafield facility as a major aspect of his planning. This included driving by the outer perimeter of the facility on two occasions in order to observe what he could of visible security measures in place there. He was also able to observe personnel and vehicles coming to and from the facility. He even spent some time in the nearby quaint village of Seascale, observing the dress and composure of the populace there. As a result, he was able to develop a general overview of the physical aspects of the facility and nearby area, details on the security makeup in and around the facility, and the shift schedule for employees there, including their work hours and days at work. By observing the vehicles going in and out of the facility, he was also able to determine the kind and optimum size of truck that would be required for the attack. The size of truck allowed him to compute the maximum weight loads for the chemicals and explosive fuel materials that would comprise the bomb that would be transported inside the truck.

However, two aspects of the attack eluded him at this point: determining the specific building to be hit in order to achieve the maximum effects from the explosion of the materials inside the truck and the driving route, once inside the main gate, to that chosen building. The attack would not succeed by just driving a truck up to the main gate and setting off an explosion. The same would apply to driving through the gate or crashing through a fence and driving up to just any building to set off the explosion.

Using the Internet, Abdul was able to acquire maps, photographs, brochures and some physical layout details for the Sellafield facility and the surrounding area. These materials enabled him to determine the specific location of the building that housed two forty-foot deep pools holding over ten thousand tons of Intermediate Level Waste (ILW) and High Level Waste (HLW)

– Building B215. One picture on the Internet even showed this easily recognizable building containing the two pools, including the area of the building where the HLW was stored in twenty one steel cask tanks inside concrete bunkers next to the pools. Looking much like swimming pools, though much deeper, as Abdul read in the brochure materials, these pools were composed of and reinforced with steel liners, steel reinforcing bars and four foot thick concrete walls. Building B215 got its recognizable shape by having an irregular L-shape to it, measuring one hundred and fifteen meters in length.

Numerous press reports indicated that the maximum capacities of these pools were reached by mid-2007. With increased amounts of HLW, composed solely of plutonium and highly enriched uranium, being shipped to the site, they were being stored in the twenty one steel cask tanks next to the pools. In all, Abdul concluded, Sellafield offered the highest potential for a disaster waiting to happen.

The one-hour drive to Edinburgh to attend the BNFL briefing went by quickly for Abdul and his fellow hospital staff members. The driver of their van let them off in front of the General Post Office Building, in Waterloo Place, where the briefing was to take place. Once inside and seated in a large hall on the ground floor of the building, Abdul looked around and estimated that about one hundred fifty people were there. Along the walls of the hall were poster boards on easels showing pictures of nuclear facilities, some including drawings and maps, from throughout the west of Scotland and England.

As the briefing was starting Abdul gazed once more around the hall and became cautiously hopeful that, amongst the posters on easels, the Sellafield facility would be included. If so, any details of the driving route to B215, housing the two pools and steel casks, would be accepted by him as a wonderful gift from the British people.

Of the five officials from BNFL conducting the briefing, the two speakers who provided the most information were physicians. They described typical medical treatment centers inside the various nuclear facilities, including the showing of PowerPoint slides on an overhead projector. Extensive discussions took place on what hospital staffs located nearby the nuclear facilities could do to assist in managing the care of radiologically contaminated patients should they be called upon to do so following accidents at any of the facilities.

Handout materials were circulated to all those in attendance. Included were descriptions of the types of accident victims and guidance on managing their care and treatment. A list was provided, showing precautions to be taken, such as shoes to be worn, masks to be used, and provisions for shielding from radioactivity. A good deal of this information was redundant for Abdul, based on his emergency room experiences and knowing how to conduct himself whenever around radiological sources.

After a little over one hour into the briefing, a thirty minute coffee break was held. This allowed the participants to circulate amongst the BNFL officials and hold conversations with them, and to view the posters on the easels around the hall. Once Abdul could see that a good number of participants were looking at the posters, and he would fit in doing the same, he moved around the hall searching out for any posters showing the Sellafield facility.

Upon locating two posters of the facility, he immediately realized they contained considerably more details than what he was able to learn from the various sites he previously had checked out on the Internet. One of the two, in particular, caught his attention. It was a schematic drawing of the entire Sellafield facility. It included a red highlighted medical building and numerous small treatment stations located throughout the facility. At the bottom of the drawing, a scale notation showed the ratio of the size of the drawing to the actual size of the facility was one half inch equals one hundred fifty feet.

Not knowing if he would be able to revisit the posters again at the end of the briefing, he knew he would have to make the most of the current opportunity. He located the main entrance gate on the drawing, along with fifteen significant plants and buildings inside, including B215. The names of the plants and buildings were all clearly shown in little boxes along the edges of the drawing. With all of the roads inside the facility clearly marked on the drawing, Abdul drew a map in his mind of the most obvious and direct driving route to get from the main gate to B215.

He visualized the route as follows: After passing through the main gate, drive straight ahead for two hundred thirty meters; turn left and go straight for four hundred sixty meters; and, turn right and proceed straight for one hundred sixty five meters. At that point, at an intersection, B215 would be the next building on the left side of the road. After entering the driveway to the building, at the corner of the intersection, and proceeding straight ahead for ten meters, the northwest corner edge of the building would be reached. This corresponded with the bottom of the "L," or vertical line running from top to bottom.

For the remaining forty-five minutes of the briefing, Abdul did not hear much of anything. Instead, his mind was filled with the details of the driving route he had committed to memory. Now he could not wait to return home in order to look at one of the Internet documents he previously printed out at an Internet café. The document was a schematic outline of the facility, but did not contain the details of what he had seen on the poster. However, it did clearly show the outlines of the buildings, including those along the driving route he had selected. By matching up the shapes and locations of these buildings, it would be easy to add the corresponding distances he had calculated. This would provide the two martyr brothers in the truck with all the necessary details for reaching the edge of Building B215.

During the drive in the van back to Paisley, Abdul hardly said a word. He was content with himself and pleased at what he had accomplished. Now a major gap in his operational planning had been fulfilled.

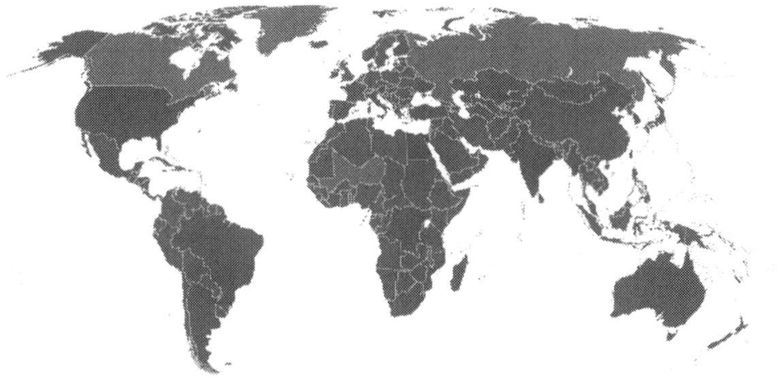

CHAPTER 15

The Winding Stair Bookstore and Café, overlooking the River Liffey, is located along a busy quayside street. As Sturgeon navigated along behind Cahill and saw him entering the store, he hesitated in his own steps, pulled-up and turned sideways, thereby able to gaze through the windows of an art gallery. This gave him the opportunity to use the glass of the windows as reflectors in order to check the direction from where he came. Through the glass, he was also able to check across the street from him, parallel to the walking route he used to follow Cahill. From this vantage point of looking into the gallery windows, he did not see anyone taking any interest in him, or Cahill. He also did not notice anyone he could recall previously, from the time he started out behind Cahill at his apartment. Since he did not know how long Cahill would be inside the store, he did not want to take the time to run a surveillance probe run into the art gallery shop next door in order to see if he could possibly draw a surveillant out of pattern to follow him inside the gallery.

After being satisfied that he and Cahill were free of surveillance, he walked up past the remaining two storefronts and entered The Winding Stair. Upon stepping inside, the first thing he noticed was stairs leading up to at least one more store level on the floor above. He proceeded straight ahead though, through the small ground floor area, noting the cramped aisles and shelves and tables packed with books, memorabilia and a few assorted antiques for sale. Fortunately, except for a couple of salespeople, few customers appeared to be inside.

When he got to the next to last aisle in the rear of the store, located on his right side, he noticed Cahill standing there ten feet away with a book in hand and leaning against one of the shelves. Sturgeon walked ahead to the last aisle, turned right and went to the end of the aisle in order to come around and enter Cahill's aisle from the far side of the store. Just before reaching the area where Cahill was browsing through a book, Sturgeon noticed above his head a sign saying, "Science & Technology Section." He also noticed that, due to the narrowness of the aisle, he would have to excuse himself if he wished to pass by Cahill.

"Pardon me, is this where books on electronics are located?" he asked.

"Yes," Cahill replied. "But you won't find much that is current."

Taking that as a cue from him, Sturgeon said, "That's OK, I collect older books, like from when we used to call it 'electrical.'"

"Me also," Cahill said. "That's what I am looking at now, but you will only find a few books here."

"Do you happen to be an engineer by any chance?" Sturgeon asked.

"You're an American, right?'

"Why yes, I am."

"Well, I'm what you Americans call a double E," Cahill said.

"What a coincidence. I am as well," Sturgeon replied.

"If you don't mind my asking, what are you doing here in Dublin?"

"I'm here conducting a survey of Ireland's electronics plants for my company in Phoenix, Arizona."

"Excuse me for not introducing myself. My name is Patrick Cahill and I work for one of those plants, locally here in Dublin – 5Com."

"Well, that is my good fortune. My name is Douglas Sturgeon. I'm very pleased to meet you."

They shook hands warmly and Cahill, looking directly into Sturgeon's eyes, said, "The pleasure is mine. Call me Patrick."

"Please call me Doug. You guys have a well developed electronics industry here now and my company has been way behind the curve in exploring it further."

"Why is that?" Patrick asked.

"Probably due to our previous dependence on fabricating mostly military specification, or mil-spec products for so many years."

"I see. What kinds of mil-spec products?" Patrick asked.

"We are primarily in the communications field."

"Like what, for example?"

"We manufacture several short-range hand-held optical laser communicating systems, a couple of infrared long-range transceiver systems, and a line of optical sensors and detectors products."

"That's very interesting."

"How about 5Com? What is your company's emphasis?"

"We are into Local Area Network products such as switches, routers and interface cards."

"That's still a good field, particularly for global marketing, where the demand remains high."

"So, what kind of a survey brings you here from Phoenix?"

"Well, we are looking for a location to set up a new division for ourselves. We would like to produce commercial versions of our products."

"Well, we are still a hot location for electronics manufacturers to set up shop."

"Look, how about I buy you a cup of coffee or a beer? I'd like to bounce a few questions off you. Do you have the time?"

"Sure, that would be fine. We can go upstairs here. Two flights up they have a small café," responded Patrick.

"That's great."

Both of them proceeded upstairs to the second floor, where Sturgeon bought the coffee. Then they went up to the third floor, a quiet area of small tables and comfortable chairs overlooking the Liffey quayside.

"What a choice spot to sit, relax and read a bit," Sturgeon said.

"I know," Patrick replied. "I try and stop by a couple of times a month."

"Are you a collector of antiquarian books?" Sturgeon asked.

"Somewhat, but I cannot afford the rare ones I would like to have."

"I am into collecting the writings of Nicola Tesla. He's my favorite visionary," Sturgeon said.

"I could not agree with you more. Electrical engineer, mechanical engineer, physicist and inventor. He did it all," Patrick replied.

"So much of his writings are now available to read on the Internet."

"Yes, I know. What are rare though, are the originals of his late nineteenth century writings and essays," said Patrick.

"I don't even want to think about what those originals would cost. I have several reprints of his writings and even they are expensive, Sturgeon said."

"I frequent a number of bookstores in Phoenix. If you give me a list of what you have in the way of Tesla's writings, I will be more than happy to see where I can fill in some gaps from the stores there."

"Sure, I would like that."

"Tell me a little about yourself. What part of Ireland are you from and where did you go to school?"

"I'll start with my schooling because it is so close by. I graduated from Trinity College, just a couple of blocks from here."

"Sure. I have already walked by it. What a beautiful campus and setting."

"It has changed a lot though since I went there. The area we now are in has gone through so much clean-up and renovation. Now it is a well-developed tourist haven and all the crowds that go with it."

"Are you from this area as well?"

"No. All of my family is from West Belfast. What do you know about Irish history?"

"I'm afraid not much at all," Sturgeon replied.

"Well, then I suppose you don't know about the Cahill name, do you?"

"I know we have many Irish Americans named Cahill in the U.S."

"We are all from West Belfast, the Catholic Belfast Republican area. I was born on Divis Street and went to St. Kevin's Primary School, on Mills road. All of my family is from that area and those that have passed on are all buried in the nearby Milltown Cemetery."

"Well then, what brought you to Dublin?"

"If you don't mind my bluntness, it's because of the harassment from the fucking Brits who still think they own the place."

"You mean you yourself have been subject to their harassment?"

"Me, and all of my family as well. It's just a constant fact of life."

"What form does it?"

"Primarily surveillance to see if we are still up to knee-capping the Protestant Loyalists and killing any Brits we can isolate and take out."

"I thought all of that died out and things were peaceful now in Northern Ireland."

"Relatively speaking, yes. In actuality though, the Brits still like to keep track of us to be sure in their own minds we are not still up to our old familial pursuits."

"Did you take an active role yourself against the Brits?"

"Only as a young boy and early teenager. At that point I was shipped off to here, in Dublin, in order to finish up my schooling and stay out of trouble."

"Your family must really have been wanting to tear down the British Empire."

"My uncle, my father's brother, was Joe Cahill. He was the Chief of Staff of the Provisional Irish Republican Army, the PIRA. He was in and out of jails in Ireland for years. He even broke out of one, ending up in the U.S., until he was extradited back to Northern Ireland."

"What a life he must have had."

"To top it all off, I am the godson of Seamus Twomey."

"I don't know of his name either."

"Well, they each followed each other as Chiefs of Staff in the PIRA. Uncle Joe was first in the early 1970's and Twomey followed him in the mid to late 1970s."

"Does any of this have any impact on you now, here in Dublin?"

"Oh, sure. Every now and then, I can spot a surveillance team on me here in town. On a couple of occasions I have even seen what I thought were British members of MI5, at the 5Com plant where I work."

"That's a shame. Has it affected your work in any way?"

"Not that I can really detect insofar as creating a problem for me. However, my immediate supervisor, along with the plant manager, does appear to be aloof or somewhat guarded when I'm around them now."

"That's not a good sign for you at all."

"I agree."

"How are you going to handle it in the future?"

"I'd like to start my own private war against the fuckers. I know how to go about it too. But, I also know where I would end up as a result."

"You don't really have many options, do you?"

"You're right. However, should it end up in a demotion, loss of income or cost me the job, I'll have to come up with some form of reaction against them."

"Look, we've only just met and you have been very forthright with me. I'd like to change gears on you."

"Sure. What are you thinking?"

"Do you feel you are knowledgeable about 5Com's competition here?"

"Yes, particularly those we compete with for the LAN, switch and router market."

"I'm going to be here for the rest of the week. I also will probably be returning within a month's time to complete my survey work."

"That's good. We should meet up and talk some more."

"After I've been here a few more days I'm sure I will have a number of questions I'd like to ask you."

"How about if we try and get together for dinner at the end of this week, if you have the time?"

"That would be fine. Let me write on my business card for you the hotel here where I'm staying, along with my cell phone number. It's the Grand Canal Hotel. Do you know it?"

"Sure. It's not far from here. Let me give you my card and I'll write my number on it for you."

"That would be great. I can't tell you how much I have enjoyed talking with you."

"Me too. Let's do it again."

They stepped outside onto the street in front of The Winding Stair. Patrick turned to his right and started up the Liffey towards Capel Street. Sturgeon turned left and headed back down the quayside, in the direction of his hotel. A feeling of pride and accomplishment enveloped Sturgeon as he made his way away from the meeting site. He didn't know where a potential operation would go with Cahill, but he knew he had laid the groundwork for working with someone who could turn out to be a quality agent, provided he was able to develop access to information of interest. He could sense that the hunt might be in the making.

CITE KINTARO 2148 042230Z DEC 11
TO: PRIORITY DIRECTOR, DUBLIN, STOCKHOLM INFO SAN FRANCISCO
S E C R E T RESTRICTED HANDLING
WNINTEL
SUBJECT: MEETING WITH SUBJECT OF REFS LEAD
REFS: A) KINTARO 2143
B) DIRECTOR 21784
ACTION REQUESTED: 1. PLEASE ENCRYPT AND PROVIDE 201 NUMBER OF REFS LEAD; 2. COMMENTS, AS APPROPRIATE.

1. DURING EVENING 04 DECEMBER 2011, CTC NOC OFFICER KINTARO MET WITH SUBJECT OF REFS AT IDENTITY. MEETING WAS HELD DURING 1950-2110 HOURS,

INCLUDING HAVING COFFEE INSIDE IDEN SITE. NO SURVEILLANCE WAS NOTED BEFORE, DURING OR AFTER MEETING.

2. SUBJECT CAME ACROSS AS FRIENDLY, CONGENIAL AND WILLING TO ANSWER ALL QUESTIONS POSED. SUBJECT ASKED A NUMBER OF OWN QUESTIONS AND APPEARED TO FULLY ACCEPT KINTARO COVER STORY.
3. KINTARO WAS ABLE TO WALK SUBJECT THROUGH EARLY YEARS GROWING UP IN BELFAST, AS WELL AS COLLEGE STUDIES AT TRINITY COLLEGE IN DUBLIN. SUBJECT PROVIDED OPEN DISCUSSION HISTORY LESSON ON THE PIRA AND FAMILY INVOLVEMENT IN ACTIONS AGAINST THE BRITISH.
4. SUBJECT EXHIBITED STRONG DISDAIN AND HATRED FOR THE BRITISH INCLUDING THEIR PAST SURVEILLANCE EFFORTS IN BELFAST AND CURRENT EFFORTS IN DUBLIN. SUBJECT CITED EFFECTS BRITISH EFFORT TO HARASS IS HAVING UPON CURRENT WORK SITUATION AND POSTURED TAKING SOME FORM OF RETALIATION AGAINST THEM SHOULD HE GET DEMOTED OR OUTRIGHT LOSE POSITION.
5. AS RESULT, KINTARO BELIEVES SUBJECT MAY WELL BE INCLINED TOWARDS GETTING INVOLVED IN ANTI-BRITISH ACTIVITIES. THIS WILL, HOWEVER, NEED TO BE EXPLORED FURTHER BY KINTARO IN TIME REMAINING THIS WEEK IN DUBLIN.
6. SUBJECT HAS AGREED AND IS QUITE FAVORABLY DISPOSED TOWARDS HAVING A DINNER MEETING LATER THIS WEEK, ONCE KINTARO CAN WORK FURTHER ON OSTENSIBLE COVER SURVEY RESULTING IN NEW QUESTIONS TO POSE.
7. HIGHLIGHTED BY COMMONALITIES IN PROFESSIONAL BACKGROUNDS PLUS SIMILAR VOCATIONAL INTERESTS OUTSIDE OF WORK.

   KINTARO BELIEVES GOOD CHEMISTRY HAS BEEN ESTABLISHED AND FURTHER BONDING LIKELY.
8. WILL ADVISE FURTHER RESULTS BY END OF WEEK.
9. FILE: 201-DEFER. E2IMPDET.

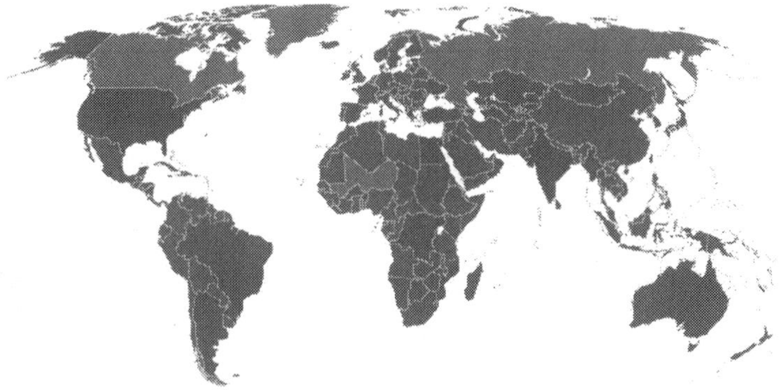

CHAPTER 16

"Dr. Ahmad, I'm sorry to have to wake you," the nurse said.

"That's alright. What time is it?"

"It's 3:15," she replied.

"Alright, what do you have?"

"A young man who says he's having an asthma attack. He's in Room C."

"I'll be right there."

"Thank you, doctor."

Abdul, who preferred to work the midnight to 8 a.m. shift, was used to being woken up to tend to patients coming into the Accident and Emergency Section in the hospital at all hours during the night. He got up, put on his lab coat and walked out of the doctor's hospitality suite into the main hallway of the emergency wing of the hospital. Room C was one of six rooms where doctors could see patients. He was one of two emergency room doctors on duty and, except for weekends, both of them could usually handle all of the emergency cases on their own.

Abdul picked up the patient's chart hanging on the wall next to the door of Room C. It listed the basic biographical data of name, date and place of birth, and purpose for coming to the hospital.

"I'm Dr. Ahmad. Please tell me your full name."

"Wahid Ali Jadoon," the young man replied.

"Tell me, Wahid, how old are you?"

"I'm 25, doctor."

The young man was struggling to raise up his chest and suck in air.

"Have you ever been diagnosed with having asthma?"

"Yes, doctor. Here's my prescription bottle. I'm all out of pills and in need of a refill."

Abdul noted the man's full name on the plastic bottle, and the name of the issuing pharmacy in Peshawar, Pakistan. The prescription was for "Medrol."

"Take off your shirt. I will need to listen to your lungs."

"Right away, doctor," he answered, still gasping for breath.

Abdul placed the end of his stethoscope against Wahid's chest wall. The breath sounds Abdul detected indicated moderate wheezing from the oscillations of narrowed airways, including the adjacent tissues. He recognized this as polyphonic expiratory wheezes and knew it to be a regular feature of asthma.

He listened a little longer in order to determine if anything else could be detected from the wheezes. He could not hear any airway obstruction, thereby ruling out, at least preliminarily, chronic bronchitis.

Before ending his examination, Abdul listened to Wahid's heart as well. He started his routine by doing an auscultation of the heart examination. He first listened in the mitral area, in order to detect the apex beat. He then turned to the tricuspid area, along the left sternal edge and fourth intercostals space. Next, he listened in the pulmonary area, at the second intercostals space that is to the left of the sternum. Lastly, he turned to the aortic area, at the second intercostals space, located to the right of the sternum. He alternated the use of the diaphragm and bell of his stethoscope in order to pick up both low and high-pitched sounds to conduct the exam. Satisfied that he had covered the full cardiac cycle in his exam, Abdul determined that Wahid was in possession of a healthy heart.

"Your heart is fine. Your lungs however, do indicate symptoms for asthma. The medicine you are currently taking I have available here. I will give you enough to get you by until you can get a new prescription filled. I see your pharmacy is in Peshawar. Do you plan on returning there soon?"

"No, doctor. You see, I'm a cousin to your brother from Mir Ali."

Abdul's eyes greatly widened in surprise, realizing he had just examined the first team member sent to him by Jamil. "Allah be praised," he said. "What wonderful news you bring."

"God willing, I'm here to help you all that I can," Wahid said.

"I take it you will not be going back then to Pakistan. Is that right?"

"That is right, my brother. I've moved here to work with you."

"It's OK for us to talk here, but I have to end this exam so that it will not draw the attention of the nursing staff outside."

"I understand. Please tell me when and where we can meet up again soon. We have much to discuss. Before we part though, let me give you this package of money from your brother in Mir Ali."

"Where are you staying and what kind of work are you able to do?"

"I've rented a small flat in East Kilbride. It's not far from here."

"What is your job situation?"

"I've been here for two weeks and have two job possibilities under consideration. I've held off taking either of them until talking with you. You may have some ideas for me to pursue."

"That's good planning on your part. What are the two possibilities?"

"One is with the City of East Kilbride. It is gardening work and involves maintaining ornamental parks and botanical gardens. The other is with a large hardware store in retail sales. I can handle either one of them easily. What do you think?"

"Does the parks and gardens job involve you working on your own and moving about town?"

"Yes, it does. I'd be driving a small truck hauling supplies and materials and placing them according to professional gardeners' specifications."

"I like that one a lot. Go ahead and try to get that job and let me know how it turns out."

"How shall we communicate?"

"Here is my hospital card. I'll write my cell phone number on the back. Do not come back here unless I ask you to. Instead, and just for now, you can call me in the evenings, before I come to work at midnight. I'd like your cell phone number as well. Now that we have met and I know who you are, I'll work up a commo plan for us to use on a regular basis."

"Whatever you say, my brother."

"Have you gone to the local mosque yet since arriving?"

"No. I wanted to meet you first."

"Good. I usually go to the Glasgow Central Mosque once or twice a week. However, except for prayers, I'm not involved in any of their activities."

"Should I be going to a different mosque from the one you attend?"

"No, you would have to travel too far for a different one. You can go to mine but I don't want you to get involved either. Some of our Muslim brothers there are too active in anti-British activities and, as a result, are under surveillance and suspicion by the police. Therefore, go to pray and nothing else. Also, if you happen to see me there, don't in any way approach or try and talk with me."

"God willing. That's what I shall do."

"Now that we've met and I know who you are, I'll not be able to write a prescription for your asthma medicine. I don't want our names to be linked in any way."

"I understand, my brother. I have plenty of capsules on hand. I just emptied the bottle before coming in order to have an excuse to be here. Your brother in Mir Ali gave me your name. He also told me where you worked. Unless you tell me otherwise, I will not be visiting you here again."

"Good thinking. We're starting out the right way."

"How will we meet next time?"

"Call me in a few days, once you have gotten a job. I hope that it will be the parks and gardens position. I'll tell you the name and address of a coffee shop where we'll meet. If I say to meet on Thursday evening, at nine o'clock, that will mean to meet on Wednesday evening, at seven o'clock. Always subtract one day and two hours whenever we talk over the telephone."

"I understand. Anything else?"

"When I see you next time I'll have a list of specific places for us to meet at after that. I'll also have a message for you to get to my brother from Mir Ali"

"I understand. Thank you, doctor."

"Go in peace, Wahid," Abdul said.

"God willing," Wahid replied.

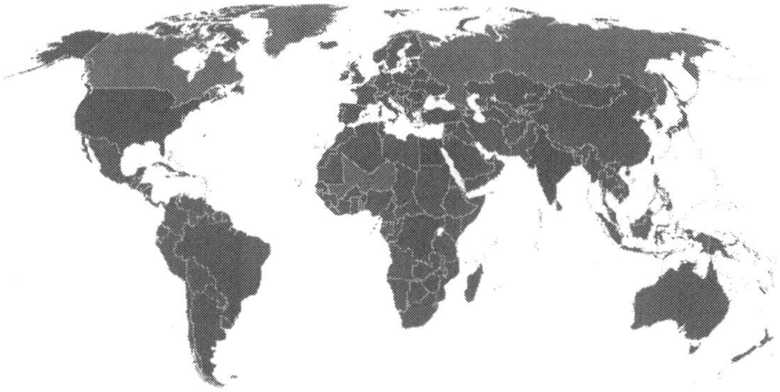

CHAPTER 17

Sturgeon hung up his hotel room telephone after the brief conversation with Patrick. Only two days had elapsed since their first meeting in the bookstore. For Patrick to take the initiative to call and ask to get together again was a good sign. This meant some commonalities had been established in Patrick's mind, and he was interested enough to seek out to renew the contact on his own. Now Sturgeon could plan the strategy for the upcoming evening meeting and set some operational goals to accomplish in order to further assess and advance the development for the potential use of Patrick in the future.

After agreeing to meet where Patrick suggested – Mulligan's Pub, on Poolbeg Street – Sturgeon booted up his laptop and did a Google search on the pub and its location. It turned out to be within a fifteen-minute walk from his hotel and still within the heavily tourist area of Temple Bar. He would have preferred to have selected the place to meet, and move to an area of Dublin on the outskirts of the city. However, this location on Poolbeg Street would suffice for this still-early stage of their relationship.

Sturgeon entered Mulligan's, glanced around the crowded, darkened interior and started working his way down the long old wooden bar towards an enlarged sitting area at the end of the room. Halfway down the bar, he spotted Patrick. They made eye contact and Patrick approached with extended hand and welcomed Mitch to what he called Dublin's finest institution.

"It may be noisy and crowded," Patrick said, "but they serve the very best pint of Guinness in all of Ireland here."

"Thank you for inviting me," Mitch replied. "I've been in a few pubs in my time, but I really like the feel of this one. Besides, who can pass up a good pint?"

"I thought we could start here, have a drink and then I'll take you down the street to a restaurant for dinner. It'll be quieter at the restaurant and easier to talk."

"Are you much for the pub scene here in Dublin?" Sturgeon asked.

"Being born and raised in Belfast, I prefer the pubs and people there. Being in the company of friends you have known all your life, means a lot more to me than the pubs here. But, Dublin has grown on me since my college days and I've a new set of friends I've gotten to know and to like."

"I can understand that. I know where you are coming from since I feel much the same way about my favorite haunts in Phoenix."

"What's it like there? What do you do when you're not working?"

"I run a lot."

"Oh, you've got the fucking Brits after you there too? I thought you kicked the bastards out for good a couple of centuries ago," Patrick dead-panned. "You look like a runner. What distances do you prefer?"

"My best distance is the 26.2 mile marathon. I try to run in at least four to six a year, depending on my work and travel schedule."

"I take that to mean you also have to run a lot in between in order to stay in shape."

"Exactly. But, look at you. You're trim and look in good shape too. How do you stay that way?"

"Some of us are just born this way. Whatever I eat or drink just does not seem to change my weight. I have a high metabolism rate that obviously compensates for what I intake."

"Does beer have much effect on you?" Sturgeon asked.

"Actually, I rarely have more than two pints a night, and that is only three or four times a week."

"Beer is alright for me also, since I do need some carbohydrate intake. But, I do have to watch any additional starches like pasta, breads, rice, desserts, and things like that."

"Now you're going to spoil my dinner. Tell me, how has your survey work gone for you since we last met?"

"Well, I still have a couple more days of work before returning to Phoenix on Saturday morning. Nevertheless, it appears at this stage that recommending to my company that a completely new division be set up here would be premature. Instead, I'm more inclined to recommend having assemblies and sub-system parts fabricated here. Upon completion, these assemblies and parts would be shipped to Arizona for final configuration into completed systems."

"Does this mean your survey effort has been less than successful?"

"No. Not at all. It means that making a major financial investment to set up a facility to manufacture complete systems here is just not yet warranted. Instead, we should start with parts and assemblies and proceed from there."

"Sounds like a good recommendation to me."

"I will still return here at the beginning of the year to further explore our options. I'd still like to think that a new division for systems manufacturing would ultimately prove to be the most cost effective move for us. I just need to do a complete due diligence study in order to fully determine what will be best for us for the future."

"I hope we can meet up again upon your return. For now however, how about some good Irish cuisine to satisfy your appetite?"

"That would be great," Sturgeon replied.

They exited Mulligan's Pub and stood at the curbside. Patrick hailed a taxi and after they climbed inside he told the driver to take them to Purty Kitchen, located in Dublin's Southside suburbs. Along the way, Patrick described his growing interest in trying new foods and restaurants as part of his self-education efforts to expand his horizons outside Ireland. Sturgeon, in reply, related his similar interests and experimentation with various cuisines found throughout the U.S.

Upon arrival at the Purty Kitchen, Sturgeon offered to pay for the taxi. Patrick refused, saying this was his evening to entertain Sturgeon and maybe he would show up some day on his doorstep in Phoenix and let him repay with a meal or two. Sturgeon agreed that would be his pleasure and he looked forward to such a visit one day.

"I know what you're thinking," said Patrick, as they entered what looked to Sturgeon to be another pub. "But this is a pub with a great kitchen and a view of the Irish Sea," he added.

After being seated in one of the upstairs dining rooms, Patrick said the most popular selections on the menu were the various fresh seafood dishes. They looked over the menu, ordered their meal and Patrick selected from the wine list a bottle of dry Italian white wine, a Pinot Grigio. After their first glass was poured, Patrick offered a toast to Sturgeon's survey efforts. Sturgeon countered with future success to Patrick's engineering career.

"I want to thank you very much for your kind hospitality and comments about my survey work here. I do indeed expect to be able to repay you in the future.

"I've enjoyed talking with you also," Patrick replied. "It's not every day I find someone with so many interests the same as mine. Based on the number of Americans I've met over recent years, it's easy to understand why we Irish and you Americans are on such good terms."

"That's relatively an easy one to answer," Sturgeon replied. "I suppose our most common similarity is we were both done in by the Brits. The main difference however, is we beat the bastards twice in war, struck out on our own and have now subsequently learned to live at peace with them. In your case, based on what you're experiencing in particular, you're still being fucked over at a cost no one should have to put up with in today's age."

"Well," Patrick said, "I thank you for your comments. Unfortunately, as if they haven't taken enough from us Irish over the many years, they still are up to practicing a perverse form of overprotecting what they view as their turf and us poor bastards within."

"What do you believe is going to happen in your job situation?"

"I suspect the current level of surveillance and harassment will continue. However, if it results in the loss of my job, I can no longer sit back and take it anymore."

"What does that mean?"

"It means I will be out of here. To date, I have enjoyed my work tremendously. I make a good wage. I am living well and have been able to save some money. I have also been able to look forward to considerable more advancement with 5Com."

"What would you do then?"

"I would hate to have to cash it all in and take up a new life of living on the edge like a number of my cousins still do in Belfast."

"You have obvious skills and talent in electronics that should enable you to get a work permit and immigrate to the US to live and work there."

"Yes, that is all true, and a possibility as well. I will not deny ultimately wanting to make such a move to the US in the future. In the meantime however, to lose what I have because of what these fuckers are putting me through is just too much to walk away from now. For me and my family, old scores and old sores require retribution."

"What can I do to help you out? You have too much going for yourself to have to make the kinds of moves you are suggesting."

"I like your friendship, but just hope and pray I don't disappear from Dublin and show up on the streets of West Belfast again. You would not like the kind of person such a move there would turn me into."

"Look, I have many good friends in the electronics industry in both the US as well as in Europe. If you are interested, let me try to work out some way to assist you. I'll be leaving Saturday morning to return to the US Would you like for me to make some inquires and let you know the results?"

"At this point, it won't hurt. Go ahead. I've yet to be called in by the bastards and questioned. But the way things appear to be heading, it would not surprise me. The Brits have a way of making things miserable for a person when they choose to do so. If they end up costing me my job, I'll have no choice but to react."

"Are any of your relatives in Belfast aware of what is happening to you here?"

"No, I haven't said a word yet."

"How do you communicate with them?"

"Usually by phone on a once a month or so basis. During the holidays, I go there by train. You've asked a curious question about talking with them. Why is that?"

"Based on what you've told me about your family background, it makes me wonder whether or not the Brits might be listening in on your conversations. Is that a possibility?"

"Certainly could be, but we long ago learned the hard way about maintaining tight discipline and security amongst ourselves. When we talk over the phone, or are in a crowd of people with whom we are not on trusting terms, or don't know very well, we carefully watch what is being said. We trust no strangers."

"Good policy to practice. I can certainly understand what you told me previously about looking for surveillance. I guess you have just plain got it ingrained in you to be alert and watchful for people paying unusual attention to you and your activities."

"You're right on the mark. It is just our way of growing up in Belfast. Be alert, be cautious and stay alive. Although things did get better and somewhat safer over the more recent years, the hounding of us by the fucking Brits has never totally ended."

"What a shame."

"As result though, we still like to let them know on occasion that we're still around. We may have gone to ground but are in no way down and out."

"I take it you would prefer not to have to go back to that kind of life. Is that right?"

"My preference is for all of us in our family to be able to live in peace and prosperity. I have been in the process of carving out a good life for myself here in Dublin. I would like to keep it that way."

"Let's stay in touch. I will let you know when I'll be returning here next month. Will you keep me advised of any changes in your situation?"

"I will. That I promise to you. I also thank you for your comments and offer of support. I knew I spotted a friend when we first met earlier at the bookstore."

CITE DIRECTOR 032657 061942Z DEC 11
TO: PRIORITY KINTARO, STOCKHOLM, DUBLIN, INFO SAN FRANCISCO
S E C R E T RESTRICTED HANDLING
WNINTEL CKCATCHER SPPROBE
SUBJECT: ENCRYPTION AND 201 FOR SUBJECT REFS
REFS: A) KINTARO 2148
B) KINTARO 2143
C) DIRECTOR 021784
ACTION REQUESTED: SEE BELOW.

1. SUBJECT REFS ENCRYPTED SPPROBE/1 (P/1) AND ASSIGNED 201-1067273.
2. HQS IS ENCOURAGED BY SIGNIFICANT PROGRESS MADE BY NOC KINTARO IN RAPIDLY MOVING TO MEET AND ASSESS P/1.
3. SHOULD UPCOMING MEETING WITH P/1 CONTINUE ALONG FAVORABLE LINES, HQS WILL REQUEST STOCKHOLM STATION AND KINTARO'S INPUT ON

TIMING FOR INSERTION OF STOCKHOLM CTC C/O BRUBACHER.

4. FILE: 201-1067273. E2IMPDET.

CITE KINTARO 2154 062310Z DEC 11
TO: PRIORITY DIRECTOR, STOCKHOLM, DUBLIN, INFO SAN FRANCISCO
S E C R E T RESTRICTED HANDLING
WNINTEL CKCATCHER SPPROBE
SUBJECT: MEETING WITH SPPROBE/1
REFS: A) DIRECTOR 032657
B) KINTARO 2148
ACTION REQUESTED: 1. HQS AND STOCKHOLM STATION INPUT RE PLANNING FOR INTRODUCTION OF STOCKHOLM STATION OFFICER BRUBACHER TO SPPROBE/1 (P/1); 2. FOR STOCKHOLM – AVAILABILITY OF BRUBACHER TO MEET WITH KINTARO PRIOR TO INTRODUCTION FOR PURPOSES OF DISCUSSING OVERALL INTRODUCTION SCENARIO; AND, 3.
FOR DUBLIN STATION - COMMENTS RE SUGGESTED VENUE FOR INTRODUCTION.

1. DURING EVENING 06 DECEMBER 2011, CTC NOC OFFICER KINTARO MET WITH P/1 AT IDENTITY A FOR DRINKS, FOLLOWED BY EXTENDED DINNER SESSION AT IDEN B IN DUBLIN SOUTHSIDE SUBURBS.
2. PERSONALBONDINGANDFURTHERINGOFOPERATIONAL GOALS WERE SIGNIFICANTLY ENHANCED AS RESULT P/1 INDICATING THAT SHOULD PERSONAL JOB SITUATION BE AFFECTED BY BRITISH INTERFERENCE WITH EMPLOYER, P/1 WOULD LIKELY RETURN TO BELFAST TO JOIN UP WITH RELATIVES IN TAKING ACTION AGAINST BRITISH INTERESTS.
3. P/1 RESPONDED FAVORABLY TO KINTARO OFFER OF WILLINGNESS TO HELP FINDING NEW JOB OUTSIDE OF IRELAND AS OPTION TO TAKING UP VIOLENT ACTS AGAINST BRITISH. P/1 EXPRESSED GRATITUDE FOR ASSISTANCE AND HOW PLEASED P/1 IS WITH GROWING PERSONAL FRIENDSHIP UNDERWAY WITH KINTARO.

GOOD CHEMISTRY AND PROFESSIONAL BONDING HAS BEEN ESTABLISHED AS EVIDENCED BY P/1 OPENING UP TO KINTARO IN DISCUSSING THE PERSONAL EFFECTS OF BRITISH HARASSMENT THAT IS UNDERWAY.

4. KINTARO ASSESSES P/1 AS HIGHLY ALERT, SAVVY INDIVIDUAL, NOT ONLY TOWARDS PROFESSIONAL WORK ASPECTS, BUT TO PERSONAL SECURITY AS WELL. P/1 EVINCES STRONG SENSE OF STREET SMARTS AS NOTED WHEN KINTARO ARRIVED AT IDEN A (CHECKING OUT WHO MIGHT HAVE FOLLOWED KINTARO INSIDE), LEAVING IDEN A, ARRIVING AT IDEN B AND SWEEPING GLANCES OF IDEN B MEETING SITE. P/1 ALSO ACKNOWLEDGED TELEPHONE SECURITY PRACTICES AMONGST FAMILY AND RELATIVES IN BELFAST, AS WELL AS PERSONAL CONDUCT WHEN IN COMPANY OF STRANGERS.
5. P/1 APPEARS TO FULLY ACCEPT STURGEON COVER STORY, ENGINEERING BACKGROUND AND EXPERIENCES. P/1 RELATED WELL TO VALIDITY OF KINTARO'S SURVEY WORK IN IRELAND AND NEED FOR RETURN VISIT TO FURTHER DETERMINE FUTURE INVOLVEMENT IN ELECTRONICS INDUSTRY IN IRELAND.
6. KINTARO BELIEVES TURNOVER TIME IS RIPE AND P/1 WOULD REACT FAVORABLY UPON MEETING WITH ANOTHER AMERICAN INDIVIDUAL WHO COMES TO LEND SYMPATHETIC EAR AND OFFER OF ASSISTANCE. QUESTION REMAINS HOW TO AFFECT INTRODUCTION, DEGREE OF DIRECT INVOLVEMENT OF KINTARO, AND/OR SERVING AS INDIRECT BYSTANDER WHO OSTENSIBLY MEETS BRUBACHER AT SAME TIME AND COMES TO SERVE IN VETTING FUNCTION OF BRUBACHER, SHOULD P/1 HAVE ANY SUSPICIONS OR QUESTIONS.
7. NO SURVEILLANCE OR UNDUE PERSONAL ATTENTION NOTED BY KINTARO AT EITHER IDEN A OR B DURING ENTIRE TIME SPENT WITH P/1. IT WOULD APPEAR P/1 NOTICED NOTHING EITHER, IN OWN EFFORTS TO DETERMINE PERSONAL SECURITY STATUS.
8. FILE: 201-1067273. E2IMPDET.

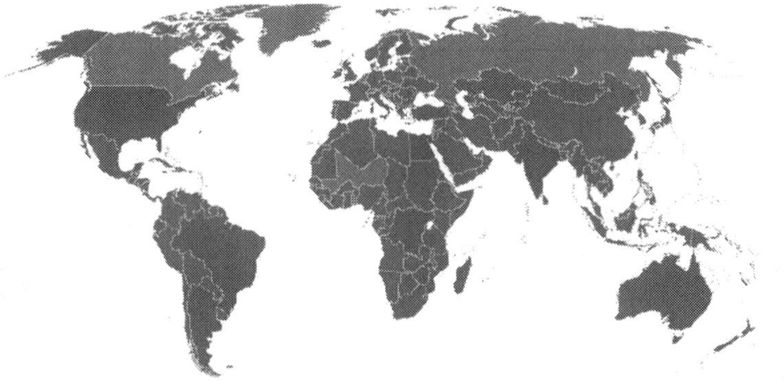

CHAPTER 18

As instructed, Wahid entered the Cherrybean Coffee Shop on Dumbarton Road, in Glasgow, at precisely 5:45 p.m. He spotted Abdul sitting at a small table in the far corner and made direct eye contact with him. Abdul smiled and motioned for Wahid to sit down at the table across from him.

"May peace be with you, my brother," Abdul intoned.

"And with you too, my brother," Wahid replied.

"I am proud that when you called two days ago and I gave you instructions for meeting here, you followed them exactly as given. That is the best way for us to begin working together."

"I am at your service, Abdul."

"Tell me, what job you were able to get?"

"The City of East Kilbride parks and gardens job. I am already feeling good about it. After one week on the job, I find that the work is not hard for me at all. I accompany two other workers and we ride around in a van tending to the parks and gardens throughout the city."

"That is great news. Allah has brought us blessings. "

"I expect that after a period of time I will be able to drive around on my own or have a worker or two accompany me."

"Do you expect to be working with fertilizers and chemicals for treating lawns and soils?"

"Oh yes, especially during the times of the year when they are purchased, stored and made ready for use in the parks and gardens."

"I would like you to be alert to, and get involved in, their purchase, handling and eventual distribution. Is that possible?"

"Yes, I believe so. The city facility that we work out of contains our office, vans, tools, equipment and storage area for all of our supplies. I already have access to fertilizer and chemicals in order to load our van and distribute as necessary. It should be easy to learn about and get involved in the movement of these materials from the suppliers to our storage site."

"Let me know as soon as you learn about where these materials are purchased from and how they are transported to your facility."

"I will let you know as soon as possible. Are we going to continue to meet in shops like this or will we be able to have more privacy?"

"Coffee shops like this will be fine for the time being. I will change meeting conditions, as necessary, in the future. It is quite natural for us to meet like this and have coffee together out in the open. We have nothing to hide. I call this the privacy of meeting in the open. I am an established Pakistani doctor living here and you are a recently arrived Pakistani worker seeking a new way of life. We have subsequently become friends and enjoy being in each other's company. We should look quite natural meeting this way. This will always be our story should anyone make inquires or question either of us. Is that acceptable to you?"

"Yes, Abdul. It is very clear and I will completely follow your instructions."

"As additional brothers are added to our team, we will continue to make use of the same story to explain away our being together. That way we will always look natural when together and always have an easily explainable reason, including the friendship and enjoyment of being around each other. As our team increases in numbers and our discussions become more sensitive, I shall move us inside more private quarters."

"Before I left our blessed land in the north, your brother from Mir Ali told me that we would be joined soon by another brother who will assist us in serving our jihad."

"Yes, I am also expecting him to join us soon. But, I am not sure if he will already be living and working in the local area here, or, coming into the country new. I hope he will be coming from home and I expect he will contact you directly and not seek me out. This is the best kind of security we can have for ourselves."

"I fully understand, Abdul."

"Once you are contacted, you should meet with him and determine that neither of you are under surveillance nor have been questioned by anyone. That will be the time for you to let me know of his presence here. I will then give instructions for you to bring him to me so that we can all meet together."

"What else can I do?"

"How soon can you take off a couple of days work and travel back home?"

"With the infidels Christmas holidays coming soon, I should be able to combine a weekend together with a Monday and a Tuesday. Will that be enough time?"

"That will be just fine," said Abdul.

"If I call my uncle in Miran Shah, and let him know the date when I arrive home, he will alert your brother in Mir Ali. That will set up a meeting with him right after I get there, and I can then convey whatever information you wish."

"That will be fine but you can only mention over the phone the date of your arrival. The only additional use of the phone later on will be to call your uncle to give him the date of out actual planned attack. I want my brother in Mir Ali to know this date ahead of time."

"I can arrange with my uncle that if I call and mention I will be arriving for the wedding of my youngest brother on such and such date, he will pass on that date to your brother. Will that be alright?"

"That will be good. The only way we will pass on any other sensitive information is via direct, person-to-person contact. No other important or sensitive information is to be discussed over phones, or even via the Internet. You must always assume someone is listening to us."

"This is obviously the best way. It will be time consuming in terms of travel back and forth, but nevertheless the most secure," Wahid replied.

"My brother in Mir Ali and I at first considered using coded words in written or spoken messages. We also thought about communicating with each other using a new model BlackBerry cell phone for making international calls. Nevertheless, I have determined none of that is secure enough.

Therefore, we will only communicate directly via you traveling back and forth, as necessary."

"That is fine with me, Abdul."

"I am very grateful to learn from you that another brother will join us soon. I know that two more will also be coming in the near future as well. Their arrival will enable me to further develop our attack plans with only limited additional help from Mir Ali."

"How do you wish I proceed regarding our previous discussion about fertilizers and chemicals?"

"Your ability in your new job to accumulate sufficient ammonium nitrate fertilizer, along with some assorted chemicals I will have you purchase, will greatly reduce our dependence on our brother in Mir Ali."

"What is it that you wish me to tell your brother there?"

"It will have to wait until you tell me when you can travel back home. Just before you leave here we will meet again and I will give you the message I wish to have conveyed."

"I fully understand, Abdul."

"We must end this meeting now. You leave first and I will pay for the coffee. Be sure and move around the streets here in the area for at least most of an hour before returning to your home. Make some stops in shops to buy things you may need, along the way. Make sure you are not under surveillance by anyone. In addition, look for any vehicles around you as you proceed. Especially note any vehicles you see that keep reappearing as you move around the streets."

"You can rely on me, Abdul. I have been well trained in surveillance tactics and have developed a keen eye for any such actions being taken against me."

"I am always alert as well, before and after all meetings," Abdul replied. "The ultimate success of our jihad will be based upon our overall security posture. Go in peace, Wahid."

"Inshallah, Abdul."

The upcoming meeting between Wahid and Jamil, in Mir Ali, would be the first chance since Abdul got approval to go ahead with his plan of attack, to report to al-Qaeda leadership on the status of the operation. Since Abdul remained convinced of being able to stage a successful attack upon the nuclear reprocessing and storage facility at Sellafield, he needed only to reconfirm to Jamil that the original target chosen remained the same. Once the date of the attack was selected, and it was imminent, he would have Wahid convey that information as well.

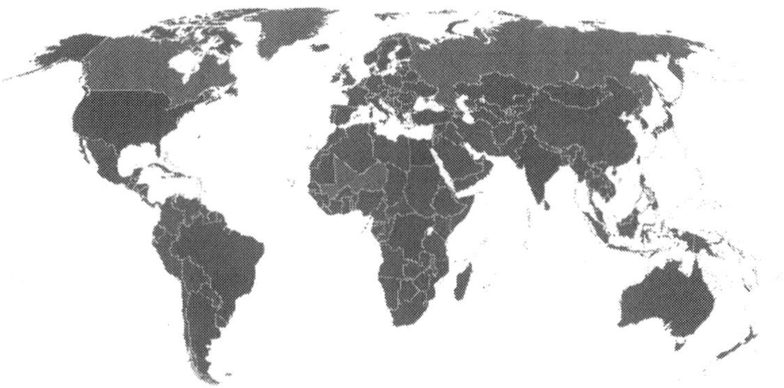

CHAPTER 19

In the weeks and days remaining in December, Mitch, Patrick, Abdul and Wahid continued on in their wide-ranging activities leading up to the coming New Year.

For Mitch, after his productive second meeting with Patrick in the outlying Dublin restaurant, it meant returning to San Francisco and his real, true name company work at M&T. He quickly got back into his daily routine in the office. In the back of his mind however, he was planning for his next meeting with Patrick at the beginning of January.

Once he worked out the details in his mind, Mitch, in mid-December, outlined his plans for the early January meeting in a cable to headquarters and Stockholm Station. He noted however, that before the introduction of Stockholm Station officer BRUBACHER (Lee Denning) to Patrick, he wanted a separate personal meeting beforehand with Lee elsewhere in Europe. That would enable the two of them to thrash out the details of the scenario for either a direct or indirect introduction of Lee to Patrick.

Traditionally, in Agency operational turnover scenarios, Lee, an inside case officer, would be introduced in an alias identity as a commercial businessperson. Lee would be with a different company from the one that Mitch, in his Sturgeon alias identity, told Patrick that he worked for.

This kind of introduction though, would not be without a significant hurdle to overcome. Namely, how plausible would it be for a commercial businessperson to have discussions with Patrick regarding making himself available to join up with a radical Islamic terrorist group?

The other possibility would be for Mitch to be meeting with Patrick at some kind of gathering where other people are present. In this case, Lee, on his own, would have to offer up some kind of excuse to approach Patrick and Mitch, introduce himself to both of them and see if enough chemistry could be established for him to ultimately be able to subsequently meet with Patrick on his own. This kind of approach also is not without a hurdle to overcome. It means Lee, without any connection to Mitch, would have to start out all over again in bringing Patrick to the point where he shows his anti-British sympathies and expresses willingness to retaliate against them. This is the kind of quandary that is always present in trying to decide how to best introduce a new officer to a target individual while at the same time having as little as possible blowback, as it is termed, against the introducing officer.

Mitch had done his work in getting Patrick to reveal his strong anti-British leanings and the willingness to seek retribution against them should he lose his job in Dublin. He also set Patrick up for an introduction of another Agency officer by offering help in finding employment should any British effort against him succeed. Patrick's response to Mitch that he could go ahead and see what kinds of positions in the marketplace might be available, signified his acceptance of Mitch's basic soft pitch. In other words, Mitch succeeding in getting Patrick to agree to be recruited for some, yet unknown position with some yet, unknown employer.

The manner in which Mitch quickly moved Patrick through the phases of assessment and development, thereby setting him up for Lee, is much the same as what a US corporation would employ to determine what a competitor corporation is doing in developing new products. In this case, the US corporation would use one of their own employees to search out amongst their known competitors a person with known access to proprietary information of interest. Provided the person exhibited exploitable vulnerabilities, he or she would be quickly developed and, in effect, recruited to provide the needed information of high priority value.

For example, if a US microchip manufacturer wants to know what Japanese chipmakers have in the way of new chips under research and development, their business plans and intentions, and timetables for introducing new products to the marketplace, they go directly to the source. The US manufacturer sends one of their electrical engineers to the Japanese chip-maker where the engineer is known and already has a business relationship with his or her Japanese engineer counterpart. By using their relationship and capitalizing on exploitable vulnerabilities, the US engineer is able to learn firsthand the latest proprietary information of interest to the US firm. It is accomplished quickly, is done thoroughly and, after enough money in discreet envelopes exchange hands, the information sought is acquired and taken back to the US firm. This kind of commercial recruitment operation is done in the corporate business world on a daily basis.

In the particular case of using Patrick to try and develop useful information on a radical Islamic terrorist group, no one person in the Agency – Mitch, Lee, or even Jack, their supervisor in CTC – is under any illusion that Patrick would become an actual actively accepted member of such a group and, as such, come to have access to high value information. Instead, it is accepted that the terrorist group will compartment Patrick from other members and severely restrict his access to their sensitive inner deliberations and planning for operations.

What is hoped for is that Patrick could be offered up as an attractive enough target for approach even if only able to work on the periphery of the group. In this case, an Irishman who harbors deep resentment against the British, and has been personally hurt by them, is seeking payback. Therefore, he might be willing to be co-opted by a terrorist group and accept tasking to further the group's own cause against the British Government. Patrick may not ever come to learn their actual identities, much less their plans and intentions, as a result of being compartmented and held on the farthest edges from other group members and their activities. However, his real value might well result in being able to learn how they are going about their planning, the destructive materials to be used, the kind of attack that is involved and, if very fortunate, a possible timetable for the attack.

These were the things on Mitch's mind as the Christmas holidays went by. He was glad to be back at work with Dane and Sumiko in the office. He attended several Christmas parties in the local business community and was also able to arrange for an all too hasty Christmas celebration with his mother in Palos Verdes. He was pleased with himself and his accomplishments during the year and, more than ever was thoroughly enjoying the wearing of two hats – the life of an undercover intelligence operative, and the work of a successful corporate executive recruiter.

* * *

Patrick's end-of-year experiences, on the other hand, were turning out very different, and very poorly. Twice within one week, he noticed surveillants watching him. The first time, upon returning home to his apartment from work, and again, two nights later, while leaving Slattery's Bar on Capel Street and walking home. In the first instance, at least three surveillants were watching him. Two of them were in a parked car across the street from his apartment building and the other one he saw standing in a dimly lit building entrance next door to his building. In the second instance, two surveillants followed him into Slattery's. One came inside, apparently to see if he was meeting up with anyone, while the other remained outside. These same two followed him back to his apartment building afterwards.

He was sorely tempted to confront the two during the second instance, but changed his mind at the last minute. However, he did get his chance one week later. Upon arriving on the third floor landing of his building after work, he confronted a burly male who tried to feign being drunk. It looked to Patrick like the fellow had just exited his apartment. Patrick put his hand up to stop the fellow, they tussled, and Patrick got in two good punches to his jaw and mid-section. The fellow went down next to the stairwell, jumped back up and quickly scurried down the stairs and out the exit door.

Patrick did not pursue the fellow outside the building. Instead, he immediately went inside his apartment and checked to see if anything was missing or if something like an audio microphone had been planted somewhere. He did not see where anything was missing nor could he find anything of a suspicious nature. He did believe however, the fucking Brits just staged a serious upgrade in their harassment campaign against him.

The final blow came at work the following week, two days after Christmas. Patrick was called inside his supervisor's office and notified of his dismissal. He was told that a decline in new production requirements necessitated laying off a number of workers. Half of his own production line was to be consolidated into another line and his position as line supervisor and troubleshooter would no longer be needed. The dismissal was on the spot and included two weeks severance pay plus vacation pay built up over the year. The supervisor, whom Patrick had considered a friend, was quite uncomfortable and aloof in talking with him about the dismissal. He apparently did not feel good at all with having to dismiss him. Patrick could sense that the dismissal was contrived and, as expected, was arranged by the fucking local British MI5 contingent.

Afterwards, Patrick called his oldest brother in West Belfast to advise him of the loss of his job, and said he may be coming home if he was unable to find a replacement job in the near future. He also sent Sturgeon an email to his Phoenix firm's email address to advise him of what had happened. Mitch checked his alias email address regularly and that is how he received the news from Patrick.

Early the next morning in San Francisco, Mitch, in his Sturgeon alias, telephoned Patrick and offered his sympathy and concern over the loss of his job. The two of them also reaffirmed their agreement to meet at the beginning of the second week in January. Patrick, obviously in very low spirits, did not hesitate to say who he thought was behind the dismissal. Sturgeon did not respond to the comment, instead saying that he had a couple of possible employment leads that Patrick might be interested in and he would provide full details when they met in Dublin.

After talking with Patrick, Mitch sent out immediate precedence cable to headquarters, Stockholm and Dublin Stations, advising of Patrick's loss of his job and suspicions of British complicity. Headquarters and Stockholm Station quickly replied, reaffirming their support for the upcoming meeting with Lee, prior to his introduction to Patrick. They both also agreed on the positive direction that the operation appeared to be heading.

Dublin Station, while also replying in the affirmative, offered up caution in continuing to meet with Patrick in Dublin, especially if a turnover were to take place there. The Station's concern centered upon the obvious stepped up British MI5 interest in Patrick, let alone interest by the local Irish police authorities. It was also noted that in the Station's liaison meetings with both British and Irish authorities, nothing to date had been mentioned about either Patrick, by name, or any US citizens that had come to their attention.

* * *

In mid-December, Abdul was summoned into the Chief Administrator's office at the Royal Alexandria Hospital, and given good news. After five full years of exemplary work in the Accident and Emergency Department of the hospital, he was promoted to senior staff status. Included in the promotion was an increase in his monthly salary. As a senior staff physician, he could now choose the hours he wished to work in the department, as well as which two days of the week he would prefer to have off. Expecting him to select the 9 a.m. to 4 p.m. weekday shift, with weekends off, Abdul, to the mild surprise of the administrator, chose to remain on the midnight to 8 a.m. shift, and continue having weekends off.

Since he required no more than five hours sleep after getting off his current midnight to 8 a.m. shift, he was able to devote most all afternoons and weekends to his primary pursuit – operational planning for the attack on the Sellafield facility. He also did not want to change in any way the established profile of his work routine and lifestyle when not working. He was quite satisfied with his acceptance at the hospital and in the local community where he lived, and did not want to do anything that might bring him to the attention of anyone.

With Wahid now in place as a member of his team, and another brother expected to arrive soon, the operation was soon going to move into a crucial stage. Abdul would now focus on the logistical details of arranging to rent two small homes between Glasgow and the seaside resort town of Seascale, located one mile south of Sellafield. These homes would be used as safe houses, and would require attached garages, if possible, as well as storage and working areas for use in the handling of bomb components. Besides bags of ammonium nitrate fertilizer, containers of chemicals and fuel oil, Abdul estimated he would require at least twenty plastic barrels for use in holding the explosives in the final assembly stage.

Making use of rented trucks was another aspect of Abdul's logistics planning. At least two trucks would be required. One to surreptitiously deliver and store the fertilizer, chemicals and fuel oil in the safe houses, via concealed delivery through the attached garages. In the final stage, just preceding the attack, a second truck would be needed to carry the assembled bomb to the targeted B215 building at Sellafield.

During the final week in December, Abdul held a meeting with Wahid in another downtown Glasgow coffee shop. Wahid reported that he had arranged for a four-day period, with two days off work, to travel back to Mir Ali, and return. With that news, Abdul then proceeded to give Wahid the information he wished to be conveyed to his cousin there.

The most important piece of information to take back was that the target facility remained the same. Although Wahid did not yet know what or where the actual target was, he did know that a fertilizer bomb, similar to that used in the Oklahoma City bombing in the US some years earlier, would be the weapon of choice.

In terms of requesting any equipment while in Mir Ali, Wahid was told to ask for only one item – A new, unused M34 Blasting Machine. This is an electric detonator that would be used to trigger the explosive charges inside the truck. It is a small hand-held device weighing only twelve ounces, standing 5 ½ inches in height, 3 inches wide and just over 1 inch thick. The device would be carried by the martyrs in the truck and detonated by hand when crashing the truck into the side of building B215 at Sellafield.

Abdul knew this type of electric device were in use in Afghanistan by the US military forces there and should not be difficult to obtain. In order to deliver the device to Scotland, Abdul suggested the best route would be to smuggle it there inside the trunk of a car, along with a jack, spare tools, etc., traveling via France and through the underwater Channel rail service to England. The reason for stressing it to be brand new and unused was that it would not have any kind of explosive residue on it. That would allow it to pass safely by the sophisticated eye of the EGIS high-tech sensing system used to screen cars making the Channel trip. EGIS sensors have the capability of detecting the minutest fragments of explosive residues.

Lastly, Abdul asked that Wahid determine, before returning from Mir Ali, whether or not the M34 device could be provided. If not, then Abdul was prepared to make other arrangements, in Scotland, for the use of a more improvised detonating device instead.

Two months earlier, while on a driving trip in a remote corner of the northwest of Scotland, he ran across an elderly Scotsman sitting on a stone fence beside his car with a flat tire. Abdul changed the tire for the old man, earning his eternal thanks and appreciation. When he had placed the flat tire inside the trunk of the car after putting on the spare tire, he noticed an opened box of dynamite containing several sticks of the explosive. The sticks looked new and Abdul asked the old man for what use he made of such explosives? The old man replied, that for years he and his family had used dynamite for clearing large stones from their farmlands. When Abdul curiously looked over the sticks, the old man asked if he would like one of them as his way of saying thanks for the assistance with the tire change, Abdul did not hesitate to accept the offer.

As he was driving back to Paisley, he felt quite fortunate having made such an acquisition. He knew he would be able use this single stick of high explosive, in conjunction with a blasting machine or similar electric detonating device, to trigger the explosive materials inside the barrels resulting in the worst disaster to happen upon the British since World War Two.

Abdul ended his meeting with Wahid stressing the need for them to get back together again immediately after Wahid returned from Mir Ali. He was pleased with having Wahid as a member on his team, and hoped that the new members to come turned out to be as resourceful and obedient. Upon returning, Wahid would be asked to assist in locating the two suitable homes to serve as safe houses.

In the meantime, Abdul would now proceed to start the New Year off by finding a suitable white-skinned European male who possessed a strong antipathy, or downright hatred, for the British Government. Having lived in Scotland for five years, he was aware of the strong anti-British sentiments expressed by many Scots and Irish. The question remained though, would he be able to summon up enough of his personal and professional skills to convince a suitable candidate to join up with him in perpetrating an act of terrorism as an expression of that hatred?

A European, compartmented from most members of the team and provided with only a limited amount of information relating to the ultimate target, would prove highly useful to Abdul. He would be able to procure a needed component or two for the bomb, as well as rent the truck to be used in ferrying the bomb to the Sellafield facility. Where an Asian might raise questions or suspicions amongst the British, for whatever reasons, a local Scotsman or Irishman would be able to go unnoticed.

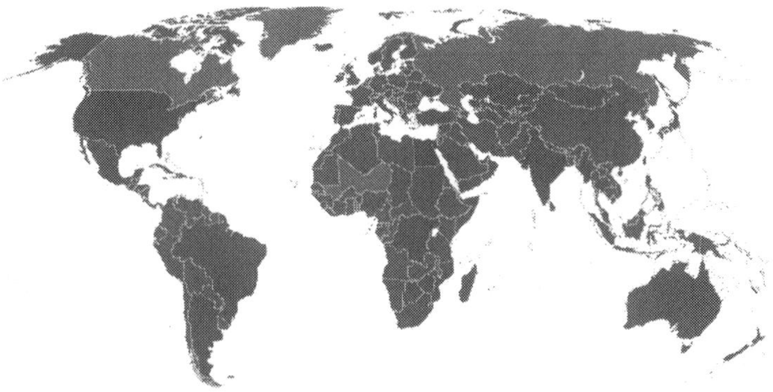

CHAPTER 20

Patrick thought it was strange to wake up on the first workday of the New Year and not have a job. He tried to go back to sleep, especially after hearing the cold wind blowing outside, but was unable to do so. He got up, made a pot of coffee, booted up his desktop computer and scanned classified ads from the websites of the *Irish Times* and *Limerick Post* newspapers.

He expected to receive a call from his new-found American friend, Sturgeon, soon, advising of his arrival back in Dublin. He looked forward to hearing some good news about a couple of job possibilities from him, but with only knowing Sturgeon for a short period of time, he was not holding out much hope. Yet, deep in his gut, he felt optimistic about the news that would be forthcoming.

Finishing up his second cup of coffee, he noted in the *Irish Times* website that The Shelbourne, a Marriott hotel located nearby Trinity College, was holding a two-day job fair. That perked up his interest, especially since it was only a fifteen minute walk from his apartment. He did not look forward to dressing up in a coat and tie, but knew that would be his standard now until finding new employment. At least for his first day of being unemployed, he would have something to do to occupy his time.

* * *

The morning Air Lingus flight that brought Abdul from Glasgow to Dublin lasted only fifty minutes. Having traded his weekend days off with another doctor at the hospital, he would now have Monday and Tuesday to visit Dublin and Belfast, before returning to Glasgow Tuesday evening. With several job fairs being held in hotels in both Dublin and Belfast during the two days, this would serve as the initial opportunity to search for a suitable candidate to assist his team in their planned mission of destruction.

The Friday before leaving for Dublin, Abdul stopped by a convenience store in Murray Square, in Glasgow, and bought another cell phone and one hour's talk-time. He programmed into the phone a voice message that requested a caller to provide a number so that he could return any calls received. Should he find a candidate that looked good, this link would provide the only form of communication he was willing to allow. He would also use an alias name with the candidate, plus a different occupation and place where he lived in Scotland. He believed this would suffice to keep any non-Muslim separated from himself and other team members, at least for the time being.

From the airport, Abdul took a Dublin Bus to O'Connell Street, and walked across the Temple Bar area to the Westbury Hotel on Grafton Street. Inside the main lobby, he found the daily events schedule posted on a marquee board. Seeing the job fair listed as taking place in the Grand Ballroom, he made his way to the other side of the lobby, entered the ballroom and found the fair to be well underway.

He noted at least thirty-five to forty people seated at applicant tables talking with an assortment of personnel recruiters, and at least another twenty-five to thirty more milling around the large room. All of the applicants were well dressed, in business attire, and appeared in the early twenties to mid-thirties age range. Comfortably dressed in a business suit himself, Abdul made his way around the floor, searching for those individuals who seemed as though they did not want to be there. They might not be dressed as well, might have facial expressions that were not overly pleasant or optimistic, and overall looked like loners who were not serious about being there in the first place.

Over the course of one hour, Abdul introduced himself to four out-of-place looking young men milling around the center of the room. All were in their late twenties to early thirties, and very Irish in appearance. When asked, he told them he was looking for employment himself, had recently lost a job in Scotland and was trying his luck in Ireland this time. The questions he subsequently asked focused on whether the man he was speaking to was experiencing difficulty in finding a suitable position or also had lost a job, were upset about it, and finding it difficult to find another one.

By the time most of the hour had passed, he determined that none of the four he talked to expressed anything at all that raised his level of interest in them. All appeared bright, eager and seriously interested in finding a suitable job they could prosper and advance in as their career choice. Only one of them bothered to ask him what kind of job he had previously lost. All of them were too much into themselves, expressing nothing negative or alerting that he could use to further question them.

Sensing that any additional effort there would not bear fruit, Abdul departed the Westbury after asking for directions to his next stop, The Shelbourne Hotel, located only minutes away, near Trinity College. Should the job fair there likewise fail to surface any suitable candidates, he planned to catch a late afternoon train to Belfast, get a hotel room for the night there, and try his luck at two more fairs the next day.

Patrick left his apartment wearing a topcoat to ward off the blustery winds that were blowing inland off the Irish Sea. He turned what should have been a short fifteen-minute walk to The Shelbourne into a forty-minute affair in order to satisfy himself that he was free of surveillance. He was curious to see if the Brits were still interested in him after succeeding in instigating the loss of his job. Try as he may, he could not detect anyone, either on foot or in vehicles, keeping track of him. He made two short stops in stores, spending five to ten minutes in each, and still noticed no one following him inside or waiting outside, as he gradually made his way over to the hotel.

The stately old Shelbourne, listed on Ireland's national historic register as dating back to the 1820s, overlooks St. Stephen's Green, a twenty two-acre Victorian park. Patrick checked his topcoat in the main lobby's cloakroom and made his way to one of the large banquet rooms where the job fair was underway. He just could not get in much of a mood for job hunting after what he had gone through.

He noted the many table and chair set-ups where company reps were offering potential candidates details on positions available. They were also handing out applications to be completed and subsequently scheduling appointments for interviews. With all of the twenty or so company reps conducting the initial screenings, Patrick was one of another thirty or more individuals milling around the center of the large room.

Not aware that his hair had become disheveled from the strong winds blowing outside the hotel, Patrick went over to a table where coffee was being served. With a hot steaming cup in hand, he turned to walk away from the table and noticed an Asian looking male, dressed in a suit, looking straight at him. The man approached Patrick and asked him if the winds were still up outside?

"They sure are, and cold too," Patrick replied.

"The wind really blew your hair around. Fortunately, for me, I do not have that problem. With mine short like this I don't have to comb it as often," Abdul said.

He excused himself, stepped around Patrick, got a cup of coffee and returned to stand next to him.

"Having any luck here so far?" Abdul asked.

"No. I just got here and really am not into this interview thing."

"Why is that? Oh, excuse me for being impolite. I should have introduced myself sooner. My name is Ali."

"I'm Patrick, and I have not had to look for a job in over five years. I cannot yet get in the right frame of mind to have to go through this process."

"What is your field of work?"

"I'm an electrical engineer."

"Well, that's good. You should have no trouble lining up an interview or two for yourself today. I noticed several of the companies were offering engineering positions."

"What brings you here?" Patrick asked.

"I live in Scotland, in Glasgow, but thought it would be interesting to see what kind of jobs are available here in Ireland."

"Do you have a job now?"

"Yes, actually I do. However, it is not a very good one. I am a biologist and work for a pharmaceutical company.

"That's a growing field nowadays. Why isn't it good for you?"

"Look at me. What do you see?"

"Well, you said your name is 'Ali,' and you obviously are an Asian. I take it to mean you are finding the Scots a difficult lot to deal with. Finding acceptance in their society has been a problem for you. Is that about right?"

"It sure is. Scotland can be a wonderful place, but too many Scots can make it very difficult for us. We actually have lots of Asians living there now, and those that have been there awhile refer to themselves as Asian Scots. Me, I am not just one of them, and never will be."

"I can understand what you're saying."

"Oh, have you had similar experiences here?"

"You better believe it. When you grow up in Belfast being called a 'Paddy,' treated with disdain and ordered around like a lackey, yes, I've had those experiences."

"I can see we do have a few things in common. I'd like to hear more. How about we go across the lobby to the restaurant and I buy you another cup of coffee?"

"Sure, fine with me. I'm not up to this interview thing today anyway."

Patrick and Ali, threw their empty coffee cups into a trash receptacle and walked out of the room and across the sparsely populated lobby to the Saddle Room restaurant. They both cast glances around the lobby area, checking to see if anyone was watching them. Both were satisfied that they were not under observation, as best could be determined in that short period of time.

In the restaurant, they took seats at a table in the corner of the room where tall windows offered a good view of St. Stephen's Green across the street. They both ordered coffee and, when it was served, resumed their conversation.

"Are you familiar with the bombing attacks in London and at Glasgow Airport several years ago?" Ali asked.

"Yes, I can recall them vividly from watching TV," replied Patrick.

"Well, I had not yet arrived in Scotland back then, but Muslim brothers took up their cause of jihad against the British Empire. How do you feel about what they were trying to do?"

"What is it you want me to say? If you happen to know anything about Irish history you know where I stand insofar the Brits."

"Have you ever thought you would like to do something about it?"

"Of course I have. However, thinking about it and going out to do something are two different things. Tell me who you are and why you sound like you are trying to provoke me?"

"I'm a Muslim with a cause and I thought we might have some things in common. Nothing else. I'm not the provoking kind."

"I think we do have some things in common but you are coming on to me like you are a snitch for the fucking peelers."

"Peelers. I don't know what that is."

"Where I come from, in Belfast, it is a slang word for British security forces. I grew up being harassed by them. I didn't like it then and don't like it now."

"Rest assured I'm not one of them. My cause is to bring them down."

"How do you plan to do it?"

"Now that sounds to me like a provocation too. I could ask just who you are as well."

"OK. When two conspirators first get together, it starts out sounding like provocations. All I am going to say now is, I'm out of a job because of the Brits and I already hated them."

"Well, we both have laid out a lot on the table about each other today. Would you be interested in meeting again?"

"I could be interested. For now though, I'm looking for a job. Making a living is of primary importance to me. Later on, if I were to get to know you better, we might talk about advancing our causes."

"How about if we exchange phone numbers?"

"Sure."

"Do you get over to Scotland very often?

"I've been over there several times in the past. Why do you ask? Do you have a job offer I just can't refuse?"

"I wish I did, but you never know when something might come up. I have some friends I'll be meeting up with soon and they might have some ideas. I'll let you know, if you do not mind my calling you."

"No, I'll not mind."

Patrick and Ali said their goodbyes and both departed the hotel to go their separate ways. At the hotel's front desk, Ali got bus directions to Connelly Station where he could take the Enterprise train to Belfast Central Station. He was quite satisfied with the results of his encounter with Patrick, but would still go to the remaining two job fairs in Belfast the next day to see who else he might be able to meet.

Patrick, on the other hand, although still facing cold winds outside, decided he needed time to figure out what had just happened with this man named Ali.

The brisk walk over to Slattery's Bar took Patrick twenty-five minutes, including one stop in a men's clothing store to check on any potential surveillance effort against him. If Ali was a provocation, surveillance would be a good possibility after their discussion. However, as best he could determine, he was surveillance free.

Along the way, while walking through the Temple Bar area, he pondered the meaning of the encounter with Ali. It looked like a provocation, smelled like a provocation. But why now? Could it be that MI5, after succeeding in getting him laid-off, was now trying to see how far he would go in planning to engage in retaliation? It did not make sense to him but, for now, a pint, or two, was in order.

"Caitlin, it has been too long. How are you?"

"Patrick, where have you been? I'd about given up all hope for you."

"First things first. Please pull me a pint of your finest. I've a real story to tell you, and it starts off with what happened to me at work a week ago."

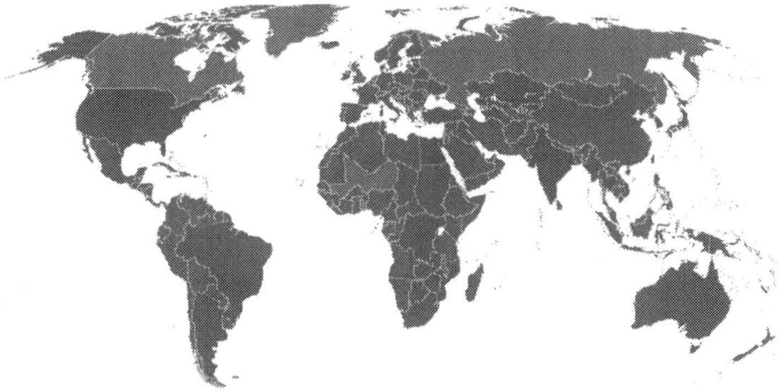

CHAPTER 21

Lee's selection of a meeting site with Mitch turned out to be perfect. The Library Bar, tucked away in the back of the main lobby of the Plaza Hotel, in Copenhagen, felt much like an old men's club. Large leather armchairs at small tables spaced around the room afforded private conversation. Subdued lighting and floor-to-ceiling shelves lined with volumes of old leather-bound books set the mood for the two ostensible business executives holding a quiet conversation.

Mitch flew from San Francisco to Phoenix, to retrieve his Sturgeon alias docs, then to New York where he caught a direct flight to Copenhagen. Lee took a short one-hour flight from Stockholm to Copenhagen, and traveled in true name. Once it was determined whether Mitch would be directly involved in introducing Lee to Patrick, Lee would be able to use either a commercial cover alias or a US Government-affiliated alias.

"I enjoyed reading your last cable on meeting with Patrick. You've made good progress in assessing him, and quickly too," Lee said.

"Thank you. I feel strongly that we can go ahead and get you introduced to him. The only issue I see is what would work best, you using an alias and me making a direct introduction of him to you, or, we work out a scenario for you to introduce yourself to him and me, with you representing someone unknown to us," replied Mitch.

"My preference would obviously be with you making a direct introduction," said Lee. "However, we both know headquarters will not buy into it given your Phoenix firm being a real business and not a made up company."

"I agree with you completely. That would be my preference as well. Even though it would allow for you to pick-up on my existing relationship with Patrick, with him knowing you're aware of his personal situation. But we still have to respect the Phoenix firm's equities."

"It would be great if he already had some form of access to a terrorist group of interest. With that, we would be able to make a direct introduction with me as government, and you could walk away."

"My bringing him along in commercial cover mode allowed for moving quickly. I think the bonding that took place also resulted in the swift pace. However, I actually would have preferred to use a non-existent commercial firm as cover with him. That way, even with or without access, I could bring you in as being with the government and we could avoid moving him through the steps of a daisy-chain."

"Well, we are stuck with what we have," said Lee. "How do you want to affect the turnover?"

"I would prefer not to use the old ploy of him and I being at some event or in a bar somewhere and you come along and introduce yourself to both of us. But what else do you think might work?"

"I'd like to avoid that ploy as well, since it means I have to start out all over again in building a new relationship with him. It would require moving him along to revealing the details of his personal situation. However, you were able to do it quickly. If I take a page out of your book, establish some chemistry and quickly bond with him, possibly I can also?"

"Obviously, Lee, neither of us is coming up with any really innovative ideas for the best way to get you directly involved with this guy."

"OK. For now, let's go with the ploy of a contrived turnover. I'll show up to introduce myself to Patrick, talk to him for a minute or two, and let him introduce me to you. If I have to start from scratch, so be it."

"Sounds good. How about I say a few things about my impressions of the guy that has not made its way into the cable traffic?"

"Great."

"He seems to have a quick mind and thinking ahead when I talk to him. He also has a wit. For example, when we were talking about what we do in our spare time, I mentioned to him that I run a lot. He said, 'Oh, you got the fucking Brits after you too.' It was a spontaneous retort."

"How about his level of intelligence? How bright is this guy?"

"He's knowledgeable and understands his field. We talked about his previous college training in engineering and subsequent work on the job. He knows his stuff. He is also current in his knowledge of technology advances in his field. He shares with me a hobby of collecting old dated early writings on things electrical. From what he said, he has troubleshooting skills for his job, and is, or was, serving as a supervisor on a production line. By the way, he is thoroughly dismayed with the loss of this job, which he is convinced is due to British intervention. As a result, he is sorely pissed off at them, and particularly, as I cited in my last cable, for the harassing tactics they have put him through."

"I can well imagine why. By the way, he has really opened up to you and it is a definite sign of the skills you've brought to bear in the way you have handled him. He has been forthcoming and you exploited him for it very well. The kudos you're getting from headquarters is well deserved."

"Thank you, Lee. I appreciate that. I've enjoyed working with him and believe you will too. He is interesting, easy to talk to, and has a very affable personality. Although he's very tightly wound up against the Brits, he has an easygoing manner. Judging by his background and upbringing though, I do believe we want this kind of guy on our side."

"Anything else that would be useful for me to know about him?"

"He shows good street smarts. It came out when discussing surveillance skills with me. He was obviously well schooled as a boy and young man in Belfast, and has kept these hard-earned skills up to date into manhood."

"Right, I remember that from one of your previous cables. It's interesting that he would tell you about learning these skills to use against the British."

"Yes, but it just shows a willingness to be open when discussing the obvious agony of what has gone on in Northern Ireland. The thoughts of young children having to learn surveillance skills does bother me."

"Well, should he be willing to work against the radical Islamic groups, he will already have a skill-set in place."

"It will certainly be of interest for you to learn from him just how well developed these skills are. Lee, I believe this is going to be a fascinating case for you to handle."

"I'm looking forward to it, Lee replied."

"How about the cable from Dublin Station expressing their concerns about continuing to meet with Patrick there? What are your thoughts?" said Mitch.

"Well, first off, they obviously call the shots on their own turf and we have to respect it. I've no problem moving future meetings offshore somewhere else."

"Well, with me bowing out after the turnover, you'll be making the decisions on meeting venues."

"Speaking of the turnover," Lee replied, "what about the upcoming meeting? Can you coax him out of Ireland for it?"

"I thought about that on the way over here. Unless I tell him that I have found a prospective employer who wishes to meet him, it probably would not sound very plausible."

"Alright then, what do you see as an alternative?"

"I believe the way to go is for me to call him and say I'll be arriving in Ireland, but at Shannon Airport, instead of Dublin. I'll tell him I have to meet with a client at a nearby factory, and will be staying in a hotel nearby the airport because I leave early the next morning for additional client meetings in the Netherlands and Belgium."

"I like it so far," said Lee, "especially since it means you can at least get him outside the Dublin area. It will not totally satisfy Dublin Station but it should allow for one more meeting inside Ireland."

"I'll invite him for dinner near my hotel to discuss what I believe is a good job prospect for him. I'll say I would appreciate it if he can join me and I offer to reimburse him for roundtrip plane, train or bus travel to the Shannon area."

"What if he asks you about resuming your company's survey work in the Dublin area?"

"I'll just say I have to put it on hold for at least a month or so."

"Given the relationship you are building with him, and the loss of his job, I doubt he would turn you down."

"Let's go with that as our plan. Tonight I'll get a cable off to Headquarters and the other stations outlining our plan and telling them you'll respond separately."

"That's good. I will be back in Stockholm by mid-morning tomorrow, and will do my write-up right away. When will you call Patrick?"

"First thing in the morning. If he's available to meet the following day, I'll get a flight to Shannon tomorrow as well, and go ahead and get set up in a hotel there.

"How about Dublin Station and requesting another in-country meeting?"

"Tonight, when I cable them, I'll ask for a reply by tomorrow morning, before I call Patrick. I don't expect they will have a problem with one more meeting on their turf."

"What about your meeting venue with him there?"

"I know of a hotel I should be able to use, especially this time of year when it is cold and the tourist trade is slow. It's just far enough from Shannon Airport to avoid any unwanted scrutiny."

"To bring me into the picture for the turnover, how about if we consider cities in the two countries you just mentioned – the Netherlands and Belgium?"

"I'm comfortable in either Amsterdam or Brussels, Lee. The choice is yours."

"Amsterdam it is."

"Are you willing to get off another cable tomorrow, to The Hague Station, briefly outlining the case and requesting approval to meet with Patrick for the turnover in Amsterdam?"

"My pleasure."

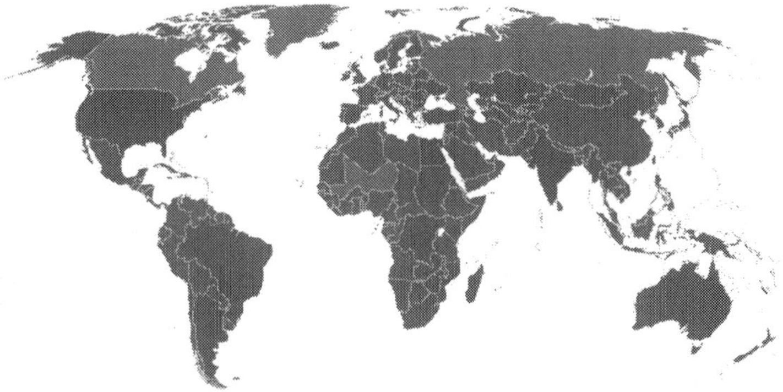

CHAPTER 22

The call to Abdul was timely. He was anxious to hear the news Wahid would be bringing from Mir Ali. After returning home from attending the job fairs in Dublin and Belfast, Abdul realized that except for the Irishman named Patrick that he met at the Shelbourne Hotel in Dublin his trip was not very productive. Now though, in the interim, he was ready to get Wahid directly involved in the next phase of the operation.

"Good to hear your voice, my brother. Peace be upon you," Abdul said.

"And peace be upon you also,' Wahid replied.

"Do you recall the pizza shop on the street corner near where we had coffee last time?"

"Yes, I remember it."

"Can you be there the day after tomorrow at eight-thirty in the evening?"

"Yes, that's a good time for me."

"May Allah guide you, Wahid."

"And you too, Abdul."

Based on Abdul's prearranged meeting instructions to Wahid, he should show up at the pizza shop tomorrow night at 6:30 p.m. In the meantime, Abdul planned to search through the classified sections of the local newspapers to houses for lease. He would focus on the area heading southward, outside of Glasgow, along the M74 motorway corridor towards the town of Larkhall.

His plan called for Wahid to find one house for use as a safe house for team members as well as the initial site location for the storage and fabrication of the bomb components. He would have Wahid give up his small flat in the East Kilbride area and move into the house. He was undecided yet whether he would have other team members move as well.

The second house should be further down the M74 corridor, in or near the town of Carlisle. It would also be for the storage of bomb components, in this case, bags of ammonium nitrate and containers of diesel fuel oil. However, according to Abdul's plan, the white European team member would live in this house alone, with none of the Muslim team members exposed to it or involved in its acquisition. Instead, Abdul would locate the house himself, making sure it meets his specifications, and then direct the European to arrange to lease it completely on his own.

The operation was starting to take on momentum. He also felt some pressure to identify and recruit the European team member. To date however, he had no way to safely check out the only potential candidate, Patrick, to determine if he was bona fide or not. Was he really without a job and wanting to seek retribution against the British? Could he actually be a provocation? Abdul was uneasy about how to proceed.

"Blessing to you, my brother," Abdul said.

"And to you, my brother," Wahid replied.

"I trust your trip went well?"

"Very well. I bring both good news and more funds for you. Your brother in Mir Ali is very pleased with both your plans and your progress. The M34 device you requested is being sent as we speak and should be arriving one week from now."

"May Allah bless you. That is wonderful news."

"While in Mir Ali I met with our new team member. His name is Rashid Inshan Khan. I believe you are going to like him. He is very bright, serious and studied computer technology in Rawalpindi. He also has a driver's license."

"Perfect. That is everything I could ask for. When will he arrive here?"

"Like the M34 device you requested, brother Rashid should be arriving in about one week's time. The device is arriving here separately and I was told it would come via car as you requested. Rashid will know the name and phone number of the person who will be receiving it. He will phone me upon arrival at the Glasgow Airport and I can either meet him there or tell him where he should go after that. I didn't want to give him my address since I had not received your permission to do so. He understands how the team members will be compartmented from each other and, as result, expects to initially be on his own. He will though, follow your guidance explicitly."

"You did the right thing. I don't want him to be aware of where you are living or even what kind of job you have. When he calls from the airport, have him take a bus to Glasgow Central railway station. You should meet him there and get an inexpensive hotel room for him nearby. He should rent the room for one week."

"I understand. I know he will have enough money to last for at least one month here. After that, I can give him additional money as you wish."

"Bring him to meet with me the evening after his arrival. Here is a list with the names and addresses of twenty-five restaurants. Whenever we talk on the phone and I refer to taking a meal together, I will mention about seeing you at bus stop number nine. That will refer to the ninth restaurant on the list. If I say to meet at bus stop number eighteen, it will mean the eighteenth on the list."

"I understand. That will be no problem at all, my brother. For the meeting day and time, I will still follow your one day and two hours earlier rule, correct?"

"Yes, of course. Make sure you explain the system we use to Rashid, as well. In addition, during the week he is in the hotel I would like you to spend your evenings with him after work. You should take him around town and familiarize him with the local area and surroundings."

"That's a good idea."

"However, before you take him to the local mosque, be sure and explain to him the limitations I want followed in not getting involved in activities there. When others there talk to him and offer to assist or help him settle here, you need to step in and make it clear you are taking care of our newly arrived brother."

"It's perfectly clear, my brother. In fact, your brother in Mir Ali asked that I reinforce with you not to listen to the mosque rhetoric being spread around about Osama bin Laden as well as the gossip about him in newscasts. He said not to pay any attention about an attack being imminent or to get ready to stand up and start our jihad by attacking the infidels."

"I understand as well," Abdul said. "We will run this operation completely on our own with no assistance or influence of any kind from other brothers that are here. We will also continue to maintain our own communications amongst ourselves and our own link, you my brother, back to Mir Ali."

"One more thing comes to mind about the M34 device. Once Rashid arrives here, make sure you bring him to see me before he calls the local number to retrieve the device. We have to be very careful about the circumstances for taking possession of it. The same applies for where we take it afterwards. The brother giving the device to Rashid should not learn any further information about where the device is going, how it is to be used, etc."

"I understand completely."

"I have another list to give you. These are newspaper advertisements and some Internet listings for houses to lease. I would like you to conduct a search for a small house that you will move into, with no more than two bedrooms. It should be located between Glasgow and Larkhall. I would prefer the house have an attached garage into which a truck can be parked. If no garage is available, a storage shed would be acceptable providing the truck can park close to it. The terms of the lease should be for three months, if at all possible. If not, six months will be all right. I realize you have only been in your own flat for a short period, but we have no choice. I need to have you living in this house."

"I will have no problem at all with moving. Is there anything else we should talk about, Abdul?"

"No, we have covered everything. Peace and happiness to you, Wahid."

"And peace and happiness to you also, my brother."

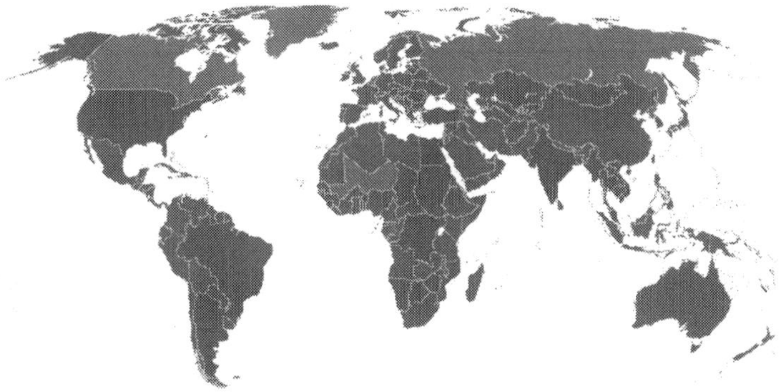

CHAPTER 23

Mitch checked into the Bunratty Manor Hotel, located on the outskirts of Bunratty Village, six miles away from Shannon Airport. Arranging for Patrick to come this far out to meet turned out to be no problem. Patrick said he was happy to get out of Dublin for a change.

The cable response Mitch received from Dublin Station, and seconded by a separate cable from headquarters, reaffirmed this should be the final meeting with Patrick inside Ireland. Due to liaison equities with both the British and Irish intelligence services being of obvious concern, it did not make sense to continue to meet on sensitive turf and jeopardize the relationships with these services by running an undeclared operation under their noses.

Another underlying issue at play here would be the future locale of any such counterterrorist operation that might be mounted by the Agency against a radical Islamic terrorist group. With an Irishman being met and developed for recruitment to work against an Islamic group, it did not mean that their terrorist attack would take place on Irish or British soil. The locale could be anywhere in Europe. This was the underlying reason behind headquarters willingness to allow the assessment and development of Patrick to continue in Ireland without saying or declaring anything to the British and Irish services.

When Mitch, in his Sturgeon alias, phoned Patrick to arrange for him to come to Shannon, he asked that Patrick meet him in a pub-restaurant just down the street from his hotel – Durty Nelly's. Located next door to Bunratty Castle, Durty Nelly's is typically a very popular tourist establishment during most of the year. However, in the winter months only a limited number of tourists visit the castle next door, much less Durty Nelly's. Instead, the Shannon's locals are the primary clientele then.

Patrick entered the pub section and immediately spotted Sturgeon standing at the bar nearest the entrance. Sturgeon ordered a pint of Guinness for Patrick, and a second one for himself. Due to the number of locals in the bar area, they limited their conversation to social chitchat, avoiding any mention of Patrick's job predicament and British harassment. Patrick picked up on what Sturgeon was doing and went along with it as they downed their drinks. After finishing, they moved to the Oyster Restaurant in the back of the pub. The Loft Restaurant dining area upstairs would have afforded more privacy but was closed for the off season. The Oyster Restaurant downstairs, being only sparsely occupied, would instead provide the privacy Mitch sought.

"Thank you for the email advising me on the loss of your job. I was very sorry to get that news. Immediately after receiving it I made some calls to see if I could come up with an opportunity or two that could be of interest to you," Mitch said.

"I appreciate all that you are trying to do to help me. I really cannot thank you enough. What I did not tell you in the email is what happened several days earlier, before I was cashiered. In fact, it was these events that probably triggered my firing," Patrick replied.

"What happened?"

"A week or so before Christmas I noticed surveillance on me again. It appeared to be a stepped-up effort this time. One night I had at least three blokes follow me home from work. Also, a couple of nights later I went to a pub and had two more on my tail. One waited outside while the other one came inside to check and see what I was doing. The real incident though was a couple of nights later. I arrived home from work and just as I came around the corner in the hallway near the door of my flat, I notice this bloke stepping away from the door and walking towards me. He tried to stagger and make it look like he had been drinking too much. I figured he had just come out of my flat. I grabbed him by the arm when he got alongside me. We tussled around and I managed to get in two good punches. He dropped to the floor but quickly jumped up, ran down the stairs and out of the building."

"What did you do next?"

"Rather than chase after him and find myself facing a bunch of fucking peas outside on the street, I went into my flat instead to see what had happened there. I could not find anything missing, nor could I see where any kind of device might have been planted."

"Any subsequent knocks on the door, a visit by the Brits, the Guarda, or anything like that?"

"Nothing at all. Except, two days later I was fired."

"Some Christmas! What a shame. Have you noticed any more surveillance?"

"Nothing at all. I've been going out of my way to check and see if they are still around, but nothing is there."

"I will tell you this: If I can help you land a new job, either in the US or elsewhere in Europe, it will not have the excitement attached to it like what you are going through now."

"I have always been one for a little excitement and change now and then, but nothing like this."

"Has anything else taken place?"

"Well, I did attend a job fair and, wait till you hear this one. I'm circulating around this hotel ballroom floor where the fair is being held, checking to see the kinds of jobs that are available. An Asian fellow approaches me. He's dressed well, is pleasant looking and comes across as a businessperson. He introduces himself and we talk for a while. Next, he suggests we go to the restaurant across from the hotel lobby to have a cup of coffee. He projects a very anti-British attitude and realizes that from what I am saying, I've no love for them either."

"How did you react to his approach and comments to you?"

"Right from the beginning I thought I smelled a provocation."

"Good for you."

"In fact, I even told him so. I asked him why he was trying to provoke me."

"Wow. Good move. What did he say?"

"Well, he said he believed we have common views and that he is not the provoking kind."

"This guy sounds real slick."

"He then tells me he is a Muslim with a cause. However, I told him that he was coming across more like a snitch working for the fucking Brits."

"Good for you. What was his reaction?"

"He reassured me that was not the case. Instead, he said his cause is to bring down the British Empire and he thought I might have something in common with him."

"Now I can understand why he was at a job fair. Obviously, he was not there representing a real company and looking for applicants to interview."

"That's right. He was walking around the floor just like me."

"Sounds to me like he's a recruiter looking for someone like you to join his cause. A cause of concern from what you're saying."

"That's the way I read it too. I even asked him how he planned on carrying through with his cause."

"Good question. What was his reply?

"He said that now I was sounding like a provocation. He was very smooth. But, I didn't grow up on the streets of Belfast for nothing. I can see a recruitment approach when it's right there in front of me."

"What were you able to learn about him?"

"He said his name is Ali, he lives in Glasgow, Scotland, and is a biologist working for a pharmaceutical company."

"Did he say why he was at the job fair if he already has a job?"

"I did just that, and he asked me to look at him and say what I was seeing. I looked at him straight in the face and said he was obviously an Asian and probably not getting along very well with the Scots."

"He was showing you that what the two of you have in common is a strong dislike for the British."

"It was about that point in the conversation when he suggested we go into the restaurant to talk further. We subsequently did so and he then asked me about the negative experiences I've had with the Brits. I told him about growing up in Belfast and having to deal with harassment. And now, after working for five years as an electrical engineer, I find myself without a job."

"Was his reaction one of empathy for you?"

"Yes, I would definitely say so. He then asked if I was aware of the bombing attacks that took place several years ago in Glasgow and London. I replied, saying yes, I did indeed remember watching what happened on TV. He said he had recently arrived in Scotland when they took place, but that his Muslim brothers who took up the cause of jihad did it. Then he asked me a curious question."

"What was that?"

"He asked how I felt about what his Muslim brothers were trying to do in their attack. I replied, saying if he knew anything about Irish history and British tactics, he would know where I stood insofar the fucking Brits."

"I would think he certainly liked hearing that response."

"He liked it alright because he then asked me if I have ever thought about doing something about it."

"He set you up nicely for that question. No doubt about it."

"Well, mind you, I revealed nothing to him about the past dealings with my family in Belfast against the Brits there."

"If you had it would serve to make him even more interested in you. What was your reply?"

"I told him that thinking about it and going out and doing something are two very different things. This was when we got into the provocation thing and went back and forth with each other."

"How did it end up?"

"Well, he said we both had laid out on the table a lot about ourselves."

"You can say that again!"

"He said he liked what I saying and would I be interested in meeting with him again so that we could further discuss our causes."

"That was a major jump forward in terms of meeting again to talk about doing something against the Brits."

"That's what I thought too. I said I might be interested, but for now, I was more concerned about making a living for myself. I did add however, that if we were to get to know each other better, maybe then we could discuss our causes."

"Patrick, you handled this guy extremely well."

"Thank you. I thought so also. We did exchange phone numbers. After that, I asked him if he had a job offer I would not be able to refuse. He said he would be meeting with some friends soon, and possibly they would have some ideas about a prospective job for me."

"What do you think is going to happen next?"

"I believe I'll be hearing from him soon. I have not met many Muslims during my life. However, this guy comes across as very polished and smooth. Especially in the way he guided our conversation. When we walked out of the ballroom and across the lobby to the restaurant, I noticed his eyes and the casual way of scanning the lobby area. I knew exactly what he was doing."

"Do you know what his approach to you could mean?"

"Sure, that he's associated with a terrorist group and is assessing me for consideration to participate in their jihad. Douglas, you have listened very attentively to everything I've said. Now tell me, why are you so fascinated with what took place?"

"Patrick, I'm going to take a page out of Ali's book. What do you want to do about it? This Asian guy, Ali, is setting you up. Therefore, do you want to get involved?"

"Now you make me wonder just who you are. I thought we were meeting here tonight and you were going to tell me about some job prospects."

"That is why we are meeting. Now however, from what you've told me, I can see that a real curve ball has been thrown at you. I actually do have a couple of job prospects for you, one in the States, and the other in Europe. This development with Ali however, fortunately or unfortunately, could change many things. It all depends on you."

"You're starting to lose me. I don't understand."

"Would you be interested in meeting with Ali again, if for no other reason than to try and determine if he is involved with a terrorist organization of some kind?"

"This is not what I had in mind as a new job prospect," Patrick replied. "Just what is it you're leading up to?"

"For now, let's set aside the two potential job interviews that I was going to tell you about. In my travels I've made contacts with all kinds of people. They are in private industry as well as government work. Awhile back, about two years ago, I ran into an American who I vaguely remember from my college days. He was a year or two behind me and I naturally lost track of him after graduating. When I ran into him, he told me that he works for the US Government, in the State Department. However, after meeting with him a couple more times in Europe, he revealed he tracks terrorist groups around the world. Are you with me on this so far?"

"Sure. And we both know who we believe he is really working for, right?"

"That's good. You are indeed with me on this. Well, if I wasn't impressed with him, and therefore believed it would not be in your interest, I would not suggest you should talk with him."

"But your government, Douglas, and the Brits, are in each others knickers. And you know how I feel about the fucking Brits."

"You are certainly right on that score. But, what if Ali is part of a group that is planning something that could affect Ireland or some other place that you don't wish to see harmed in any way. Remember, he may have told you he lives in Scotland, but you met him here in Ireland."

"Man, now you're pulling on my heart strings. We call that Celtic solidarity. We want no harm to come to the mother country."

"That's right. When events can strike close to home, of course it affects us in the heart."

"OK. What is it you're suggesting that I do?"

"I would think these things can move pretty fast. What does your schedule look like for the next several days?"

"Well, since you don't have a job for me to interview for in the next few days, I guess I am readily available."

"I'm impressed with your humor. Don't stop it now. I will make a call tonight and find out where my friend is and how soon we can meet up with him. I assume he is in Europe somewhere. Do you have a passport and national ID for traveling outside Ireland?"

"Sure do."

"I'm going to reimburse you for your travel here to Shannon and back, plus additional Euros to go and meet with my friend if he is available. I'll cover all expenses until you return to Dublin, since he will reimburse me."

"That's fair enough. Now I have one last question for you."

"That's fair enough too," Sturgeon replied. "What is it?"

"How many other blokes have you introduced to your friend like this?"

CHAPTER 24

With headquarters and stations concurrences in hand early the next morning, Mitch departed Shannon Airport mid-day for Amsterdam. He arranged for Patrick to fly there, via Dublin Airport, the following day. Lee was due to arrive in Amsterdam the same day as Mitch, via Stockholm-Arlanda Airport.

Headquarters and Stockholm Station cables offered strong encouragement to go ahead with the introduction and turnover of Patrick to Lee as soon as possible in view of the approach and soft recruitment pitch made by Ali at the job fair in Dublin. In view of MI5's interest in Patrick, along with the meeting between Ali and Patrick in Dublin, headquarters stressed the need for stringent operational security measures for the introduction and turnover, noting the step-up in the tempo of the operation based on Ali's overture to Patrick.

As result, Lee, in alias, made a reservation at the Lloyd Hotel & Cultural Embassy, located on the outskirts of Amsterdam's city center. This would be the location for the introduction and turnover meeting. The hotel's location alongside the harbor, instead of the city center part of the city, afforded a better opportunity to surveill Patrick coming to and leaving the hotel.

Mitch had Patrick make his own reservation at the Groenhof, a small family hotel located in the heart of city center, on the Vondelstraat near Leidsplein. This hotel, with a large park across the street, would allow both Mitch and Lee, from separate vantage points, to observe Patrick arriving and determine his surveillance status at least from the time of his arrival in Amsterdam. Both of them would also engage in counter-surveillance of Patrick at other times during his two-day stay in the hotel as well.

Mitch made a hotel reservation, also for two days, at the Jolly Carlton, on Vijzelstraat, and within a ten-minute walk to Patrick's hotel. This location would place Mitch nearby in order to observe Patrick on the second day of the introduction and turnover, when he would be going to and coming from his meeting alone with Lee.

Mitch's plan called for him to introduce Patrick to Lee on the first day. That evening, after the introduction and dinner, he would excuse himself and say his goodbyes to Patrick, as if leaving Amsterdam early the following morning. Instead, Mitch would remain there to observe Patrick during the second day, including him leaving Lee's hotel to return to his own.

All went smoothly and according to plan with the introduction of Lee and discussions leading up to and including dinner in Lee's hotel room suite. After dinner, Mitch excused himself, said goodbye to Patrick and left the meeting. Afterwards, he observed Patrick leaving the hotel and making his way across one of the canals to his own hotel in the city center. Mitch then returned to Lee's hotel room.

Lee answered the door with a wide grin on his face.

"I can tell already that things went well," Mitch said.

"You got that one right. This guy is really something. I cannot get over the pair of balls he is packing. He talked about growing up in West Belfast and what life was like there, including treatment at the hands of the British."

"That's great," Mitch said. "So, why don't you back up and start with right after I left."

"Well, first off, he had no qualms at all about your departure after dinner. He has a great sense of humor. The warming-up time the three of us spent together during the day went a long way to set the stage for a successful turnover."

"Do you think he realizes I set him up for you and we have an obvious connection?"

"Yes, and apparently he has no problem with it. He also seems to recognize that you fully briefed me on his situation. By the time he started talking about Ali's approach, he knew I was fully aware of what happened."

"Well, that saves you a lot of time in discussing where he goes with you from here."

"Yes, that's definitely the case. Originally, my game plan was to tread lightly with him until some degree of trust could be established. However, based upon your own reasoning with him prior to my entering the picture, it turned out much like when a good friend introduces another good friend and a degree of trust is transferred."

"That's great."

"In fact, because of his upbringing in Northern Ireland, and the training he received in working against the British, the police constabulary and Protestants there, he already has an idea of what needs to be done insofar dealing with Ali."

"In other words, what you're saying is that in Patrick we have an already partially trained agent to do the job we want of him," Mitch said.

"It may well be more than partial. You and I might characterize his years in West Belfast as a young gun-toting urban terrorist serving the IRA. But to himself, Patrick was a young paramilitary soldier carrying on God's work against the evil empire."

"Wow," Mitch replied. "That almost sounds like a young radical Islamic terrorist carrying out a jihad."

"I know. I know. I have to be cautious and circumspect with him. I have to avoid at all costs a situation where he ends up translating the terrorists' jihad, on behalf of Allah, into his own cause against the Brits and their minions."

"In my earlier meetings with him, I found that he responds to fact-based arguments. Perhaps due to his training as an engineer. You cannot avoid the closeness of the US-British relationship. However, you may well be able to play the Irish card instead. In other words, if it turns out Ali has a plan for a terrorist act against Ireland, or even possibly Scotland, you should be able to distance yourself from the British connection. You may even be able to play up our long and close ties with the people of Ireland."

"I believe that with careful reasoning, I should be able to get to him before he makes up his mind. In fact, that is an imperative. By playing up to his knowledge and background of what he learned in Northern Ireland, I hope to move him to want to work with me to uncover Ali's plans, whatever they may be. I need to keep him in the clandestine mode he knew in his youth and continues to practice to this day. In fact, we still don't know yet that Ali even is a terrorist."

"I agree. This could be the way to go into your next discussions with him."

"You should have seen his eyes when I asked him about the kinds of training he was given in West Belfast. He just lit up."

"From the way he described it to me previously," Mitch replied, "he does indeed have surveillance skills. What else?"

"Namely, small arms and demolitions training. Here he is, a young kid growing up and being exposed to that kind of training. I smiled at him and asked, what, no heavy weapons training? He broke into a laugh, said no, shoulder-fired weapon systems were reserved for the older guys."

"Sounds like you have a Celtic Tiger on your hands."

"We also talked about the various hand guns he is familiar with, his ability to fabricate pipe bombs, grenades, and even working with det. cord. As a 13-year-old, he helped to assemble fertilizer pipe bombs."

"What a way to have raised a child. We don't realize how lucky we were to not have lived under basically wartime conditions as children," said Mitch. "Were you able to learn anything more from him about Ali?"

"No, nothing further unfortunately"

"How did things wrap-up?"

"We ended on very good terms. He's a factually oriented person, he makes no quick decisions. It showed in the way we agreed to move forward. He is the deliberative type and will quickly sense if I try and push him too fast."

"You have him well pegged already."

"He sees you as a very good friend, Mitch. He expressed admiration for your background, your work and, particularly, your willingness to help find him another job. He is very appreciative of your efforts on his behalf."

"I tried to be as accommodating as possible with him. In our short times together, I also have come to like him as well."

"Mitch, should it turn out we have a real operation involving this Ali character, you may well be staying. This could turn out to be a team operation, as much as we thought it would be a singleton op with him and me instead."

"Yeah, I thought about that once he told me about Ali. However, let's see what lies ahead. Tell me, did he accept tasking from you?"

"Yes, he did. You know the old saying about the duck taking to water. It's almost as if he's groomed for our kind of work. Patrick would not commit, however, to anything more than trying to learn additional details about Ali and his plans. He would not sign up yet to direct involvement in any kind of operation against Ali. He is smart and obviously is taking his involvement a step at a time."

"How far was he willing to go?"

"He will return to Dublin and call Ali indicating his willingness to meet with him again. Then he will call me with the details. After his meeting with Ali, we'll quickly meet and I'll debrief him."

"Some potential problems come to mind here," replied Mitch. "What if he says the meeting with Ali is in Ireland? Or, worse yet, what if the meeting is to be in Scotland, directly on the Brits turf?"

"What can I say? We'll have to see what Ali tells him. This whole thing has the potential to start moving very fast for us, including the host service issue involving the British and the Irish."

"I definitely sense this thing starting to move now. But, between you and me, with our commo capability to keep everybody on board, we should be able to move as necessary."

"I agree."

"What exactly did you task him with for his next meeting with Ali?"

"I suggested that Patrick convey to Ali his confusion with Ali's approach during their meeting in Dublin, in terms of what it meant for his involvement. Namely, what kind of role did Ali see for him to play in any kind of subsequent operation, if indeed an operation is being planned?"

"Good move. You're taking him in the right direction."

"Meanwhile, I asked him to try and gather further details about Ali. But I stressed he should appear casual and cautious in the questions he asks. For example, while I want to know who Ali really is, what is his background, where does he currently live, that may not be possible."

"Yes, but these are the right questions at this early stage. It's not as if we will get answers to the key questions, like what is the projected type and location of any planned operation, including, hopefully, the target? Even if we did, I would expect them to be false and diversionary."

"However, if we're fortunate and he can learn additional details, we should be able to set up our own surveillance team as a starting point for mounting a full-scale counter-terrorist operation."

"Getting Ali to respond to those kinds of questions will be difficult for Patrick. Obviously, we don't want him to appear to be asking too many questions of the vetting type that you and I know so well."

"I agree," Mitch replied. "Too many of the hard and fast-type questions could spell a quick ending for Patrick. For starters however, we need to learn much more about Ali."

"I don't know if it's Patrick's self-confidence, or street smarts, or whatever, I just have a good feeling about him."

"I know just what you mean," Mitch said. "That's why I really enjoyed my meetings with him. How did he respond to you tasking him with obviously sensitive vetting-type questions?"

"It was as if he was totally aware of the direction I was taking him. He responded as if, okay, I can do this."

"In other words, he sounded like he was a professional taking his tasking and ready to go work on it."

"That's exactly right."

"It is really unusual for a new potential agent source to be moved along this quickly, with him being so adept and willing to go along with us."

"Nevertheless, it all goes back to his Northern Ireland street smarts," Lee said. "As a result, I can understand his ability to quickly move with us in this scenario."

"I know. But, since I moved so fast in bringing him to this point, we still have more vetting to do on him ourselves. You'll need to be alert to his willingness to cooperate and degree of accommodating to the requirements and tasking you give him. In particular, be alert to any unusual questions he may ask of you. I had just such a case last year and it turned out the agent was doubled back on me."

"I respect the time you have spent to bring him this far along. Be rest assured, I understand what we have to look out for, and will move forward with caution in dealing with him. The primary goal for now is be sure that we have on our hands a vetted agent with the potential to penetrate a radical Islamic terrorist group."

"How did you leave it with him insofar as getting back together again?"

"We exchanged cell phone numbers and established a pre-arranged commo plan."

"How are you handling the locations to meet?"

"We will use the old A, B, and C's. If I mention to meet in Amsterdam, it will mean Brussels. If I mention Brussels, it will mean Copenhagen. If I say Copenhagen, it will be Amsterdam. That will get us started. Until we can learn more about Ali, and determine if indeed something is in the offing, these locations will suffice initially."

"You can be sure that if Ali is a terrorist," Mitch said, "he will create conditions early on that will enable him to place surveillance on Patrick as part of his own vetting process. If we get lucky though, and Patrick is able to learn at least the country where an incident is planned for, I would not be surprised if the whole scenario for meeting arrangements and conditions will change."

"I agree. What are your plans for leaving here?"

"I have a flight out tomorrow morning to head straight back stateside. Since we have no idea how this is going to play out, I will say my goodbyes to you now. It has been great working with you on this case. Your ops experiences really came through in the way you handled Patrick today. I look forward to reading your cable write-up to headquarters on the turnover. CTC will really be pleased to learn how well today's meeting went. I can just see Jack's face as he reads the cable."

"I will be leaving in the morning as well, and will send out the turnover cable as soon as I get back in the station. Mitch, it has been a real pleasure for me in working with you as well. We teamed up very nicely on Patrick and I am sorry it has to end. Who knows though, maybe it has not ended after all."

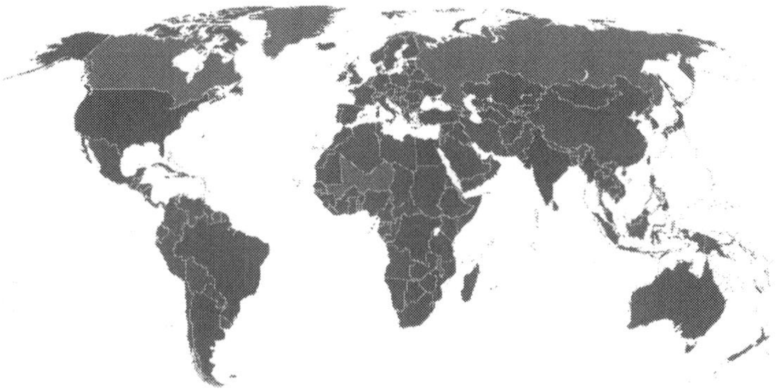

CHAPTER 25

When Wahid called Abdul to report that Rashid had arrived and was able to get a hotel room nearby to the railway station, Abdul referred him to number eighteen on the list of restaurants as the place they would meet the following evening. As usual, Wahid followed their meeting arrangements plan precisely, and showed up as agreed upon at the Spice of Life restaurant, located on Argyle Street, in Glasgow. He had a beaming smile on his face as he escorted Rashid over to Abdul's table in the far corner of the restaurant.

"Peace be upon you my brother," Wahid said to Abdul

"Peace be upon you also," Abdul replied.

"I want to introduce to you our brother from home, Rashid Inshan Khan."

"I am pleased to meet you, Rashid, and very happy you are now here with us."

"May Allah guide you, my brother," Rashid said to Abdul.

"Both of you, please be seated. We have much to discuss," Abdul said. "Before we go any further though, let me mention to you, my Rashid, what the conditions are when Wahid and I meet. The three of us will now use the same cover story whenever we are together. Wahid and I have used this same one ever since we first met. You will know me as a doctor working at a hospital here in Glasgow. At this stage, there is no need for you to know the name of the hospital. I treated Wahid once there, when he came in as a patient. I took a liking to him right away since we are from the same area in North Waziristan. As he settled down here and found a job, we have continued to meet on occasion, much like we are doing now."

"I understand, my brother," Rashid replied.

"You will be a good friend of Wahid's, and he has brought you here tonight to meet me, his friend who also is living here. We will use this simple cover story whenever we are together. Is everything I have said clear to you?"

"It is all very clear, Abdul. I fully understand."

The three of them proceeded to make their dinner selections off the menus given to them by a waiter and, for the next ten minutes, listened to Rashid as he brought them up to date on events taking place back home in Pakistan. Of particular interest to Abdul, were Rashid's descriptive comments of their Muslim brother's successful attacks against Pakistani Government troops in the tribal areas, near the border with Afghanistan. Once their dinner arrived and they started to eat, Abdul turned the conversation to the planned jihad operation that brought them together.

"Wahid, have you explained to Rashid about familiarizing himself with the Glasgow area and what you will be doing with him in the evenings as this week goes by?"

"Yes, Abdul, I have. He has a good map of the city and surrounding area and knows I will be with him each evening."

"I understand you have a background in computer sciences. I am very interested in learning the details of your training and work experiences. However, before going into that, I would like to explain to you some of the operational guidelines under which Wahid and I live and work under here. In planning for our operation, these guidelines offer the best means of achieving maximum success."

"I fully understand," replied Rashid.

"We dress only in European clothes, conservative clothes at that, with no bright or outlandish colors that would only serve to attract attention. We have no beards or shaved heads. We do not engage in any work or other activities at night that might attract unwanted attention. We always strive to appear as pleasant and polite as possible when dealing with other people. Do not hesitate to speak to people and be friendly. Where we can express kindness, and be helpful to others, do so. We do not exhibit any kinds of nervous behavior, like looking over our shoulders or looking too intently at other people. I assume you have had training in surveillance detection. Is that correct?"

"Yes. I received several weeks of training in the camps. I have continued to maintain these skills in my daily life."

"Excellent. We are at war against the infidels but we must not show it. With the grace of Allah, we will bring down all of our enemies. The jihad operation we are planning will be against the British, who are the number three enemy after the Jews and the Americans. I understand Wahid has explained to you how we conduct ourselves at the mosque. Is that correct?"

"Yes, my brother," Rashid replied. "If I should see either of you there, I will avoid you completely. I also will not get involved with any of the groups there, nor engage in any mosque activities. Like many attending the mosque, I will be going for my prayers only."

"Excellent. That is fine. Now, tell me about your computer skills background."

"I obtained a Bachelor of Sciences Degree, in Information Technology, from the National University of Sciences and Technology, in Rawalpindi. That was four years ago. I subsequently earned certifications as a Citrix Administrator, a Cisco Network Associate, and a Microsoft Systems Administrator. For the past two years, until called back home for additional training for jihad, I worked in Rawalpindi as a supervisor in a large computer store."

"I could not have asked for someone with more skills than what you already have. I am very pleased to have you with us, Rashid."

"I am here to serve and succeed in our jihad, Abdul."

"And that you will, Allah willing."

"Would you be able to open a small computer service shop, for repairs and troubleshooting, in a one-man only operation?"

"Yes, of course. That would be easy for me."

"It will be in a small town and you would be on your own except for visits by Wahid. All of the money you will need to set-up a shop and live in the town will be provided of course."

"This will be no problem for me. I take it that you wish me to lease a small amount of space in the business part of the town."

"Yes, exactly. You will also need to purchase a motorbike there. This will be for moving around the area, including picking up and delivering the computers that you troubleshoot and repair. You should offer door-to-door service and, projecting that positive look you have on your face, freely move about the place at will. You should come across as a friendly and personable young man starting up his own business to serve the people. How does that sound to you?"

"This sounds very good to me. Will Wahid be my point of contact and means of communicating with you?"

"Yes, he will. He will also have you purchase a new cell phone and instruct you in the personal security protocols we maintain when using it."

"Wahid, when this coming week has gone by and you have the weekend off work, have Rashid check out of his hotel. I then want you to take him by train southwest of here to the town of Seascale. This is a small seaside village town located in the northwest of England along the Cumbrian coast. It is a two and a half hour drive from here, whether by motorcar or train. Leaving from Glasgow Central Station, I believe you will change trains in Carlisle in order to get to the Cumbrian coast, where Seascale is located. You cannot drive your car there since that could serve to compromise your security by showing you were there in the area nearby where the attack is going to occur."

"I agree and understand completely. What else do you want us to do?"

"Survey the town and any other village towns nearby. I would like Rashid to have his shop in Seascale, if at all possible. Check out the kinds of business establishments that are there, looking for a small facility. If it has living quarters in the rear, or upstairs, that would be perfect. If not, locate a small apartment nearby that would be suitable. For the shop and the apartment, Rashid, on his own with no direct involvement on your part, should seek a three-month lease for one or both sites, as need be. If necessary, a six-month lease is acceptable as well."

"What if no business space is available in Seascale?" Wahid asked.

"Expand your search to the nearby villages that are the closest to Seascale. Whether it is the shop or apartment, I would like one of them to be in that village."

"I fully understand. Any other instructions for us this evening?"

"This will be it, for now. Rashid, do you have any further questions?"

"No, none at all. Everything is clear to me."

"Would you be able to make your way back to your hotel on your own? I have a few additional details I wish to talk to Wahid about."

"Yes, I can find my way back easily from here."

"May Allah bless you, Rashid."

"May Allah bless you too, Abdul."

Once Rashid had departed, Wahid handed Abdul a wrapped package containing money, in both Euros and British pounds that Rashid brought with him from Mir Ali.

"Please be sure and tell me, Wahid, as soon as you learn that the M34 device arrives."

"Rashid should receive a call on the cell phone that he brought with him from Mir Ali. The caller will have the device and will be asking how and where to deliver it."

"OK. That will be good. I want you to pick out one of the indoor shopping malls in the Glasgow area where the delivery can take place. Select a bench inside, near a particular store of your choice. The bench in front of the store will be the location where Rashid tells the brother he will meet him to get the device. Make sure you have a suitable vantage point nearby where you can observe the bench and Rashid when he arrives there. Give this exact location to him and make sure he understands this is where he will meet the brother with the device. You will also have to give Rashid directions on leaving the mall with the device. I want him to travel along a route out of the shopping mall that will enable you to observe him and provide counter-surveillance. You will be looking to see if anyone, or a team, places him under surveillance. He must not go directly back to his hotel. Have him stop in a particular coffee shop, again with you in a position to observe him."

"How about the brother who brings the device to Rashid?" Wahid asked.

"I don't care about trying to surveill that person at all. My interest is in making sure that Rashid is free of surveillance after he takes delivery of the device. If you notice surveillance of any kind on him, let him go ahead and make his way to the coffee shop. Once he is seated inside, you should call him and give instructions to go to a new location where he can maneuver himself around a corner or through a doorway where he is out of sight of surveillance. If you recall from your own training, I believe it's called temporary loss of the eyeball. It is also known as getting into the gap. You can be waiting there, where both of you will be out of sight, to get the device from him. This new location should be another shopping mall, or a hotel with shops, anything where you can find one of those turns that places both of you together for just a couple of seconds, out of sight of anyone else."

"I understand the maneuver. If it becomes necessary to use it with Rashid, I will make sure it works."

"Should you notice any surveillance, get physical description details on anyone you see who appears to be watching him."

"That I will do, Abdul. If Rashid and I have to make this change, I will brief him on where he can go afterwards, to another part of the city, where he should be able to lose any surveillance he has attracted."

"Let us hope he receives the device surveillance free and can proceed to give it to you. Then, he can take a leisurely walk, and a bus ride or two, making his way back to his hotel."

"I shall pray to Allah that will be the case."

"Once you have the device in your possession, have Rashid take the SIM card out of his cell phone and smash it, and the phone as well. Have him throw both away into two different trash bins located blocks apart in the city. He will have the new cell phone to use until he gets settled, hopefully in Seascale. Once settled, he is to destroy the new phone and buy another one there."

"I understand," Wahid replied.

"Now, Wahid, tell me how your search for a house turned out?"

"I have good news. I checked out nine houses in the areas you specified. The one I believe will be most suitable is located in Larkhall. It is a small bungalow with two bedrooms and an attached garage in the rear of the driveway. This garage has an inside door leading to the laundry room and kitchen. It is in a mixed ethnic neighborhood, including some Muslim brothers, but they are located five to six blocks away."

"I like what you are saying. Please go on."

"The lease price is four hundred fifty pounds a month, for a six month period, including an option to renew. The house is partially furnished, including the living room, dining area and one of the bedrooms. An inspection of the inside of the house, by the property rental company, will occur once every three months. The house is now vacant and is available immediately. What do you think?"

"Tell me more about the garage. Will a truck fit inside?"

"Yes, but it will depend upon the size."

"It will be a small moving van, delivery type truck, with a box on the back measuring ten feet long, by six feet wide and six and a half feet high above the rear axle."

"Yes, it should not be a problem from the eyeball measurements I was able to make when the property manager was showing me around. The width and depth of the garage will be fine and, as best I could determine,

I am quite sure the height of the door will allow for the truck to fit inside."

"Provide me with the address and driving directions, and I will check out the house tomorrow. I will just drive by the house, look it over plus check out the surrounding neighborhood as well. If it looks suitable, I will call you immediately so that you can go ahead with the lease arrangements. I believe the Larkhall area is about sixteen to eighteen miles from here. Am I right?"

"Yes, that is correct. From here to the house is eighteen miles."

"Is there a possibility you can use your work van to move your things into the house?"

"That should be no problem at all. I use the van alone now regularly, for the smaller gardening and planting jobs in the local parks. I should be able to move my things into the house during work hours."

"Should you be successful with the lease arrangements and move in, I would like you to start buying the large plastic drum containers, with tight-fitting lids, plus the five gallon jerry cans we talked about previously. Each drum and each can should be bought from a different store. You will need to pay for all of them in cash only. You can't leave any kind of credit card trail."

"I completely understand."

"The same will apply for making purchases of the fifty-pound bags of fertilizer. Buy no more than three bags per store. Determine from the bags of fertilizer you currently work with on your job the color of the prills, the little beads of fertilizer. These will either be gray or white in color."

"We actually use both colors, in separate bags, of course."

"That's good. From amongst your suppliers, see if you can determine who sells the gray ones and who sells the white ones. My interest is in the supplier of the bags with the white prills only. When you can find out whom that supplier is, we need to know what other vendors stock those bags for sale to the public. For example, if the local DIY chain stores throughout the area stock the bags with the white beads, that is where you will go to purchase them, three bags at a time. The same will apply if other garden or hardware stores stock the same kind of bags."

"What is the importance of the white beads?

"Prills are actually hollow inside. The difference between the gray and white ones is in the size of the hollow cavity inside of each bead. The white beads are slightly larger in size, meaning the hollow space is larger. The beads themselves are made of ammonium nitrate. For our purposes of constructing a bomb with the most destructive amount of outward blast power, the white beads with larger space inside provides more oxygen to mix with the fuel oil. This results in a greater blast when compared to the smaller gray beads."

"I am learning much from you, Abdul."

"When do you think you will have the information about the suppliers and stores selling the items I want you to purchase?"

"It should be easy for me to learn all of this information in a day or two. What about the number of plastic drums, fuel cans and bags of fertilizer you want me to purchase?"

"For the plastic drums with lids, the number to buy is twenty. For the five-gallon fuel cans, buy twenty as well. You will also need to go to a sporting goods store and purchase a pair of wooden or plastic oars. They will need to be at least four and a half to five feet in length. We will need these when we mix the fertilizer beads and fuel oil together. This will give us the desired consistency, or slurry, when we are in the final stages of preparation. Lastly, the fifty pound bags of fertilizer. I would like you to start with buying one hundred bags. I still have a few calculations to work out, and the number of bags, I am sure, will increase. However, one hundred will be a good start."

"Now I see why I will need to buy a car."

"Yes, exactly. It will get you to and from work and enable you to make these purchases. Each day, after work, you will need to go to different stores to make your purchases and bring them to the house for storage in the garage and inside the house. Remember though, buy one plastic drum at a time, and no more than three bags of fertilizer at a time. The fuel cans are to be bought one at a time as well. Hold off though, on buying the actual fuel oil. We will do the mixing of the fuel and fertilizer at the end of our preparation stage. You should make sure the size of the trunk of the car is big enough to hold one of the plastic drums. That way each one bought can be concealed there when driving to your house for storage."

"Is anyone else going to be involved in making purchases of all of the components that you require?"

"Yes, of course. I am working on bringing to our group a white European who, among other assignments, will purchase the additional bags of fertilizer, above the initial one hundred I wish you to buy."

"How else will you use this person?"

"He will be used for renting the moving truck we will use in the attack. Rest assured though, I will be keeping him strictly separate from you, Rashid and our brother martyrs after they arrive."

"I feel very good about your planning, Abdul. Allah willing, our jihad, I know, will succeed."

"Allah is with us. We will succeed. I know you are going to be very busy from this point onward. Let me know once you have moved into the house and have returned from taking Rashid to Seascale. I will need the details on where he is going to live and work. Once known, I will then be able to have you task him on what further information we need on the Sellafield facility."

"Long life to you, Abdul. Success is from God. We shall walk through the gates of heaven."

"And God's blessing to you too, Wahid."

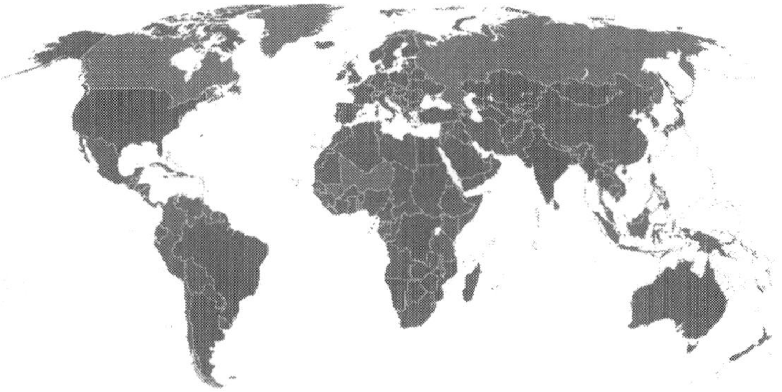

CHAPTER 26

The flight back to San Francisco, via Phoenix, in order to exchange alias for true name docs, was a letdown for Mitch. The turnover of Patrick to Lee, in Amsterdam, as successful as it turned out, left Mitch feeling removed from an operation that offered good promise. However, this type of turnover was just one of many that he had done in the past and it certainly would not be his last one. Nevertheless, dropping out of an operation was a disquieting one. Just when he could sense the excitement of an operation getting off the ground and the fortuitous turn of events of Ali approaching Patrick, with the accompany kick-in of momentum, he leaves it.

As he usually catnapped on long flights, Mitch let his mind wander. He needed to get back into his work routine at M&T, and to be brought up-to-date by Dane and Sumiko on recent developments. He was also restless, eager to get back behind the wheel of the new toy he purchased six months previously, a 2012 BMW 8-Series 760LI Sedan.

After two days back at the office, he called his mother to say he wished to come home for a visit. Overjoyed, she said to come as soon as possible. Driving the BMW overnight to her home in Palos Verdes, he left San Francisco around midnight in order to better enjoy the light traffic heading south on Highway 5. The four hundred mile trip took only five hours, and consisted of pure, smooth enjoyment.

Although he had several cars in the past, the performance of this one was unmatched. On turns and switchback curves, it tightly hugged the pavement. Feeling the acceleration grab hold of his body when a light turned green, he become melded together with the ergonomic leather seat. He hated thinking of the car remaining parked in the underground garage of his apartment building, with a cover over it, during his frequent trips out of the area.

After spending two pleasant days visiting with his mother, the return drive back to San Francisco in the middle of the night was, once again, a sublime experience. Following three more days of meetings at the office, and interviewing several new clients, Mitch was ready for Saturday night to come around.

He spent the morning hours getting his car detailed at a shop out on the avenues, near Fleischaker Zoo. The shop workers attention to detail in the cleaning and polishing of every inch of the car pleased him to no end. In the afternoon and early evening, he read and responding to cable traffic from headquarters and a number of stations around the world. Several new assignments were being offered up, requesting that he travel to three countries and initiate start-up work against Islamic terrorist groups operating there. His interest was piqued and he would be responding favorably to all of them.

By the time he left home, drove across the Bay Bridge and arrived at his favorite milonga, his watch showed just a few minutes after 11 p.m. He turned over the keys to the valet parking attendant in the lot next door, and once again entered the Las Canitas Tango Club. After exchanging greetings with several acquaintances from earlier visits, he made his way to the bar and ordered a glass of red wine.

With the melodic sounds of an accordion-like Bandoneon wafting through the room, Mitch intently searched the dance floor, trying to catch a glimpse of Maria Luiza. He scanned a dozen or so women sitting and standing alone along their customary wall on the other side of the room. He did not see her amongst any of them.

Mitch turned back to his glass of wine on the bar. Glancing down the side of the bar he saw Paulie, Maria Luiza's brother, working and walking toward him with a bottle of liquor in one hand and a glass in the other. As Paulie stopped in front of Mitch, and greeted him with a pleasant smile on his face, Mitch caught a mild scent of sandalwood perfume from over his shoulder. Without their bodies touching, he knew it was Maria Luiza and she was standing directly behind him. He turned around and, seeing a seductive smile on her lips, turned his gaze directly at her eyes.

"What did I do to be so fortunate this evening?" he asked her.

"You came to dance with me," she replied.

She stepped forward into Mitch's embrace as they stood together at the bar. Their chests touched and they came together as of they were one person. It was as if they were on the dance floor without their arms around each other. From above the waists they were connected together. From below the waists, they were not. Without any movement on their part, they were already starting to transcend into their tango heaven.

"Would you like to have a drink?" Mitch asked.

"I would like a kir, please," she replied.

"Why is it I'm always together with you when I'm here?" he asked with a grin on his face.

"It is because I am the only one you can see when you are here."

"I should have realized that a long time ago."

"Thank you for the beautiful bouquet of roses you sent to me for Christmas."

"That is the least I could do for such a beautiful and wonderful dancer."

"My mom and dad believe I now have a secret lover and wonder when I will bring him home to meet them. I think Paulie has told them about you but, obviously, all he can say is that we dance together a lot."

"The next time I drive over from the city, let's go out for dinner. If you like, I can stop by your home beforehand and meet them."

"Yes, that would be nice."

After finishing their drinks, Mitch and Maria Luiza spent the next hour and a half on the dance floor. Unlike when they first met and started dancing together months earlier, their moves and steps were now much more in total harmony with each other. He was finding magic in her responses to his moves. Holding her in a close embrace, he invited moves from her. She responded and then he moved with her. That was their tango. She had become one with Mitch because she was with him in his way. At the same time, they both had become vulnerable. They were feeling the power of tango.

The floor became more crowded and their gestures had to draw in tighter. As a result, the more formal precision required in tango moves gave away to more intimate contact in their movements together. A new group of musicians were appearing at the club, and they played the five set pieces of music in a slower fashion. The elegant simplicity of Mitch and Maria Luiza's moves became more subtle and refined as they revealed themselves to each other. They relaxed in their embrace and were in full contentment with the music and each other.

They forgot all the other dancers around them, because they had their own warm lair with which to glide. The occasional bump from another couple was meaningless. They had found that tango heaven as they moved slowly in the counter-clockwise ronda. The softness of her breasts rubbing on his chest began to arouse him. Succumbing to her own desire, she encouraged Mitch through a delicate swaying of her thighs during those infrequent times when their bodies touched below the waist.

These were not the tango moves they had learned in the pursuit of the dance. With no words, they agreed it was time to leave. Maria Luiza told Paulie she would not be coming home with him after the club closed. Mitch phoned a nearby hotel to make a reservation, and went to get their jackets from the cloakroom. In the cold, brisk air of a late-January evening in the Bay Area, they walked next door to the parking lot, got into Mitch's car and drove away.

The Waterfront Plaza Hotel, located in downtown Oakland, at Jack London Square, accepted Mitch's request for a penthouse suite overlooking San Francisco Bay. They arrived at the hotel just after 2 a.m., and within fifteen minutes of Mitch calling-in his request for a reservation. The sleepy-eyed clerk at the front desk checked them in and pointed out the elevators against the north wall of the lobby.

The fifth floor penthouse suite provided an excellent southwesterly view, with the city of South San Francisco on the other side of the bay awash in sparkling orange and white lights. Mitch ordered a bottle of champagne from room service, and turned on the electric fireplace in one corner of the suite. Maria Luiza was standing in front of the fireplace when the room service attendant arrived and set the tray with the champagne and glasses on the coffee table in the middle of the suite. He handed the check to Mitch for signing and left.

With the lights in the suite turned low, and the long bay window curtains open, a relaxing scene of subdued illumination took over. Mitch popped the cork on the bottle of champagne, poured each of them a glass and said to Maria Luiza: "What should we drink a toast to?"

Without hesitation, she replied, "Bailemos."

Caught off guard, Mitch hesitated, and then said, "Of course, let's dance."

They eagerly tossed back their champagne and set the glasses aside. She turned away and motioned for him to follow her into the bedroom.

Standing together at the foot of the room's king-sized bed, the two of them embraced and kissed longingly for the very first time. The spirited exploration of each other's mouth with their probing tongues provided instant realization of what each of them knew was going to be a wonderfully long early morning together.

They ended their kiss and Maria Luiza stepped back. She pulled at the thin cloth belt around the waist of her dress and let it fall to the floor around her ankles.

"Would you mine if I take the lead for this dance?" she asked, motioning for Mitch to sit down on the edge of the bed.

He sat down and, looking up at her five foot nine inches of a gorgeous, well-proportioned body, replied, "The pleasure will be mine."

No sooner had she quickly helped him to undress, than she noticed his large erection showing through the front of his shorts. She then said to Mitch, "The pleasure is going to be mine too."

He slipped his shorts off and moved his body all the way up on the bed with his head on a pillow. She laid down alongside him and tenderly started kissing his neck and ear. As she moved her lips across his cheek, they once again brought their lips together for another long, deep kiss. She moved her right hand down his chest, found his groin and slowly began stroking his stiff erection.

He reached over and brought his left hand slowly over her right breast. In the light Mitch could see and feel a very large erect nipple. Gently massaging the breast with his hand and the nipple with his fingers, he tried to turn over and position himself on top of her. However, she would have none of that. She pushed him back and softly whispered in his ear, "I'm still leading."

Sensing that he was about to explode, Maria Luiza rolled on top of Mitch and effortlessly slid his pulsating erection inside herself. She let out a low groan, arched her back and rose up and down in six long undulating motions of her thighs and upper legs. They both came at the same time, each with their bodies shuddering. Laying down besides him, they stared at the ceiling together for what seemed to be no more than five minutes as their breathing returned to normal.

With no words spoken, Mitch gently moved on top of her and, after no more than a minute or two of kissing her breasts, experienced the pleasure of having another erection. Back inside her again, he could feel her contract and relax the muscles of her pelvis as he continued to thrust softly into her depths. Feeling her shudder several times, Mitch felt himself reach his point of release at the same time.

Rolling off of her, they both faced each other and lay on their sides with their arms entwined. In soft spoken words, as her breathing was getting back to normal, she whispered in his ear, "You have made me very happy."

Mitch, his breath normal now, gently stroked her long black hair and said, "A week ago, flying back home from Europe, I dreamt about our relationship changing. Tonight the dream came true. I am very happy too."

With their arms still entwined, they both dozed off to a light sleep in what was left of an early Sunday morning, the lights still aglow across the bay.

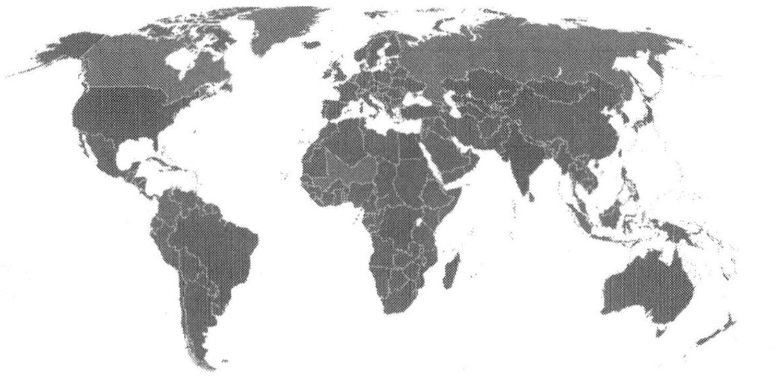

CHAPTER 27

Following his return to Dublin after meeting with Mitch and Lee in Amsterdam, Patrick stayed close to his apartment during the following week. He mulled Lee's proposal that he get involved with a group of possible Islamic terrorists. Since he agreed to at least another meeting with the man he knew as Ali, he would go ahead and try to find out more information on whether a terrorist operation was indeed being planned. If so, it would be up to him to decide on any further involvement. He accepted enough Euros from Lee to live on for at least a month, until such time that he came to his decision.

Late in the afternoon of a cold and blustery day, he left his apartment to go to Slattery's Bar for dinner and drinks. He checked for the presence of any surveillance as he made his way out of his immediate neighborhood. About half way in his walk across the Temple Bar area, his cell phone rang. He was not surprised at all that it was Ali calling. After a polite exchange of pleasantries, Ali asked Patrick if he would be willing to fly to Glasgow the following day to meet with him. He said he would pay for all of Patrick's expenses and made it clear he wished to continue their previous discussion on the commonality of views they shared about their enemies.

Without sounding overly eager, Patrick said he had nothing planned for the next couple of days and was agreeable to a meeting. Ali asked that he try to catch a flight that would arrive in Glasgow around noontime. Once the flight's arrival time was known, Patrick should call him and he would then give directions on where they would meet for their discussions. This alerted Patrick further to Ali's security consciousness,

Lee had told Patrick to purchase a new cell phone from a local convenience store in Dublin, with at least two hundred minutes of airtime, and make sure the phone was not attributed to him by name and address. Once the arrangements were made to meet with Ali, Patrick was to leave his own personal phone in his apartment and make subsequent calls, to both Lee and Ali, on the new one. Patrick readily agreed since he knew that the British Government had extensive capability to intercept and track cellular telephone calls.

So after ending the call from Ali, Patrick turned around in the middle of Temple Bar and headed back to his apartment to retrieve the new cell phone, canceling his plans for the evening at Slattery's. Once he had the new phone, he went down the street to a local coffee and sandwich shop to call Lee about Ali's call, and the limited details for their meeting the following day in Glasgow.

In Lee's cable write-up for headquarters after the Amsterdam meeting, he outlined the successful turnover and change of responsibility for Patrick, from Mitch to himself. He also pointed out the obvious step-up in the speed in which the operation was progressing now. This included the distinct possibility of new meeting venues that could mean Scotland, plus back into the Republic of Ireland, or elsewhere in Europe, depending upon what Ali told Patrick.

What Lee was not aware of was headquarters reaction to his cable. Jack, and the Director of CTC, Keith Holloway, read the cable and knew the operation was on the verge of taking on increasingly heightened sensitivities due to the intelligence liaison equities with Her Majesty's British Government. After being invited to the seventh-floor offices of the Director and Deputy Director of the Agency, they knew that decision time was near on informing the British on developments that could possibly take place on their soil.

They spent an hour working out the details of how Jack would continue to provide the headquarters management of Lee's handling of Patrick in whatever might develop with Ali. It was agreed that should a terrorist attack be in the planning stages, depending on new information learned by Patrick,

Steve would exercise his position as DDCIA to inform his British liaison counterparts of a potential terrorist operation shaping up on their shores. Without being willing to expose Mitch, Lee or Patrick to the British, Steve would inform them of the limited information currently available on what was known about Ali, and his claim to live in Glasgow. Steve would also tell them that Ali had discussions with an Irish national, expressing interest in wanting to conduct an attack against them. He would not reveal however, where the meetings between Patrick, Ali, Lee and Mitch had taken place, nor the frequency of those meetings. Steve would offer to provide any additional information obtained from Ali as the operation developed, particularly should the information become critical to British interests.

At Steve's strongly worded suggestion to Jack, at the end of their meeting, they agreed that should Patrick meet with Ali and develop any significant information of high priority interest, Jack was to be prepared to move a team of CTC officers to one of the European stations, offshore from the UK This team would provide on-the-spot management and logistical support toward working against any possible operation Ali might be planning. Steve also instructed Jack to put together his best counter-surveillance team available, and place them on short notice to move to Europe at any time. They were to be prepared to operate as both singletons and as a team on British soil, without British knowledge if necessary, against a potential terrorist threat there. As Jack, Keith and Steve were well aware, they would be operating contrary to agreed upon-norms with the British intelligence services. However, due to the quick moving nature of the operation, and the need to protect the identities of Agency officers and recruited agents, Jack was given approval to proceed along these lines. Jack and Keith walked away from the meeting satisfied that both of them continued to have the full confidence of the seventh floor.

Jack sent an immediate cable to Lee advising him of headquarters approval to proceed as planned. He included telling Lee of seventh-floor concerns and sensitivities, and the need to keep headquarters informed on an immediate or, if need be, flash precedence level on all cable traffic. If nothing else, Lee was to utilize his cell phone capability should the need arise, although it would have to be later backed up by cable traffic for record keeping purposes. As a courtesy to Mitch in San Francisco, Jack sent him a copy of his cable to Lee.

Jack also informed Lee that he was approved to travel to Scotland in commercial alias, once Patrick informed him where he would be meeting with Ali in Glasgow. At Lee's discretion after learning the meeting location, he could request that the counter-surveillance team standing by move to a location there where Lee believed they could best serve to locate Ali and place him under surveillance.

While waiting to hear from Lee for additional details on Patrick's meeting with Ali in Glasgow, Jack sent another cable to Mitch in San Francisco, as a follow-on to the cable sent to Lee. Jack asked Mitch to go into stand-by mode, in the event it became necessary to bring him back into Lee's new operational relationship with Patrick. In the back of Jack's mind was Mitch's ethnicity as half-Arab and half-Italian, which could be useful in placing someone close in on the ground where Ali might be operating in Glasgow. Should Ali be found there, and he used his advantage of being more familiar with the area, including moving about in the Muslim neighborhoods, Mitch would offer more potential to getting closer to him than in Lee's case.

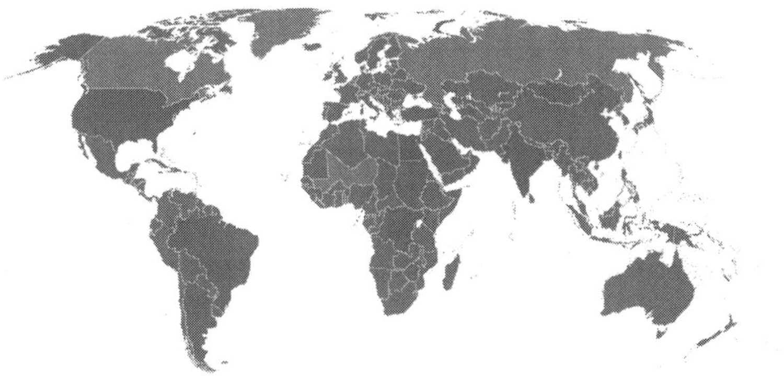

CHAPTER 28

When the call from Patrick came through to Lee, informing him of meeting with Ali the next day in Glasgow, the adrenalin quickly started to flow through Lee's veins. It would require him to get to Glasgow ahead of Patrick's arrival there, and try to set up some form of surveillance of Patrick exiting the airport and moving towards a meeting site with Ali. Rather than send a cable to headquarters, Lee decided to call Jack to inform him of Patrick's call and let him know he would be traveling to Glasgow first thing in the morning and wanted the surveillance team on stand-by to immediately deploy there.

Patrick arrived at Glasgow Airport the next morning at 11:10 a.m. When he called Ali back the previous day to give him the flight arrival time, Ali told him to exit the terminal building and look for him at the taxi rank outside. Upon exiting the terminal doors at 11:25, he spotted Ali standing near the end of a short queue of people in the rank, waiting for taxis. They both made eye contact and Ali immediately took up the last position at the end of the queue. With only five people ahead of him, Ali noted the long line of taxis moving quickly forward to pick up people in the rank. By the time Patrick walked the seventy foot distance to where Ali was moving forward in the rank, he joined up alongside Ali and they both stepped into a waiting taxi. It all happened so fast, Patrick did not even notice Lee starting to move towards him from a short distance away.

Lee had arrived at the airport a full hour before Patrick. After learning of the arrival at the gate of Patrick's flight from Dublin on time at 11:10 a.m., he took up a standing position eighty feet behind the end of the queue line at the taxi rank, with his back up against the front of the terminal building wall. When Patrick called him the night before, advising of the taxi rank meeting location, Lee was able to sense the foul-up that was to come. The surveillance team members were not due to arrive until several hours later and, to make matters worse, of all the locations that could serve to easily lose a surveillance tail, an airport taxi rank was one of them. Now, as he watched the taxi, with Ali and Patrick inside, pull away from the terminal, all he could do was get a partial on the taxi's license plate. He got the first letter, followed by three numbers, but could not make out the remaining three letters, as if it would have done him any good. It was obvious to Lee that he was not up to the task of trying to conduct surveillance alone, as a singleton, on British soil. Without the knowledge or benefit of any of the intelligence or police services there, he was left in a quandary. The opening kudos went to Ali for quickly moving Patrick away from their initial meeting location.

Now, with the surveillance team yet to arrive, Lee knew he would be out of position to do anything until he heard from Patrick. It would be a long shot at best to get the team on British soil and in position to pick up on Patrick and Ali in time. All he could do now was wait for Patrick's call and, if able, subsequently stakeout a position on Ali and place him under direct observation.

Lee went over to the same taxi rank where Ali had been standing, and took a taxi into Glasgow City Centre where he would wait for a call from Patrick. During the short twenty minute ride into the city, he stewed over the overall sloppy way he had handled this opportunity. If this had been any kind of joint operation with the British, the taxi picking up Ali and Patrick would have been completely under their control. Utilizing a radio-frequency identification (RFID) license plates system on vehicles throughout the UK for the past five years, they would have been able to track the vehicle wherever it was going. This would have even included the possibility of learning from the driver of the taxi the location or address where Ali asked to be taken to, without his knowledge while he was still riding in the back seat with Patrick.

Once the team arrived from the US, Lee would feel a lot better. Although they would not have available to them any kind of RFID system, they would have with them the Agency's most up-to-date secure communications equipment. The team themselves would also represent five people with more than one hundred years of surveillance experience between them. The team would range in ages from twenty-five to seventy-five, and would pass themselves off as a retired couple on vacation, a graduate student working on a doctoral dissertation, an American Scot doing genealogy investigative work and a travel agency representative scouting out new package tours for inland trekking and sports venues.

Once in Glasgow, Lee had the taxi driver drop him off at Central Station, on Gordon Street, in the City Centre. Although not knowledgeable at all about Glasgow, he thought that the center of the city would offer him the best location from which to move once he got a call from Patrick. When he stepped out of the taxi, in front of the station, Patrick decided he did not want to go too far from the taxi rank since he would quickly need another taxi to take him wherever Patrick said he was meeting with Ali. Noticing a coffee shop across the street from the station, he headed there to await the call.

Patrick and Ali, in their taxi ride from the airport into the city, made small talk about the cold weather this time of year in Scotland. Ali told the driver to take them to the west end of the city, but gave no specific location. Ali rebuffed Patrick's questions about where in Glasgow he lived and worked, as if he did not hear him. As they moved closer toward the center of the city, Ali told the driver to take them to the Buchanan Bus Station on Killermont Street.

They got out of the taxi in front of the bus station, and the taxi sped away. Ali and Patrick walked inside, where Ali bought a newspaper. They exited the station through a side door and proceeded on foot several blocks away to the Buchanan Galleries Shopping Centre. Patrick could tell from Ali's eyes and head movements that he was still obviously concerned about possibly being under surveillance. The weather was downright cold, hovering just below freezing. They walked briskly and did not speak a word to each other. Patrick was biding his time until he could find an excuse to get away from Ali for a few minutes to call Lee on his cell phone and let him know where they were located.

Upon reaching the junction of Sauchiehall and Buchanan Streets, they entered the shopping center and Ali motioned for them to take the up escalator. With the escalators, up and down, being juxtaposed towards each other, Ali was able to easily see from the second up escalator if anyone was following them upwards from the first floor escalator. Alighting from their escalator in the food gallery area, Ali directed Patrick to the Café Italiano where they were shown to a table and given lunch menus.

They both ordered light lunches consisting of salad and pasta, plus coffee.

"First of all, I want to apologize for putting you through all this, but I believe you can understand the reasons why," said Ali. "I cannot take any chances insofar our security is concerned."

"I understand that, no apology needed," Patrick replied. "I share your concern about surveillance. You did a good job of getting us here under what I believe are surveillance-free conditions. I thank you for that. Before we go any further, I do have to relieve myself. I will be right back."

Patrick noted the sign in the rear of the café showing where the toilets were located, and headed straight for them. Shutting the men's room door behind himself, he immediately pulled out his cell phone and, using the pre-programmed number for Lee's cell phone, was connected to him within a few seconds.

"Lee, this will be quick. We are in the west end of the city, in the Buchanan Galleries Shopping Centre, second floor food gallery, Café Italiano."

With that, Patrick hung up and barely had time to place the cell phone back into his jacket pocket when, as he expected, the outer door opened and inside stepped Ali. While remaining standing at the urinal, with his back to Ali, he continued with what was by then, one substantially long piss. Ali stepped up to the urinal next to him and not a single word was spoken between them. They finished, washed their hands and returned to their table for lunch.

Within a minute of returning to their table, their lunch dishes were served. They had just started to eat, when Ali said to Patrick: "I realize this may surprise you, but I would like for us to get up and leave right away."

"It is no surprise to me. You are carrying a cell phone with you, right?"

"Yes, I am," replied Ali.

"Me too. For that reason alone, I have no problem leaving now. We both could have used them in that brief span of time we were out of eyesight of each other."

"You're right, Patrick. Let's go."

They pushed their plates aside, stood up and Ali left enough pounds to cover the costs of their meal. They retraced their steps, this time down the escalators, exited the shopping center and Ali hailed another taxi. Ali told the driver to take them to the Tesco Extra Supermarket, on Dalmarnock Road. As they crossed Glasgow to the southeast side of the city, they talked in muted tones in the back seat and reached a mutual understanding. It was that neither of them would make a move to use their cell phones, under any circumstances, while they were together.

After a twenty minute ride to the Tesco Extra, Ali paid the driver and they entered through the main doors at the front of the store. Just inside, to the right of the doors, was a large coffee and pastry shop area where they both sat themselves down next to each other, at a small table with their backs up against a wall. This position gave them both direct line of sight views of the main entrance doors they had just come through. They ordered large cups of coffee, looked at each other and resumed their conversation from where they had left off at the Buchanan Galleries.

Lee, in the meantime, quickly caught a taxi at the Gordon Street taxi rank, and asked to be taken to the shopping center on Buchanan Street. When he asked the driver how long it would take to get there, the driver said no more than ten minutes. Thinking this would be soon enough for him to get there and place himself in a position to observe Patrick meeting with Ali, he sat back in the taxi and briefly relaxed.

After arriving at the Buchanan Galleries, he quickly made his way up the escalators to the food gallery. With the two of them having already departed the area and on their way to the southeast side of Glasgow, Lee did not even come close. The Café Italiano had customers at about half of their twelve tables. Neither Patrick nor Ali was to be seen at any of them. As he was descending the escalators Lee knew he had his job cut out for himself. Unless Patrick could get back in touch sometime soon, it was going to be a long afternoon and a much longer night.

In the freezing cold, with a light wind blowing that made it feel even colder, Lee hailed another taxi and headed back to city centre, and another coffee shop. Before searching out a hotel nearby to spend the night, he made a secure cell phone call to Jack at headquarters to bring him up to date and find out the arrival times for the surveillance team. Jack informed him that with the five team members were shortly due to arrive in Glasgow, and he provided their cell phone numbers in order for Lee to be able to call them and provide meeting instructions.

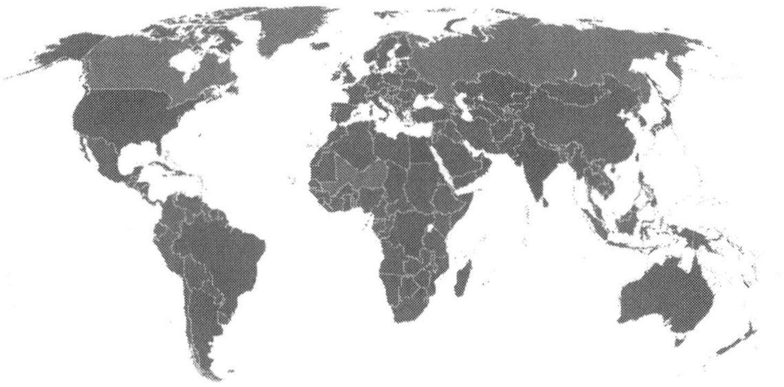

CHAPTER 29

"Director Capps, I have London on line one for you."

"Thank you, Molly," replied Steve.

Steve was in the office earlier than usual, at 6 a.m., in order to have two calls placed to both of his counterparts at MI5 and MI6, in London, before they went out for lunch. Without going into the specifics of who was involved and where the meetings were taking place, he wanted to inform them of Agency counterterrorism operations officers meeting with a source of information on possible radical Islamic terrorism in Europe.

"David Neville here."

"David, this is Steve. Good to hear your voice. How are you and Robin doing?"

"Steve, you old bastard. You always have to inquire about my wife. Robin is just fine. Are you and Kathleen still married?"

"Thanks sport. Yes, we indeed are still together. She never lets me forget it either."

"What can I do for you today? As you can expect, Her Majesty's Secret Intelligence Service continues to keep me gainfully employed. How much longer I'm not sure."

"I want to give you a heads up on a possible operation that may be starting up for our guys in the counterterrorism center. Two of our officers have been meeting with an Irish national, in Europe, who apparently has been approached by a Pakistani Muslim there who claims he wants to enlist support for terrorist acts against both of our governments."

"I hope you have more than that for me. What else can you tell me, may I ask?"

"Little else at this point, David. We do have the Irish national going to meet again with the Pakistani who, at this point, we only know as Ali, and try to develop more information. I know this is very sketchy, but this is all we have."

"Does Ali Baba have a full name and nationality? Can you give me the name of the Irishman? Where do these two characters live?"

"David, I'm giving you this bit of information now so that you are not blindsided later on, should something more come out of it."

"Has your headquarters traces on these guys revealed anything?"

"No, without having full names to work with, we have nothing more. That's why we have the Irishman going back for more info."

"Do you know if the Irishman is a Muslim?"

"No indication of that at all."

"Might he be one of these Irish zealots we still have to deal with on occasion?"

"Not that we can tell, at this point."

"I also take it that you have no details yet on specific targets in either of our countries?'

"The targets, of course, are at the top of the list of requirements given to the Irishman to fulfill. I'm going to paper over our conversation with a cable to you from our UK desk immediately. I also promise to quickly let you know as we learn any further details."

"My dear old chap, why do I still bother talking with you? Steve, please advise soonest as you learn more since we would like to trace and vet these characters as well."

"Will do, David. Again, I apologize for not having more. Take care of yourself and give Robin the very best of regards from Kathleen and myself."

"The same to Kathleen, Steve. I looked forward to hearing back from you soon."

Steve hung up the phone and sat back in his chair wishing he had been able to be more forthcoming.

"Director Capps, I now have MI5's Ian Campbell on the line for you."

"Thanks again, Molly."

"Hello, Ian. This is Steve. How are you?"

"Well, if it isn't my favorite Yank. Steve, I'm just fine. How about yourself?"

"Doing well, Ian. All is well at this end of the pond. I just got off the line with David, and wanted to give you the same heads up as well."

"Why do I feel I know what may be coming?"

"You mean David got to you that quick?"

"Of course not, old sod. What have you got for me?"

"We have a couple of our operations officers meeting with an Irishman in Europe who claims to have been approached by a Pakistani Muslim who has some apparently serious gripes about our two countries."

"Your Irishman, is he one of ours from Northern Ireland or from the Republic?"

"That much is not yet clear."

"Can you be specific on where this Irishman is being met?"

"Not yet, Ian. I have another liaison service's interest in Europe to protect."

"My dear old cock, I thought we were at the top of your list. Next you're going to tell me you don't want to see us blindsided here on this side of the pond, right?"

"Ian, we have the Irishman going back to meet with the Pakistani again, in order to develop further details. We don't even have enough full names to run complete traces."

"How about sharing what little you have and give us a shot at them?"

"The Pakistani is only known as Ali. We don't even know his nationality, at this stage."

"How about the Irishman? What have you got on him?"

"I expect to have more details soon and will get back in touch with you right away."

"How many meetings has your guys had with this Irishman?"

"I believe he has only been met twice, so far."

"Might you have at least a first name since you have two of your officers meeting with this guy?"

"So far we only know him as Patrick."

"A fucking Paddy, you mean I'm surprised its not John or William. All right, Steve, please be your usual prompt self and let us know when you learn more."

"That's my promise to you, Ian."

"Each day, you know, I get fucked over at least once. I didn't expect it before lunch today. You've given me that distinct bad feeling in my water. Anything else, old sod?"

"That's it, Ian. I'll be talking with you again, soon."

Steve hung up his phone and kicked over the wastebasket behind his chair. Deception is an integral part of the intelligence game and, unfortunately, at times it has to extend to friends. At some point soon, however, should Lee learn from Patrick that this Ali character is real and does indeed have plans for an attack, wherever it may be, he would call David and Ian back again, fill them in and provide as much in the way of details as possible. Taking a page from Ian's lexicon, Steve did not like that feeling in his water either.

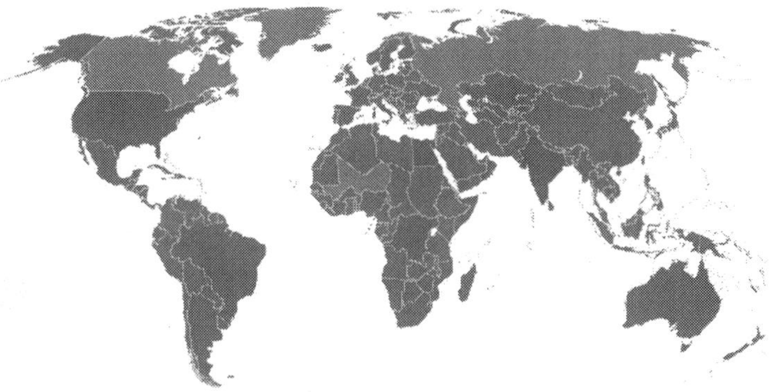

CHAPTER 30

With two steaming hot cups of coffee in front of them, the two men scanned the main entrance doors of Tesco Extra. Ali was satisfied that he and Patrick were in the black, clear of surveillance, and could now talk together alone. Patrick, also trying to appear satisfied, had concluded that Lee would not be able to find them at their new location.

"Patrick, when we talked last month in Dublin, you indicated willingness to meet again to further discuss our common enemies. I hope that is still the case and you will listen to what I am going to ask of you and give it serious consideration."

"If I were not interested in continuing our discussion I would not be here. How far I am willing to go to assist or take part in an operation you may be planning, will depend upon your proposal. Is that a fair response on my part?" Patrick replied.

"Of course it is. Before I go any further however, I need to know a little more about you."

"That's fine. I also would like to know a little more about you as well."

"Patrick, you previously told me you were from Northern Ireland, and you showed a lot of disdain for the British there. Are you from a family that has been active against the British?"

"Yes, active for many, many years. I come from a family of ultra-Irish nationalists who remain vehemently opposed to the British. For me, it started when I was seven years old and became actively involved against them. It ended when I turned fourteen, and was sent to Dublin for further schooling. Being sent away served to keep me out of jail."

"Can you tell me your family name?

"Let's just say our family is well known in Ireland, dating back into the 1800s, as being consistently involved in fighting against the fucking Brits there, including the local police forces under their control."

"Are you wanted by the British or any of the police forces there?"

"I know what you're thinking. If they want me there, they would want me here too. The answer is, no."

"I'm glad you appreciate my position and can understand that I don't want surprises of any kind. I can't have you joining up with me and my Muslim brothers only to find you are a wanted man."

"If I decide to work with you, rest assured I'll have documentation showing me as a different person; a clean person without a record or any warrants outstanding."

"What do you mean? You have the capability to document yourself in another identity?"

"Exactly. Do you know what the word quartermaster means?"

"I believe that is a person who takes care of and provides the provisions, equipment and supplies."

"I could not have defined it better myself. In the IRA, quartermasters take care of all the logistical needs our people require. We actually don't have many of them right now, but every now and then a new one is appointed to take the place of one of the older ones who can no longer handle the job."

"How does that apply to you and documents?"

"I've an uncle, twelve years older than me, who was recently made a quartermaster. Because we are family, all I have to do is ask and he will see to it I'm supplied with whatever kind of documentation I need."

"What is it you think you would need insofar as working with me?"

"Basically, and unless you see things differently, I can think of three things: first, a UK passport in a new name; second, a national identity card; and third, a Northern Ireland Driving License. All three would be in the same name. Where a home address is listed on the documents, it would be a real address in Northern Ireland, where people living there would say that I also live there."

"For starters, Patrick, all three will do quite nicely. Are you confident these documents would look genuine and withstand scrutiny?

"They will indeed be genuine. Tell me, Ali, what kind of documents are you carrying?"

"Since I'm a foreign national here, I am not eligible for a UK passport. However, I do have my UK national identity card along with my own country's passport."

"Which country is that?"

"Pakistan."

"I don't suppose you want to tell me your real name either?"

"That's correct. Like you, it is best for both of us not to be aware of each other's true identities."

"Alright, but tell me, Ali, are you really a biologist living here in Glasgow?"

"Yes, indeed I am. Are you really an electrical engineer from Dublin?"

"Very much so. An unemployed engineer at that, unfortunately."

"I'm hoping you will let me become your employer. I'm in a position to help you out, while at the same time achieve retribution against the British. Once our jihad against the British succeeds, if you wish, you can work with me further to engage in another jihad, in this case against the Americans."

"How about spelling out the role you want me to play in these jihads?"

"That's fine. You're being very direct with me, and I'll be the same with you. I'm planning on two operations in the UK. One will be in England, and the other here in Scotland. After that, once we succeed with both of them, and I know our jihad will indeed be successful, we will proceed to the US and achieve an even bigger jihad there."

"What can you say about the 'we' part of your plan?"

"You, I and several of my brothers will be able to manage all three operations as I presently have them planned. If more brothers are needed, so be it. I can have them brought here from Pakistan, or elsewhere, at any time. I'm sure you understand it when I say I'm keeping all of them, as well as yourself, as separated from each other as possible. Protecting all of our identities is of utmost importance if we are to succeed."

"Of course I understand. What's your timetable, especially as it applies to my getting involved?"

"I'd like you to start as soon as you can get your documentation in another identity and return here."

"I should be able to do a turnaround and be back here in no longer than a week. Getting new documents will take me no more than five days. Is that acceptable to you?"

"That will be fine. Once you return, I'll be directing you to a particular area here in Scotland to lease a house. I'll then have you rent a truck and procure a number of local supplies. These will include large plastic barrels, smaller fuel cans, fuel oil and ammonium nitrate fertilizer."

"I see. This means the attacks are going to involve ANFO bombs delivered to their target by truck. Am I right?"

"Yes, that is correct," Ali replied. "And the term ANFO is correct too," he added.

"ANFO is what I've decided to use for the first two attacks here in the UK. With what you have just said however, I've another request to ask of you. Do you think your uncle, the quartermaster, might be able to help out on a couple more items besides the identity documents?"

"What might these items be?"

"I'll require four blasting caps, two of which must be electrical caps. The only other item would be a small amount of detonation cord. If these items are available to you, would it be possible for you to bring them over here to Scotland?"

"Both the caps and det-cord, should be no problem at all. However, I would not bring them over myself. I would have them brought over separately, on a fishing boat that I would meet here on the Scottish coast. I would then retrieve the items and bring them to you, or whomever else you wish."

"It sounds like you and your family has a very well developed organization in place in Ireland."

"It's not the large organization it once was, but we still manage to play a good size role in it. How much det-cord will you require?"

"What I already have on hand will not be enough for both attacks. I'll require a single fifteen foot length. Would that be possible?"

"That should not be a problem."

"I'd like you to give me a fair price for the blasting caps and det-cord, plus any other expenses involved in getting these items to me."

"For the caps and det-cord, I'll only have to pay to replenish our stocks. The expense to the fishing boat captain will be separate. I should be able to let you know before I return back here."

"I take it then, that you are agreeable to everything I've proposed and will be willing to bring both our jihads together for the common good?"

"The more you tell me about your plans against the bastards, Ali, the better I like it. For that reason alone, you can count on me."

"I'm confident that working together like this will ensure our success."

"I take it that, since you have not asked for any further items to build the actual bombs, you must have everything else you need to initiate the charges and set-off the ANFO. Am I right?"

"Yes, I've everything else that is needed. Once you return here and get settled in a house, we can start putting everything together and fabricate the actual bombs."

"What can you tell me about the timetable for the two attacks and the actual intended targets?" Patrick asked.

"Because of the amounts of ANFO to be used, it'll take some time, possibly a month or so, to buy up the ingredients in small amounts from different suppliers, in order not to arouse any suspicions. I'll not be rushed to move any too quickly. I would say the first of the two attacks would take place by mid to late February. As for the targets, leave that up to me."

"I understand. By the way, I forgot to ask earlier, what size truck are you going to want me to rent? The size will determine the type of driver's license I'll need to have documented in my new name."

"It'll have to be a delivery truck, or small moving van, with a capacity to hold at least 4,500 kilos, or about ten thousand pounds."

"Good."

"I have nothing further to cover with you. Do you have anything else, Patrick?"

"No, Ali, I am satisfied with all that we have talked about."

"Here is an envelope that contains four thousand pounds. Use this for whatever costs were involved in your travel here and for going back to Dublin, returning here again in a week, plus to pay for the items we talked about. When you return I'll be giving you more funds to cover a house lease, the truck, supplies, etc. Does this sound fair to you?"

"Thank you, Ali. Yes, that certainly is fair. For communicating with you in the meantime, I assume you want me to let you know when I'll be returning here and also when the fishing boat will be arriving as well."

"Yes, we should both continue to use our cell phones."

"By the way, Ali, I've a new cell phone number to give you. My old one was just that; it was not working well anymore."

"That's funny, Patrick. The same thing happened to me. I also have a new number for you."

They both exchanged their new numbers and glanced around the front of the store. They were fixing in their minds the physical descriptions of some of the people standing around. Once out of the store and making their way to transportation to leave the area, they would check to see if any of the same people exited the store and started to move in front or behind them. All that was on Patrick's mind however, was the need to get back in touch with Lee.

"Patrick, would you mind waiting here for a few minutes and let me depart first?"

"No, not at all. Do we need to get together tomorrow for anything else?"

"No. This will be it."

"OK. I'll get a hotel room for the evening and then return to Dublin first thing in the morning. Once I gather up a few things there, I'll be off to Belfast to begin pulling together the items we agreed I would handle. I'll give you a call two nights before I'm ready to leave and return here. How does that sound?"

"Excellent, Patrick. That'll be fine. Through your efforts and contribution, we'll be successful. For all of us it will be ours for the taking. Go in peace."

"Peace to you too, Ali."

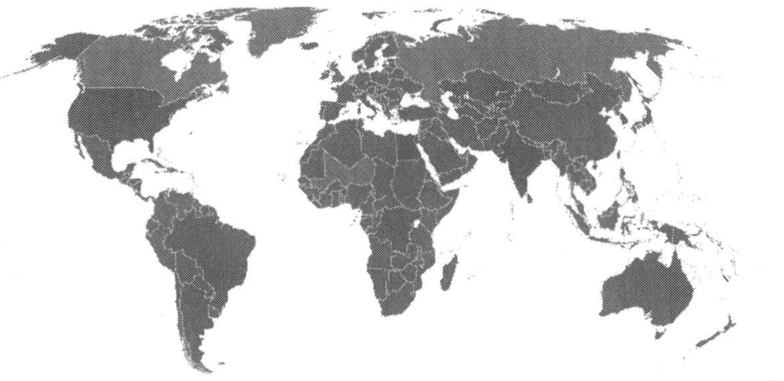

CHAPTER 31

Lee was taut and visibly shaken with worry after informing Jack of losing Patrick and Ali at the airport's taxi rank. He could only hope that Jack would understand how quick events had moved there. .

Following Ali's request to Patrick to remain behind after they concluded their meeting at Tesco Extra, Patrick walked around the store for ten minutes before exiting to catch a taxi. He knew it was best not to follow Ali outside the store in the event Ali waited around to see if he would attempt to do just that. Wandering through the lumber and woods crafts section in the rear of the store, Patrick placed a call to Lee to let him know what had happened.

After several cups of coffee and a long wait back in Glasgow's City Centre, Lee was relieved when his cell phone rang and it was Patrick calling. They agreed to meet later in the evening, after dark, in an area Lee was able to check out earlier in the day. He instructed Patrick to stand on the northeast corner of Meadowpark Street and Craigpark Drive. After spotting Lee diagonally on the southwest corner, he was to proceed to follow Lee, from a discreet distance, to the Tibo Coffee House, located about ten short blocks away on Duke Street.

It was a cold evening with a brisk wind blowing, but Lee wanted to ensure himself they were free of surveillance. This particular area of Glasgow, a residential district of flats and townhouses located on the eastern fringe of the center of Glasgow, was suitable for being able to confirm their surveillance-free status. Lee was able to place himself between two buildings of flats and observe Patrick arrive on the northeast corner of the two streets, as instructed. After looking around and becoming satisfied of Patrick's black status, Lee moved from between the two buildings to the southwest corner where Patrick could see him. After sundown during this time of year, most of the residents were buttoned up inside their warm flats and townhouses. With the streets being virtually deserted, this allowed for Lee and Patrick to notice any movement around them as they started their walk to Tibo.

Upon arriving at Tibo and finding it had a good selection of dinner items on the menu, they ordered drinks and a full meal. By the time Patrick revealed to Lee the details of his meeting with Ali, Lee quickly concluded that with anywhere from one to possibly three terrorist attacks being planned by Ali and his co-conspirators, this represented a most serious threat to both the UK and US Governments. The worst part of the scenario to him was that one of the attacks was being planned against the US. Lee knew he had to immediately convey this information to Jack at headquarters, and let him deal with senior Agency management and the highest levels of the government as to how best to proceed. He knew what he would be doing, once the surveillance team arrived and was able to take up their positions in and around Glasgow.

The gravity of the situation was further heightened when Lee considered the effects of ANFO bombs on gatherings of people and public infrastructure, regardless the countries involved. He commended Patrick for the way he handled his willingness to get involved in Ali's plans, particularly insofar learning of Ali's need for some of the components for the bombs. They both noted and agreed that, as expected, Ali provided no details or mention of who would be driving the trucks used to deliver the bombs to their ultimate targets. This prompted them to look at each other and, slowly moving their heads up and down in unison together, they formed the word martyr on their lips.

Patrick and Lee realized that, besides Ali saying the timetable for the attack was about one month away, little more was learned about Ali himself. Except for him saying he was from Pakistan, and was indeed a biologist living in Glasgow, nothing further in the way of new biographical details had been obtained. The lack of this kind information placed them at a distinct disadvantage in trying to identify and track him and his co-conspirators down. Now, more than ever, it would be up to the surveillance team to learn Ali's true name identity and details on the other people involved in his attack plans. Lee would not rule out British assistance as well, but that would be a headquarters decision by people at a much higher pay grade than himself.

Lee decided he wanted to get more of a feel for Patrick's way of thinking about what Ali's said his role would be in taking part in his planned operations.

"Patrick, how do you think Ali perceived your indication of willingness to become part of his attack group?"

"I certainly know that I cannot trust him. At the same time, I believe he feels the same way. I'm also sure he realizes I look upon him that way too. Ali needs me to acquire some of the bomb components, lease a house and a truck That'll be the extent of my initial use. After that, I may well be of no further use. Should the first attack succeed as planned, that'll determine any need he was for me in the second and third attacks."

"That's a very pragmatic way to view your involvement," Lee said.

"It's just the way you go into these operations. Whenever an outsider is needed, the degree of that person's access and involvement is severely limited to what only is absolutely necessary. This is what I experienced in Northern Ireland as a young man. Outsiders are just that. Only family and the closest of long-time friends are trusted. I expect to be totally compartmented off from other members of Ali's group, and even said to Ali that I expected as much of him if he was to securely plan and conduct a successful operation."

"What was his response?"

"His answer was a nodding of the head and a slight grin on his face."

Lee realized that Patrick was showing a very mature and well-developed understanding of the way terrorists think and plan their actions. Patrick was quite forthcoming about how Ali was giving him a limited number of details as related to Patrick's involvement in the operation. To Lee, this meant that Patrick's openness was a sign of them bonding closer together as their relationship was developing.

Based on Lee's previous experiences working counterterrorist operations of this kind, the quick movement of people and resources to counter the threat was now of paramount concern. Also, informing all of the necessary senior government officials, in this case both the US and British Governments, was an absolute necessity. He excused himself from Patrick, and the dinner they were just finishing, saying he needed to step outside and call headquarters immediately.

Jack, upon hearing from Lee all of these details, likewise sensed the seriousness of the situation and the need to quickly place in motion all of the resources available to him in CTC, as well as elsewhere in the government. He also knew that his old friend and colleague, Steve, up on the seventh floor, would be faced with some difficult choices in dealing with the British. Working with liaison on a counterterrorist operation on their soil would require some adroit footwork. He hoped Steve would be up to the task.

Lee, feeling the coldness of a Scottish winter night, stepped back inside Tibo and finished dinner with Patrick. They agreed that Ali knew how ANFO bombs were constructed. Patrick pointed out though, that an initiator of some kind would be required in order to fire the blasting cap that would subsequently set off the det. cord. Since no mention was made of one, they concluded Ali already had one, or, had another means of obtaining it.

Patrick noted that with Ali saying he would task him with purchasing plastic barrels and fuel cans, no mention was made of how many barrels would be required. Knowing the number of barrels would serve to indicate the size of the bomb. The size of the truck however, was indicative of a bomb that could be up into the ten thousand pounds range. Both Mike and Patrick did some quick calculating, concluding that the explosive force of such a bomb could be similar to what occurred at the Murrah Federal Building in Oklahoma City seventeen years earlier, in 1995. If Ali wanted to produce a bomb of that size, close to two hundred bags of ammonium nitrate would be required, along with at least fifteen or more barrels to hold the fertilizer and the fuel oil.

In the absence of any information on who Ali actually was, and where he could be located, it was agreed that any further efforts to track him down would have to wait until Patrick returned from Belfast with his new identity documents. Once he learned from Ali when and where they would next meet, the surveillance team's effort could begin. Lee did not tell Patrick about the team coming into Scotland and not arriving in time to pick-up on him and Ali at Glasgow Airport.

Patrick however, asked Lee to make sure that his identity, in true name as well as the new identity he would be traveling in from Belfast, not be revealed to the British. He acknowledged that with him coming back to Scotland in a new identity, and picking up the blasting caps and det. cord from a fishing boat, he would be particularly vulnerable should the British be aware of his presence. Lee reassured him that no information about him would be shared with the British.

They ended their meeting by going over details of Patrick keeping Lee informed when he would be departing Belfast, where he would meet the fishing boat for picking up the materials for Ali and, most importantly, when and where he and Ali would next meet. They agreed on words and phrases to be used on their cell phones to set-up their own meetings, including a brief encounter meeting before Patrick was to see Ali.

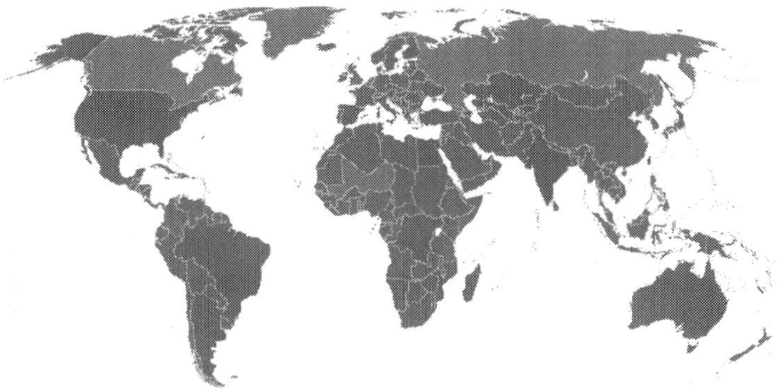

CHAPTER 32

Returning to his nightly graveyard shift during the workweek at the hospital in Paisley, Abdul was able to shed the vestiges of his Ali alias as he went about tending the emergency room patients. Following his meeting with Patrick the previous day at the Tesco Extra however, he found that he needed time to pull together all of the information he had revealed to this non-Muslim outsider, and consider the degree to which it posed a threat. When he finished his shift the morning after meeting with Patrick, Abdul returned home and compiled a mental list of the details about the operation he had discussed with him.

Although he was only planning one attack in the UK – at Sellafield – he alluded to three attacks in his discussion with Patrick. The first would take place in England. A second non-existent one, shortly afterwards, would be in Scotland. The third, and final attack, would be in the US. For the first attack, the one for which he primarily sought Patrick's assistance, it would be the ANFO bomb delivered by truck.

He avoided any mention of the specific locations of the targets. The only information he gave Patrick on the timetable for the attacks was mid to late-February for the first one. That meant that in about five weeks time, based upon what he told Patrick, the first truck bomb would be delivered to its intended target in England.

Abdul pondered at what point this amiable yet very sharp Irishman would become expendable. He knew he could never come to have any degree of full trust in this non-believer. He could never allow him to become knowledgeable of other team members or safe houses. Nevertheless, in Patrick he found the means of acquiring the remaining components for the bomb, plus his ability to move around the UK countryside blending in as he went about leasing a house, renting a truck and purchasing locally available components.

Abdul decided that he, along with Wahid, would have to make an effort to place Patrick under surveillance once he returned from Belfast in his new identity. This would include following him from the house he would acquire, as he made his way to meet with Ali, as well as departing the meeting area to go elsewhere.

After a hectic night at the hospital, followed by this mind exercise about Patrick, Abdul was just about ready to doze off for some needed sleep when his cell phone rang and brought him fully awake. A confident and happy sounding Wahid was on the other end, saying he was doing well in his job, making a lot of progress to advance himself there, and was hopeful they could meet soon. With a week and a half gone by since they last met, Abdul provided the time they could meet for dinner that evening and the bus stop where they would link up together. Since the bus stop number corresponded to the name and location of a restaurant, according to their list of pre-arranged meeting venues, nothing else needed to be mentioned over the phone.

The Chicken Ranch, located on Cathcart Road, south of the River Clyde, in Glasgow, was a suitable location for two Pakistanis to have dinner. Wahid showed up precisely on time, and both he and Abdul selected Halal certified chicken dishes from the menu. Abdul had dined there six months previously, and this time selected a chicken wrap. Wahid, at Abdul's suggestion, ordered the fried chicken, a well-known specialty of the house.

"I could tell from your voice over the phone that you sounded pleased with your progress for our cause," said Abdul.

"Yes, I have much to report, and it is all quite good," Wahid replied.

"Did Rashid get the call saying the M34 device had arrived?"

"Yes," Wahid replied. "He got the call and immediately informed me. He followed your instructions for him to meet the brother with the device in one of the shopping malls here, exactly as you requested. Rashid did so, and

I was able to observe him receiving the device. As he departed the mall I was able to determine that no one else followed him."

"Good. Tell me what you did next?"

"I was able to get ahead of him and go to the coffee shop where he expected to meet me. I positioned myself across the street when he arrived. Again, he was alone. After he was inside, I called his cell phone number and gave him directions to an alley six blocks away. It was a long alley between two buildings and had an s-shaped turn in the middle. It was a perfect location for getting into an unobservable position in the middle of the turn in the alley. Nobody was around at all to observe Rashid brushing past and handing me the package. He continued on to the end of the alley and there is where I lost sight of him. Later, he told me he made his way to another small shopping mall for a while, before returning to his hotel. In my own case, I was able to enter an open rear door in the alley that led down a hallway and into a hardware store. I looked around, purchased a couple of small gardening tools and exited through the front door of the store."

"Are you satisfied neither of you was under any kind of surveillance?"

"Yes, perfectly satisfied. I have the device here with me. You just tell me when you want me to hand it over to you."

"For now, let us continue with our meal. We have much more to discuss. Tell me about taking Rashid to Seascale."

"On a Saturday morning, we took an early train from the Central Station here and went to Carlisle where we transferred to the train going to Seascale. All went well and I am satisfied we did not draw the attention of anyone else. Seascale is a small seaside resort village, and this time of the year, it is very quiet. By mid-afternoon, we had walked through just about every street in the village. On one of them, Gosforth Road, we spotted a small vacant store for rent, located next door to the Seascale Health Centre. This is on the main road leading out of the village to the small town of Gosforth."

"That sounds good. Was that about it in terms of finding a place for rent?"

"That is all that we found. While I walked away from the storefront towards the beach area, I had Rashid go into the Health Centre next door. It is a medical clinic for treating out patients. He asked if anyone was doing computer servicing and repairs in the area. He was told that only one such business existed, several towns over to the east. He then inquired about the storefront for rent next door. They gave him the telephone number of the property owner living in a cottage several blocks away. Rashid caught up with me down in a teashop next to the beach. After explaining what he had learned, I had him phone the owner and arrange to view the storefront later in the afternoon."

"You handled all of this just right. Then what happened?"

"With me staying completely out of the picture, Rashid met the owner at the store, where he was shown the insides of it. It is a small store but upstairs, he learned, was a small room for sleeping, along with a kitchen area and a toilet with a shower. It turned out perfect for Rashid and our purposes. He explained to the owner the kind of computer shop he would open there, noting that it even sounded like his first customers would be the people working next door in the clinic. Rashid and the owner agreed on an initial three-month lease of the shop, and Rashid paid him the full amount and got a copy of the lease."

"That's excellent news."

"Later in the afternoon, we found a bed and board facility further up Gosforth Road, where Rashid was able to stay for two days before moving into his new shop. By the time I caught a late evening train for Carlisle, we agreed that he would visit the larger towns just to the east of Seascale, purchase a motorbike and necessary computer equipment and supplies to outfit his shop. Within three days after I returned back here to Glasgow, he called to say he was all set up in the shop, had made some flyers and was going around the village introducing himself and his new computer service and repair shop in Seascale."

"What has happened since you received that call?"

"Based on instructions I gave him for making it a routine to ride once or twice a day past the main gate at the Sellafield facility, he wasted no time to call and ask to meet the following weekend. As a result, we each took a train to Carlisle where we met in a pizza shop for lunch near the train station."

"Neither of you has wasted any time at all. This is wonderful news."

"While eating lunch, Rashid reported that he already is doing computer servicing and repair work at the golf and country club located on the north side of the village, between Seascale and Sellafield. This allows him to plausibly drive by the main gate area and observe what he can of what appears to be the procedures for entering and exiting the facility, plus view the physical barriers that are in place just inside the main gate. It turns out that he has some well-developed observation skills."

"How so, Wahid?"

"I told him that in no way was he to actually approach the gate and the guards there. He also was to make no calls or inquiries at the facility about offering them his computer services. Instead, he said, he stopped one afternoon across the street from the gate, and got off his motorbike to ostensibly adjust the wooden box of computer tools and parts fastened above the rear wheel of the bike. From that observation point he was able to see what the barriers were like inside the gate."

"This is an example of using one's own imagination to learn what could be a treasure trove of useful information. He has the basics down and you briefed him up well ahead of time."

"Here is his overhead sketch he made of the main gate and guard booth entrance area. As you can see here, just next to the guard booth inside of the main gate, is a series of bollards, or Jersey wall barriers, that are made of concrete. They measure about three and a half feet in height and are at least twelve feet, maybe twelve and a half feet in length. These barriers face end to end to each other and line both sides of the single lane used for vehicle traffic entering the facility. As you can tell, the barriers zigzag for approximately sixty feet or more once inside the gate, in order to prevent a car or truck entering into the facility at a high rate of speed."

"I know exactly what Rashid is talking about," Abdul replied. "A couple of months ago, when I made two drive-by passes of the main gate while traveling to and from Seascale, I noticed them inside the gate but nothing in the way of barriers outside the main gate in the forty to fifty foot distance from the gate to the roadway on which I was traveling. From the looks of the sketch Rashid gave you, that is still the case."

"Yes, that's the way it looks. You'll notice though, what apparently used to be two lanes for vehicles from the main road leading to the main gate, is now just a single lane. When you reach the main gate itself, a sliding metal fence gate has been pulled across the outer lane."

"What are these little circles or dots he placed on the entrance lane, both outside and inside the main gate?"

"He said those are numerous rough spots or small potholes in the lane due to overuse and probably heavy loads carried on trucks entering and exiting the facility."

"Now that is the kind of information that represents pieces of gold to us. Can you see why, my brother?"

"No, what do you mean?"

"It means you must get back in touch with Rashid immediately and encourage him to continue to make his drive-by of the facility, as long as he has plausible reason, due to his computer servicing work. He is to look for the very first signs that a re-paving effort is going to begin at the main gate area."

"I will contact him immediately after we finish our meeting."

"You should tell him to look for a truck with a crane to be used for moving the heavy concrete barriers, plus paving trucks, possibly a steamroller, etc. This also means that both of us are put on notice that we must re-double our efforts to bring together all of the components we require for the bomb we will use to start our jihad."

"Allah almighty is your guardian, Abdul, and he will guide both of us through to success in our jihad."

"Now, please tell me about the progress you have made here in bringing together the components we need."

"As I was able to get across to you over the phone just over a week ago, I leased the house in Larkhall that you had selected. I moved all of my things in, and purchased a used car, a four-door Mitsubishi Colt. Since then, I've been steadily making purchases of plastic barrels and fuel cans. So far, I have accumulated ten of the large plastic barrels you requested, all with lids. I also have bought twelve fuel oil cans."

"That's wonderful news. Now this is what I would like you to do next: Go ahead and buy eight more barrels and eight more fuel cans, as I originally requested."

"I should have the remaining barrels and cans within a few more days."

"Now tell me, What about your purchases of the ammonium nitrate fertilizer?"

"I learned that the fertilizer with the white beads, or prills, that you told me about, have been used for many years here in the coal mining industry as an explosive component. They are no longer being manufactured here though, due to government restrictions as result of the Irish nationalists using this kind of fertilizer for making bombs. Now, only the grey prills are manufactured and sold here now. Just as you told me previously, the grey prills do not have the same explosive power as the white ones. At my job site, we still have in our inventory at least four hundred to five hundred of the bags of white beads since they are still available on the local market. Once the market depletes their stocks, only the grey beads will remain. When I go into each store now to purchase three of the bags at a time, I can recognize the older bags with the white beads inside. When the stock of them runs out, only the bags with gray beads will remain. No one has noticed my checking on the bead type before I buy the bags."

"How many bags have you purchased to date?"

"I hope you will not be upset with me, but with the purchase of the barrels and cans, I have only managed to accumulate seventy-eight of the one hundred bags you requested. Now however, with so few barrels and cans to buy now, I will easily be able to step-up my purchases of more bags. Between the many DIY chain stores in and around the Glasgow area, along with the many hardware and garden store outlets, it is easy to move from store to store each evening after work to make the purchases. I could actually take some bags with the white beads from my job site as well, if it becomes necessary."

"No, Wahid, you must be careful and not engage in any stealing. It is important you continue to have your job and ability to move around the city as much as you do."

"What will be the total number of bags of fertilizer that you want me to buy and store at the house?"

"Originally, I was hoping to have a second house and another person making similar purchases like yours. However, for the time being, I am going to hold off on that and, instead, have you continue with the fine job you are currently doing. For the total number of bags, I would like you to set your sights on a goal of two hundred bags. At fifty pounds a bag, and along with the fuel oil, that will give us a bomb of almost ten thousand pounds. That will be just right in providing us with the kind of bang I want to start-off our jihad."

"Oh, before I forget, I also bought a pair of five-foot long plastic oars, as you requested. Regarding the fuel cans, do you want me to start buying the fuel now?"

"Yes, in about one week's time, you can start filling the cans with diesel fuel from the many gas stations around the area. That means one five-gallon can of fuel for each station where you stop. Once filled, the cans will need to be stored inside your house and not in the garage. Also, make sure the caps on the cans are tightly secured. We don't want any smell of the fuel to get outside of the house into the local neighborhood. We don't need to attract that kind of attention."

"Tell me, my brother, what else do you want me to do?"

"Before I answer, let me say that you are doing an outstanding job for our jihad against the infidels. Your efforts are going to make it possible for us to succeed in our battles against all of our enemies. What I need for you to do next, however, is to plan another trip back home to see your cousin, our brother in Mir Ali."

"I should be able to book a flight this Friday, after I finish work. Will that be soon enough?"

"Yes, that will be perfect. When you meet with him, I want you to say it is time to send us two brothers selected for martyrdom. I would like them to be here within three weeks, if possible. Both should have drivers' licenses and at least one of them should be able to drive a truck. We will also need additional funding in order to complete the final stages of our plan. An amount equal to what you brought to me last time will be just fine."

"What about when our brother martyrs arrive here?"

"They should arrive on separate flights, a couple of days apart. You should have them meet you in town, away from the airport. Pick a location you are comfortable with, a separate location, for each of them to meet you. However, stay away from George Square in the City Centre. The police presence there, and the closed circuit television cameras used for surveillance purposes throughout the square, is overwhelming. After you have met them, bring them to your house and call me as soon as you have both of them there. You should continue to use your cell phone to keep me up-to-date, for example, when you depart for Mir Ali, when you return, when we should next meet, etc. In the meantime, please continue the great job you are doing to make the remaining purchases of the components we still require."

"I would not expect to be able to meet our brother martyrs this weekend in Mir Ali, since my trip will be on such short notice. However, after they arrive here, is there anything you wish for me to convey to them?"

"Yes, there is. I would like you to tell them I will be coming to spend time with them as the time nears for the start of our holy war. We will all be together for the final assembly of the bomb at your house. Let them also know it will be my honor to bathe each of them, according to our wudu custom in the Qur'an, before we say our last prayers together and they start their voyage to Paradise."

"It will be my pleasure to tell them this news, Abdul. I will go now. Here is the package with the device you requested."

"Thank you, Wahid. May Allah guide you and keep you safe from every pain, sorrow and distress."

"May Allah bless you, Abdul."

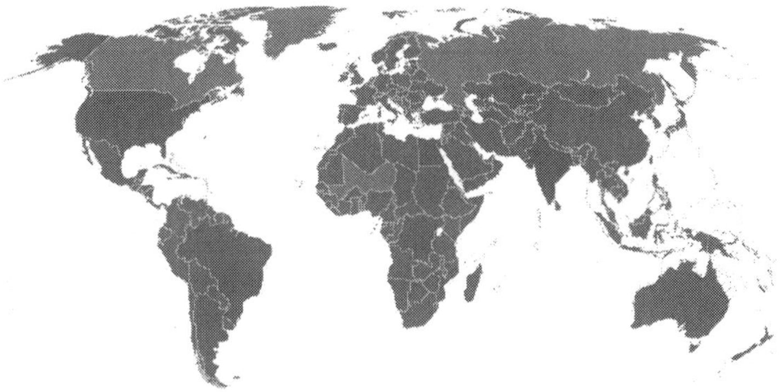

CHAPTER 33

Once again, Steve had Molly place a call to London, this time a conference call, to talk once again with his old colleague friends from Washington days, David from MI6 and Ian from MI5. Only this time he was not looking forward to what he was going to tell them. A number of years earlier, when Steve was serving as the Agency's Director of Clandestine Operations, David was the former MI6 representative, or Station Commander, at the British Embassy in Washington. At the same time, Ian was posted to the embassy as well, as The Security Service representative, which was the equivalent to the senior most FBI Legal Attaché posted to a US Embassy abroad. Steve worked hard to cultivate personal friendships with both of them, and it paid off when they all subsequently rose to their current senior positions in the US and UK Governments.

"Ian, David, I hope both of you are well," Steve said to them.

"Barely a week has gone by and I take it you are ready to live up to the promises made in your last call. Right, Steve?" David asked.

"Fellows, it looks like we all are able to play in this one. I still don't have the kind of biographic information we need, but I do have details on a terrorist operation that could be in the planning stages. I'll, as usual, have all of this papered over with an immediate cable to both of you after we finish here."

"Steve, old sod, please don't kick us in the goolies on this one," Ian replied. "May we chime in with questions as you proceed?"

"Of course, please do. Our source on this one is an Irishman from West Belfast by the name of Padraig Cahill. He is meeting with a Muslim who claims to be a Pakistani. The Muslim, only known as Ali, says he's a biologist working for a pharmaceutical company in Glasgow, where he claims to live, as well. Cahill has been pitched to join up with Ali and several other unidentified Muslims to carry out three separate operations."

"Steve, how old is your Paddy?" Ian asked.

"Our officer's estimate he is circa thirty-four years old. Cahill claims to be the nephew of the IRA's late Joe Cahill. That may help for you to clearly identify him," Steve replied.

"If that is the case, we'll have full book on the bloke. Steve, go on where you left off on the three separate ops," Ian said.

"Ali told Cahill that the first attack will be in England, the second in Scotland and the third in the US No further details were learned about where specifically the attacks would take place."

"Steve, what is the timetable," David asked.

"Mid to late February, for the first attack. That's all Cahill could get out of him."

"Methodology, Steve, what kind of attack and how is it to be delivered?" Ian asked.

"For at least the first attack, an ANFO bomb delivered by truck. Cahill, who obviously has been brought into this op because he will not attract the attention an Asian would, is to be tasked with procuring ammonium nitrate and fuel oil, leasing a house and renting a truck."

"How big is the lorry going to be?" Ian asked.

"It should be able to handle a load up to ten thousand pounds. I know where you are going with this, Ian. It sounds like the 1995 Oklahoma City bombing all over again. It does have a few different wrinkles, however," Steve replied.

"How's that?" David asked.

"Cahill was not able to learn what the initiator for the bomb is going to be, but he's been asked to obtain a two electric and two non-electric blasting caps, plus fifteen feet of det. cord."

"Blooming Christ," Ian thundered over the phone. "I next suppose you're going to tell us you're going to let this fucking Paddy give these things to these fucking Pakis?"

"Ian, we have an opportunity here to intercept them and render the caps and det. cord inert. I'd think you should be interested in doing so."

"What else are you saying I should be doing, Steve? Will we be doing it on UK soil with your people leading the vanguard?" Ian blurted out.

"Ian, take a hold man," David responded loudly. "I'm as brassed off as you are at what we're hearing. Let's hear Steve out and then we can think this thing further through. I don't like what Steve is telling us at all. Sorry my dear Yank friend, but what else might you have to make for a real dog's dinner of a day for us?"

"Cahill is back in Belfast now, where he claims he has an uncle who is an IRA quartermaster. The uncle is going to supply him with a new set of identity docs, along with the blasting caps and det. cord."

"Now you're giving us something we should be able to quickly act upon," Ian replied.

"Cahill," Steve continued, "plans on returning to Glasgow in four to five days time, and pick up the caps and det. cord from a fishing boat along the Scottish coast. He'll then bring the items to Ali somewhere in the Glasgow area."

"Steve," David interjected, "how will Cahill return to Scotland and what kind of commo plan have you set-up with him?"

"This case has moved so fast for us, we don't even have Cahill fully vetted. We have no idea how, nor exactly when, he'll come across from Northern Ireland. We have issued him nothing in the way of secure comms. Our case officer and Cahill use their cell phones with pre-arranged meeting locations, key phrases, code words, etc.," Steve replied.

"Now if that isn't a splendid cock up," Ian replied. "You've a UK citizen on your hands, this Cahill, and you obviously have recruited and trained him up to at least a minimal level. You're also tasking him but, until now, you've yet to come to us, supposedly your most friendly of liaison partners, and revealed your relationship with this Paddy."

"Ian, when we learned that these attacks are being planned against the US and the UK, we indeed went ahead and proceeded to run Cahill on our own," Steve replied.

"For all you know, Steve," David responded, "Cahill could be our own recruited penetration of the IRA, let alone being run against the radical

Islamic elements in the UK. He also could be regularly reporting to us on what your plans are for him?"

"David, that possibility has crossed our minds. Again, events have moved so fast on this one. With the prospects for an ANFO attack in the UK, and not knowing any further details of what may be planned for the US afterwards, I allowed our officers to move forward," Steve replied.

"So then, my dear Yank, how are you now proceeding, particularly as it applies to operating on UK soil?" Ian asked.

"We would like to work with you at two different levels on this one"

"You mean a joint op on our turf?" David asked.

"A joint op on the turfs of both of us," Steve replied.

"As if you have not dropped a clanger on us already," Ian said, "would you mind telling us what you are proposing?"

"I know you will not like this but, as we speak, we have two counterterrorist case officers plus a five-person surveillance team already in place in the Glasgow area."

"Bollocks you say," Ian hollered over the phone.

"Cahill says that Ali is six feet tall, about 170 pounds, light olive complexion, clean shaven, and with no facial hair of any kind. He also is extremely street smart, regularly going to the extreme to detect and evade surveillance of any kind," Steve said.

"So are a lot of the other two million Muslims we now have living here in the UK," David replied. "You better hope we get lucky and find out that one of them is a Paki biologist working for a pharmaceutical company in Glasgow, my dear Yank."

"I don't buy his story about being a biologist. He's too smart to give that kind of checkable information away to a non-Muslim. Therefore, I'm proposing that our officers already in Glasgow take the lead in finding Ali. They'll work on their own but maintain a secure commo link at all times with your own people on the ground."

"What if, by chance, you locate this Ali character before we do? What then do you propose to do?" Ian asked.

"Ali told Cahill that except for being a resident in Scotland, he is a Pak citizen. Therefore, should we apprehend him on our own, we will immediately move to render him to the US There he'll be interrogated in order to obtain full details on his plans for attacks in the UK, as well as in the US," Steve replied.

"You fucking bastard," roared Ian.

"Ian." David said. "My knickers are in a twist just like yours, but I want to know from Steve just what he bases taking that kind of action on our soil."

"David, you and Ian should both remember that five years ago, in 2007, my government made it quite clear in your Court of Appeal in London that under American law, the US Supreme Court sanctioned us to kidnap and render to the US any terrorist suspects facing criminal charges. Our law actually includes British citizens, and anyone else suspected of a crime. This applies even if a person is a resident in the UK. We want to work with you on this one and stop any attack planned in your country. Since we are already running the source of the information, Cahill, we have a chance to intercept the caps and det. cord, and render them useless before they are given to Ali. If we succeed, we may be in a position to learn the ultimate target of the attack."

"Steve, first of all, and I'm sure Ian agrees with me on this, whether you call it kidnapping or extraordinary rendition, it's a highly repugnant concept for us here in the UK. You should also note that doing so on our soil has yet to be challenged in our court system. Therefore, old sod, while I'm willing to accept working with you on this operation here, in order to prevent an attack on our soil, proceed with extreme caution and be very careful of the implications of your actions. I hope, Steve, I have made myself clear. Ian, need I ask what you have to say?"

"Bloody hell. I do have something to say. I've just had placed in front of me the long list of names of Cahill's involved in both the Troubles of the past, as well as actions against us up to recent times. Included are their mug shots as well. Amongst them is your one and only Paddy, Padraig Cahill. He was thirteen years old when the picture was taken. Another more recent picture, taken in Dublin, is probably too grainy to be used for identification purposes. A slight resemblance is there, but not all that much, unfortunately."

"Ian, can I count on you to support our people now on the ground in Scotland, as they work to intercept these explosive materials from Cahill and make a substitution?" Steve asked.

"I'll agree to it provided you give us the name Cahill will be using on his new identity documents, plus the cell phone number he is using with your people. I would also like the cell phone number of this Ali character as well."

"Ian, I can have the cell phone numbers for you in a matter of hours. The new identity is something else. Until he lands back in Scotland in that identity, and call our case officer to arrange to meet, we will not have it. Once he does so, I will have it turned over to your people there, on the spot. Cahill is highly surveillance conscious and street smart. If your people try to monitor our meeting with him, or try to intercept him, he'll get spooked and neither of us will see him again."

"Steve, as much as I detest being told how to run an operation here, I want this Ali character as much as you do. I will not allow bloody radical Islamic terrorists to commit any further acts of terrorism on our soil. The killings here in London in 2005, and the failed attempts here in 2007, followed by the Glasgow Airport incidence shortly afterwards, have totally soured me on our so-called tradition of tolerance. We used to criticize the melting pot of crime and vulgarity your country had become. Now we look at ourselves, and find we have turned into our own version of the same, with too many outcasts, particularly of the Muslim variety, safely ensconced here. This is my country and I'll not allow this extremism to go any further."

"David, I take it then that I've your support as well?"

"Yes, Steve. You do. Both Ian and I will brief up the head of Scotland Yard's anti-terrorism branch, and I'll also bring my own MI6 anti-terrorism people up to date as well."

"Steve," Ian said, "I'll go ahead and make the appropriate arrangements with our MI5 anti-terrorism people, including arranging a point of contact for your case officers in Glasgow. If you'll call back with the secure communication numbers for them, I'll have a link established with ours in Glasgow. I'll also arrange for the full cooperation of both the City of Glasgow Police and the Strathclyde Police there as well."

"Ian, thank you very much," replied Steve. "I cannot thank both of you enough."

Steve hung up the phone and sunk down heavily into the lowest reaches of his leather armchair behind his desk. He turned the chair around and looked out the seventh floor windows across the Potomac River. It was bitter cold outside, with close to a foot of snow on the ground. By the time this heated discussion with David and Ian had ended, Steve felt not heat, but the coldness outside his windows. He knew he was on the verge of losing whatever degree of friendship he previously had with two professional intelligence colleagues he had come to respect and admire.

With Ian's MI5 having responsibility for protecting the UK against threats to national security, Steve knew his security service would be the primary interface for the Agency's counterterrorism officers now in Glasgow.

David, on the other hand, was focused on his intelligence service's global covert capability to defend the national security of the UK. As such, while Ali and his co-conspiratorial terrorists were inside the UK, David's service would be playing a secondary back-up role to MI5.

The question in Steve's mind now however was, if both of them would honor their agreement to let the Agency take the lead in trying to stop Ali before he could stage his first attack. He didn't like the feeling that was swelling up in the pit of his stomach given he had just blown the identity of Patrick. With Patrick's information indicating a terrorist operation was underway in the UK, Steve took the position that his responsibility to protect the liaison relationship with a close ally had become more important than protecting the identity of the source of the information. What this would mean to Lee and Mitch's operation would now become the focus of his attention.

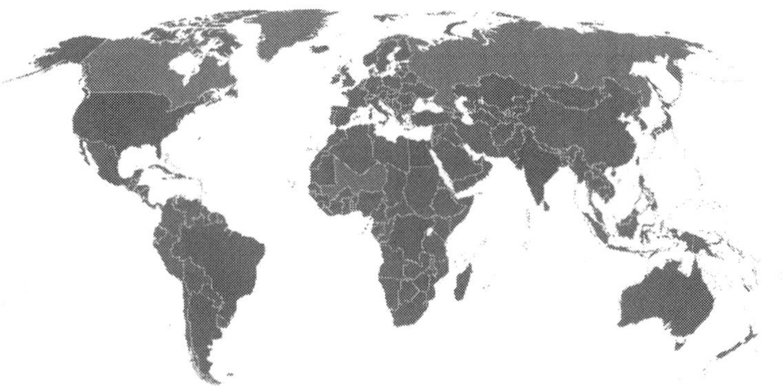

CHAPTER 34

Edinburgh Airport was shrouded in fog, and a light rain was falling, when Mitch's early morning Swiss Air flight arrived from Zurich. After receiving instructions from headquarters to resume work in the Patrick Cahill case, he wasn't pleased at all to read the cable traffic sent to the Station that papered over the conference call Steve held with his counterparts in MI5 and MI6. By revealing Patrick's identity to them, Steve placed him in jeopardy, casting serious doubt on his ability to work with Agency officers positioned in Scotland to track down Ali. It resulted in Patrick now becoming a hunted man.

With Lee arriving from Stockholm at noon of the same day, Mitch planned to link up with him in downtown Edinburgh. They worked out their game plan via secure comms the night before. It called for them to rent separate cars in Edinburgh and drive to the outskirts of Glasgow. After renting rooms in separate hotels, they would await word from Patrick that he had returned from Belfast with the blasting caps and det. cord.

Their plan was to meet up with Patrick before he called Ali to arrange to give him the explosives. This would enable Lee to substitute inert versions of the caps and det. cord beforehand. Mitch could tell from Lee's voice during their call the night before, that he could use his help in tracking Ali down after the fiasco at Glasgow Airport the previous week. Lee had the inert versions of the explosives sent to London Station by courier, and they were hand-carried to him at his hotel in Glasgow. They both coordinated their plans, again via secure comms, with the surveillance team of five that was now on-site in Glasgow awaiting instructions.

Meanwhile, Jack, in headquarters CTC, was instructed by Steve to fly immediately to London and report to the Chief of Station at the US Embassy in Grosvenor Square. Located across the street from the park at Grosvenor Square, the embassy chancery building occupies an entire city block. After arriving at the embassy, he went to the COS' office located on the sixth floor and brought him up-to-date on headquarters position on the case and the overall status of the Agency's efforts to track down Ali and break-up his plans for staging a major terrorist attack in the UK.

The COS was relieved to have a senior counterterrorism officer like Jack there to act in his place in dealings with the UK Government. With only six months remaining on his two-year tour there, the COS was in no mood to even think about a terrorist attack in the UK, much less having seven additional Agency officers running around the UK planning the kidnapping and extraordinary rendition of Ali to the US.

The COS London position is a plum assignment for the Agency's senior-most career operations officers who are usually destined to retire at the end of their tour there. The position has yet to attract an officer with any notable experience in counterterrorism operations. The current COS was no exception. Intent to finish his tour quietly, he did not relish having to deal with MI5 and MI6, much less the US Ambassador, on the subject of additional Agency officers on their soil and contemplating rendition. After talking it over with Jack after his arrival, it was agreed that the COS would handle the ambassador, while Jack was left to deal with MI5, MI6, Scotland Yard and assorted city police commissioners around the country.

Unless it became necessary to travel outside of London, Jack chose to remain there and coordinate directly with Mitch, Lee and the surveillance team leader via secure comms. Steve told Jack to stay in the UK as long as the terrorist threat remained and Agency officers were actively involved. Jack was glad to be back in the field and taking part in an ongoing operation. Supervising terrorism cases from headquarters was not his first choice of things to be doing.

By the end of the week, when Patrick was tipped off to what had happened to his family members in West Belfast as a result of the raids by the police and MI5, he set into motion his plan to turn against and wreck vengeance on the perpetrators – the fucking Yanks he previously thought were his newfound friends. With the blasting caps and det. cord in his possession, along with his new documents identifying him as Sean Fleming, Patrick found himself on the southeast coast of Northern Ireland, holed up in the fishing village of Portavogie. However, based upon what he learned from his uncle and IRA quartermaster, Joe MacKenna, a fishing village is the last place where he should be hiding.

As Joe described it, one day after giving Patrick the explosives and identity documents, all hell broke loose in West Belfast, particularly in the Andersonstown areas of Falls Road and Divis Street, where the majority of the Cahill family members lived. Fortunately for Joe, he escaped the police sweep made on family members by remaining just across the Irish border in the town of Dundalk, where he maintained one of the IRA's weapons caches. No sooner had Steve given up Patrick's identity to Campbell during their conference call, when Northern Ireland Police Service and MI5 officers raided and began rounding up all adult men, women, and children from nine years old on up, with any association to the Cahill family, and taken into custody for questioning. The sought after target was, obviously, Patrick Cahill. If Campbell hadn't acted so precipitately in ordering the raids, instead making full use of the extensive technical collection and surveillance capabilities available, Patrick may well have been uncovered and apprehended before he could go to ground.

Patrick was furious that he was betrayed. After thinking through his options, his plan was to quickly leave Portavogie and make his way south to Dublin, where he would catch the Dublin Swift ferry and slip back into the UK at Holyhead, in North Wales. Before leaving however, he removed the SIM card from his cell phone, smashed it and, along with the phone itself, threw them both away at two separate locations in the village. He knew the phone was compromised and would give away his location, and anything he said on it, to the Brits and the Yanks. He found a convenience store next to the bus station in the village and purchased a new one with one hundred minutes of talk time on it. Instead of returning to Scotland from Belfast and retrieving the explosives from a fishing boat along the coast, he would carry the explosives himself and land in the UK at Holyhead. That would give him the best chance to avoid arrest.

Best of all, Lee did not know the new alias identity he would have. He knew he was now a wanted man in Northern Ireland, the Republic of Ireland

and throughout the UK in his true name identity, or any other name for that matter. However, if he could make it back to Scotland to meet with Ali and give him the explosives, retribution against both the Brits and Yanks was a distinct possibility.

Dressed in workers clothing, and posing as a painter in his new Sean Fleming alias, he carried a heavy duty cloth satchel bag containing two one-gallon cans of paint, three assorted sized brushes, a plastic stirrer and some rags. Both of the cans contained paint, as stated on the labels. However, only one was full. The other one, instead, was only three-quarters full. In the bottom quarter of the can was a concealment device containing the caps and coiled fifteen feet of det. cord. The bottom of the can was actually a large screw cap and, when turned in a clockwise motion, it would open up, revealing the contents inside.

Arriving safely in Dublin by bus from Portavogie, he walked the short distance from the bus station to the nearby Port of Dublin. Encountering two uniformed Irish officials in the short line of passengers at the boarding queue next to the ferry, he was asked for his identifying documents. He showed them his alias Northern Ireland-issued identity card, along with a UK Passport. With electronic biometric chips on both documents that contained biographical data in his new alias, along with his fingerprints and a picture, his uncle assured Patrick that the documents would pass electronic scrutiny. However, neither of the two officials, one a Garda police officer, and the other an immigration officer, had any kind of electronic device to use in checking documents. They also had not received any kind of alert to be on the look out for someone fitting Patrick's physical description. Both officers glanced at Patrick and his picture in the passport, and motioned for him to board the ferry for the one-hour and fifty-minute crossing to Holyhead.

After arriving and disembarking the ferry, he spent five minutes walking along Victoria Road to the train station. He distinctly noted the absence of police in the area. Once at the station, again, except for one police officer standing off to the side of the entrance to the building, no other police were present. He boarded the afternoon train to Glasgow, which was scheduled to arrive there just before nine o'clock in the evening. However, along the way, he decided to leave the train at the final stop just before Glasgow, in the town of Carlisle. Rather than take the chance of the Glasgow Central Station having police there on the lookout for him, going by bus into Glasgow was a safer alternative.

After arriving in Carlisle, Patrick caught one of the National Express buses heading northwards to Glasgow. He got off on the outskirts however, in the town of Larkhall, and then took one of the many Glasgow area local buses for the remainder of the trip. Arriving at the Buchanan Street Bus Station, he immediately headed over to the west end bar known as Jinty McGinty's, located in Ashton Lane. Remembering an old friend from Dublin who six months earlier had taken a job at the bar, Patrick was hopeful she would be able to help him out with a place to stay for a couple of nights.

As his Irish luck would have it, he spotted her right away, waiting on tables. As he glanced around to see who else were amongst the patrons that late in the evening, she caught sight of him and immediately came over to him next to the bar. Sorcha McLaughlin, at thirty years of age, with long, flowing blonde hair and a pure white complexion, remained as stunning as Patrick remembered her.

"Jeanie Mac!" she exclaimed. "How are you?"

"Is that you?" he replied.

"Come here young fella," she said.

"What about ye?" he replied.

"Since I left Dublin, I've been thinking about you."

"Me too."

They embraced, and as they stepped back, he met her emerald green eyes for a lingering look. "Aye," Patrick said.

"I've got to keep working, but will you stay awhile?" she asked, and turned and went back to her work of taking orders and serving patrons.

Patrick ordered a pint and settled himself at the bar. Within an hour, the bar was starting to close down and she returned to his side.

"What brings you here?" she asked.

"I need a place to lie low for a couple of days. Can you help me out?"

"First off, answer this question: Are you still single?"

"Of course. No change for me."

"If that is the case, I have only one reply."

"What's that?"

"Stay with me."

"Thank you. I'd like that very much. But tell me, have the Peelers been around asking about me?"

"No, not at all. It would not make any difference anyway," she replied. "You are still my fella."

After the bar closed, Patrick waited for Sorcha just outside the door. A couple of minutes later, in the cold darkness of the lane with its shuttered storefronts, she stepped out through the bar's door and they walked arm-in-arm to her second story flat above an art gallery, located just three short blocks away on Creswell Lane. In what remained of the night, Patrick and Sorcha made passionate love to each other, rekindling past passion. By the time they both awoke in the mid-morning, he brushed her sweet-smelling hair from across his face, looked into those gorgeous green eyes, and said: "Wet the tea, please, you beautiful creature. You have made me a very happy man, and enough so as to wonder why I did not follow you over here from Ireland in the first place."

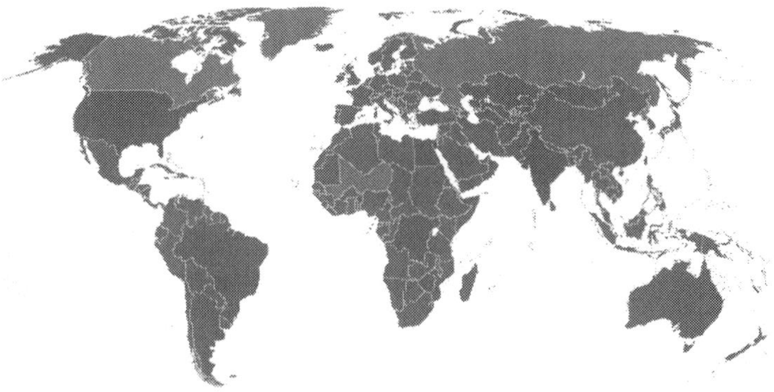

CHAPTER 35

"Peace be upon you, my brother. I almost did not make it back in time tonight to call you," Wahid said to Abdul.

"And peace be upon you also, Wahid. What happened?" Abdul asked.

"The flight was overbooked and departed late as well. With all the marriages that take place this time of year in our homeland, it is not surprising to have these travel problems."

"Nevertheless, I knew you were looking forward to attending your cousin's wedding."

"Even though I was only able to attend two of the three days of celebration, I was still glad to be there. Everything went very well and I will tell you all about it when we meet."

"How about if we have dinner together tomorrow night, at eight o'clock?" Abdul asked.

"That is good for me. Where shall we meet?"

"Let's meet at bus stop number eleven. Is that convenient for you?"

"Perfect, Abdul. May Allah bless you."

"May Allah bless you too, Wahid."

Abdul was glad that Wahid made it back from Mir Ali. He looked forward to hearing the news about the brothers who volunteered for martyrdom, and when they would be arriving in Glasgow. He finished dressing and prepared to leave for his Sunday midnight shift at the hospital.

With his plan for the attack continuing to move forward, Abdul knew he must go to great lengths to assure he was not under any kind of suspicion by the Scottish authorities. He made sure he maintained his record of spotless service at the hospital, especially after being selected to be a regular staff member there. He continued to work hard to be looked upon as a highly professional and congenial physician by all of his colleagues.

It was now almost five years ago that foreign doctors in Britain were determined to have been behind the car bombings that took place in London and Glasgow. This included a doctor from his own hospital in Paisley. Fortunately, with Abdul arriving at Royal Alexandra after that tumultuous period, his devotion to work had come to earn him the respect of the staff and elevated him to a position of being beyond reproach. He was fairly sure that, during his time at the hospital, he had been well vetted by MI5 and the local Strathclyde Police. Nevertheless, when off-duty he continued to regularly perform surveillance detection routes, on foot and in his car, to reassure himself he was not being followed or checked upon in any way.

The following evening, on Monday, he met up with Wahid at the previously agreed upon meeting site, Neelim's Indian Restaurant on Dumbarton Road in Glasgow. They greeted each other warmly, sat down at a corner table near the front windows, and ordered their meal. Wahid handed Abdul a package containing the money he requested from their brother in Mir Ali, and proceeded to report on the status of the two brothers who volunteered for martyrdom.

"My cousin was very pleased to receive your request for the two brothers. He said to tell you there's no shortage at all of brothers desirous to take part in a martyrdom operation. He expects to have two highly motivated ones seeking their place in Paradise to arrive here within no more than two weeks."

"My thanks go out to you, Wahid, for handling this most important task. Will they arrive separately, as I requested?"

"Of course, Abdul. They will arrive two or three days apart from each other. I gave my cousin two locations in Glasgow, away from City Centre, where I will pick them up and drive to my house. Once they call from the airport after arriving, we will only have to agree on the time to meet. No mention of where to meet will be necessary."

"Excellent, Wahid. How about Rashid? Do you expect to hear from him soon?"

"Yes, he should be calling me either tonight or tomorrow and will provide the latest news on the status of the entrance to our target facility. He has really become enthusiastic about running his own small business in Seascale. He said he thoroughly enjoys moving about the village and the surrounding areas, and is actually conducting enough business to appear quite legitimate."

"That is good news to hear. Be sure and let me know if he learns any new information. Now tell me, how about you? Are you up to resuming your purchases of the remaining supplies we need?"

"Oh yes, very much so. By the time our two brothers arrive from home, I should have all of your requested materials in the house. I still have plenty of space inside to accommodate everything."

"Good. Once you have the materials together, it will only take a couple of days to assemble all the components and be ready to stage the attack. All that will remain is good news from Rashid that, due to new road paving repairs, the barriers inside the entrance to the facility have been removed. As a fall back position, should the barriers be put back into place, I do have another option. It is another gated entrance that is closed and locked, and no longer in use. It is located closer to the sea, along the railroad line on the west side of the facility. It will only require crashing through the unmanned and locked cyclone fence gate to get inside the facility. However, the driving distance to the B215 target building inside is somewhat longer. Let us pray to Allah, however, that such will not be the case and we will be able to use the entrance at the main gate."

"Who will be involved in the final assembly of the bomb?"

"You, the two brothers who will soon be arriving, and myself."

"And what about the truck, Abdul?"

"It looks like I've found a European who will be used to rent it. We'll only have to keep it at your house for one or two days, in order to load it and prepare for driving to Seascale. Although the two brothers will be making the final drive through the gate of the facility to the target building, I will ask you to drive part of the way there since you are so familiar with the local roads and motorways. In order for you to be satisfied that their driving skills are up to the task, however, you can have both of them drive nearby where you live beforehand as a test of their abilities to handle a fully loaded truck.

For the final drive, however, you select which brother will drive the truck into the building and which one will sit next to him and activate the blasting machine upon impact. Obviously, you'll be getting off the truck prior to entering the target area. This will allow for you to have time to clear out and place some distance between yourself and the facility."

"How about Rashid?"

"We'll give him enough notice so that he can depart the area as well. Tell me, have you ever been to Canada or the US?"

"No, I haven't been to either. Does this mean you have further plans for me?"

"Yes, indeed I do, Wahid."

"We should finish up our dinner now and leave. You go first and take your usual precautions when clearing out of the area. I look forward to being with you again soon. Please let me know if you learn any further news from Rashid. Long life to you, Wahid."

"Blessing to you too, Abdul."

Abdul waited for ten minutes before paying the dinner bill and leaving the restaurant. He returned to his flat and expected to receive a call anytime from Patrick, saying he had returned to Scotland with the explosive materials. He thought through his plan for the subsequent meeting with Patrick and taking the materials off his hands. He actually reached a decision on Patrick the previous weekend, when he went to the east end of Glasgow and walked around The Barras Market.

On that Saturday morning, he left his car parked in the back of his flat building in Paisley, and took a local bus into Glasgow where he got off at the Kelvinbridge Underground Station. Glasgow's subway system is known as The Clockwork Orange. This is due to its distinctive bright orange passenger cars that follow a circular route consisting of two dual tracks. One track travels in a clockwise direction, and the other in a counter-clockwise direction.

Whenever Abdul went anywhere of an operational nature related to the upcoming attack, he purposely left his vehicle back at the flat. He didn't want to be spotted doing something considered suspicious and make it easy to be identified by driving his own car. So he varied his travel routine by making use of both the bus and the subway line, instead. He knew to avoid parking his car in one of the subway system's numerous parking garages. All of them are equipped with closed-circuit TV surveillance cameras. Combined with the cameras found along many of the major streets as well, there is always a possibility of being spotted and monitored by the police whenever out and about in the city.

Boarding the underground at Kelvinbridge Station, he rode eastward to St. Enoch Station. A short five-minute walk from there brought him to the entrance arch of The Barras Market, with its multitude of lanes and rows upon rows of shops and stalls numbering over one thousand in number. Spending a good thirty minutes wandering around amongst the vendors displays, he did not detect the presence of any surveillance cameras. The only uniformed police officers he noticed were two standing next to their car at the entrance to the market.

One of the small shops tucked away at the end of a rather crowded lane stocked all kinds of hunting knives; some new, some of antique value, and others, because of the low prices, probably counterfeit. He glanced at, but dismissed showing any interest, in thumb knives. Deadly and quick to bring out of the pocket; it takes no more than a simple thumb rotation to unleash the blade for ready use. This kind of knife, however, would not be suitable for the particular kind of use he had planned.

Instead, what caught his attention was the assortment of dagger knives that were on display. During his medical school training in Pakistan almost ten years earlier, Abdul was fascinated with French and Italian historical knives dating back to the Middle Ages. This interest came about while learning the correct ways to hold and make use of surgical cutting tools.

Picking up a rondel dagger knife from a display case, measuring approximately twelve inches long, he noted that its double edges were both quite sharp, and it had an ice pick-type grip handle. The Scottish shop proprietor told Abdul the blade was made of the finest hand-forged carbon steel. However, with Abdul not seeing anything stamped on the blade indicating the steel maker, or historical markings of any kind, he figured it was probably a reasonably high quality counterfeit dagger.

The handle consisted of two rondels, both oblong in shape and positioned above and below the grip. This provided a very strong grip for the hand, particularly when thrusting forward and parrying to either side. In addition, in a stabbing motion, whether it be point up or point down, great penetrating power is possible with this kind of blade. The dagger came with a leather scabbard that had a single stitched seam running up the back of the sheath.

Abdul looked it over carefully and, expressing his interest, asked the proprietor for the best price possible. When told he could have the dagger and scabbard for fifty pounds, Abdul knew he had found what he was looking for, even if it were not of any antique or real historical value. Instead, he looked upon it as strong, sturdy and able to serve its intended purpose quite well. Not wanting to appear gullible and willing to accept the first price quoted, he countered with a price of forty-five pounds, which was quickly accepted by the Scotsman. Abdul gave him the money and the proprietor wrapped the knife and scabbard in brown paper and handed it to him in a small-unmarked white plastic bag.

When he left the market, just at noon, it had become thoroughly crowded with shoppers and curiosity seekers. He took a circuitous route back to his flat by retracing his steps to St. Enoch Station, and then took a bus to the Western Infirmary, located near Queen Mother's Hospital. Checking for surveillance as he walked along the perimeter of Glasgow University over to the hospital, he boarded another bus, this time for Paisley and his flat.

* * *

On Tuesday morning, after spending a second night of passionate lovemaking with Sorcha, Patrick departed her flat, promising to be back in a couple of days. Carrying his cloth satchel bag containing the cans of paint with the concealed explosives, he stepped outside to find it was near freezing with a light fog and mist in the air. Walking several blocks away to the Byres Road shopping district, he turned northwards and headed towards the intersection with Great Western Road. Just before the intersection, he found a coffee shop that had only a few patrons inside. He went in, ordered a cup of coffee and sat down in a comfortable chair behind a small table. Half way through the coffee, he called Ali to find out where and when they would be meeting.

Still seething with rage over being betrayed, he looked forward to revenge with his newfound Muslim cohort. While having a taste of revenge and the spreading of terror against the fucking Brits, he never had an inkling he would join up with Muslims engaged in their own jihad. He could recall the stories of his legendary uncle, Joe Cahill, in particular one of how he smuggled a shipload of weapons, including shoulder-fired missiles, into Ireland from Libya. As he thought more about what his uncle had done, joining up with the Islamic cause was not such a bad idea after all.

"Ali, my friend, this is Patrick."

"Patrick. Good to hear your voice. I take it you are back in town. Did everything go alright?"

"Yes, it certainly did. I look forward to telling you all about it."

"OK. I can't remember the name, but do you recall where we last got together in that large store, the one where we sat in the front, near the entrance, and drank coffee together?"

"Sure. I remember it well."

"Good. Can you be there in about two hours?

"Fine with me."

"Let's meet then, just outside the main door entrance."

"OK. See you there."

After finishing the call, Patrick left the coffee shop and headed to the bus stop at the Great Western Road intersection. He looked over the posted routes and figured out the best way over to Dalmarnock Road and the Tesco Extra Supermarket where they previously met almost two weeks ago.

* * *

Lee and Mitch were now beside themselves. Having checked into hotels near Glasgow's City Centre three days earlier, they spent time together each day trying to figure out why Patrick had not called. They could only conclude that it had something to do with the DDCIA, Steve Capps, having revealed Patrick's identity to the Brits. Jack, still positioned at the embassy in London, was also trying to pick-up any bits of information through the station's sources, including one high value unilaterally recruited agent that was a penetration inside the Police Service of Northern Ireland.

The agent, a senior police superintendent involved in working closely with MI5, reported to his Agency case officer in London Station the initial information regarding the joint MI5 and Police Service raid against Cahill family members. Other than reporting that Patrick was not amongst the Cahill's rounded up, he had no further information. It appeared that Patrick had disappeared into his new alias identity and, like Ali, had the street smarts and operational skills to remain on the run and confound attempts to apprehend or bring him under control.

MI5's Ian Campbell, who was now Jack's primary point of contact in efforts to track down Patrick, as well as capture Ali, tried his utmost to badger him much like he tried with Steve upon learning about the Agency recruiting Patrick and running him on British soil. Jack however, could only quite honestly plead ignorance of knowing anything more. With Lee, Mitch and the surveillance team members waiting it out in Glasgow, unless Patrick suddenly reappeared and made contact, all they could do at this point was to sit on their hands.

Except for Ali now, no one knew Patrick had successfully crossed the Irish Sea and made his way back to Glasgow undetected in his new identity. Likewise, no one knew of Ali's true name identity, occupation or actual location in Scotland. Nothing was known about the other radical Muslim extremists that were part of Ali's operation either. The British, for their part, figured they had put the queer on the Agency's op following the Cahill raid. It would effectively serve to eliminate the Agency's capability to run the op on their soil. At headquarters, Steve, believing he had covered the Agency's ass by revealing Patrick's identity, could now only question his action and whether anything was left of an op gone sour, as if it was much of an op in the first place.

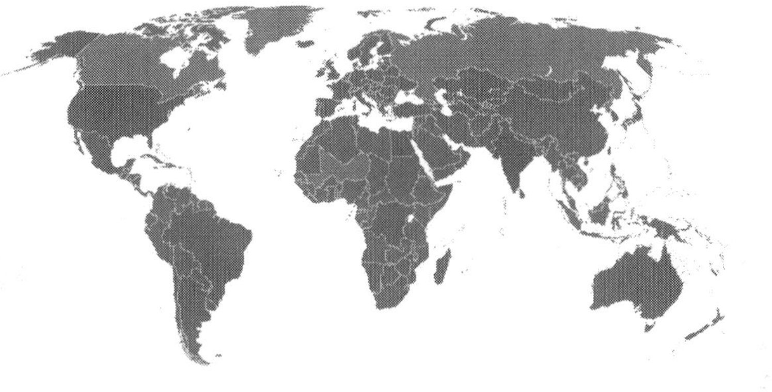

CHAPTER 36

Ali stood just inside the large glass entrance door of the Tesco Extra, waiting for Patrick. It was a cold and blustery morning with the temperature several degrees below freezing. The heat coming from the overhead air blower felt good and he did not mind the wait. He glanced outside the door and looked to his left across the parking lot toward the fish and chip shop where he would be sending Patrick for their meeting. He could barely make out the shop's sign on the rooftop above the vehicle traffic flowing by on Dalmarnock Road.

At 11:35 am, he spotted Patrick stepping off the bus that had stopped at the entrance to the parking lot directly in front of the store. Patrick was carrying in his right hand a brown cloth satchel. As Patrick walked across the parking lot toward the entrance door, Ali checked for anyone else getting off the bus or getting out of a car from behind the bus. Seeing no one, he then scanned the parking lot for any cars that had just pulled in, particularly any where the people remained in the vehicle. Again, noting no one else, and believing Patrick to be free of surveillance, Ali stepped outside the entrance and moved about ten feet away from the door to his right, towards Patrick.

"It's good to see you again," Ali said.

"And I'm very happy to see you too," Patrick replied.

"I've a spot picked out for us to have lunch together. I'd like you to walk alone over to my left, and go straight ahead to the far side of the parking lot. When you reach the street, turn right and go to the intersection with Dalmarnock Road. There, if you look across the road to your left, you will see a shop about fifty meters up with a sign on top of the roof. The sign says Fish and Chip Shop Andrea Crolla. Go inside and take a seat. The shop is just opening up for lunch. I will be coming in behind you in a couple of minutes."

Without turning his head to look in the direction Ali asked him to take, Patrick nodded his head and headed off.

Ali turned around and walked back into Tesco Extra. He noted that Patrick was proceeding to the side street at the end of the parking lot. At that point, two people, a male and a female who were together, walked past Ali and exited the store. As they proceeded straight ahead to their car in the parking lot, Ali fell in a dozen paces behind them.

When he reached the road, at the parking lot entrance, he glanced to his left and caught sight of Patrick crossing the intersection of the street with Dalmarnock Road, and headed towards the fish and chip shop. Not seeing anything unusual in the movement of people on foot or vehicles heading towards Patrick, Ali crossed over the road and turned to his left to walk in the direction of the shop.

Having been in the shop a month earlier, Ali was familiar with its layout. It consisted of a small counter in the front, for ordering and picking up take-out meals, and eight tables, with chairs, for eating inside. The kitchen was in a closed off area behind the counter. On the right side of the shop, behind the tables, was a hallway along the wall leading to the restrooms in the rear.

As he neared the door of the shop, Ali checked the placement of the rondel dagger, in its scabbard, that was duct taped to the left arm of his shirt inside his winter jacket sleeve. He wore the dagger in the scabbard upside down, with the handle grip nearest to his wrist and hand. The sharp stiff tip of the dagger securely pointed upwards towards his elbow. He was comfortable carrying the dagger this way and had practiced many times over the quick removal of it from the scabbard while wearing his jacket.

Ali entered the shop, and could see that Patrick had seated himself at one of the tables along the right hand side, against the wall. Ali knew from his previous visit that a young man served as the waiter, while the apparent owner of the shop was the cook back in the kitchen, as well as handling the cash register behind the counter. He could see the cook in the back, but did not see the waiter at all. Patrick was the only patron seated inside. This boded well, he thought.

The cook had his back turned and was busily working in the kitchen area. The aroma of hot cooking oil permeated the air. As he neared the table where Patrick sat, they made eye contact. Ali glanced at the satchel bag next to the chair. He nodded his head in the direction of the restrooms in the rear and began walking toward them. Patrick stood up, picked up the bag and followed behind Ali. It appeared to Ali that he might well have been able to enter the shop and walk past Patrick toward the restrooms without anyone else seeing him, including the cook in the kitchen.

The first door down the hallway was to the men's restroom. As Ali reached it, he took the door handle in his right hand, took one step back and opened the door so that Patrick, with the satchel bag in his right hand, could enter first. The small restroom consisted of one urinal, one toilet behind a metal door and metal wall partition, and a washbasin.

Once both of them were inside, Patrick pulled open the metal door to the toilet to see if anyone was inside. He turned to Ali and said, "It looks good. We're alone."

He then set the bag down next to the metal partition, with his back to Ali. He had to stoop down somewhat to place the bag on the floor. Although Ali could not see the contents of the bag, it was obvious that what was inside was reasonably heavy. Patrick straightened back up, saying to Ali, "I need to show you how to unlock the bottom of one of the cans inside."

"Go ahead, let's see," Ali replied.

With that, Patrick stooped over to undo the leather latch on the bag. Ali, looking down at Patrick's back and exposed neck sticking out from the top of his jacket, delivered a strong rabbit punch with the back of his right hand to the cervical area where the top of the spine meets the head. Patrick sagged forward and dropped to his knees on the floor. He reached out with both arms in a futile attempt to prevent his head from going all the way down and hitting the floor just in front of the urinal.

Although momentarily stunned and not totally unconscious, he went down seeing nothing but bright flashes, like soundless fireworks in the sky, going off inside his head. Knowing that he had to move quickly, Ali used his right hand to slip the dagger out of its duct-taped scabbard from inside his jacket sleeve. Seeing Patrick starting to stir but still facing the floor, Ali leaned over and, using his left hand to hold Patrick down by the shoulder, plunged the blade of the dagger downward its full length to the rondel on the guard. The blade penetrated all the way through the triangle of the trapezius, collarbone and neck. With the tip of the blade penetrating the brain stem and pithing the brain, all that remained was to slide the sharpened blade horizontally to the left and then back to the right, much as the motion used when shucking an oyster. Patrick died instantly as his spinal cord was severed.

Using a knife to sever the spinal cord in the cervical region, Ali selected what is probably the most reliable method to produce instant death. He had initially thought of severing the jugular vein and carotid artery on either side of the windpipe, but dismissed this method due to the large flow of blood that would immediately spurt out all over the place. It reminded himself of an emergency surgical procedure he had performed at the hospital the previous year on a severely injured woman. In that case, he combined an aortic value slicing and root remodeling for an ascending aortic aneurysm that turned out to be a very messy operation. Unfortunately, the patient died on the emergency room table.

Ali stood upright and surveyed the floor and his clothes to see how much blood had spread around the area. Wearing black shoes, dark blue pants and jacket, he appeared untouched. With a large pool starting to form on the floor around Patrick's face and neck, Ali reached for the bag of explosives next to the body and lifted it upwards and away before any of the blood could reach it.

He set the bag on top of the ridge of the washbasin, looking it over to make sure no blood was visible on it. He then rinsed off the blood from the blade of the dagger with water, and wrapped it in five pieces of paper towel taken from the dispenser on the wall. Placing the paper-wrapped dagger inside the bag and closing the leather latch shut, he looked himself over closely in the mirror to be sure he could not see any telltale signs of the violence that had just taken place. He took two more pieces of paper towel from the dispenser and wiped off the faucet handle used to turn on the water and rinse the blood off the blade.

Ali took one last glance back at Patrick lying face down on the floor in front of the urinal. The pool of blood on the floor was quickly increasing in size around the body. He checked the bottoms of his own shoes for blood and to make sure he left no footprints on the floor.

Carrying the bag in his left hand, he quietly opened the door of the men's room. Using the two papers towels to wipe down the handles on both sides of the door, he walked down the hallway towards the front door of the shop.

Pocketing the paper towels in his jacket pocket, he looked at his wristwatch. It was 11:55 am and no other patrons were in the shop, either seated at the tables or standing at the counter. Not wanting to make any kind of eye contact with the cook in the kitchen, he did not even glance back as he opened the door and stepped out into the freezing cold wind blowing outside.

Turning to his right and walking eastward further down Dalmarnock Road, away from the direction he originally came from, Ali did not notice the young male Scot waiter crossing the street to enter the shop. Arriving just in time to start his noon to 8 pm shift, the young man was not looking forward to another day of waiting on tables and smelling the hot oil that got increasingly pungent as the day and evening wore on. The waiter paid no mind to the lone individual coming out of the shop carrying a bag and heading away from him.

Opening the door of the shop, glad to get out of the cold wind, the waiter went into the kitchen where he reported to the cook for work, hung up his winter jacket and donned an apron. He made his way amongst the empty tables of the shop and down the hallway to the men's room to wash his hands. There were curdling screams as the waiter ran from the men's room down the hallway and into the kitchen where he collapsed on the floor in front of the cook.

Leaving him sobbing on the floor, the cook ran to the men's room and took in the bloody carnage of a dead man lying in a massive pool of blood in front of the urinal. Without touching anything except for the doorknob to enter the room, the cook ran back to the kitchen and dialed 999 for emergency services. The young waiter had picked himself up off the floor of the kitchen and was sitting in a corner chair, his sobbing reduced to low-murmured whimpers.

By the time the Strathclyde Police and Scottish Ambulance Service vehicles arrived eight minutes later, Ali was on a bus heading in a northwesterly direction back toward the center of Glasgow. By 2:30 pm, after two additional bus rides, he made his way back to his flat. After spending thirty minutes in the bathroom carefully examining all of his clothes and shoes, checking for any traces of blood, he burned the paper towels from his jacket pocket and those used to wrap his choice of weapon for the murder of Patrick, the dagger. He would now have to give some thought as to how to securely dispose of the dagger soon. The scabbard and duct tape used to hold it to his shirtsleeve, he decided, would be taken to work with him that evening at the hospital, and placed inside an extreme high-heat incinerator used for tissue disposal. As he laid down to rest up before his midnight shift, he quickly dozed-off believing he had left the Fish and Chip Shop Andrea Crolla unseen and successfully disposed of the only threat to his jihad operation so far, Patrick Cahill.

* * *

Sorcha, after finishing up her work late that night at Jinty McGinty's, walked home in the cold, starless night, wondering when she would be able to see Patrick again. If only they had been able to spend more time together and build a lasting relationship back in Dublin, she thought. At last, she believed Patrick was the one she could spend the rest of her life with, loving him to the fullest. She did not sleep well that night, tossing and turning and, occasionally, crying to herself.

* * *

Lee and Mitch spent a good part of that evening in Glasgow's west end pub, Uisge Beatha, for drinks and dinner. They both were still at a loss to explain the absence of contact with Patrick. With no way to determine if he had returned to Scotland, or where he would be staying if he did, they had nothing to go on. Repeated attempts to call him on his cell phone were fruitless. As best they could determine, the phone was out of service.

Early the next morning, Lee received a call from Jack at the embassy in London. Jack gave him the direct telephone number for the Chief Constable of the Strathclyde Police, and said to call him as soon as possible. Apparently, the body of a man murdered in a fish and chips shop in Glasgow's east end had become an anomaly in terms of learning his real identity. He told Lee to fill Mitch in on their conversation and noted that since Glasgow was still viewed as the most violent, crime-prone country in the developed world, followed by England and Wales, chances were there was no connection to Patrick.

Lee called Mitch and, within fifteen minutes, he was knocking on Lee's door. After giving him the details of Jack's call, Lee called the Chief Constable's office and learned that the identity card and passport found on the murdered man's body identified him as being from Northern Ireland. A birth record existed in the name of Sean Fleming that exactly matched the birth date found on the identity documents of the murdered man. However, according to a thorough check of the records in Belfast, the Sean Fleming with the same birth date died when he was two years old. Other records existed with the same first and last name, but none having a birth date that was even close to this one.

The constable gave Lee the name and telephone number of the Detective Chief Superintendent in charge of the Strathclyde Police's violent crime unit, suggesting he call to learn any additional details. Lee and Mitch quickly concluded that further details were indeed needed and agreed that Lee would be in the best position to go to the police since, being an inside operations officer, could reveal himself to the Strathclyde Police for follow-up.

Prior to calling the detective in charge, Lee called Jack in London and filled him in on the information learned and the plan to meet with the detective for further details and to provide any assistance that might be necessary. Jack concurred with this plan of action, but warned Lee about dealing with not only the Scottish authorities, but any MI5 types that might show up as well. Obviously thinking of MI5's number two, Ian Campbell, Jack wanted Lee and Mitch to be fully aware of British sensitivities of Agency officers treading on their soil.

Lee next placed a call to the detective in charge and arranged to meet with him early that afternoon at Strathclyde Police Headquarters, located in downtown central Glasgow. Arriving precisely at 2 pm, he was ushered into the detective's office and introduced to William MacKay.

"Detective MacKay, a pleasure to meet you. I am Lee Denning."

"Call me Billy. Lee, how do you do? The pleasure is all mine."

"Billy, I am an operations officer with the CIA's Counterterrorism Center. Have you been briefed on my presence here in Scotland and what I have been doing?"

"Oh yes, indeed I have. My colleagues in MI5 have been all over my superiors on this one. In fact, I had to stress to them that we are only in a very preliminary stage on identifying the body that was found yesterday. I also told them, particularly the MI5 blokes who love to jump into our knickers and interfere, that with our climbing violent death rate due to booze, drugs and knives, this one is probably in no way connected to your case."

"I am glad to hear that. How can I be of assistance?"

"Lee, I would like you to look at a couple of very grainy pictures I have here that were faxed over from Belfast late this morning. They show a young man named Patrick Cahill, the chap you are handling and trying to run against radical Islamic terrorists here."

Lee looked closely at the two pictures, neither of which were direct face shots. Beside being old and very grainy, both were taken at oblique angles that only showed the sides of the face more than anything else.

"I can see some similarities to Patrick but not conclusive," Lee said.

"OK. Now here is the photo ID and UK passport of the murdered man, Sean Fleming."

"Oh, my God. This is Patrick."

"For the sake of positive identification, I would like you to accompany me downstairs to view the body."

"Certainly," Lee replied.

"Have you ever done this kind of identification in the past?"

"Yes, a couple of times in agent cases and operations I have handled."

Lee went with Billy downstairs to the Glasgow Central Morgue, where he positively identified the body as Patrick Cahill. Seeing Patrick lying on a stainless steel table, laid out face up, was a terrible shock to Lee.

"Billy, what can you tell me about the cause of death?"

"Our lead forensic physician has listed the cause death due to the severing of the spinal cord in the triangle of the trapezius with a long sharp bladed instrument, probably a knife or dagger. The blade entered the back of the head at the bottom of the brain stem."

"What a horrible way to die," Lee replied. "What else can you tell me about the circumstances? Has anyone been apprehended or found to be involved in the murder? Also, what was found with the body?"

"The doctor told me that death was instantaneous and a very large loss of blood occurred on the toilet floor. He was not robbed. His wallet, money, a watch and a ring, were found on the body. We don't have a motive so far. What is it you're looking for that might have been in his possession?"

"Unless he was able to stash it somewhere, he may have been carrying explosive materials."

"I was not aware of that. The MI5 types are not all that informative with us sometimes, particularly regarding what I've heard about this case."

"I'd like to stay in touch should any further information be developed. Can we exchange cell phone numbers?"

"Of course, Lee. Oh, by the way, the doctor also said it appeared that no struggle was involved. To me, that means that since the entry of the blade or very sharp instrument was in such a precise location from behind, Cahill might well have known the person who attacked him. This person may also have some medical knowledge."

"Like being a doctor or a medical technician?"

"That is a possibility. This isn't the typical booze and blades case."

"Billy, thank you very much for what you have done to help me understand what has happened here."

"Lee, you have my number. Don't hesitate to use it if I can help you out in any way."

Lee proceeded upstairs from the morgue, grateful to step outside into the cold afternoon air and clear his head. First, he called Jack to give him the bad news, and then Mitch to arrange to meet back in his hotel room. They had a lot to talk about but not much at all to consider in terms of where the operation would proceed to next.

Lee knew that he and Mitch would be in full agreement on the major aspect of what had happened to their operation. Namely, the fucking loonies in MI5 had acted prematurely in conducting their raid on the Cahill's in Belfast. It resulted in spooking Patrick into fleeing back to Ali without first calling to arrange a meeting to switch out the explosive materials. What was shaping up as an operation with an agent serving as a penetration of an Islamic terrorist group, had been reduced to knowing a terrorist attack was being planned, explosive materials were in the process of being assembled, and nothing could be done about it.

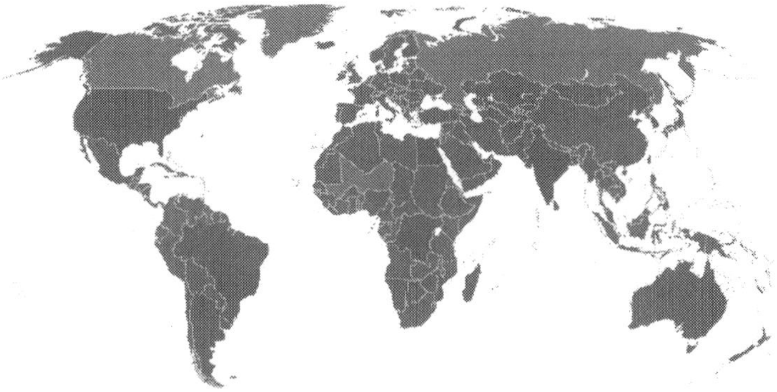

CHAPTER 37

Lee and Mitch speculated that if Patrick believed they betrayed him, he might have decided to jump ship and join up with Ali, for real this time. That could explain why he did not call after arriving back in Scotland. Whatever the case, the Agency and the British had both lost out and faced the possibility of being unable to prevent Ali and his brothers from attacking.

They reminded themselves that British liaison and the police authorities had to be brought into the operation and know what the Agency was doing. However, when an opportunity presents itself of penetrating a terrorist group, an intelligence organization like MI6 is much better prepared to understand and run a penetration operation through to a successful conclusion of preventing an attack. MI5, on the other hand, being more concerned with protecting national security and the British homeland, exhibited a thoughtless thug mentality in this particular case and proceeded with the raid to capture Patrick instead. The failure of MI5 leadership to think through the results of their action and consider the benefit of allowing Patrick to return unimpeded to meet with Ali, left a situation that was going to turn critical.

* * *

The following day Jack had the unfortunate task of talking with MI5's Ian Campbell on a secure phone at London Station.

"Jack Benson here. What can I do for you?"

"This is Ian Campbell. I take it you're still the chap speaking for Steve, your number two at Langley. Is that correct?"

"Yes, that's right, Director Campbell. I'm still assigned to liaise with you on this potential terrorist attack unfolding in the Glasgow area. I'm the Agency's counterterrorism officer responsible for penetrating radical Islamic terrorist groups."

"I like that, a potential terrorist attack." Campbell replied.

"Sir, I believe I am up-to-date on events leading up to the murder and the identification of Cahill yesterday in Glasgow. Do you have any new information?"

"Hell with new information. I rounded up the bloody bastard's family but, unfortunately, just happen to have missed out on catching your Paddy . Too bad about what happened to him, but what do you expect when they are all working against us?"

"Did it occur to you." Jack replied, "that with the raid on the Cahill's in Belfast, and the subsequent murder of Patrick Cahill in Glasgow, we may well have lost all chance of running down the Muslim terrorists planning to wreck havoc on your country?"

"How dare you question what we determine is the best course to insure our internal security. Where in the fucking bonkers do you get off, Yank?"

"No one is questioning what you can do on your own soil. We happen to be here working to stop an attack not only upon your country but possibly ours as well. Do you understand what I am saying to you?

"Look Yank, we agreed to a joint operation that allows you to run amok around our country trying to stop what you purport is going to be an attack against us. However, while we will provide any support you require, we'll see to it you don't get out of hand. Am I clear on this score?"

"Yes sir, that is quite clear. It is just unfortunate however, that you didn't have the foresight to avoid interfering with our meeting with Cahill so that we could have switched out the explosives and continue on with a good chance of a solid penetration of this terrorist group."

"What do you mean a good chance? That chance has fallen to the way-side at the foot of a pisser in a fish and chips shop. You are in my country now, Yank. I control what you and your fucking people are going to be able to do from here on out. Don't forget it."

"I will forget it because you don't have a clue about what it takes to track down a determined Muslim terrorist that is intent on killing people and destroying property."

"Well, I do believe we have cleared the air a wee bit. You know what, Yank? I'm looking forward to meeting up with you one of these days. What do you say? It will be interesting to see you face to face."

"Let's instead wait for a few more days and give our officers in Glasgow time to regroup and see where we go from there."

"You make it sound as if you people are the only ones that know what is happening up there. Tread lightly, my friend. We are closer to you than you think. Keep me informed."

"My pleasure, Director Campbell."

* * *

As soon as he had gotten word that Lee had identified Patrick's body, Campbell pulled together the sparse leads on Ali and his plans provided by the Agency, and ordered his MI5 subordinates to coordinate with police forces throughout the UK in running these down. He was intrigued by the manner in which Patrick died: namely, the skillful placement of the dagger blade into such a vulnerable spot at the top of the spine where it meets the brain stem. This could well indicate knowledge of human anatomy. Campbell surmised that Ali probably did not give Patrick an accurate description of himself, and fabricated a cover story instead. This includes the possibility that Ali may not even be a Pakistani. Therefore, starting with the greater Glasgow area, Campbell ordered that a list be drawn up of all Asian and Arab males with biological, pharmaceutical, and medical backgrounds. In particular, he wanted to know who these individuals are and what were they doing at the time of Patrick's death, sometime around noon on Tuesday.

An additional lead worthy of follow-up is the major component for the bomb: ammonium nitrate fertilizer. All commercial outlets selling fertilizer, along with companies and organizations making use of large amounts of it, were to be identified and contacted, again, starting with the Glasgow area. Campbell realized this was going to be a long list that would require a lot of footwork on the part of law enforcement officers. Nevertheless, a lead is still a lead and he knew it has to be run into the ground.

As for the use of a truck to transport the bomb, all truck rental firms were to be contacted to determine if a person of Asian or Middle Eastern descent had rented a truck with a capacity of around ten thousand pounds. This will be a shorter list, Campbell surmised, but definitely could be a solid lead for follow-up. Noting what Ali told Patrick about the timing for the first attack, mid to late February, the rental firms would be queried on trucks currently out for rent, as well as being alert to any new reservations placed for a truck starting around the middle of the month.

Lastly, he considered the ultimate target for the attack. It was the one bit of information that Ali never revealed to Patrick, at least according to what the Agency has said. As a result, according to Campbell's way of thinking, speculation and imagination now come into play, including taking past terrorist attacks worldwide into account. Due to what appears to be plans for a large bomb, a target that involves killing many people would be a distinct possibility. Major indoor and outdoor sporting events and concerts, taking place during the latter half of February, for example, would be taken into consideration as potential targets.

With only a two-week window now, leading up to mid-February, Campbell knew that time was not on the UK Government's side. As for dealing with the Agency in his directives for following up on these few available leads, he decided he would closely monitor their activities but not directly involve any of the Agency people currently in-country at all. He knew that the Agency indeed has some unique capabilities that could be brought to bear through the seven officers currently in Glasgow. However, by holding them at arms length while on British soil, he would be able to remain in control. The only capability that was used by both the UK and US Governments in this operation was the highly effective monitoring of phone calls. He could live with that since he had no choice. In the end however, he believed, the dogged work of MI5 and police authorities throughout the UK would prevail, and they would be able to apprehend all of the Muslim extremists involved in this planned terrorist attack against the UK

* * *

Jack, Lee, and Mitch soon knew they were being totally kept in the dark by MI5, MI6 and the local police authorities. Jack placed a call to Steve at headquarters, asking him to query MI6 directly, based on his excellent relationship with their Deputy, David Neville. Unfortunately, Steve reported back that MI6 was sitting this one out on the sidelines due to MI5's in-country jurisdiction on all internal security matters.

With nothing tangible being gleaned from telephonic intercepts of calls in and around Scotland, Lee, Mitch and the five surveillance team members were basically on their own to try and run down Ali. Lee used his newfound relationship with Detective Chief Superintendent Billy MacKay to see if he could provide any useful information. However, according to what Billy told him, he had no real access to the orders coming out of MI5. All he could tell Lee was that extensive legwork on the ground was taking place involving MI5 and police forces throughout the country. He said that pharmaceutical firms, medical institutions, fertilizer dealers and truck rental firms were all being queried about involvement of any kind with Asian and Arab males. Unfortunately, he added, he was not aware of any results. He would let Lee know should he learn anything more, but he did not hold out much hope.

Forty-eight hours after Patrick's death, Lee held a meeting in his hotel room with Mitch and the surveillance team. After looking over detailed street maps of Glasgow and the surrounding area, they decided to divide the total area up into seven quadrants, one for each of them. Maintaining regular contact with each other using their secure transceiver phones, they would drive individual streets, and in some cases walk through particular areas, checking to see if any Asian or Middle Eastern males they noticed warranted further attention. That was about the best they could do given the few leads that had to go on.

Included in their efforts would be looking for rental trucks, and who was driving them, plus following anyone fitting the profile who looked like they were doing something of a suspicious nature. In the evening hours, they would shift their attention to residential areas, particularly where they spotted Asian or Middle Eastern males, since they concluded that the materials for the bomb would take up a lot of space and a home or garage would be a likely choice for storage and assembly purposes.

Prior to setting off for their assigned quadrants, Lee called Jack, in London Station, and advised him of their intentions.

"Jack, Mitch and I have met with the team and decided to conduct a detailed search of Glasgow and the surrounding area for a one-week period. After that, if nothing of interest turns up, we will re-group and consider shifting to other parts of Scotland, if not head southwards into England."

"That sounds good. How will you divide yourselves up?"

"Each one of us will cover a specific quadrant and maintain regular contact so that we can come together should something of interest be spotted."

"How about giving me a call every other day?"

"Will do. Have you learned anything more from headquarters?"

"No, not really. I know you and Mitch are upset about Steve revealing Patrick's identity to MI5 and MI6."

Jack knew from the pause on the line that Lee was not particularly interested in going over this issue.

"Jack," Lee replied, "I can't believe what Steve did. It explains a lot about what has happened here, but I still can't believe he would do this to our operation."

Following another pause, during which Jack could hear Lee talking to someone, Mitch came on the phone.

"Jack, this is Mitch. Do you realize that what we now have left is virtually nothing? A liaison relationship is one thing, but I fail to understand the price we have paid for it. And Jack, also look at the price Patrick paid for it."

"Mitch," Jack said, "I understand how you guys are reacting and, believe me, I can share your anger as well. But, Steve made the decision and went ahead anyway. I do know that he didn't feel right about it either."

"Jack, rest assured Lee and I will slog onward. To what, and to what end, I'm not sure. Unless we spot something, and soon too, this op is all but over. Goodbye, Jack. Talk to you later."

Mitch turned off the phone and handed it back to Lee. They ended the meeting with the other team members and encouraged them to start the search of their assigned quadrants.

"Lee," Mitch said, "I feel like we've been fucking over royally. Done in and betrayed by the very organization we owe our allegiance. What have you got to say?"

"I completely agree with you but, you know what? It's happened to someone else before us, and it will happen again to someone in the future. It's the fucking nature of the beast."

"If I were Steve," Mitch said, "I would have handled it differently and probably never gone to the Brits in the first place. But, that's not the way we play it sometimes with our allies. In this case, while Steve no doubt was optimistic that a better response was on the horizon, the Brits charted a different course."

"I couldn't agree more," Lee replied.

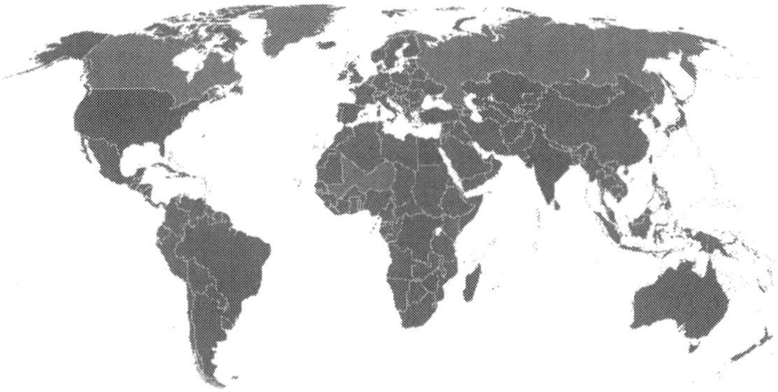

CHAPTER 38

The call from the hospital administrator's secretary came through to Abdul as he was finishing his midnight to 8 a.m. shift and getting ready to return to his flat for some much needed rest. A number of traffic accidents and burn cases brought into the Accident and Emergency Section had kept him busy throughout the night. The secretary apologized for the request, but asked him to return to the hospital at 1 p.m. for a meeting with Strathclyde Police officials who were conducting a series of interviews.

Knowing better than to panic at prospects of a police interview, he nevertheless felt quite sure it had something to do with the death of Patrick. This served to further convince Abdul that the decision to eliminate him was the correct one. When he was meeting with Patrick upstairs in the pizza shop of the Buchanan Galleries Building, his suspicion that the Irishman was being run against him was just too much to let pass by. He felt sure that when he followed him into the men's room, he caught him finishing up a call on his cell phone. If he had not gone to check on him, Patrick would still be alive and serving as a penetration of Abdul and his jihad operation.

Abdul finished work and returned to his flat. Before lying down to sleep, he went over in his mind the cover story for meeting with the police in the afternoon. If he were asked about his whereabouts on the day of Patrick's death, he would maintain that following his shift at the hospital he returned to his flat alone and slept for at least six hours. That would provide an uncheckable alibi that would cover him at least until two or three in the afternoon. A check with his neighbors, should any of them happen to have noticed him returning from the hospital, would confirm that between eight and nine in the morning, he parked his car in the back of the flat building and entered for his usual morning rest after his shift.

Recalling what happened in the UK during the 2007 bombings, he knew that obviously, once again his hospital in Paisley was under investigation due to the number of physicians and technicians having Asian nationalities. He believed he would have to rethink his upcoming plans for the attack based upon the information he previously revealed to Patrick. The police would be looking for Asian or Middle Eastern males, accumulations of fertilizer and explosives, plus the use of a rented truck.

Having rested for several hours, Abdul departed his flat and drove the short distance to the hospital for his 1 p.m. appointment. The incriminating evidence left behind in the flat – the blasting machine, detonator caps and det.cord – were secreted away in a hollowed-out hole underneath a twelve inch by twelve inch piece of parquet flooring and the sub-flooring in the darkened hallway between the bedroom and living room. He was satisfied that the skill he used in making the flooring removable would be unnoticeable. The other incriminating items that would link him to Patrick's death were already disposed of safely. During the early morning hours of the day following the murder, the cloth satchel bag, the scabbard, duct tape and paper towels were all disposed of in the hospital's incinerator. Using a hammer in his kitchen, the dagger itself was broken into three pieces and thrown into the River Clyde at three different locations. One piece he threw into the river nearby the Clyde Maritime Centre. The second piece he threw off the quay below the Finnieston Crane on the north bank. The third piece he threw into the river along the quay at the Braehead Shopping Centre.

Having been ushered into the offices of the hospital's Chief Administrator, Dr. Angus McGurk, Abdul was directed into the conference room next door where he was introduced to three Strathclyde Police officials, including Detective Chief Superintendent Billy MacKay. The interview started with Dr. McGurk introducing Abdul as a superior physician with five years of exemplary service that included having recently been made a permanent staff member. Dr. McGurk then left the room and what followed were twenty minutes of the kinds of questions Abdul had fully anticipated. With no surprise questions asked and no difficulty at all in answering those that were posed to him, Abdul was told the interview was over and he could leave.

On his way out of the hospital, he stopped by the Accident and Emergency Section to say hello to his colleagues working the eight to five shift. He confirmed that every one of the forty-seven physicians and technicians of Asian and Middle Eastern nationalities on the regular staff there either had been interviewed already or were scheduled to be. This did not include several dozen more physicians who were serving as consulting physicians to the hospital.

Having no illusions that he was no longer under suspicion, Abdul returned back to his flat fully alert and on guard. Being placed under surveillance was a distinct possibility, as was having his flat and personal possessions scrutinized in his absence.

Over the next three days, while awaiting the latest word from Wahid, Abdul kept a low profile, going to and from work and running a limited number of personal errands around the local community of Paisley. When Wahid finally did call, Abdul was glad that he had a pre-arranged meeting time and location chosen instead of needing their usual procedure of mentioning a numbered bus stop as the key to where they would ultimately meet. Should their phone conversations be monitored, it made more sense to change and vary their meeting arrangements and avoid sounding too cryptic or secretive sounding during their conversations.

Wahid sat down in the booth opposite Abdul at The Royal India Restaurant located in the Southside Glasgow district of Newton Mearns. Abdul could tell from Wahid's effusiveness that he had good news to report.

"Rashid called last night and he had new information. In addition, one of our martyr brothers arrived yesterday and I brought him to my house last night. I am also pleased to report that I have all of the needed materials inside the house and ready for assembly."

"I could tell from your voice on the phone," Abdul replied, "that you had this kind of good news. Splendid, my brother. Now, tell me the details."

"Based upon our pre-arranged list of topics we would discuss over our cell phones, Rashid was able to get across to me that the truck with a crane on it that he previously was tasked to look for, has been placed next to the inside of the gate entrance to the target facility. It would appear that it will be used to remove the concrete traffic dividers in order to resurface the roadway inside and outside the gated entrance."

"How did you leave it with him on reporting further progress at the entrance?"

"I asked him to call me as soon as the barriers are moved off to the sides and the entrance roadway leading into the facility is straightened out, with no barriers to impede a rapid drive through the gate."

"If it takes another day to remove the barriers, that would be followed by bringing into place all of the equipment necessary for the removal of the broken surfaces of the road and preparing it for re-surfacing. That should give us the weekend after that as our target window for launching the attack," Abdul speculated.

"Yes, that would seem to be about right. How long will it take us to assemble the materials in the truck and be ready to go?"

"With all of us working non-stop late in the evening, we should be able to have the truck ready to go in just a matter of a few hours."

"That means next weekend, on a Saturday or Sunday, is a good possibility."

"Yes, I agree. My primary concern is having a straight drive through the entrance and a weekend timeframe when the area is quieter, with less traffic and people being around."

"When do you want me to rent the truck?"

"We have a change of plans for the truck. I recall you telling me in the past about the vehicles that your parks service employer in East Kilbride maintains and you use on a regular basis."

"Yes, I normally work from either a van or small truck, but sometimes I drive a larger truck."

"Since you don't work on weekends, do these trucks remain unused at the storage site?"

"Yes, and we make sure that every Friday, before we finish work, we have all the vehicles fueled and ready to go on the following Monday."

"What about the keys for these vehicles?"

"Duplicates and some triplicates for all the keys are hung up on a wall inside our office at the site. However, occasionally someone forgets and takes the keys home over the weekend. But, it is not considered a serious mistake since the trucks are seldom used during the weekends."

"Would you be able to enter the gated area on a Friday or Saturday night and drive out one of the trucks of the size we need?"

"I could do it, but I would not have a plausible excuse for doing so. If I was caught in the act, and I said I needed a truck to move some possessions, for example, it would probably cost me my job on the spot."

"As you know though, after the weekend you won't be going back to your job anyway. Therefore, are you confident you could do it anyway and not be caught removing the truck either of the two nights?"

"Yes, I am quite sure. All of us groundskeepers have our own keys to the gate. I will just need a moment or two in the office at the end of a Friday afternoon to remove a set of keys from the board on the wall."

"If the roadwork at the facility's entrance in Seascale goes according to plan, next Friday night, or Saturday night at the latest, will be the date for you to remove a truck and drive it to your house where we can do the assembly of the bomb for our jihad."

"May Allah bless you, Abdul. We have a plan."

"Now, please tell me about the brother you brought to your house last night."

"His name is Hamza. Hamza Masood. He asked many questions that I had to defer until you can meet and talk with him. When will that be?"

"I was hoping to be able to meet with him, and the other brother due to arrive shortly, as soon as possible. However, I may have to wait until I come to your house next Friday or Saturday for the assembly work. Can you keep him occupied in the meantime?"

"Of course, that should be no problem. He said he spent today reading the Qur'an, praying and watching an occasional TV program. I should think it would be the same when the other brother arrives in a day or two. As you have instructed, I will keep them inside the house until we are ready for them. Hamza appears very serious, introspective and intent on his mission to reach Paradise."

"I hope, Wahid, you understand what this change in plans for the truck will mean for you."

"Yes, I believe I do. I will still do most of the driving to Seascale and only turn the truck over to our two brothers a few miles before the target. I have a simple map for them to follow and will see to it they fully understand the directions to the main gate. They will also have the map and directions you had me prepare for them to use once inside the gate. I will have them memorize the buildings to drive by, the number of streets to take, and the necessary turns in order to reach the target building. It should actually be easy for them to follow."

"Thank you, Wahid. I will see to it they understand how to operate the blasting machine once they are ready to impact the building. I will also show you how to arm it just before you leave the truck. Now tell me, what are your plans once you get out of the truck?"

"I will get out of the truck in one of the villages before Seascale, one that has a train station heading south towards London. If I can time it right, I should be on the train before our brothers hit the target building. Once in London, I have a very close cousin who will take care of me for a day or two, until I can leave the UK and make my way back home to Mir Ali. With Allah's blessing, I will make it there and look forward to being with you again soon. What are your plans, Abdul?"

"Similar to you, I also will get out of the country as soon as possible and make it back home as well. Make sure you have enough money available to live on and for your travel, as long as you think necessary. Let me know if you need any more."

"I hope that when we meet up back home you will include me in your next jihad operation. I now have the address for my cousin who lives in the US. This is the cousin I told you about previously. I hope to be able to personally introduce you to him. If that is not possible, all you have to do is mention my name and tell him his father lived a glorious life of which he should be so proud. That will signal to him that he is to fully cooperate in whatever you ask of him."

Wahid handed him a slip of paper with the name and address of his cousin. Noting that the address was in Herndon, Virginia, he asked Wahid, "This is your cousin that works at Washington Dulles International Airport, correct?"

"Yes, he is the one who works as a maintenance engineer there and is responsible for heating and air conditioning equipment throughout the airport."

"Excellent, Wahid. You continue to do well in all that I ask. Long life to you. May Allah guide you in all that you do. Please let me know when you have further word from Rashid. Peace be upon you, Wahid."

"And peace be upon you also, Abdul."

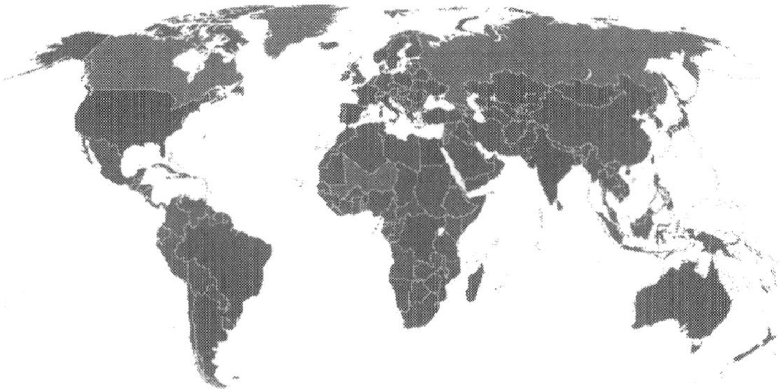

CHAPTER 39

With the arrival of the second martyr, Salman Jafari, at Glasgow International Airport on Sunday evening, Abdul's team was now complete. All that remained was word from Rashid in Seascale that the main gate barriers at the target facility were removed. With that, the last remaining task of bomb assembly could take place and the attack would be launched.

Wahid picked up Salman late Sunday evening in downtown Glasgow and drove him to the house in Larkhall. There he joined up with Hamza and they spent their few remaining days together indoors in prayers, meeting with Wahid in the evening after he returned from work. Each evening he brought the finest of halal foods to the house and the three of them enjoyed each other's company as they talked late into the night.

Abdul continued his graveyard shift at the hospital, more alert than ever to being under the watchful eye of MI5 and the local police. Twice during the week, he thought he caught a glimpse of people sitting in cars inside the hospital parking lot as he exited in the morning to drive back to his flat. The cars did not follow him, but on one of the two occasions, upon arriving at the flat, he noticed a car with two people sitting inside parked nearby.

Midway through the week, Wahid called Abdul to say that Rashid had called with good news. The barriers had been removed and it was a straight drive through the main gate. The repair of the road surface would start next and should not take more than a day or two. As a result, Abdul selected Saturday night for the assembly of the bomb, with the attack on the B215 target building mid-morning the next day, on Sunday.

Abdul's plan was to drive his car to the downtown area of Glasgow and leave it there early in the evening. From there he would make his way by bus and on foot to Wahid's house in Larkhall. If all went according to this plan, Abdul would never return to his car, much less his job at the hospital. Instead, after the dispatch of Wahid, Hamza and Salman in the truck, he would go by bus to the airport where he would catch an early morning flight to Amsterdam, ostensibly to attend his brother's funeral. From there, he would make his way back to Pakistan a day or two later.

* * *

For Mitch, Mike and the surveillance team members, it was turning out to be an uneventful week. A number of times each of them spotted either rental trucks or people of interest. However, each turned out to be a dead end. A multitude of Clarkson, Thrifty, Portman, Ryder and Enterprise rental trucks were spotted in the Greater Glasgow area, all to no avail.

Patrick had reported that his earlier meetings with Ali all took place during weekdays and during daylight hours. Combining that with the method of Patrick's death being the skillful placement of a knife blade, Mitch and Lee surmised that Ali might be a hospital worker. All seven members of the team spent four days hanging around hospitals in the area. They focused on late evenings, when swing-shift personnel would be getting out of work, and early morning hours, when graveyard personnel would be finishing work. Once having surveilled a particular person to see where they lived, one of them would remain behind to wait and watch to see where that person went and did when not working. However, considering the thousands of Asians and Middle Easterners living in Scotland, including many working in the medical field, this became a thankless task.

On a number of occasions, a team member believed they had found a person of interest for follow-up. Other members were subsequently called in and they formed a four or five person team that was able to mount both foot and vehicular surveillance efforts against the person to see what might turn up. Again, no results worthy of additional follow-up.

Late in the week Mitch found himself driving in South Larnarkshire, a part of the greater Glasgow area that includes the city of East Kilbride. This had not been a good week for him at all. A gnawing feeling in his stomach, the uneasiness in his mind, all serving to convince him that Steve had royally screwed up the operation by giving up Patrick to the Brits.

The successful practice of espionage, Mitch learned when dealing with agents and targets of interest, is to make glory of vice. If you can't cheat, lie, steal, bribe, suborn, burglarize, mislead, seduce, blackmail and kill successfully, you are in the wrong business. Manipulating the agent, by whatever means possible, is standard practice. But being manipulated by your superiors instead, left Mitch feeling used and dangling on the end of a line.

Braking for a stoplight at a four-way intersection, a small step-up delivery-type truck pulled alongside him on the left side of his car. He glanced over to see who was driving, noting it was an Pakistani appearing male. Looking toward the back of the truck, he could see it was not in the ten thousand pound weight capacity class. Besides, it was not a rental vehicle either. The truck was dull white in color and had no writings or markings on the side. Instead, an emblem was on the driver's side door. Underneath it were the words, East Kilbride Park Services.

Mitch looked back up at the driver. Their eyes met for a few seconds. Mitch could see that he was clean-shaven with medium length wavy black hair combed straight back. He judged his age to be between thirty and thirty-two years old, with no distinguishing marks on the face. Mitch nodded his head up and down, as if to acknowledge the driver's presence, or as a form of greeting. The truck driver, while looking straight at Mitch, did not return the gesture, but instead briskly faced forward as the light changed.

After proceeding through the intersection, Mitch slowed down and dropped back behind the vehicle. The truck slowed down and proceeded to make a right turn into a large park entrance area with a sign in front saying, Calderglen Country Park. Mitch continued to drive straight ahead, not giving any further thought to what had occurred, except for what he observed about the man's face. By instinct and his constant operational work over the years, it was easy for him to remember a face, especially after being able to lock on it for a few seconds.

Continuing on for another couple of miles, Mitch drove past Hampden Park Glasgow, which includes the Scottish National Football Stadium. With a seating capacity of just over fifty-two thousand, the stadium holds both major football events as well as many sold out concerts featuring world-class performers. Mitch thought of kind of toll in human lives a truck bomb could do to such a stadium. He headed back toward his hotel with another day of negative progress behind him, further cementing in his memory bank the image of the Pakistani driver's face.

* * *

It was just past four in the afternoon on Friday when Wahid called Abdul. By a pre-arranged choice of words, Wahid said it was unfortunate but he would not be able to meet Abdul for dinner on Saturday night. It turned out he would have to work all day on Saturday, plus into the early evening hours because of a major preparatory effort to prepare a city garden for a botanical show due to start on Sunday. Abdul replied that they should try to reschedule for dinner the following weekend. That was the extent of their brief conversation.

Those words indicated to Abdul that Rashid had reported in with additional news meaning that with the barriers temporarily removed, and a straight drive through the main gate now possible, that the weekend would be the best time to launch the attack. Starting on the following Monday, the repair work on the roadway would take place and in the meantime, except for the metal chain-link gate at the entrance, nothing would hinder a straight drive through the gate. This also meant that Abdul, having the next two evenings off, would not be due to report back to the hospital until Sunday night at midnight. With that, he called the hospital to tell the supervisor on duty in the administration office that his brother, who lived in Amsterdam, had passed away. Abdul said he would be leaving for the funeral the next day and would not be reporting for duty until midnight on Tuesday.

After all of Abdul's planning, plus the dedicated work of Wahid and the valuable contribution on the part of Rashid, it was all now coming together in the final culmination that would result in the launching of their jihad operation. Within thirty-six hours, Abdul would be giving instructions to Hamza and Salman, resulting in their martyrdom and new life in Paradise. In forty-eight hours, he would be in The Netherlands where he would see the results on TV and all the newscasts about the horrific destruction caused by a major terrorist bomb attack at a British nuclear reprocessing facility. Shortly after that, he would be back in Pakistan and his home village in North Waziristan

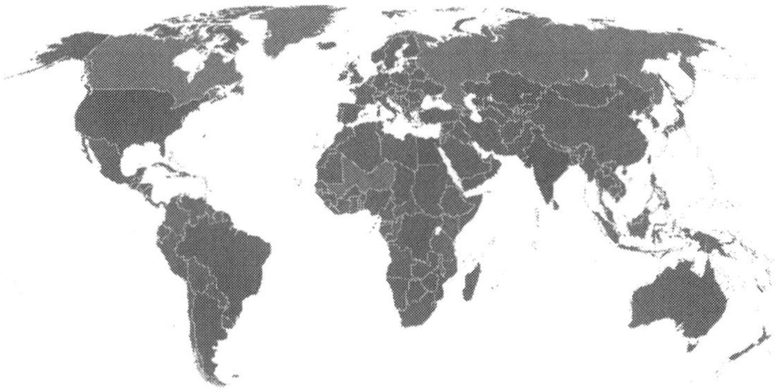

CHAPTER 40

Leaving his flat on Saturday evening for the last time, Abdul carried a garment bag containing his personal items, a suit and two sets of business casual clothes. Separately, in a supermarket shopping bag, he carried the blasting machine, four blasting caps, a stick of dynamite and coiled det.cord. He drove his Vauxhall Tigra into downtown Glasgow after determining the route he had taken left him surveillance free. By the time he parked the car, walked to a bus stop and rode south to Larkhall, it was nearing 9:30 pm. Walking the remaining distance to Wahid's house, he arrived at 9:50 and found Wahid, Salman and Hamza all in high spirits and a celebratory mood.

Meeting with Salman and Hamza for the first time, Abdul immediately noticed the level of deference and respect they showed towards him. Obviously, Wahid prepared them well in advance as to all of the planning and work that had gone into the operation. After sitting down and sipping glasses of warmed, sweetened tea, Abdul explained what they all would be doing for the rest of the night in preparation for launching the attack.

Wahid apologized for not having the truck available beforehand in order to have Salman and Hamza show their driving skills. Having just arrived at the house with the truck an hour earlier, after taking it from the storage yard in East Kilbride, he did not want to chance taking it back out on the streets of Larkhall with the two brothers inside it. But, he explained to Abdul, earlier in the week, before Salman had arrived from Mir Ali, he took Hamza out one evening and had him drive his car around the local area. As a result, Hamza would be the driver of the truck for the attack, once they arrived near the Seascale area.

Not wanting to take up any more time sitting in the house, Abdul said that their first task was to load the truck with the empty plastic barrels and fill them with fertilizer and fuel oil taken from inside the house. After that, he said he would configure the det. cord around as many of the barrels as possible, starting with the first row of barrels placed inside the cargo compartment behind the cab. The blasting machine would be set-up inside the cab of the truck with two long firing wires ready to be connected to the two terminals on top of the machine. The other end of the wires would be run through a small hole in the back of the cab into the front of the cargo compartment box where they would be connected to the blasting cap that was to be inserted into the stick of dynamite.

After all of these tasks were completed, he said they could rest for a short while and then proceed with the Wudu' ablution washing ritual, as their act of purification and preparation for their final morning prayers together. Wahid said that he had checked the prayer schedule in the Glasgow latitude for the next morning, and the time for the Fajr, or first dawn prayer, was at 5:46 am. With that, they all went about their tasks as assigned by Abdul.

Wahid had the truck backed up all the way into the rear of the driveway and up against the open doors of the garage near the kitchen door and backyard of the house. The height of the back of the truck was six inches higher than the garage door opening.. They worked in silence and almost darkness, guided only by a limited amount of ambient lights from the neighborhood and star lights in the sky. With all of the twenty barrels stored inside the house, Abdul and Wahid carried them out through the back door of the kitchen and into the garage where they placed them inside the rear of the cargo compartment. Salman and Hamza then placed them four to a row starting against the front wall behind the cab.

Next, they followed a precise recipe to obtain the correct ratio of fertilizer to fuel oil. In order to enhance the level of explosion and achieve the maximum destructive effect, the major source of oxygen is found in the fertilizer beads. Abdul directed Salman and Hamza to empty four bags of fertilizer, at fifty pounds apiece, into each of the barrels. This was followed by pouring exactly four gallons of fuel oil into each of the barrels. The fuel oil would serve to provide the only explosive compound in the bomb so far. With each of them using an oar, they proceeded to stir the fuel oil around the fertilizer beads inside the barrels, turning the contents into a slurry mixture. By adding four more bags of fertilizer and four more gallons of fuel oil to each barrel, stirring as they went, the barrels were filled to the brim and the desired slurry consistency was achieved.

By the time all twenty barrels, in five rows of four barrels each, were inside the truck and loaded with fertilizer and fuel oil, three hours of dedicated work in silence had passed by. They worked in unison with each other, with Salman and Hamza filling all of the barrels and doing the stirring.

Once all the barrels were filled, the plastic covers were tightly secured on top of each. All of the two hundred bags of fertilizer that Wahid purchased were used to fill the barrels, along with 160 gallons of diesel fuel oil. Based on Abdul's calculations, the overall bomb weighed almost exactly ten thousand pounds. When looking at the space inside the cargo compartment however, the barrels did not completely fill the inside of it. Four feet of empty space remained between the last row of barrels and the rear doors of the truck. To keep the barrels in place, and prevent them from shifting during the drive to the Sellafield facility, Abdul took six of the long coils of canvas straps hanging inside the truck and tied them down to the slats that ran along the sides of the compartment. This would serve to hold the barrels securely in place.

With Jafari and Hamza going inside the house to wash off the residue fuel oil and fertilizer beads from their hands, Abdul climbed inside the cargo compartment and, using an ice pick, opened up a small hole in the front metal wall of the compartment, just above the first row of barrels. From there, he continued pushing the ice pick forward into the back of the metal wall of the cab. He then took a screwdriver and poked it through the holes to enlarge them to a quarter of an inch in diameter. This was accomplished soundlessly, metal on metal, by slowly forcing the screwdriver through the holes of both walls and into the cab.

Next, he took the ends of two five-foot long metal firing wires and poked them through the holes from the compartment into the cab. Taking the ends of the two wires in the compartment, he attached them to the two leg wires extending from the end of one of the electric blasting caps. With Wahid looking on and acutely observing every move that Abdul made, he took the screwdriver and proceeded to gouge out a two and a half inch long hole into one end of the stick of dynamite. Inserting the blasting cap into the hole, he duct-taped the wire end of the cap to the dynamite. He then duct-taped the dynamite to the side of one of the filled barrels located in the second row behind the cab.

Taking the fifteen-foot long coil of det. cord, he wrapped it around as many of the inner barrels of the first three rows as possible, ending up with each end of the cord next to the dynamite. This was followed by duct-taping the two ends to the dynamite, as well as taping the cord to each of the barrels it passed by, about one-third down from the top of their rims.

Abdul explained to Wahid that when he was nearing Seascale, and planned to leave the truck in Hamza's hands for the final portion of the drive to the target, he would have to climb back inside the compartment to check and make sure everything inside was still in place. He would need to be sure that the wire coming into the compartment from the cab was still attached to the blasting cap and all of the duct taping was secure as well.

With Salman and Hamza returning to the garage, and looking on very attentively, Abdul placed the blasting machine inside the cab of the truck and showed Salman how to use it. He explained that by holding it upright in one hand and strongly depressing the attached handle against its side, an electrical current would be generated to the two terminals on top of the machine. As they neared the main gate entrance to the facility, he was to take the two wire leads coming through the hole of the cab and attach them to the two terminals. This would complete the arming circuit for the now fully assembled bomb.

In the final act of martyrdom and achieving their entrance to Paradise, Abdul explained that just as Hamza was about to crash the truck into the side of the B215 target building, Salman was to quickly and strongly depress the handle of the machine to set off the bomb. As Abdul spoke these words to them, he studied their eyes. Judging by what he could see, he understood their deep commitment to Islam and determination to succeed in their martyrdom. They both seemed relaxed and had a look of inner peace on their faces. He was so impressed by what he saw that he wanted to talk with them further about their preparation for the roles they would be performing. However, standing in the garage next to the truck was not the place to do so. They closed the door on the back of the truck, as well as the doors of the garage, and all went back inside the house.

It was three-thirty in the morning. Salman and Hamza went to their bedroom where they placed clean sets of clothes on their beds in preparation for the Wudu washing ritual. Hamza undressed first and went into the bathroom where Abdul was waiting for him. This act of purification would be done before their last time of praying together. It involved the washing of separate parts of the body three times each. The hands were first, followed by the mouth, nose, face, arms, head and hair, ears and finally, the feet. Abdul dutifully cleansed Hamza as an act of honor to bestow upon a brother soon to be martyred. After Hamza was finished and returned to the bedroom, Salman came into the bathroom and Abdul repeated the honor on him. Afterwards, Wahid went into the bathroom and cleansed himself, followed lastly by Abdul.

With all four of them in clean clothes, they reassembled in the living room where Wahid had their prayer rugs on the floor facing east, in the direction of Mecca. This room would serve as their temporary mosque for this final act. At precisely 5:46 am, they began their prayers, starting with the Salah ritual prayer, followed by the Fajr, or dawn prayer. One hour and ten minutes later, the prayers ended at just ten minutes before sunrise.

With both Salman and Hamza tucking small versions of the Qur'an into their shirt pockets next to their heart, they were ready to begin their journey that would end with the pressing of the handle on the blasting machine, thus opening the door to Paradise. Earlier in the evening, Wahid gave Hamza a map and a simple set of directions for what to do upon crashing the truck through the main gate at the Sellafield facility. He went over it several times in order to satisfy himself that Hamza should not encounter any problems following it.

Abdul had hoped to talk further with Salman and Hamza about their Shahada, or concept of martyrdom. As a physician and a scientist, he was curious about the level of dedication and spiritual commitment they had made. However, after watching their faces earlier, when he was explaining about the use of the blasting machine, as well their personal manner of performing the washing ritual, he realized the totality of commitment both of them had already made. No further discussion on his part would be appropriate.

First, Abdul spoke to Wahid. "Allah Almighty is your guardian and caretaker. May you remain safe from every pain, sorrow and distress. Peace be upon you."

"And peace upon you also, Abdul my brother," Wahid replied.

They firmly shook hands and then Abdul turned to Salman and Hamza, saying, "May Allah bless and guide you. God is Great."

Together they both replied, "Peace be upon you, Abdul."

With a bright morning sun rising above the horizon behind them to the east, the three of them, with Wahid driving, rode west for three blocks before turning south and onto the M74 Motorway heading for the town of Carlisle. Abdul, bundled up in a warm jacket to ward off the early morning cold of February, walked east to the local bus stop. Carrying his bag of clothes and personal items, he was seeing Glasgow for the last time as he made his way to the airport and the short flight to Amsterdam.

Maintaining a consistent driving speed of fifty miles per hour on the M74 to Carlisle, followed by forty to fifty miles an hour on the A596 and A595 to Gosforth, Wahid expertly drove the heavily laden truck in a smooth, steady manner. After two hours and forty minutes of a trouble-free ride, he told Hamza to get ready to take over and drive the rest of the way. Reaching the village of Gosforth and taking the turnoff for Gosforth Road, he pulled over to the side of the road. He showed Hamza on the map how he was to follow the road westward, straight into Seascale. From there, he pointed out on the map where to turn northward and head past the golf club to the main gate at Sellafield.

Wahid stepped down from the driver side of the truck and walked to the rear, where he opened the back door. Climbing inside, he made his way to the front where he checked all of the duct taping and the wires running from inside the cab through to where the blasting cap remained attached to the stick of dynamite. Satisfied that everything was secure, he dropped out of the compartment, closed the door and walked around to the passenger side where Salman was sitting. He opened the door and stood up on the step and looked at Salman. Wahid asked if he was comfortable in knowing what had to be done in attaching the two wires to the leads on top of the blasting machine.

Salman smiled and said, "Brother Wahid, all is well and I know just what to do. We will not fail, that's for sure. We'll see you one day in the future."

Hamza leaned over and said to Wahid, "Long life to you, brother Wahid. Keep your efforts going to establish our Islamic Caliphate. Peace and happiness to you."

"Peace be upon both of you, my brothers," Wahid replied.

Carrying a small bag of his personal belongings, Wahid made his way back to the motorway, walked under the overpass and into the quaint Cumbrian village of Gosforth. Within a few minutes, he was aboard the Gosforth Minibus heading southeast to Ambleside. He figured that within ten to fifteen minutes, Salman and Hamza would have entered Paradise. He glanced at his wristwatch. It was twenty minutes past ten o'clock on a quiet, cold and rainy Sunday morning.

Purposely driving easily within the local speed limit, at twenty-five miles per hour, Hamza drove down Gosforth Road into the scenic seaside village of Seascale. As he made his way through the village towards the Irish Sea, the weather was taking a turn for the worse. The rain showers increased as he neared the beach area. The morning air had turned overcast with dark, cumulus clouds filling the sky and a distinct chop showing on the sea. Reaching the end of the road at the far west end of the village, he turned right and headed northward toward the Sellafield facility.

Salman held the map and printed directions in his left hand, and the blasting machine cradled in his right hand. Protruding over his left shoulder, between him and Hamza, were the two wires coming into the cab from the cargo compartment. They both had smiles on their faces as they drove past the Seascale Golf Club, nearing the main gate at Sellafield.

By this time, Wahid, still the lone passenger riding in the rear of the minibus, was heading eastward, out of the area and just past the village of Boot. His thoughts turned to Rashid. He had given Rashid just over twenty-four hours notice of what was going to happen with a call that he expected a cousin from Islamabad to arrive the following day, probably in the morning. Those words would tell him to leave the area. He had previously instructed Rashid to throw away his cell phone just before leaving as well. Wahid knew he no longer had any way to check on his whereabouts. However, he was optimistic they would soon be together again in Mir Ali or one of the nearby villages of their homeland.

Turning left off the road and into the access road in front of the Sellafield main gate, Hamza could see ahead for sixty yards to where the metal gate was closed across the road. Except for the gate itself, he did not see any barriers, concrete or otherwise, on either side that would prevent a drive straight through. As he speeded up to gain as much momentum as possible in driving through the gate, the only thing he noticed was that the road surface was slightly rippled and mottled in preparation for re-surfacing. It was not noticeable enough, fortunately, to cause the truck to have to slow down.

Barely glancing to his left at the guardhouse next to the closed gate, he smashed the truck straight through, splintering metal shards from the metal chain links and supporting metal rods; forcing them forward, up and into the air, as well as to both sides of the truck.

The slumbering guard inside the gatehouse barely had time to look up upon hearing the truck bearing down on the gate. By the time he stood up, the truck was half way through in the shattering, shrill sound of metal upon metal. Grabbing for his British-made L1A1 SLR automatic weapon, the 54 year-old, overweight guard barely had time to click off the safety and loose a burst of ten rounds before collapsing back against the gatehouse door.

Neither Hamza or Salman heard or felt the impact of two of the ten rounds that struck harmlessly into the rear door of the truck. Both rounds hit high in the door at an upwards angle and pierced through the top of the truck. With Hamza calling out distances and buildings he could recognize on the map Abdul had given them, they drove straight ahead for 230 meters to an intersection with two buildings on each corner of the left side of the road. Braking and slowing down from forty-five to fifteen miles an hour to make the left turn, Hamza felt in full control of the truck. He also knew they did not have much more than seconds to reach their target, building B215.

Recovering alongside the gatehouse, the guard stood back up straight and reached for the walkie-talkie on his belt. He could feel his heart pounding in his chest, as if it would burst through his shirt and jacket and he would die instantly. Alone, with no other personnel from the facility in sight, he called both of the roving security patrols that were on duty for the Sunday dayshift. Both patrols, consisting of one man each in a Land Rover, and also carrying L1A1 SLRs, were at opposite ends of the Sellafield site consisting of four hundred buildings squeezed into four square miles of land. Both patrols quickly responded to the guard's call for assistance. He told them the truck that crashed the gate went straight ahead down the entrance road and took a left turn at the first intersection. He was unable to provide any further information except to say he thought the truck was white and traveling at a high rate of speed.

Having made the left turn, Salman told Hamza to continue to drive straight ahead, until he reached the second right turn. The distance to the turn would be 460 meters down the road. They passed a number of buildings and plants along the way and, after turning, only 165 meters remained to their final destination. Again, with more buildings on both sides of this road, Salman said he was able to see the B215 target building on the left side at the next intersection. He had Hamza increase the speed of the truck and head straight ahead.

The security guard driving one of the Land Rovers spotted a truck coming directly toward him, but it was more than half a mile away. The truck was just starting to turn right for the remaining 165 meters to building B215. The guard, not knowing the intention or final destination of the truck, would be nowhere near the truck in time to do anything about it.

Coming to the final intersection, and reaching a speed of forty-five miles an hour, Hamza angled the truck to the left side of the road as he crossed the intersection and into the small empty parking lot area up against building B215. Surprised at how easy it had been to crash through the main gate and get this far into the facility, Salman, who had already screwed the two wires from behind his shoulder into the terminals on top of the blasting machine, held it tightly in his right hand.

With the truck now hurtling across the parking lot in its final few seconds of earthly existence, Salman turned his head toward Hamza. Knowing they would be entering Paradise together, in fulfillment of their commitment to jihad against the infidels, Hamza likewise fixed his gaze on Salman. As the truck was about to hit the corner of the L-shaped building, they smiled at each other and cried out in unison as Salman depressed the handle of the blasting machine, "Allahu Akbar" – God is great.

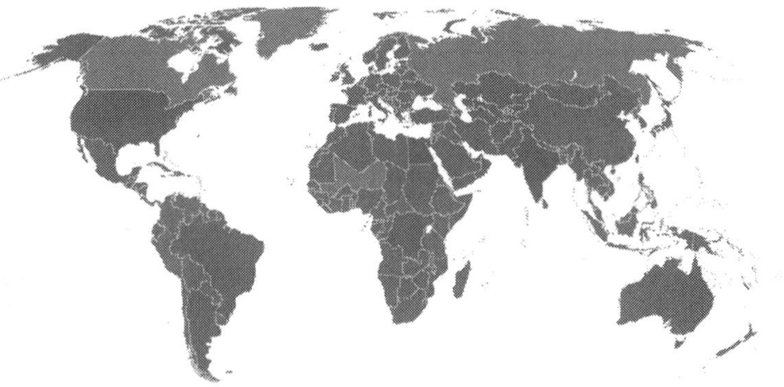

CHAPTER 41

The resulting blast, as the truck struck the five-story building at the bottom left side of the "L," shook the ground violently as a mushroom-shaped fireball immediately rose two hundred meters into the cold, windy and rainy morning air. The truck and its total contents were instantly vaporized. The entire northwest corner of the building disappeared.

The explosive impact sliced through the thin outer metal skin of the building like a hot knife through butter. Inside this corner of the building, the forward momentum of the blast directly affected a five-inch thick walled-off room of concrete that held thirty-five above-ground steel casks full of liquefied high level radioactive waste. These tightly sealed casks, in the recently enlarged concrete room, contained reprocessed nuclear fuel waste in the form of uranium and plutonium, in one the most dangerous concentrations of radioactivity known to humanity.

Of all the buildings in Sellafield, B215 was considered the most critical since it held the largest inventory of nuclear materials in all of Europe. Of all the areas inside the building, this corner at the bottom of the L, containing the concrete room of steel casks, was considered the most sensitive. Inside the casks were just over 1,800 cubic meters of hot, acidic liquid waste. Within the liquid was over 2,700 kilograms of the highly radioactive isotope cesium-137.

The impact from the blast popped the tops off three of the casks nearest the corner of the building, immediately spewing the contents upward into the column of smoke, fire and debris that quickly rose into the atmosphere. Four additional casks remained intact but were blasted out of the concrete room and into the nearest of two forty-foot deep pools of water taking up most of the rest of the space inside the building. The remaining twenty-eight casks, bruised and scarred from the effects of the blast, stayed in place in what remained of the shattered concrete room.

The two pools inside the building contained highly radioactive spent fuel assemblies that consisted of additional cesium-137. Following the explosion, the oxygen-rich ammonium nitrate fertilizer beads fueled the resulting fire. The potential existed that with the subsequent fireball tumbling over and around the concrete room, a major conflagration could occur that would spread throughout the building. If either of the two pools had been damaged, causing cracks that resulted in the loss of water, the exposure of the spent fuel assemblies to air could lead to a catastrophic fire. Since a fire of this kind is inextinguishable, it could rage on for days until burning itself out. If that had happened, more cesium-137 would have been released into the atmosphere.

However, such was not the case. The actual triggers used to ignite the bomb, the stick of dynamite and the det.cord, were not powerful enough to take full advantage of the large amount of oxygen inside the fertilizer beads. Building B215, although severely damaged, remained standing and the two pools intact, as the surrounding countryside quickly become highly contaminated with radioactivity.

As the smoke, debris and cesium-137 rose into the air, they mixed in with the cold rain and strong winds blowing from the southwest off the Irish Sea. It resulted in the cesium-137's deadly atmospheric plume blowing all the way across the north of England and all of southern Scotland. Cesium-137 has a half-life of thirty years. Coming down out of the atmosphere, it strongly adheres to whatever it lands upon – people, animals and the land – giving off intense amounts of beta and gamma radiation.

Several studies were written up years earlier, all postulating on the after-effects of major releases of radioactivity on the populace and the land. One study was done on the explosion of a steel tank of high-level waste at Chelyabinsk, in Russia, in 1957. Another study was done on an accidental release of radioactivity from an accident at Sellafield, in 1977. In addition, a study was written on the major release of radioactivity from the deadly

Chernobyl reactor accident, in Russia, in 1986. All three of the studies would be looked at again, in depth, as a result of this terrorist attack upon Sellafield's B215.

The British Nuclear Fuels Limited complex at Sellafield would never be the same again. The size of a small town, it comprised many different kinds of facilities and plants for the production and processing of nuclear fuel. The facility also served as the storage site for reprocessed spent fuels. Spent nuclear waste at Sellafield was not just from UK power plant reactors, processing and enrichment facilities alone. Highly toxic waste was brought in by the shiploads to docks at the site from BNFL's clients in the countries of Germany, Switzerland, The Netherlands, Italy, Spain, Sweden and Japan.

* * *

The KLM non-stop flight from Glasgow to Amsterdam took off on time at 9:30 am, barely an hour before the attack at Sellafield. Abdul, sitting in economy class, felt content, relaxed and satisfied in knowing he could do nothing further to assure the success of Hamza and Salman. Arriving at Schiphol Airport at 10:50 am, he proceeded into the immigration arrival hall and presented his passport and UK identity card to one of the officers on duty. Not being a national of one of the European Union countries, he was required to pass through one of the non-EU member booths in the hall.

Amsterdam Schiphol Airport is one of the most securely maintained airports in the world, thanks to the Israeli firm that oversees the security controls and screening system used throughout the facility. Abdul purposely chose Schiphol as his gateway into the European mainland, on his way back to Pakistan, and he had his cover story rehearsed and at the ready.

"What's the purpose of your visit to The Netherlands?" the security immigration officer asked.

"I'm here to spend time with a friend in Amsterdam."

"What do you do for a living?"

"I'm a physician."

"Where do you work?"

"At the Royal Alexandra Hospital in Paisley, Scotland. It is a suburb of Glasgow."

"How long have you worked there?"

"Five years."

"How long will you be here?"

"Four or five days. I am unsure."

"Let me see your air ticket."

"Certainly. Here it is." Ahmad took the ticket out of his jacket and handed it to the officer.

"Do you know where you'll be staying?"

"Yes. I have the address of my friend, here in my bag. He lives in Amsterdam."

"I see you have an open return on your air ticket. Why is that?"

"Because I don't know yet whether I will be here for four or five days."

"Welcome to The Netherlands."

Ahmad proceeded through the immigration arrival hall and outside into the main part of the airport terminal. As he was walking past a stand-up bar and snack stand towards the exit doors, he noticed a number of men standing there intently looking up at a TV screen behind the bar. He stopped, looked up at the screen, and heard the words from a BBC commentator describing the horrendous explosion that had occurred earlier in the morning at the Sellafield nuclear site in the northwest of England.

The warmth feeling of release in his groin felt better than any orgasm he had ever achieved in his lifetime. It provided him with a wonderful feeling of accomplishment. With a satisfied grin on his face, he made his way out of the terminal and across the street to the train station, where he caught a train for the short nine-mile ride into central Amsterdam. After checking into a third rate hotel in front of one of the ring canals near the Central Station, he walked to a nearby travel agency that was open for business on a Sunday, and booked a one-way reservation to Islamabad, late in the afternoon of the following day.

After spending several hours watching the TV in his hotel room describing what happened at Sellafield, he fell into a long, deep sleep, satisfied that he had covered his tracks quite well in the way he departed Scotland. By his next scheduled shift, Tuesday at midnight, he would be arriving in Pakistan instead. Once the hospital authorities reported him as missing, he could be traced to his flight to Amsterdam, ostensibly to attend the funeral of a relative. After that, he could be traced on an additional flight to Islamabad, where his trail would go quite cold.

As far as he was concerned, his existence as Dr. Abdul-Karim bin Ahmad was over. He left nothing in his flat in Paisley that would incriminate or connect him to Sellafield, much less to Wahid, Rashid, or the two martyred brothers, Hamza and Salman. He was satisfied that he would only remain of interest to the UK authorities as a Pakistani physician who failed to return to his job at the hospital.

Once back home in his North Waziristan village of Mir Ali, he would immediately start planning the next jihad operation. By altering his appearance and traveling with a new set of documents in an alias identity, he was quite confident of succeeding again. This time it would be against the number one target in the world after the state of Israel – the US.

The following day, just after noon, he caught a KLM co-share flight with Pakistan International Airlines from Amsterdam to Islamabad, via a short stopover in Abu Dhabi. Settling back into his seat, he browsed through several of the newspapers offered him, both in English and Arabic. The headlines and stories within were just now starting to describe the destruction and estimated horrendous toll from the blast against building B215.

The first estimates provided were for the effects caused by the radioactive plume sweeping across northern England and Scotland. Based upon the rupturing of the three steel casks containing cesium-137, the estimate was that just over 232 kilograms were released into the atmosphere. The most heavily contaminated area, spreading eastward from Sellafield, was being estimated to cover over three thousand square kilometers of land. All of the human population, along with animal life in the area, was being evacuated. It was projected that it could take up to four centuries for life to return to normalcy in the area.

The attack was described as the worst terrorist incident ever in the UK. In the meantime, the cesium-137 atmospheric plume was to carry downwind to the east, outside the UK and across the English Channel into all of Scandinavia, the Baltic States, northern Germany and parts of France and Poland. The area to the west of Sellafield, across the Irish Sea to Ireland and Northern Ireland, was spared, at least for the time being, the immediate effects of the blast. If it had been a liquid release of the cesium-137 westward into the water, the whole of the Irish Sea would have been contaminated.

The UK's National Health Service initial plan for dealing with such a catastrophe was reported to have been found very inadequate. The few people immediately affected that were being treated at local hospitals had to subsequently be moved, along with complete hospital staffs and existing patients, due to the radioactive fallout that had forced the evacuation of the entire area. Once the realization set in that the degree of cesium-137 contamination was going to make such a large area uninhabitable, whole villages and towns throughout Cumbria, the third largest county in England, would have to be moved further south into England and Wales. Likewise was going to be the situation through a sizeable portion of southern Scotland.

The populace, upon learning about what had happened, were in a panic trying to flee southward. Traffic accidents by the hundreds were occurring within a few hours after the attack as people were rushing to leave the area. By midnight Sunday evening, roads, railways, boats and planes that could leave, were all jammed with people seeking to head south. An intense fear set in as people rushed about, trying to avoid any kind of exposure, whether through contact with the skin, internal exposure through breathing or ingesting contaminated liquids internally. From this day onward, the attack at Sellafield would become the most serious tragedy unleashed upon the country since World War Two.

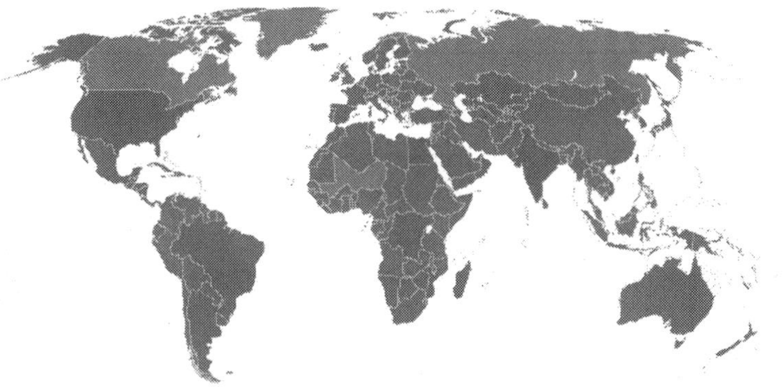

CHAPTER 42

Although nothing was written up in the press reports that Abdul had read during his flight to Islamabad, by the end of the second day after the attack, Scotland Yard's Counter-terrorism Unit and MI5's Centre for the Protection of National Infra-structure had developed significant information on specifically who was behind the attack. How far that information would go to apprehend those involved however, would be another matter.

The security guard at the main gate of Sellafield was only able to provide a partial description of a white truck, thought to be in the ten thousand pound weight class, that had crashed through on its way to B215. The roving guard in the Land Rover, because of the distance between him and the truck turning a corner in front of him, could only say it was white and with no markings on the side except for an emblem of some sort on the driver's side door. The wreckage found at the blasted-out corner of B215 revealed part of a rear axle but little else.

Scotland Yard and MI5 officers trained in how to deal with terrorist incidents involving weapons of mass destruction, all wore protective clothing and, along with Sellafield site radiation specialists, probed the site for evidence. The investigation however, was extremely complicated due to the high levels of radiation permeating the entire scene of the attack. The Yard and MI5 officers all had to be flown to Sellafield by helicopter due to the jammed roads leading out of Cumbria.

On Monday morning, just over twenty four hours following the attack, Wahid's supervisor at the East Kilbride Parks Service reported to the Strathclyde Police that a ten thousand pound class truck was missing and presumed stolen. He also reported that Wahid had not shown up for work that morning. A subsequent police search of his Larkhall house by early afternoon revealed a few dozen small ammonium nitrate fertilizer beads on the garage floor near the front door. In addition, a number of body hairs were found inside the house, in the bathroom. The empty bags for the fertilizer were found stacked in one of the bedroom closets, and the empty cans for the fuel oil in the closet of the second bedroom. Only a slight lingering smell of the fuel oil could be detected.

A check with the neighbors on both sides of the house revealed neither unusual noises nor gathering of people in and around the house in the several days prior to the attack. Wahid's car was parked inside the garage. The keys to it were on a countertop inside the kitchen.

By Monday evening, with a picture provided by his East Kilbride place of employment, Wahid's face was emblazoned all over TV newscasts, newspapers and tabloids throughout England, Scotland, Wales and Northern Ireland. An arrest warrant was issued for him based upon the traces of fertilizer, empty bags and fuel oil cans found in his house and garage, along with the theft of a truck from his place of employment and strong suspicion that the same truck was used in the attack. At this point, the authorities had no indication whether Wahid was alive, or had died in the attack.

By Tuesday evening, the body hairs collected at Wahid's house was determined to have come from four separate individual males. By comparing one set of the bathroom hairs to hair found in his car, as well as the minivan he regularly used at work, Wahid was positively identified as one of the four sources. No sooner had Wahid been singled out, when investigators at Sellafield located a severely mangled portion of a license plate over three-quarters of a mile away nearby the entrance road leading to the Seascale Golf Club. The plate was identified as having come from the East Kilbride Park Service truck.

The other three sets of hairs found in the Larkhall house were unidentified until the end of the week. Strathclyde Police Detective Chief Billy Mackay, acting on a hunch after the Royal Alexandra Hospital chief administrator reported Abdul missing, collected hair samples from Abdul's personal locker in the hospital's Accident and Emergency Section. As a result, within twenty four hours a second set of hairs from the Larkhall house would be identified.

The following day, on Saturday, another picture, this time of Dr. Abdul-Karim bin Ahmad, would be plastered throughout the UK and the rest of the world, as a suspect terrorist accomplice wanted for questioning in the attack. Although Det. Mackay had previously interviewed Abdul as a possible suspect in the death of Patrick, that detail was left out of the press release. Abdul did not count on being publicly identified, at least so soon after the attack. In the meantime, the remaining two sets of hairs found in the house would remain a question never answered.

* * *

Like Abdul in his effort to get out of Scotland and back to Pakistan, Wahid, so far, was faring well. Upon reaching the village of Ambleside, Wahid thanked the driver of the minivan for his service and exited the vehicle. Following the directions the driver had given him, he only had to walk ten yards across the street and down the sidewalk a short distance to the bus stop. Just as he reached the sign for the Coniston Rambler Bus Service, a large boom could be heard in the air from over his shoulder. With that sound, he knew that Hamza and Salman were martyred and had entered Paradise. The sound of the blast had barely subsided when the bus arrived. Wahid stepped inside, paid the fare, and was on his way to the Windermere Railway Station where he would catch a train for London's Euston Station.

By two o'clock in the afternoon, after transferring trains in Preston, Lancashire, he arrived in London. His cousin, Mahmood Hussani, lived in east London, in the borough of Newham, where he worked mostly night shifts as a pizza deliveryman. Not having seen each other in over two years, they would spend the rest of the day and late into the night in animated conversation. Having grown up together in the same house, they were as close as brothers could be. In fact, they even looked similar, in build and facial appearance, except that Mahmood was two inches shorter, wore glasses and sported a beard.

Mahmood called his employer and said he was too sick to come to work that evening, so they could continue talking and watching the TV coverage that was just starting to be shown about the attack. He agreed to return the next day for both an afternoon and evening shift of delivering pizzas. Wahid confided in Mahmood his involvement in the jihad attack, saying that is why he had come to London. He asked that Mahmood let him stay in his small flat where he lived alone. He said he would not show his face outside and would only be there for a few days until the coverage of the attack subsided and he could leave for Pakistan.

By Tuesday, when Wahid's picture appeared on TV and in the press being circulated throughout the world, Wahid could only hope that he would not be traced to London. Before his cousin left for work that evening, they worked out a plan for Wahid to take Mahmood's identity documents and use them in the next few days to leave London and work his way back to Pakistan. When Mahmood told him he had a couple of friends from the local mosque who could be relied upon to assist in getting him out of the country, he firmly said, no thank you. No trusted outsiders were to be privy to what had happened and none would become so in the future. Wahid would remain loyal to the dictates of Abdul as a continuing sign of his devotion to him. Mahmood completely understood.

Purposely not shaving now for close to one week, a good growth of black hair was taking form on his face. Following their agreement to use Mahmood's Pakistani passport and UK identity card to leave the country, he started to trim his beard and hair to match Mahmood's in the documents. He also started practicing a slumped over walk in order to appear a couple of inches shorter, to match the physical description listed in the documents.

By the beginning of the weekend, on Saturday morning, when Abdul's picture, description and Wanted for Questioning notice was in the press and on TV, Wahid and Mahmood agreed that the following Monday would be the time for Wahid to leave. Mahmood called the London office of Eurostar and made a reservation for Monday morning at 6 am, for the first train of the day leaving London St-Pancras Station for Brussels. He paid for the ticket using his credit card, and then gave it to Wahid, along with his passport and ID card. This would enable Wahid to travel, in his place, for the return home. Wahid reimbursed him for the ticket, and gave him three hundred Pounds representing most of the money that remained from the last stages of planning that went into the attack.

In the darkness of the early morning hours on Monday, Mahmood drove Wahid to within one block of St. Pancras and they said their goodbyes. Subsequently, Mahmood would wait a couple of days and, claiming his identity documents had been stolen, apply for a new identity card. He would hold off for a couple of days on reporting the loss of the passport and credit card, per Wahid's request. Without experiencing any problems at all, Wahid boarded the train for the short two-hour trip to Bruxelles Midi Station in Brussels, with only cursory glances given to his ticket, passport and identity card.

Looking quite similar to his cousin, and exhibiting the same mannerisms, Wahid effortlessly carried off the impersonation as he made his way through a one-night hotel stay in a run down section of Brussels, followed by a Turkish Airlines co-share flight with Pakistan International Airlines, to Islamabad, via Istanbul, the following day.

* * *

The whereabouts and life of Rashid, unlike that of Abdul and Wahid, turned out quite differently in the aftermath of the attack. He carefully thought through all that he had done in Scotland since his arrival less than two months earlier. Being a well-trained computer specialist ostensibly seeking a new life in the UK, he believed he could succeed in remaining behind and take his chances with the authorities.

Unless he could be identified as being associated or seen with either Wahid or Abdul, there would be no evidence connecting him to the attack. Having had only one meeting with both of them together, over dinner in a Glasgow restaurant shortly after his arrival in Scotland, this would be a tenuous link at best. Further, unless someone could come forward and identify him as an associate of Wahid through the limited time spent together in public in Glasgow, or during the less than full day traveling together to Seascale, that as well was a weak link.

Having been given twenty four hours notice by Wahid that the attack would be taking place the next day, on Sunday, Rashid planned to be on his motorbike south of Seascale and the neighboring Sellafield site, scouting out new business opportunities. Early that morning he rode to the towns of Barrow-in-Furness and Ulverston. He had planned to also visit an additional town, Grange-over-Sands, but found plenty of things to occupy him in the first two.

He found Barrow-in-Furness to be a larger town than expected, especially after the village of Seascale. It was an old-established shipbuilding town with considerable work taking place there so he located a number of information technology businesses, including several that provided the same kinds of computer services he offered. It was just before noontime, and he decided to stop at a small restaurant for a drink and a snack before riding over to Ulverston. The few patrons and employees inside the shop were glued to the TV, watching the coverage just starting to come in on a terrorist attack that had taken place up north at Sellafield. He placed his order and joined in with the others watching the TV. Shocked but eternally grateful for the success of the jihad operation, his order arrived and he took his time eating, while continuing to watch the TV. After finishing, he paid the bill and left the restaurant.

By the time he had ridden his motorbike the short ten miles to Ulverston, along A590, he noticed a distinct increase of people, cars, trucks and a few buses coming into town from the north, along A5092. It was early afternoon and he spent about an hour riding around the town seeing where various businesses and residential areas were located. He found that Ulverston also had a number of competing businesses like his, much like what he found in Barrow-in-Furness. He concluded that it would take more investigation to see if he should start offering his computer services there.

As he was leaving town and had turned onto Soutergate to head north towards A5092, he continued to see the influx of traffic coming from the direction he wished to go. Just before reaching A5092, a Cumbria Constabulary traffic police officer stopped him to ask what his destination was. He told the officer he lived in Seascale and was returning home. She told him that Seascale was being evacuated and he would be unable to return there. She gave him directions to the nearby Ulverston Victoria High School, where people from the evacuated areas to the north could find temporary shelter.

Arriving at the school, he reported to the community service personnel operating the shelter in the school's gymnasium. He provided his name, address and business details, including showing his UK identity card. Shown to a cordoned off area of the gym for single men, he would spend the next three days there, with a canvas cot to sleep on, three hot meals a day, and uninterrupted hot showers.

He made several new friends there, including several with laptops who enjoyed talking with him about their computer pursuits. Two husband and wife couples that he met there had been customers of his in Seascale. Without exception, all of the people there, from a number of villages and towns along the Cumbrian coast and Lake District inland, were fraught with worry about their return to their homes and businesses and prospects for their future lives.

On the morning of the third day at the school, three law enforcement officers visited Rashid. They took him to a nearby classroom where each identified themselves, one from Scotland Yard, the second from MI5 and the third, a Cumbrian Constabulary officer in uniform, and working at of the Barrow-in-Furness office. By this time, having already seen the picture of Wahid several times on the TVs set up in classrooms near the gym, he feared for his cover story and decision to remain behind.

After thirty minutes of questioning had gone by, Rashid realized his story had held up, made sense and the officers had no further reason to continue questioning him. The constabulary officer, in particular, appeared to be very polite and understanding. He acknowledged that he was aware of the computer services that Rashid offered in the Seascale area, and that he was viewed by the people there as polite, serious, and accomplished in his work during the short period he had lived in the village. The Yard and MI5 officer, having neither anything positive or negative to say about him, said he would be advised when he could return home.

After spending two more days in the gym, all of the people there were allowed to return home to their villages and towns in the north, depending upon the levels of remaining radioactivity. They were advised of the cleanup and remediation efforts going on in the north, and the likelihood that those choosing to return there would be subject to regular testing for levels of radiation as new medical treatment facilities and procedures would be available to them through the National Health Service. With that, Rashid decided he would be among those returning and would continue, at least for the time being, operating his business in Seascale. At an appropriate time in the future, he would make his next move and return home to Pakistan for a visit and to make himself available for the next jihad against the infidels.

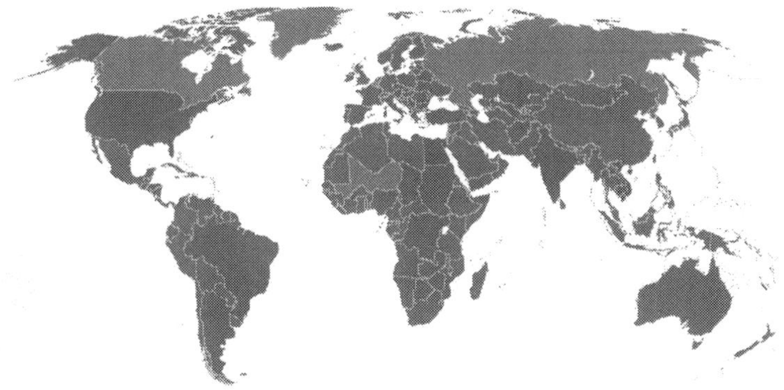

CHAPTER 43

Ordering a crackdown on the movement and travel of Pakistani/Asian males throughout the UK, MI5's Ian Campbell, along with his counterpart at Scotland Yard, instituted searches of homes, places of business and employment, and even mosques. Having identified two of the individuals believed to have been involved in the attack, Wahid and Abdul, at least two additional persons were believed to be involved, as based on the two remaining sets of body hairs found at Wahid's house. With at least one person driving the truck into building B215, that could possibly account for the third set of body hairs. Another possibility was that Wahid and Abdul perished in the attack and the remaining two individuals were accomplices that were not directly involved. Needless to say, no DNA or body parts of any kind were found at the blast site.

When Mitch saw the picture of Wahid in the newspapers and on TV, he recognized him as the Asian male he had spotted the previous week in East Kilbride driving a small delivery truck. He discussed it with Lee and the team members, followed by a call to Jack in London Station. Jack reported this to Ian Campbell, who thanked him for the information. Campbell noted however, that this simply confirmed that Wahid did indeed drive a truck for the East Kilbride Park Service, and Mitch happened to have made direct eye contact with him several days prior to the attack.

Recognizing that they were not advancing the case at all on their own, Mitch and Lee held another secure call with Jack to discuss their next moves. They all agreed that having no information indicating a second attack in the UK was imminent, it was no longer necessary to remain there. With Patrick's murder, and the subsequent identification of Wahid and Abdul, the latter of whom was certainly a suspect, no further options were available to them. In all probability, they believed, Abdul was Ali, Patrick's point of contact with the radical Islamic terrorist group responsible for the attack at Sellafield.

Lee informed the team members that the five of them could make their air reservations and leave Glasgow to return to the US at any time. He made his own reservation to leave Glasgow and return to Stockholm the following morning. Jack, likewise, made plans to leave as well. Lee also arranged for a London Station support officer to travel to Glasgow to pick up the semi-automatic handguns that he, Mitch and the five team members all carried during their time there. These would be returned to the Station's logistics and support office in the embassy.

If there were to be any kind of additional attack on the part of Abdul in the U.S., no information was available. That part of Abdul's operational planning, as he previously described it to Patrick, was now totally unknown. Lee, before departing, placed a call to Det. Billy MacKay, thanking him for his assistance. He also informed him of Mitch's recognition of Wahid several days before the attack, as driving the East Kilbride Park Service truck. They agreed to stay in touch should any additional information be developed. The chief detective had been the kind of invaluable personal contact that intelligence officers working against the terrorist target regularly hope to cultivate.

For Mitch's part, he spent his final restless night in a Glasgow hotel room thinking about how Abdul, as the probable leader of the terrorist group, would now proceed. He knew from experience that Abdul, having several other people taking his direction, would not have sacrificed himself in the attack. At least one martyr was used to drive the truck into building B215. With both Abdul and Wahid now identified as Pakistanis, and probably both surviving the attack, they would be long gone now, back to Pakistan or elsewhere in the region.

Thinking back to what Patrick had said about Abdul planning three attacks and having asked him to consider involvement in all of them, Mitch speculated that Abdul must have been working on some kind of timetable.

He decided to search on the Internet for the regularly published government counterterrorist journals listings the anniversary dates for previous terrorist events, along with the groups and nationalities involved. Getting out of bed and booting up his laptop to review these journals, he found nothing useful that would help take him in a new direction. Returning to bed for a remaining three hours of fitful sleep before leaving for the airport and a long flight home, Mitch was certain that the world had not heard the last of Abdul.

* * *

For the past five years, following the assassination of former Prime Minister Benazir Bhutto and the return to power of her Pakistan Peoples Party, further lawlessness and corruption increased. By 2010, The Federally Administered Tribal Areas of North Waziristan and South Waziristan fell completely under the separate control of al-Qaeda and the Taliban. The entire Swat Valley area in the North-West Frontier Province likewise fell under their control. The Pakistani military no longer held even a bare foothold in these areas.

It was to one of these areas, and the town that had become the virtual headquarters center for insurgent activity there, Miran Shah, that Abdul returned. When Jamil Amin passed word to his immediate superior, Dr. Ayman al-Zawahiri, who was still serving as the deputy to Osama bin Laden, he rejoiced to hear the news. Jamil had kept Ayman up to date on Abdul's planning for the attack, and he was ecstatic to learn it had succeeded.

Abdul arrived in Miran Shah and found that little had changed since his last visit a five months earlier. He made his way across town and to the nearby village of Mir Ali, where his family ancestral home was still located. All that remained of his relatives living in the home were two cousins and their families. With his picture now just starting to appear the world over in the press and TV, he was welcomed as a hero. However, he knew that he must quickly go into hiding once word spread that he had returned home.

US Special Forces teams and commandos from the French Foreign Legion still regularly came over from the Afghan side of the border to visit a good part of North and South Waziristan, along with the Frontier Province, in search of high priority targets. If they could get a reliable lead from a well-placed informant to an al-Qaeda or Taliban high-value target in one of these areas, missions were planned that made use of sophisticated infrared laser target designators to "light up" the house or vehicle the target was inside. This would enable an Agency unmanned Predator aircraft, overhead on station, to fire a missile into the target. It was only during the past two years that the teams and the commandos pulled back from openly operating in and around Miran Shah, as a result of the insurgents taking complete control there as they interspersed themselves among the populace.

While spending two hours with his relatives celebrating the success of his jihad operation, arrangements were made for Abdul to stay out of sight in the home of a nearby tribal elder. As he was preparing to leave to walk the quarter mile to the elder's house, a courier came from Jamil to arrange for Abdul to meet with him that evening. He knew that for obvious reasons of personal security, he would be prevented from meeting with Ayman himself. Nevertheless, to meet again with Jamil, the de facto number three in al Qaeda, was still quite an honor.

After settling-in at the elder's house and performing minor medical exams on the old man and two of his children, Abdul was escorted to the nearby house of another tribal elder from Mir Ali. Within a half hour, Jamil and his assistant arrived in an old beat-up pickup truck, following their one-hour horseback ride from a safe house on the Afghan border.

"Jamil, I'm honored to have you visit me," Abdul said.

"The honor is mine, Abdul. Congratulations on your success at Sellafield. The infidels have suffered a major setback."

"I had just arrived in Amsterdam when I heard the news. I was overcome and at the same proud that our two brothers had found Paradise."

"Osama and Ayman were overcome as well and offer their highest of congratulations. Jihad is the path to freedom and your success is from God. God is great."

"God is great," Abdul said.

"Now tell me, my brother, what's your plan for the next operation against the infidels? We'll provide whatever support you require."

"Thank you, my brother. I want to strike at the heart of the Great Satan, in Washington, DC."

"That will be a difficult task. Tell me more."

"Just outside of Washington, in the Northern Virginia suburbs, is Washington Dulles International Airport. The attack will be a biological one involving weapons-grade anthrax spores. It will take place late in the afternoon, a busy weekday, when the airport has its peak number of passengers arriving and departing inside the main terminal building. Along with airport workers and well-wishers greeting passengers or saying their goodbyes, tens of thousands of people will inhale the spores."

When Abdul said the attack would involve anthrax spores, Jamil's eyes sparkled and a large toothy grin appeared.

"Abdul, my brother, are you familiar with the Iraqi effort to produce weapons-grade anthrax at their al-Hakam biological research facility southwest of Baghdad during the 1980s?"

"Yes," Abdul said. "I know a Pakistani microbiologist from medical school who had done extensive research at al-Hakam. I have been back in contact with him and he is willing to assist in preparing the anthrax bomb for the Dulles operation."

"Would you be interested in having another participant in your preparation plans, also a microbiologist who had worked at al-Hakam?"

"Yes, my brother. I definitely would be interested. When and where can I meet with him?"

"He is an Iraqi researcher living in one of our most secure safe houses along the border not too far from here. I can arrange for you to meet with him in two days time."

"I'll be pleased to meet with him and learn the degree to which he can assist."

"I'd like you to work up a list of what else you will need for the operation, including money for all of your expenses."

"I'll have that for you before we finish tonight's meeting, my brother. It's all but completed now."

"Pictures of you, along with your physical description, have appeared all over the world on TV and in the press. How do you plan on dealing with this for the next operation?"

"I'll have minor cosmetic surgery that will involve suturing a black silicon mole, the size of pea, to my cheek. The unattractive mole will serve to distract from the rest of my face and, along with wearing glasses and a short-trimmed beard, enable me to pass through immigration and customs while traveling and moving about on city streets undetected."

"Your planning is excellent, my brother. I received word that Wahid is due to arrive nearby in a day or two. Will he be involved in your next attack?"

"I hope so. I'll need to talk with him about it since pictures of him also have been publicized around the world. He was invaluable during the Sellafield attack and I wish to use him again if possible."

"After he arrives, I'll arrange for our documents specialist to meet with both of you and create new identity documents, as needed."

"Jamil, my brother, I'll also need someone who can fabricate a concealment device in a carrying case. This will be used for hiding the anthrax spores I'll be carrying to the land of the Great Satan."

"Such a specialist is also available and I can have him here to meet with you in no more than two days time. You can discuss with him what you require and he'll be able to come up with whatever you wish."

After enjoying a sumptuous celebratory meal together, with the tribal leader hosting them, Jamil and Abdul said their farewells. Abdul returned to the other elder's house, which was made out of mud bricks and located in a compound that was large by local standards, and included several other mud brick buildings and huts, one of which afforded Abdul a good night's sleep. He awoke in the morning and immediately went to work contacting another medical school colleague he had trained with years earlier, to arrange for the cosmetic surgery.

Late that evening, the elder came to Abdul's hut and asked him to come to the front gate of the compound to see someone who was asking for him. Stepping up to the gate and peering through the slats, Abdul could see a bearded male who was standing somewhat hunched over. He looked intently at the face peering back at him. No words were said, but after about ten seconds, Abdul broke into a wide grin and welcomed Wahid home.

The following morning, they agreed on a limited role for Wahid to play in the Dulles operation, primarily to make the introduction of Abdul to Wahid's cousin, in Northern Virginia. With the change in appearance based on his beard and manner of walking to make himself appear somewhat older and shorter, Wahid convinced Abdul of his ability to travel anywhere in the world using a new set of alias documents.

By early afternoon, a courier arrived from Jamil's safe house on the Afghan border. He gave Abdul a small leather satchel of money, in US dollars and Pakistani rupees, for use in covering future expenses. The courier also reported that the two specialists, one for producing new alias identity travel documents, and the other for fabricating a concealment device, would be arriving later that afternoon.

While they waited, Abdul asked Wahid about Rashid and if he had any idea if he stayed behind in Seascale, or, would be making his way back to Pakistan soon. Wahid said he could only speculate on what Rashid would do. He said it would not be surprising if Rashid decided to remain in the UK since he was establishing himself as a real businessperson there. However, since few Pakistanis lived along that part of the Cumbrian coast, he might have to undergo some serious police questioning following the attack. He added that the cell phone link between them was lost when they both agreed to destroy their phones just prior to departing the area.

With the arrival of the two specialists, the alias documents person showed Abdul several legitimate passports, with photographs removed, of business people who no longer needed them for travel outside Pakistan. Abdul picked out the one belonging to a cosmetics salesman who had previously only traveled outside Pakistan twice, both times to other areas in the Middle East. The physical description was close enough but the date of birth was eight years older than Abdul. It was decided that a little touchup of the beard and sideburns with some grey hair coloring would be enough to place him in the right age bracket. Some hair coloring was sent for in Mir Ali and subsequently brushed lightly onto Abdul's hair, sideburns and beard. Afterwards, passport photos were taken of him on the spot.

The specialist then proceeded to write down details on Abdul so that cosmetic company business cards, stationary and other identifying pocket litter could be printed up showing him as a bona fide cosmetic salesperson. It was agreed that within a week or less, when the specialist returned, he would have with him the passport showing Abdul's picture, several extra passport photos, a driver's license with his picture, a Pakistani national ID card, and the cosmetic company business materials. Also included would be would be an address and two telephone numbers from the Islamabad-Rawalpindi area that would be backstopped in acknowledging that Abdul, in his new alias identity, did indeed work for a cosmetic company.

Next, the concealment device specialist took over and talked with Abdul about the size specification that was required, as well as the type of carrying case that would be the most suitable for him to use when traveling abroad. Abdul described wanting to have a black leather sales representative case, approximately eighteen inches long, ten inches wide and twelve inches in height. The concealment area should be in the bottom so that when the case is turned upside down, a lever could be moved that would allow for the whole bottom of the case to slide open revealing an area 17 ½ inches long, 9 ½ wide and ¾ inch in height.

Abdul then asked the specialist if he could arrange for a glassmaker to manufacture a flat bottle of two sheets of molded, tempered glass, with an opening at one end in the shape of a pourer. In effect, as he described it, it would be a rectangular shaped bottle, the size of which would fit inside the concealed area at the bottom of the case. Without saying what would go inside the bottle, he asked that the inside capacity of the bottle be able to accommodate approximately a half to one liter of either a powder or a liquid.

To Abdul's surprise, the specialist said he should not have any problem with either the concealment case device or the glass container. He said he would need one week back at his shop on the border to fabricate the leather case. The glass bottle however, would have to be manufactured in Islamabad, but would probably take no more than a week as well. Abdul expressed his sincere gratitude since the bottle was something he expected to have to make arrangements for on his own.

After the two specialists departed, Abdul and Wahid further planned their separate itineraries for travel to the US, and how they would link up when it was time for Abdul to be introduced to the cousin in Northern Virginia. With at least one more week remaining in Mir Ali, they would both continue to stay out of sight in the tribal elder's compound. Abdul's medical colleague would be visiting the compound during that period to do the implant of the silicon mole on his cheek. If all went according to plans, their next jihad operation would be shortly underway, this time against the very high priority target, the Great Satan, the US.

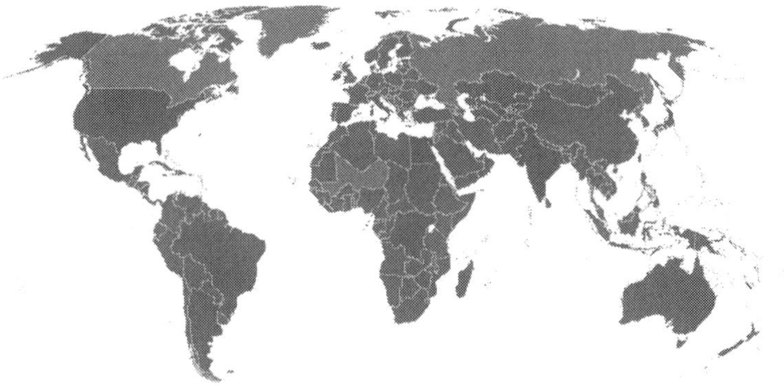

CHAPTER 44

Over the course of the remaining week that Abdul would spend in Mir Ali, he still had much work to do on the configuration of the anthrax bomb. He had already done a lot of research and planning for what would be required to produce a devastating bomb of frightful and epic proportions; a bomb that he would have never thought could be so effective, had it not been for what Wahid told him about his cousin working at Dulles airport. Ingenious bomb, yes. A deadly bomb, yes, that too.

It would all hinge on the extent of the cousin's access. From the way Wahid described it, his access was apparently excellent. As a maintenance engineer, the cousin had direct access to the airport's air handling systems for the heating, ventilating and air conditioning throughout the airport. The remaining aspect for success in the jihad operation would be Abdul's ability to bring the bomb safely and securely across international borders to the US. After that, once the cousin was able to place the bomb into the main duct of one of the air handling systems, the release of the deadly anthrax spores would go completely undetected by anyone.

As a form of terror, few biological weapons can be said to be perfect. However, not so in the case of weapons-grade anthrax spores. First, they are easily concealed and transportable for delivery. Secondly, because such a small amount is needed for a lethal inhalation, anthrax is also highly potent.

Once Abdul decided upon the use of anthrax spores for his bomb against the US, he first thought the concealment and delivery could best be accomplished in aerosol metal cans. This form of anthrax, referred to as aerosol anthrax, is invisible as well as odorless. As a result, it is a stealthy killer. However, transporting metal cans of anthrax across international borders presents problems that he believed would be too difficult to overcome given the stringent restrictions on what can be carried aboard aircraft in either checked luggage or hand-carry items.

For this reason, he developed his idea for making use of a concealment device and a flat glass bottle container for transporting the anthrax. He believed that by dropping the glass container of the anthrax spores inside the air-handling duct, breaking upon impact, the spores would be released into what would become a form of aerosol release that would spread throughout the atmosphere inside the cavernous high, open spaces of the main terminal at Dulles. Given the internal capacity that he specified for inside the glass bottle, between a half to one liter in volume, it would be more than enough anthrax spores to infect and ultimately kill hundreds of thousands of people.

In furthering his operational plan, Abdul learned that Dulles, during the previous year, handled more than three thousand flights a day involving over 350,000 passengers alone, not including airport workers, flight personnel and visitors. The capacity of the glass bottle, Abdul concluded, would suffice quite nicely. With all the passengers having to move in and out of the main terminal, regardless of flying into or out of the two outlying terminals, the inhalation of the anthrax spores would start to take place upon the breaking of the glass bottle.

Abdul focused his thoughts on the aftereffects of the breaking of the bottle. The first symptoms to appear on those infected would not commence for two days, at the earliest. By that time, passengers and crews would be well beyond the airport to, in many cases, far-flung regions of the US and the world. These initial symptoms would be in the form of fever, coughing, chest pains and, in some of the victims, shortness of breath.

Many of those infected, believing they caught a cold, a virus or the flu from other passengers, would turn to over-the-counter remedies. Others would seek advice over the phone from their doctors or visit their doctors or clinics wherever they were at in the world. Influenza would be assumed, with bed rest and fluids prescribed for many of those infected. Of those that required hospitalization, they might have blood cultures drawn or undergo chest x-rays. At this point, following laboratory analysis, it would be possible that a physician might notice the telltale signals that anthrax carries. The problem here though, is that since these patients would be seeking treatment in locales all over the world, connecting their illness to a biological terrorism attack at Dulles, might take some figuring out. In most of the cases, with subsequent health care provided by so many different sources, no kind of serious health emergency would even be detected. Until a major uptick in the number of anthrax cases were reported internationally, by this time victims would begin experiencing severe breathing problems, followed by going into shock, coma and finally, death.

A major health emergency would be detected three or four days after the attack among airport workers or visitors who lived in the region around Dulles. Their sheer numbers in seeking treatment would provide the first real clue of what had taken place at the airport. With doctors, clinics and hospitals within a limited geographical area noting would provide the first real clue of what had taken place at the airport. With doctors, clinics and hospitals within a limited geographical area noting a distinct increase of serious upper respiratory illness, with deaths by the dozens now starting to occur, state health departments and the Centers for Disease Control and Prevention (CDC) would be called in for further advice and diagnosis.

With each day passing, the number of people seeking medical care would at least double, regardless of their previous state of good health. People from all age groups and economic sectors would be succumbing to what now would appear to health authorities and the general populace as the spreading of a fatal illness. Local deaths would begin to skyrocket, with no clear diagnosis except for some unexplained upper respiratory infection. Likewise, similar unexplained deaths would be occurring throughout the world.

For the anthrax spores remaining in circulation inside the airport building in the days following the attack, they would continue to do their deadly work. Until it was determined that an anthrax attack occurred there, passengers, visitors and a dwindling staff of workers would still be inhaling decreasing amounts of the anthrax-laden air. Once that determination was made, the airport would have to be completely shut down in a state of total quarantine. In the meantime, even though anthrax is not contagious, and therefore cannot be transmitted from one person to another, widespread panic would now have become commonplace. From Northern Virginia, the panic would spread outward as bus, train and air traffic throughout the Northeast and mid-Atlantic areas of the US would be disrupted. In those cases that would go untreated, the fatality rate for inhaled anthrax spores would be approximately 90 per cent.

The state of the US public health system before the September 11, 2001 attacks, followed by the anthrax incidents that took place in October 2001, was in a deteriorating condition that was going nowhere except down. Going into 2012 however, even with all of the fifty states having much improved health departments capable of dealing with pandemic or biological attacks, it would still remain for CDC, in most cases, to be able to determine if such an attack took place. Only a few laboratories and health departments in the US had developed the capability to look at a sample from a patient or deceased victim and quickly detect and process it as a biological agent such as anthrax.

The alarm bells of the anthrax attack at Dulles would only go off, for example, when an alert technician in a local medical laboratory in Northern Virginia tests a blood culture from a now-deceased airline check-in attendant at the airport five days after the attack, and makes a preliminary diagnosis of anthrax. At that point, the world would finally become aware of what took place there. The following investigation and interviewing of those infected would reveal they were all at Dulles within the same twenty four to forty eight hour period. All that subsequently could be done at this stage, however, would be to administer antibiotics, preferably before the symptoms began to appear, or in the earliest hours after they appeared. With at least a dozen kinds of antibiotics available for use against anthrax, successful treatment is possible if administered in time.

Abdul estimated that this next successful jihad operation, using an anthrax bomb, would cause the ultimate deaths of tens of thousands of people who all shared one thing in common – having passed through the doors of Washington Dulles International Airport. In an article he had read recently on the airline industry and airport security, an airport security official was asked to name the safest airport in the world. His reply was "the one that is closed." Ironically, in the case of Dulles, it would only be closed after a devastating attack took place there. As another day went by for Abdul, he moved closer to leaving Pakistan and traveling, with his concealed biological weapon, to the US.

* * *

It was a chilly afternoon when the three doctors met inside the tribal elder's house in the compound where Abdul was staying. He enjoyed spending an earlier two hours with his medical school colleague, Dr. Kamram Rabbani, and catching up on their professional activities and accomplishments since graduation. Once the microbiologist that Jamil promised to send to Abdul arrived, Dr. Sa'eed Jassim al-Naseri, the three of quickly settled down to discussing the main topic that brought them together – Bacillus anthracis.

Once Abdul described what he needed in the way of anthrax spores, and the ability to configure them for transport inside a flat glass bottle, Dr. Rabbani volunteered both a limited quantity of the spores and the facility for safely configuring them inside the bottle. He described the medical supply and laboratory company he started and operated in Islamabad and, without learning from Abdul what the target was for the attack, revealed he could provide at least twelve milligrams of anthrax spores from his firm's culture collection.

The offer was graciously accepted by Abdul who knew that twelve milligrams, while not as much as he wanted to acquire, would nevertheless still wreck havoc at the airport. At that point however, Dr. al-Naseri removed from his briefcase a small wooden box containing a sealed glass vial and placed it on the table in front of them. He explained that under the late Iraqi President, Saddam Hussein, he worked as one of the chief researchers at the al-Hakam Institute outside Baghdad. When Saddam ordered the closure of the institute, and the removal of all evidence of a weapons of mass destruction program, he personally carried the vial, along with other biological cultures from the institute's collection, across the border to Syria.

Dr. al-Naseri remained in Syria for almost ten years, continuing to grow the culture collections at a secret facility built by the Syrian government northeast of Damascus. Working alongside him was an Iraqi researcher who convinced him to relocate, along with their collections, to an al-Qaeda safe house on the Afghan border with Pakistan several years ago. He said that what he had in the vial in front of him was 226 grams of anthrax spores, roughly eight ounces. He added that Dr. Ayman al-Zawahiri himself asked that the vial be made available to Abdul for his next jihad operation.

By late afternoon, after several rounds of celebratory tea and sweets, Dr. Rabbani departed Mir Ali for Islamabad, carrying the wooden box with the vial of anthrax spores inside. It was agreed that once he received the flat glass bottle, which was also being fabricated in Islamabad, he would place the 226 grams of anthrax inside and seal it. Once Abdul received the leather salesman's case with the concealment device and was ready to depart Pakistan, he would arrange to meet with Dr. Rabbani in Islamabad and pickup the bottle of anthrax on his way to the airport.

Given the lateness in the day, Abdul arranged for Dr. al-Naseri to stay in one of the tribal elder's spare rooms for the night and return to his safe house across the mountains early the next morning.

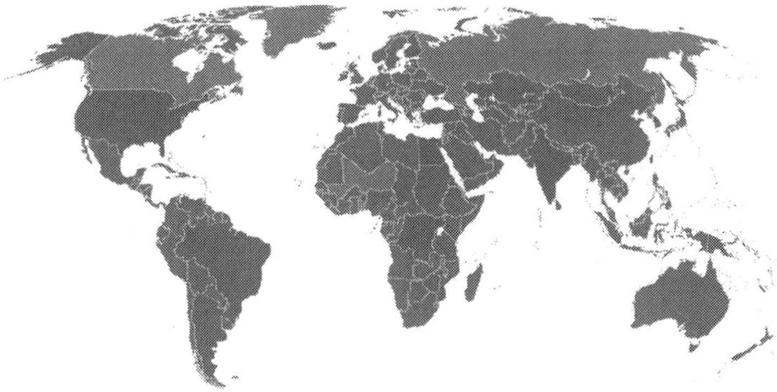

CHAPTER 45

While remaining out of sight in the compound, Wahid watched, with keen interest, the black and white remake of The Hunchback of Notre Dame, starring Charles Laughton. If he could further perfect how he walked and carried himself, it would detract people from paying too much attention to his facial features during the jihad attack against the US. Seeing Charles Laughton, as Quasimodo, the deformed bell ringer, climbing around the bell towers of Notre Dame Cathedral in Paris, gave him some ideas that he would incorporate in his newly disguised appearance.

The tactical deceptions he decided to employ was feigning a limp in his right leg, holding his head tilted slightly to the right and continuing to walk in a somewhat stooped over position. Concentrating on remembering to tilt his head and walk slightly stooped over would be no problem for him. The limp however, would take a little more effort on his part. He started by making use of some props.

Finding a water-worn smooth flat stone near an old creek bed at one end of the compound, measuring two inches in diameter and half an inch in height, he placed it inside his right shoe. Even though the stone was inside his sock, next to the skin, it had a tendency to move around and feel uncomfortable. To remedy that, he duct taped the stone directly to the skin in the middle, or arch portion of his foot. He then put his sock back on, followed by his shoe.

He practiced walking around by taking a step with his left foot, followed by gingerly easing his right foot to the ground. After a few minutes of doing this, he found it worked best if he lifted his right foot up quicker, as if favoring it, compared to his left foot. At the same time, he noticed that by putting the left foot down harder, as in light stomping, he could exaggerate the limp.

After walking around the compound for twenty minutes, he had perfected the deceptive limp to his complete satisfaction. He removed the duct-taped stone from the bottom of his right foot and was able to continue walking around with the very same limp as if the stone were still there. Combined with the slight tilting of his head to the right and stooped over position of his right shoulder as he walked, he looked as if he had suffered some kind of traumatic injury that left him deformed. He laughed to himself about not wanting to appear as bad as Quasimodo in the movie, but just deformed enough to cause people to notice more of the injury and less of his facial features. With his beard now trimmed to about one inch in length, and the addition of clear glass plastic rimmed glasses, he was ready to leave Pakistan for the US.

* * *

Three days following the meeting with Dr. Rabbani and Dr. al-Naseri, the concealment device specialist arrived back at the compound with the black leather case. He unwrapped its paper covering and proudly presented it to Abdul, who looked it over slowly and carefully before asking how to open the concealment portion on the bottom. The specialist turned the case on its side and showed him how to turn one of the four small round protective coasters that were on each corner of the bottom. This unlocked the bottom section and allowed it to slide open revealing the thin, narrow storage cavity inside.

The specialist also gave Abdul a package containing his new identity documents consisting of a barely worn looking Pakistani passport, a national identity card, a driver's license, two credit cards, a stack of one hundred business cards showing Abdul as a cosmetics sales representative, and assorted company literature and pamphlets. With their business concluded, Abdul expressed his gratitude and the specialist departed for the trip back to his safe house on the border.

Later in the afternoon, a messenger arrived from Dr. Rabbani, saying the package was available for pickup anytime, meaning the anthrax spores were inside the sealed bottle. That evening, while packing his clothes and personal items for the trip, Abdul placed a variety of small sample bottles of cosmetics inside the bottom of the leather case. These would serve to substantiate his cover story of being a salesman and also to further conceal the bottle of anthrax spores during routine airport security screening during the trip.

* * *

Before going to the airport on the day of his departure, Abdul met with Dr. Rabbani in an empty office space the doctor rented out near his medical supply and laboratory. The doctor gave him the sealed glass bottle and Abdul placed it inside the concealment device.

His subsequent travel to the US went off without a single problem. None of the airline check-in personnel, airport security people, or immigration and customs officials anywhere along the route of travel, offered up any serious questions at all. With just over three weeks having passed since he had departed the UK following the attack, his trimmed beard had grown sufficiently thick. The unattractive mole sutured to his cheek received numerous glances and, combined with the black plastic rimmed glasses and neatly trimmed beard, served their purpose well. He did not look anything like the pictures of him that appeared in TV newscasts and newspapers all over the world following the attack at Sellafield.

After the hotel stay in Vancouver, he entered the US in Seattle by stepping off a Victoria Clipper ferry at Pier 69, following a pleasant three-hour cruise from Victoria Harbor, in British Columbia. He presented his Pakistani passport and national identity card to the Immigration and Customs Enforcement (ICE) officer on duty at the pier. He held the driver's license openly in one of his hands, but the officer said it would not be necessary for him to see it. Since the US and Pakistan signed an accord three years earlier upgrading their relationship, Pakistani nationals no longer required a visa to enter the US for tourist purposes. Abdul was asked the purpose of his visit to the US, the hotel in Seattle where he would be staying and when he would be leaving the US.

After answering the questions, the officer asked to see his airline ticket. Noting the ticket was for a round-trip and showed a return to Pakistan from Vancouver in two days time, the officer accepted that Abdul would just be visiting Seattle for a day or two and then returning to Canada. Earlier, when Abdul first arrived in Vancouver and changed his ticket to an open return, he did so over the telephone. As a result, the airline ticket he showed the officer still listed the flight number and date of departure as originally made.

Wahid's travel to and entry into the US, using his new alias identity documents, also went as smooth as could be expected. While the ICE officer at the El Paso border crossing noticed his limp and apparent injury to the right side of his body, he was basically only asked the same questions that Abdul experienced. When asked the purpose of his visit to the US, Wahid said that this trip was the first real vacation in his life and that before returning to Islamabad he would attending his brother's wedding in Frankfurt as well.

Following his arrival at Dulles Airport, after flying from El Paso via Chicago, Wahid took a taxi to a Courtyard by Marriott Hotel in Reston, Virginia, a short 10 minute walk from his cousin's house in Herndon. Not wanting to take any unnecessary chances of being seen with his cousin in public, Wahid called and arranged for him to come to the hotel instead. Within fifteen minutes, Mohammad Shirazi arrived at the hotel room door and they greeted each other warmly, once he got over the shock of seeing how Wahid looked. The beard, glasses, walking with a limp and stooped appearance caught him by surprise. The both laughed a lot together while Wahid explained his disguises.

Mohammad said he had seen the pictures of Wahid on TV and read in the newspapers about the Sellafield attack. As a result, he said he actually was not surprised at the change in appearance. The two of them had not seen each other for three years and had much to talk about since they had grown up together since infancy as virtual brothers.

After having pizza and cokes delivered to the room, Wahid brought the subject around to the planned attack at Dulles Airport. While he knew of Mohammad's belief in the obligation to wage jihad against the infidels, he was surprised to hear about the examples of ethnic discrimination that Mohammad had experienced from workers at the airport and neighbors around where he lived. It served to further convince him that Mohammad would be willing to carry the anthrax bomb inside the airport.

Wahid told Mohammad that the remaining details for the attack would have to wait for the arrival of Abdul, whom he described as the other face that was shown on TV and in the newspapers. He said that Abdul was a noted physician that was totally committed to waging jihad, and was a brilliant mastermind when it came to planning these kinds of operations.

Before Mohammad returned to his apartment that evening, he agreed to meet with Abdul after he arrived, and hear the full details of the plan for the attack. Wahid said that he expected him to arrive in a day or so and would probably want to have the attack launched in a day or two after that. He suggested that Ali, without doing anything in the meantime that would appear unusual, get his affairs in order and plan to leave his job and the area following the attack.

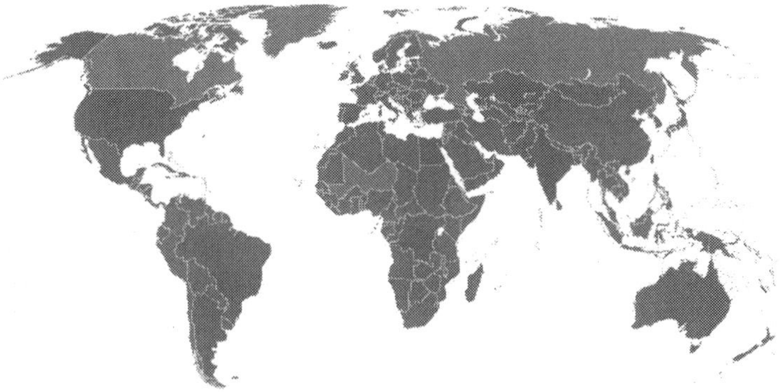

CHAPTER 46

Mitch had only been back on the job at M&T in San Francisco for three weeks when he received a call from Jack to fly to the East Coast to meet and discuss what was taking place regarding the possibility of another attack, this time in the US. Jack said he also was having Lee fly in from Stockholm to join their meeting as well. It was agreed they would meet in Philadelphia, in a safe house provided by the local office there.

Mitch had been in turmoil and conflict since his return from Scotland. He felt betrayed and at a loss over Patrick and the attack at Sellafield, which he felt totally helpless to prevent. If ever there was a time to question continuing his work as a NOC for the Agency, this was it.

Never forgetting his mother's words of respect for the Quran, he was raised to truly have faith in whatever he decided to do with his life. If he could not have faith in what he wanted to do, he should break out and do something else. Having unshakable faith in himself, she taught him, is what the game is all about. He remembered now, in this time of difficulty, it would be in the virtues of the Quran that she so firmly believed in that he could turn to.

During those three weeks in the city, which seemed to Mitch to have gone by much too quickly, he worked an average of sixty hours per week, exclusively engaged in meetings with Dane and Sumiko, their Chairman of the Board, Mac McKinsey, and holding a number of interviews with assorted job candidates. On the one weekend he found time to get a complete detailing job done on his BMW, he could not find additional time to take it out for a long drive, either north or south along the coast, as he usually liked to do in order to clear his mind and to relax.

He made two calls to Maria Luiza, over in Oakland, but since she had come down with a bad case of the flu, they were unable to get together. For each of the three weeks he was in the city, he sent her a bouquet of long-stemmed red roses, and notes filled with kind, soothing words to see her through the ordeal. He knew that soon they would be back in each other's arms.

When he received Jack's call requesting he come to Philadelphia, Mitch knew crunch time was on his doorstep. Should he accept the Agency's decision to sacrifice an agent, in this case giving up Patrick to the Brits resulting in his murder at the hands of Abdul, and move on with his life of dedicated service? Or inform Jack of his decision to sit this one out while he considered resigning from the Agency? He had watched the operation in Scotland slip away. Why risk it happening again with what looked like prospects for another terrorist attack in the US? Mitch focused his thoughts and made his decision, knowing that in the daily tug of war that is the fight against terrorism, losses of life and occasional compromising of principles are sometimes unavoidable. He could only hope that the days ahead would turn out to be better than those experienced in the UK.

* * *

The safe house in Philadelphia was located in an upscale condominium building in the city's old historic district. The leased condo was nicely furnished and the refrigerator was packed with sandwich fixings and a case of ice-cold Iron City Beer, Jack's favorite. Mitch, Lee and Jack made themselves comfortable following their mid-day arrival, prepared their own sandwiches and, along with the cold beer, began their discussion.

Jack started by expressing his appreciation for their extensive, but unsuccessful efforts in Glasgow to locate the infamous Ali, now identified as Dr. Abdul-Karim bin Ahmad, and his obviously close associate terrorist, Wahid Ali Jadoon. He showed them blown-up nine x twelve inch color photographs of Abdul and Wahid, taken from their identity card pictures of Royal

Alexandra Hospital and East Kilbride Park Services, respectively. Mitch, looking at Wahid's picture, said he would not soon forget this face, particularly since he looked straight at him while they waited for the light to change along Strathaven Road, in East Kilbride.

Mitch said that with only six feet or so separating them, Wahid looked as if he didn't even notice him in response to when he nodded his head as if to say to Wahid, "What's up?" Mitch added that when someone rebuffs you like that, you remember that look you received.

"I wonder," Mitch theorized, "what this guy would look like now if he were in the US and taking part in another terrorist attack?"

"I for one," Jack replied, "would grow a beard and try to change my appearance as much as possible. Hey, I'm preaching to the choir. You guys already know that for starters, that's just the beginning of altering an appearance."

"Jack," Lee offered up, "how about having these photos touched up to reflect beards and glasses, and distributed to the appropriate agencies you are working with at Headquarters?"

"Its already being done all over the place and I'll be getting copies to you guys shortly."

"What is the latest news you have since getting back from the UK?" Mitch asked.

"This is where it gets murky, yet interesting," Jack replied. "The most intriguing news is the chatter that the National Security Agency (NSA) is picking up from overhead cell phone traffic emanating out of Pakistan and the Afghan border region. The code words for bomb has been heard several times, but nothing descriptive at all relating to the kind of bomb. Likewise no mention of the method of delivery, or the ultimate target. Whoever has been doing the talking seems to know a bomb has been prepared and the target will be in the US."

"To me," Mitch said, "that implies the bomb had already been fabricated and is on its way or already here in the US."

"That could also say something about its limited size as well," Lee added.

"Has their been any reference to the Great Satan, or the target being number one, or number two?" Mitch asked.

"The Great Satan," Jack said, "has been mentioned twice in the chatter. From the NSA analysis of the traffic, it was cellular calls between the North Waziristan area of the border and the center of Islamabad. But with terrorists and their supporters buying, stealing and throwing away their cell phones on a regular basis, it would be impossible to track any of them down."

"Anything else in the chatter?" Mitch asked.

"One reference was made to the work of the mastermind doctor," Jack said. "It was unclear however, if it was in reference to the attack at Sellafield or the new attack to come."

To the three of them however, that could mean the doctor, Abdul, whom they all fervently sought to apprehend.

"What about the possibility that Abdul and Wahid are already here or about to arrive?" Mitch asked.

"Two senior ICE officers sit near me in CTC at headquarters. They are in regular real-time contact with virtually every ICE and Border Patrol officer throughout the 320 border crossing points in the US. This includes all international airports, seaports and land crossings in Canada and Mexico. The touched-up photos I mentioned have been sent to every one of these border crossing points."

"Lee and I," Mitch said, "are still convinced Abdul murdered Patrick and is the leader of the radical Islamic terrorist group we are now facing."

"The question is," Lee interjected, "what spooked or convinced Abdul into committing the murder."

"Once Abdul knew Patrick had with him the blasting caps and det. cord, he might well have concluded that Patrick was no longer a useful member, albeit a compartmented member, and would have to be eliminated," Mitch said.

"I can buy into that theory," Jack replied. "It was a very unfortunate turn of events and I remain completely baffled by Ian Campbell's actions in ordering the roundup of the Cahill's."

"With that," Lee said, "everything starting to unravel."

"I just want the two of you to understand and accept," Jack said, "that insofar Steve's actions at headquarters he was placed in a tight spot after revealing to MI5 and MI6 that you guys were operating independently on British soil. He had no choice but to reveal Patrick's identity to them. I might have been less honoring of the liaison relationship and not have said a word. I did however, expect a more professional response from Campbell, particularly along the lines of letting Patrick continue the penetration of the terrorist group as far as possible."

"With the exception," Lee said, "of Strathclyde Police Detective Billy MacKay, this was an overall horrendous experience. His cooperation is what dealing with law enforcement is supposed to be."

"Lets hope the three of us never have to work another case on British soil again," Jack said. "Especially if Ian Campbell has anything to say about it."

"What we need now is a break that leads to either Abdul or Wahid, or hopefully, both of them," Mitch said.

"Jack," Lee said, "would it be possible for Mitch and I remain behind here for a couple of days, in order to see if that break might occur?"

"I see no problem with that at all," Jack replied.

Little did Jack, Mitch and Lee know that a break indeed was coming their way. The question was however, would it arrive in time to do any good? With literally nothing to go on in the way of even a single lead, all they could do was wait for that break and hope it would come soon.

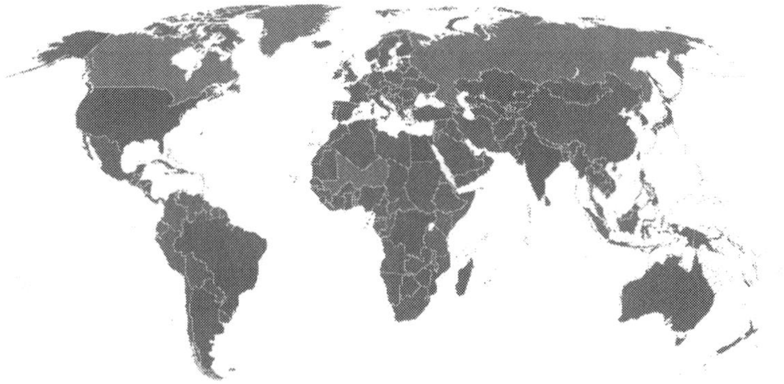

CHAPTER 47

The same afternoon that Jack, Mitch and Lee were meeting in the Philadelphia safe house, Abdul arrived in Charles Town, West Virginia, following the short bus trip from Pittsburgh. Finding himself in the middle of the small downtown area, he immediately called Wahid at his hotel in Reston and arranged to be picked up early in the evening, after Wahid's cousin, Ali, returned from work at the airport. With a couple of hours of waiting ahead of him, Wahid found a bookstore to browse in on West Liberty Street, followed by dinner in a restaurant on South George Street.

Just a few minutes past seven, he stood on the northeast corner of South George and West Washington Streets and immediately spotted Wahid in the front passenger seat of Mohammad's Volkswagen sedan as it pulled up to the curb in front of him. Abdul climbed inside and was introduced by Wahid to Mohammad. However, except for talking about Wahid and Mohammad's childhood days of growing up in North Waziristan, little else was discussed during the drive into Northern Virginia.. Abdul sat in the backseat with the black leather salesman case alongside and said nothing about the attack soon to occur at Dulles.

After arriving in Herndon, Wahid and Mohammad sat outside in the parking lot while Abdul checked in to the Holiday Inn Express, on Elden

Street. After placing his luggage inside his assigned room, he called Wahid on his cell phone to give him the room number where they could come to talk about the attack plans. In their subsequent discussion, Abdul found that Wahid's previous description of Mohammad was quite accurate. He was pleasant and easy to talk with and definitely knowledgeable about his job and responsibilities at the airport.

Based upon what Wahid earlier told Abdul about Mohammad's commitment to jihad, Abdul was not surprised that he readily accepted playing a role in the operation. Mohammad had also revealed to Wahid that he was looking forward to returning to Pakistan after his less than satisfying experiences in the US. This was an opportune time for him and he had no problem to making this kind of commitment.

Abdul asked Mohammad to walk through his daily routine at the airport, and what he was required to check on and service during a normal workday. Mohammad did so, including his daily access to the numerous HVAC systems located in secure areas throughout the main terminal and the outlying two additional terminals. When asked if any single one of these air handler systems, in the main terminal, would be better located to more completely saturate the atmosphere, Mohammad immediately replied that the system located in the physical center of the main terminal would be the optimum choice. This center system, while the same size as the others in the main terminal, had its air duct system designed to flow upward and out into both sides of the middle of the terminal. As a result, better coverage would occur using this particular system when compared to the others on each side of it.

Abdul then asked how he would plan to enter the secure area of the terminal where the system was located and break the glass bottle of anthrax spores inside the air handler system. Mohammad said he had given it some thought and had a plan figured out that he believed would work. With that, Abdul brought the sealed bottle out of the concealment device and set it on the hotel room table in front of Mohammad. Abdul looked into Mohammad's now wide-open eyes staring at the bottle, and asked him to proceed with describing his plan.

Trying to focus more attention on Abdul, rather than the bottle, Mohammad said he had a backpack that he carried to work each day. He used it for his lunch, consisting of usually a sandwich, some fresh fruit and a thermos full of hot, sweetened tea. He said the backpack could easily hold the glass bottle as well. With the HVAC central utility maintenance office located behind a four digit keypad lock door into a secure area of the ground floor terminal, he would bring the backpack to the office and store it in his lockable locker next to his desk there. The office, he said, was actually just adjacent to the center air handler system.

For maximum effectiveness, when the passenger traffic was starting to reach its peak, the best time to break the bottle would be starting around mid morning in order to allow for full circulation of the spores leading up to the most crowded time between two and six in the late afternoon. From the mid-morning period onward he would be alone in the office. His supervisor always spent mid-morning to early afternoons in the other two terminal buildings and they maintained contact via their cell phones. He would be able to walk undetected over to the air handler system with his backpack, and break the bottle inside, just above the filters that are scrubbing incoming fresh air for passage upwards through the ducts into the main terminal upstairs.

Once the job was done, he continued, he would immediately leave his office and the terminal and, while taking an airport service minivan to the employee's parking lot nearby, call his supervisor to say he must have ate something real bad for lunch and needed to go home since he had become sick to his stomach. Abdul asked what would be the supervisor's reply. As an infidel, Mohammad said his supervisor would laugh and say he needed to stop eating that shit-laden Arab food anyway. He added that his supervisor would not have any problem with him going home early for that kind of reason.

Abdul was most impressed with this plan of action and wanted it to be carried out exactly that way. He suggested however, that Mohammad modify his reasoning for calling the supervisor before leaving the airport. He said it would be better if, when he called, he told the supervisor he had just received word from Pakistan that his father had passed away. As a result, he was returning home to arrange to travel there immediately. Mohammad agreed that would make more sense and would be plausible for him to remain away from the airport for at least a week.

When Abdul asked if the attack could occur as soon as the following day, a Thursday, Mohammad said that would be as good a day as any. He added that he had taken all but a few dollars from his savings account in a local bank the day before, and could easily have a few clothes packed in preparation for the following day. Mohammad noted he would not be able to leave from Dulles for Pakistan, obviously, due to the anthrax contamination.

Instead, he would book a flight from Reagan National Airport, to JFK, in New York, and then fly back home to Pakistan via Frankfurt.

The rest of their final evening together, in the small town of Herndon, only minutes from Dulles, was spent drinking cokes and reminiscing about their past and what they contemplated would be their futures. Mohammad agreed to return to the hotel room the next morning and pick up the glass bottle to take to the airport.

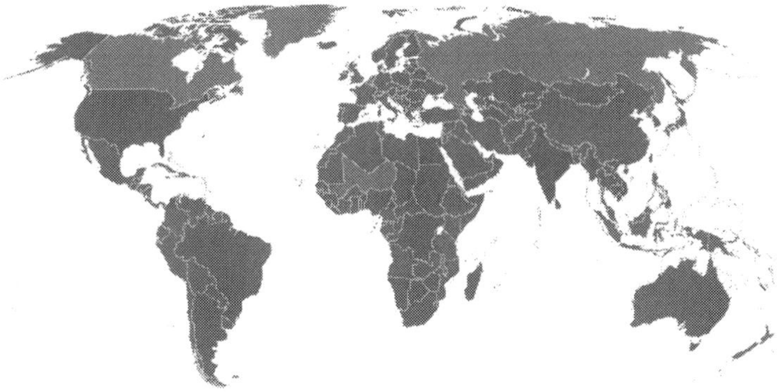

CHAPTER 48

The twenty-eight McQuay Vision Customized Indoor Air Handlers installed at Dulles International Airport in 2009 are capable of circulating more than four hundred thousand cubic feet of air per minute efficiently throughout the main terminal building's two levels. When Mohammad reported to work that morning carrying his backpack containing the glass bottle of anthrax spores, his mind was focused on just one of those air handlers – the one nearest his office located in the airport's Engineering and Maintenance Department on the lower level.

Wearing his green bordered badge that provides full access to all areas of the airport, Mohammad punched the four-digit code into the Trilogy Pushbutton Lock on the door leading into the secure area and his office just inside. After placing the backpack in the bottom of his locker, and locking it, he proceeded to perform his usual daily activities as a HVAC Utility Operator responsible for the maintenance and safe operation of all HVAC equipment throughout the airport. With five years experience beforehand, maintaining high temperature and pressure hot-water boilers and chillers, Mohammad was in his third year of working at the airport. While often at the butt end of anti-Muslim jokes from his supervisor, he was nevertheless viewed as a competent and reliable employee.

The morning wore on slowly for him as he made his rounds checking and servicing equipment primarily in the lower level of the main terminal. When mid-morning came around on that fateful Thursday, Mohammad found himself checking on a thermostat that required replacement upstairs on the main floor behind the Delta Airlines check-in counter. After finishing the job and starting to make his way downstairs, he noted the increasing crowds and noise level of passengers departing and arriving in front of the security barriers on the main floor of the terminal. That was his signal indicating the opportune time was at hand.

Returning to the office and walking toward his desk, he glanced over to his supervisor's desk, which was located separately behind a glass window and open door. No one was there. As he turned toward the row of six lockers positioned along a wall near his own desk, his cell phone rang. His supervisor was calling to say he was just about finished changing a filter in an air handler out in Midfield Terminal C and would be returning to the main terminal in about a half hour.

With a look of determination on his face, Mohammad opened his locker, took out his jacket and put it on, and picked up the backpack. Exiting the office, he walked down the hall to the screened-off portion of the area where the air handler was located. Using his key to unlock the metal screen door, he stepped inside and stood next to the toggle switch that opened up the one-foot by three-foot metal unit door. He kneeled down and removed the glass bottle from the backpack. Unlatching the toggle switch, he opened the door and allowed it to swing downward on its spring hinges. Looking inside, he peered down to see the metal grate two feet below and the roll of filter material underneath it.

Feeling the pleasantly warm air coming upward through the grate and striking him in the face, he quickly threw the bottle inside and heard the glass shatter on the metal grate. Immediately, he closed the door and fastened the toggle switch. Exiting the cage area and locking the door behind him with the now lighter backpack slung over his shoulder, he moved rapidly out of the secure area and into the lower level section past where a multitude of arriving passengers were taking their luggage and personal items off of the revolving baggage carousels. He exited the main terminal glass doors and quickly took in a deep breath of the chilly morning March air.

Rather than walk to the eastern end outside of the terminal where he could catch a small van for the employee parking lot a mile and a half away, he instead went straight ahead, past the waiting taxis, and climbed aboard a passenger shuttle bus that would take him to the parking lot next door to where his car was located. Just before boarding the bus, he called his supervisor to say he had been notified that his father had passed away and that he was going home to make preparations to return to Pakistan.

With a wry grin on his face, Mohammad knew he would never be returning to Dulles Airport to work, ever again. He also knew he would not have to put up with his supervisor's harassing remarks anymore. The supervisor did not know it yet but hopefully, Mohammad thought, this stupid man barely had a week or so to live once he came back from Terminal C and began to inhale the anthrax spores now spreading throughout the main terminal building.

The first of the one hundred thousand plus passengers and people at the airport that day to inhale the deadly spores would be those either sitting on or walking by the air duct grates that line all four of the glass windowed walls of the main terminal building on the upper floor. These grates are on the floor alongside the glass windows and stand fifteen inches in height. People like to sit on them while watching or waiting for others at the check-in counters a few meters away. The warm air rising up and out of the grates from the air handlers below feels comforting during the winter months. This day however, they would be spewing out their invisible deadly spores.

This chilly March day would forever be remembered since it would come to mark the most devastating attack from a biological weapon ever to be loosed upon the US populace. There was no explosion or loud noises of any kind indicating a bomb had gone off, or that an attack had taken place. Instead, following the breaking of the glass bottle, the deadly anthrax spores went about their way, thoroughly circulating throughout the air inside the cavernous high-ceiling main terminal and then down the center of the building into the lower level.

The invisible cloud of spores consisted of particles ranging from one to five microns in size. That is about one-millionth of a meter for each particle. No air handler filter is available that can prevent spores of this size from passing through. While some of them would eventually fall to the ground, most would remain suspended in the air and be continuously circulated. Of those that did land on the ground, a good portion would be kicked back up into the air by people walking by, and further circulated.

No one who was breathing the air inside the terminal that afternoon were going to fall over, go into uncontrollable coughing spasms, collapse, gasp for air or go into a coma and die. None of that would occur that day. However, for the majority of those infected, that is what they could look forward to happen wherever in the world they ended up following their time spent at Dulles Airport.

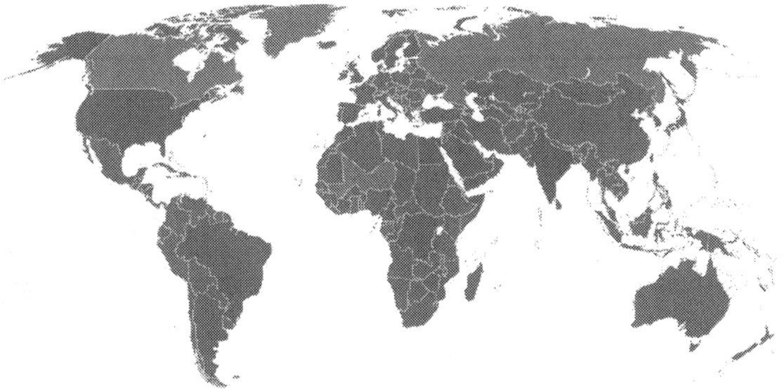

CHAPTER 49

After Abdul gave Mohammad the glass bottle early that fateful morning in Herndon, and sent him off to work and jihad, he took a taxi downtown to Washington, DC, where he boarded an Amtrak train for New York City. After a one-hour layover there, at Penn Station, he boarded another train for Niagara Falls, New York. Two hours after the train departed Penn Station, Abdul's cell phone rang. Wahid was calling to wish him a safe trip back home. That served to indicate Mohammad had called in to report that everything had gone according to plan at the airport in the morning.

In an obvious celebratory mood and, regardless being a Muslim, Abdul went into the train's bar car and indulged in an occasional treat that he developed for himself while living in Scotland. He ordered a malt scotch, straight up, and slipped it slowly. He followed it with one more before returning to his seat and quickly falling asleep for the remainder of the trip. After an 11 pm arrival in Niagara Falls, he found a rather seedy motel near the train station where he spent the night.

The next day, while attempting to walk across into Canada via the ICE border inspection point on the US side of Rainbow Bridge, he was taken out of the primary inspection line and escorted into a large separate office for what is referred to as a secondary inspection. The referral was prompted by the ICE inspector, during primary, imputing Abdul's passport details into the nationwide ICE computer database and finding an anomaly that needed resolution. Showing no signs of concern or nervousness, Abdul stood across the counter from another ICE inspector who rechecked the database for Abdul's record of entry five days earlier in Seattle.

Abdul, standing there in front of the inspector, was confident that his beard, glasses and distracting mole on his cheek would serve to conceal his real identity, regardless of his picture being displayed around the world. Even if Interpol had issued a Red Notice and picture as well, seeking his arrest and extradition, he was willing to take his chances in trying to return to Pakistan.

The inspector, having glanced at the biographic details inside Abdul's Pakistani passport, peered intently at him for a few seconds, and began his questioning.

"Where were you born?"

"Sir, I was born in Pakistan," Abdul replied.

"Of what country are you a citizen?"

"Sir, Pakistan."

"What was the purpose of your visit to the US?"

"Tourism, sir."

"The database shows you entered the US almost week ago in Seattle. Is that correct?"

"Yes sir, that's correct."

"It also shows you to have said you would remain in the Seattle area for a few days and then return to Vancouver for your return to Pakistan."

"Sir, that was my original intention. However, I decided to take another week and remain in the US and travel by train across the country and see as much of it as possible before returning. This is my first time here and I've enjoyed it very much."

"What's your occupation?"

"I'm a cosmetics salesman."

"What kinds of cosmetics?"

"Cosmetics manufactured for Asian and Arab women."

"How much money do you earn a year?"

"In US dollars it would be about $35,000 per year, plus another $7,000 in commissions."

"How do you plan to return to Pakistan?"

"I have my air ticket with an open return that I'll change so that I can leave from Toronto and return home through Dubai, instead of going back through Vancouver."

Handing his passport back to him and continuing to look directly into his eyes, the inspector said to Abdul, "Have a nice day."

"Sir, thank you very much," he replied.

The remaining time Abdul spent in North America went by quickly and no further problems were encountered. On the Canadian side of Rainbow Bridge, Abdul showed his Pakistani passport, driver's license and his air ticket to the immigration officer He was quickly admitted and he proceeded to take a bus for the short one-hour drive to Toronto. Before leaving Niagara Falls, he called the Emirates Airline and made a reservation to return that evening from Toronto, via Dubai.

* * *

For Jack, Mitch and Lee, the long sought-after break that they were hoping for did not occur until Saturday, two days after the attack at Dulles. And again, unfortunately, it was after Abdul had just arrived safely in Islamabad.

Following Mohammad's departure from Dulles, and his plan to fly out of Reagan National Airport for his return to Pakistan the next day, he met with Wahid at his hotel in Reston to say goodbye and plan for their linkup back home in North Waziristan. He also filled Wahid in on the details of how he went about launching the anthrax bomb into the air handler system. After he was finished, Mohammad said goodbye and departed the hotel for the airport. Wahid also was making plans to fly out of Reagan but did not want to leave from there the same day as Mohammad. He would leave the following day, on Saturday.

* * *

ICE Deputy Port Director, Jerry Finkelstein, the number two officer in charge of immigration and customs enforcement at Dulles, was driving his SUV to the airport that Saturday morning from his home across Route 7, in Great Falls, Virginia. As his usual custom, he stopped for breakfast at the Silver Dollar Diner on Baron Cameron Avenue, in Reston. Finishing his two fried eggs, rasher of bacon, toast, and first cup of coffee, he ordered another cup and leaned back on his counter stool to wait for it to come.

Wahid, still walking with his perfected limp, entered the diner carrying his small luggage bag for the trip back home. He sat down at the end of the counter about twelve feet away from where Officer Finkelstein, in civilian clothes, was sitting. He did not pay much attention to Wahid, with his beard and plastic rimmed glasses, since he is accustomed to seeing many Asian and Arab males regularly arriving at the airport on a daily basis. However, Officer Finkelstein was an acute observer of human behavior, having been well-trained to detect deception on the part of the various people he encounters attempting to illegally enter the US at the airport.

Wahid ordered toast and coffee for himself not noticing that Officer Finkelstein had started to take an interest in him. Having recently read the wanted notices and seen the pictures of both Abdul and Wahid, the officer focused his mind on a blank sheet of paper and began a mental sketch of the person, in this case, Wahid, without the beard and glasses. When finished, he then formed in his mind what he could recall of the two pictures he had recently seen of Abdul and Wahid. Finally, he placed the picture of Wahid without beard and glasses alongside that of the wanted poster picture.

Turning his stool to the side, with his back to Wahid, Officer Finkelstein called his boss at the airport, the ICE Port Director, on his cell phone and requested that he and the FBI officer assigned to Dulles immediately come to the diner, about twenty minutes away. He told the Port Director that he believed he had found one of the terrorists wanted for the Sellafield attack. He also said he would be calling in local Fairfax County Police officers for backup as well.

Officer Finkelstein, 54 years-old, six foot two inches in height, and with a trim yet muscular body, was an imposing looking figure. With a full head of close cropped light silver gray hair, he carried himself with a serious demeanor at all times. Wahid did not notice that the officer finished his cell phone call and was walking slowly toward him. When off duty and in civilian clothing, the officer always carried a .38 caliber Smith and Wesson snub-nose revolver in an ankle holster above his left foot. He made no move at all to remove the weapon and instead, took his gold and silver ICE law enforcement badge, in its black leather holder, from his left rear pants pocket.

He stopped close to Wahid, who remained sitting in his counter stool and, from a distance of two feet away, identified himself as an immigration law enforcement officer. Asking Wahid to stand up and come outside of the diner with him, he detected a noticeable exhaling of air from Wahid's lungs and he appeared to slink downward into the stool. Offering no resistance at all, but still using his well-practiced limp, he picked up his bag and allowed the officer to take hold of his left arm just above the elbow as he was led outside and to the side of the diner.

When asking the officer if he had done something wrong, Finkelstein asked to see some identification. Wahid gave him his Pakistani passport, identity card and driver's license. Officer Finkelstein carefully looked at the pictures on the two documents and asked Wahid to remove his glasses. Comparing Wahid's eyes to those in the pictures, he asked for the glasses that Wahid had just removed. He held them up and glanced through the glass. It was obvious they were not prescription glass, but just thin, nonprescription plain glass instead.

With that, Officer Finkelstein dropped the glasses to the ground and quickly spun Wahid around so that he was facing the side of the diner. With one hand, he grabbed hold of Wahid's jacket collar at the nap of his neck. With the other hand he took hold of his belt and top of his pants and marched him forward and up against the side wall of the diner.

At that point, with Wahid forced to lean spread-eagled, with his hands up against the wall, two Fairfax County Police cruisers pulled alongside them in the diner parking lot. Officer Finkelstein immediately identified himself and turned back to begin his frisk of Wahid and his clothing.

* * *

The first Jack heard about the apprehension of Wahid was through the FBI and ICE officers assigned to his office in CTC. Having driven back from Philadelphia and his meeting with Mitch and Lee the day before, he went into headquarters CTC early Saturday morning to read cable traffic and catch up on developments there. After learning about the apprehension, Jack immediately called Mitch, only to find that Lee had already left for Stockholm. He then told Mitch that he was sending a car to Philadelphia to pick him up and bring him to the Fairfax County jail facility, in Alexandria, Virginia, where Wahid had been identified and was in the custody of the FBI. Mitch could have made it down to Alexandria quicker on his own, but knew it was best not to compromise his identity by purchasing a traceable air ticket or renting a car.

By the time Mitch arrived late that afternoon and met with Jack at the jail facility, Wahid's beard had been shaved off and his identity, as Wahid Ali Jadoon, confirmed through his fingerprints and pictures from the East Kilbride Park Service records in Glasgow. Wahid sat in a steel chair at a steel table with his wrists and ankles chained to the floor in front of him. Now however, knowing it was all over for him, he set a strident and defiant tone when talking and responding, mostly evasively, to the questions asked of him.

Two FBI officers escorted Jack and Mitch into the interrogation room. All four of them sat in chairs across from Wahid. Jack asked about the two MI5 officers who were due to arrive from London. One of the FBI officers said they were due on a special flight early the next morning and would be taking Wahid into custody for the attack at Sellafield. Both Jack and Mitch knew this was an FBI show now and they would not even be required to take part in any extradition or subsequent prosecution of Wahid. If so, they would only appear in court in camera, and their identities as Agency officers would be fully protected.

With no knowledge at this point that another attack had already occurred, their interrogation of Wahid focused on any upcoming attacks in the US. Also of primary interest, of course, was the whereabouts of Abdul. Wahid had not given up information to the FBI about Abdul.

Because of Mitch's work against Abdul's ring of terrorists, his handling of Patrick until his untimely murder, and the actual sighting of Wahid in Glasgow, Jack asked for and received approval from the FBI to have Mitch question Wahid.

Mitch knew that unless he was able to get Wahid to reveal information of vital importance, like current threat information or the location of Abdul, he would not be spending much time with him now. He stared into Wahid's eyes, saying, "Do you recognize me?"

"No. I don't know you."

"Don't you remember me from when you were driving your East Kilbride Park Service van near Calderglen Country Park?"

"No. I don't remember you at all. If I did, it would mean nothing to me. You're just a infidel who is not worth remembering. You are only worth destroying."

"If you're so fucking smart, Wahid, why are you sitting on that side of the table in chains?"

With eyes now widened, he replied, "What does that mean?"

"It means that you and your inept terrorist brothers were so stupid, you left all the identifying hairs of your assholes all over the bathroom floor of your house in Larknell."

"Yeah," replied Wahid, 'but our jihad was a success. Do you have any idea what this means to all of you infidels?"

"No, tell us," Mitch replied.

"It means that this is your wave of the future. This is what you bastards all have to look forward to from now on. It is going to be jihad after jihad."

"Well, what about the next one? You are caught now. What other stupid mistakes are going to be made next?"

"You don't need to be worried about that now," Wahid replied.

When they all head the word "now," the FBI officers quickly stepped in and said they would resume talking with Wahid alone. That key word had given them a completely new line of questions to pursue with him in terms of the next attack to come. It would only be a day or two before they and the whole world realized what had already happened at Dulles Airport.

Jack and Mitch walked out of the jail facility and towards the waiting car to take Mitch back to Philadelphia so that he could catch a plane to the West Coast.

"You have many other fights to fight in the future," Jack said.

"I'm not so sure, Jack."

"I know what is going through your mind now after Scotland. Unfortunately, it happens to all of us on more than one occasion. We serve at the wishes of the service, starting from the President on down. Buckle up, Mitch, turn your back on this one and look forward."

"I will, Jack. I know I will. The hunt is too challenging to walk away from it now."

"It's in your blood, Mitch. I know the feeling."

"When Wahid mentioned about the wave of the future, he reminded me of something from not too many years ago."

"What was that, old friend?"

"When I was about to join the Agency, the contracting officer handed me the US Government secrecy agreement and employment contract for me to sign. She smiled and told me that of us new people coming on board the Agency, those that are destined to become NOCs will be the future of the Agency. Because of the deep cover arrangements afforded by working for actual commercial firms," she said, "you are going to be the wave of the future."

With that paradox in hand, Jack and Mitch said goodbye to one another until the next fight to fight.